SONS OF GOD

TO WIELD THE WORLD

Rebecca Ellen Kurtz

Rebecca Ellen Kurtz
June 3, 2014

Published by: Ephesus, LLC

Ephesus, LLC

(visit our Ephesus Media Group website at rebeccaellenkurtz.com)

Publication Date: April 7, 2012

Jacket design, illustration and book design by REK

Copyright © 2012

Book formatted by REK

Manufactured in the United States

10 09 08 07 06 04 03 02 01

ISBN: 978-1491045695

ISBN-10: 1491045698

The paper used in this publication meets the minimum requirements of

ANSI / NISO Z39.48-1992 (R1997)

SONS OF GOD

TO WIELD THE WORLD

Rebecca Ellen Kurtz

DEDICATION PAGE

To Elohim,
who freed me from deception,
restored my faith,
and brought beauty back into my life

Special Thanks To

To my family, the most loving and supportive family an artist
could hope for: Ken, Ruth, Janine, Denise, Michael, Elizabeth,
Tim, & Kristen

REBECCA ELLEN KURTZ

REBECCA ELLEN KURTZ

1500 BC, CANAAN

Darkness enfolded him in its seductive, cool embrace, allowing ignorance to be counted as bliss. It eased his soul, somehow soothing it from what he witnessed in the bright light of day...

This is how he had been raised. This is how he had been taught to believe. Every once in a while, a tradition or ritual seemed a bit illogical or historically invalid, but who was he to trust if not his mother? When he asked, she would just shrug and say, "That's the way it has always been done," or she would say, "What is important with the holiday is what it means in your heart."

Caleb inhaled the cold, wet air and waited for the most important religious holiday to commence: the Festival of Ishtar. It began every year before the sun rose on the spring equinox.

The masses could be heard moving about, positioning themselves for the spectacle soon to take place. For forty days, they had been preparing themselves. Women had sat outside their houses each sunrise, crying and lamenting for the resurrection of their beloved sun god Tammuz, who was the son of the Queen of Heaven and Mother of God, Ishtar. Men, to show their mourning, had given up hobbies, certain foods, and sexual activities with their wives. The men only found release at Ishtar's Temple, where priestesses normally procured tithes to their goddess in exchange for sex. But during the forty days of lent, the priestesses were not allowed to perform these acts. Because the Mother of God decreed that only she could be immaculate or unsullied, the virgins scheduled to be married that year, stayed at the temple to perform their sacrifice. Each virgin had to be breached by a stranger, most by caravan drivers or visiting dignitaries and Nephilim, but after that, the husbands of the town could take their pick. For many of the virgins, the forty days were long and arduous, each day commemorating one year of the sun god's short life, but his resurrection would bring them rebirth and renewal. Just as the Mother of God mourned for her son to be resurrected, so did they. On the seventh day of the week, the children had run to gather wood, the fathers had kindled the fires, and the women had made cakes to the Queen of Heaven. The round cakes were leavened bread with emblems of a cross on them. The children had spent the day decorating eggs for everyone in their family, and everyone now held that egg in their hand. All waited in anticipation for the resurrection of the sun god, Tammuz.

Caleb had decorated his mother's egg. He had carefully dipped it in molten gold and strung it around her neck. His mother, Ishtar, the self-proclaimed goddess of this area, was the embodiment of the mystic egg to the peoples. All through the lands, different female Nephilim were enacting this ritual for the masses, their names ranging from Astarte, Isis, Ashtoreth, and more. Their sons also partook in this ritual, an event depicting the sun god and the Mother of God.

Caleb had heard the legendary tales of how Ishtar survived the flood and helped to replenish the earth. Ishtar, along with the other Nephilim and humans, were supposed to be executed in the Creator's world-wide deluge, but instead, she had saved herself and blessed the world with her womb, giving the mortals what they needed most, the sun. Her son had turned back the wrath that had started the deluge and defeated anyone who chose to subjugate humans. He was their savior, their mediator, and their hope for life. His bright rays and love wiped out the cold barren winter, and dried up the wrathful waters of the Creator who had turned his back on them all... The Creator who had spurned them and chose favorites to cherish in an arc, leaving everyone else to fend for themselves. So their hope lied with the sun.

Dawn's light came creeping over the magnificent stone city, a city built by Nimrod himself, a man Caleb had always wanted to meet, a man the Creator, Elohim, had called the greatest hunter of all. Caleb ran his eyes over the majestic city before spotting a bowl of water on a window sill. It was common for children to float an egg in such bowls of water to show their devotion to Ishtar. It represented how their mother, the blessed one of the mystical egg, had protected her fertile eggs during the flood. The legend stated that during the flood, in an immaculate conception, Ishtar had created life and birthed their savior, the sun, who defeated the one who had sent the Great Flood. Caleb knew the tale was false. Ishtar was born after the flood and there had been no immaculate conception, but the masses loved these rituals, and it gave unity to the tribes coming out of seclusion of winter as they gladly celebrated the arrival of spring.

A wooden crate brushed against Caleb's leg. A child was getting impatient. The boy shifted from one foot to another, terrifying his bunny within the cage. His mother leaned down and whispered, "Stop. You'll break your egg or make the bunny so sick, it won't hop off for you to chase. Then what will you do? Your father will not be pleased if you come home early."

The boy let out a big sigh and forced himself to stop fidgeting. Stringed instruments slowly built in volume to the east where the sun would rise. A haunting melody full of mystic charm flowed over the masses. The seductive beating of drums soon joined the stringed instruments before the sullied virgins began to sing. The words were full of anguish and sorrow from their own soiled bodies longing to be cleansed by the Immaculate Mother. They cried out to be freed and forgiven for defiling their future marriage beds. They prayed that Ishtar would show her forgiveness in their fertility with their husbands.

The sun finally crested over Ishtar's Temple. The fiery orange globe splayed its rays far into the horizon. Within the sun, Caleb could see his mother, Ishtar, seductively dressed in seven sheer orange veils that reflected gold dust. Her hands lovingly rested upon her nine month pregnant belly. Her eyes, gazing at her engorged womb, slowly looked up to gaze compassionately at her children. She was breathtaking. Her skin glowed like a milky orb that dusted the sky at night, and her golden hair blew gently in the breeze. Her emerald eyes slowly closed. She tilted her head to the heavens and raised her hands in preparation to give of her divine self. She stood in the position of a cross, perfectly in line with the fiery orange sun behind her, her veils blowing immodestly around her. It was the mystic symbol of the sun god, a cross within the sun, and she was ready to sacrifice for the good of the world once again. Everyone stood transfixed. Ishtar always planned this perfectly. It was just nine months ago that the most beautiful shepherd boy had been selected by her. She had lain with him until impregnated, then offered him up to his people to be sacrificed. Immediately afterwards, his blood and flesh were offered on a platter for Ishtar to nourish herself with. It was his son who was about to be born, but his son's birth represented his own reincarnation. He had planted his seed within the mother goddess of earth, nourished her body during the winter months with his own flesh and blood, and slept protected deep within her womb, awaiting his resurrection. Her body, like mother earth, became the rejuvenating paradise where his spirit dwelt in peace before his resurrection.

As the sun rose, so did Ishtar. She perfectly paced her levitation in accordance with the rising of the sun, keeping her form in the center of it. Her body convulsed, yet she kept her arms open wide beside her. She was forcing her own body to begin contractions.

"My children, take from my body what you need," Ishtar spoke. Her voice supernaturally echoed through the town. "I present to you my son, the vanquisher of your guilt. He will mediate and save you from the Creator who has turned his back on you. He will prepare an army of gods to do your bidding and rid you of all obstacles. Not only has the sun defeated death and the winter of the soul, but he has resurrected himself within me as he may resurrect himself in you and for you."

Another sharp contraction wracked her body, twisting her body back in pain. "Here is the hope for immortality." She spread her legs. "And the sun will sustain you. He is your only hope for deliverance."

Caleb's eyes fell to the glittering golden egg he had made for her. It laid at the hollow at the base of her throat, like a pendant of a choker. Her skin sweated profusely, only adding to her normal ethereally glowing appearance. The sun was almost too bright to continue watching.

The masses lifted their decorated eggs towards her and chanted in one accord, "May your womb be blessed forever. May your divine eggs continue to replenish the earth. May your fertility be an example to us all."

The women and girls chanted, "May our eggs be as yours, each one giving of life."

Ishtar screamed in pain. Her arms shook but remained outstretched.

"May we procreate as quickly as your divine bunnies," the men chanted.

"May we grow to maturity and be chosen as your consort," begged the young boys.

Ishtar screamed, "It is the rebirth!"

"Oh Mother of God, Queen of Heaven, we yearn to be reborn as well. We pray to you to bless our wombs and make us fertile. May your sun deliver us from the dead, the winter of our souls. In commemoration, we will eat of the cakes of heaven and drink the blood of your sun as you have done. We pledge our oath in this symbolic eating of your egg, ingesting your soul and spirit deep within us. May we be reborn as we meditate on this." Each citizen of Nineveh cracked his egg open above his mouth and slurped in its content. Bowing, they meditated while Ishtar let out her last scream, slipping a babe from her womb to be caught by the priestesses below her. Slumping, Ishtar fell backwards to the ground.

The children cheered and opened their rabbit cages. Bunnies ran free and fast, causing many to laugh in glee. Each rabbit had a ribbon tied onto its foot that matched the ribbon of the child who had set it free. All the children excitedly began chasing after their bunny knowing that if they found it before the sun set, its foot would bring them good luck for the whole year. The husbands and wives quickly returned home to see if Ishtar would bless their womb, for a child conceived on this day would bring their parents good fortune.

The betrothed women, who had just given their virginity away during lent, walked to the center of town to begin their duty. Their fiancés had hunted down wild boars to be eaten on this holiest of days, and the future brides were responsible for pitting the pigs and roasting them for the entire city.

"Well, wasn't that a wee bit o' a show."

Caleb turned and took in the most wildly appearanced man he had ever seen. He had long burnished copper hair and the most amazing eyes - a seemingly molten swirl of gold, orange, red and green with a speckling of those same colors in his pupils. He smelled oddly of a crackling bonfire. The Nephilim asked, "Are you one of Ishtar's consorts?"

Caleb's sapphire eyes narrowed. How could this male know he was a Nephilim? It was apparent that the stranger himself was a Nephilim, his otherworldly burning eyes gave him away. The Nephilim were half-breed children, the byproduct of mixing mortals with a spirit being or another created race. Ishtar was a second generation, giving her a shining, luminous appearance as well as many supernatural abilities like her ability to levitate. Caleb was only one generation away from aging. His height was much less than the average height of a Nephilim which normally ranged between nine and twelve feet. Caleb's eyes were his only feature that alerted anyone that he was a Nephilim. All Nephilim had eyes that resembled precious gems. The stranger was short like him, six foot four or so.

Caleb answered hesitantly, "Son."

"Ah, and who be yer da?" the mysterious Nephilim with burning eyes asked.

"Madai. Who are you?" Caleb retorted a little put out that the other man seemed to be controlling the situation.

"Loki. So, ye're Noah's grandson, one of Japheth's?"

Caleb nodded his head. "I've never seen you before."

"I roam a lot. Been down in Egypt seeing the most amazing things. Elohim plagued the pharaoh and forced him to let his chosen people depart." Loki shook his head. "Ye should have seen what all he did. And then he allowed Ah-Mose to part the Red Sea and everyone walked over on dry ground, but the waves came crashing in when pharaoh's army chased them down. His army's gone. Finished."

"Elohim? My mother hates Elohim. He turned his back on us," Caleb warned.

"Your ma dinnae scare me, lad." Loki flung his arm out and pointed towards the heavens. "Right now, Elohim abides above his chosen mortals as a hovering, sparkling cloud during the day and as a flaming fire at night. That's how he guides them. Ye should see it." Loki's eyes twinkled. "It is Elohim ye should respect, not yer ma."

"Why do you concern yourself with them?" It annoyed Caleb that Elohim would choose weak mortals to be his chosen people. Didn't he care about them too? And what was to happen to everyone else? Did they not deserve to be noticed by this God of the gods? Favoritism had never set well with Caleb.

"The Hebrews?" Loki asked amused. "Ye should be concerning yerself with them. They're heading this way to take back their land. After what I've seen, your ma doesnae stand a chance." Loki chuckled.

"Loki," a seductive purr sounded.

Caleb didn't know why, but his mother's purposeful sensuality always bothered him. He knew that she was the goddess of sex and fertility, but did she have to be so wanton? She was his mother, for goodness sakes. It roiled his stomach.

"Ishtar." Loki curtly nodded his head. "Quite a show. Feeling *enamored* by yer adoring masses?"

"Why yes, thank you. Would you care to be my next adoring fan? I would love to be worshiped by... your body." Ishtar stepped around Caleb to stand directly against Loki as she gazed up at him longingly. "Our child would be a god like no other."

Loki stepped away, but couldn't help looking at her pouting lips. "Nay, but I would suggest ye prepare yerself fer war."

She spoke seductively, "If that's the way you want it. I'm always up for a good tussle before the pleasure."

Caleb sighed. "That's not what he meant. Elohim's leading the Hebrews here and has promised them victory. They've already defeated the Egyptians."

Ishtar stiffened. "We have nothing to fear. All the male gods will come to my aid. I do believe I have loved them all." She ran her eyes over Loki. "Well, almost all."

"I'm nay a god and dinnae claim to be," Loki replied brusquely before taking in Ishtar's beauty and shaking his head. She was stunning and the most powerfully blooded female Nephilim. A thought crossed his mind. "Yet, I am without a helpmate. If ye were to have a daughter of your beauty, a pure virgin, and dinnae think that I wouldn't check first, Ishtar. I would betroth meself to her." Loki looked out at the remains of the morn's activities. He wouldn't want her marred by the depravity he saw here. "She would have to be sent to me young, very young. I will educate her in all she needs to know."

Ishtar rolled her eyes. "So patriarchal, Loki." She smiled. "But I like that in a male. What would I get for my daughter?"

Loki remained quiet for several moments. "An alliance... of sorts."

Ishtar bristled. "Of sorts?"

"I will give ye information that I know of concerning the Nephilim to the north," Loki explained.

"And aid me in my war against Elohim?" she bartered.

"Nay. Information on any Nephilim I encounter," Loki added onto his first offer.

"Aid when the Hebrews try to conquer my people? Take back our land?" Ishtar pushed.

Loki noticed her eyes held a bit of fear within them, and they should. She wasn't stupid. Loki reasoned with her. "I will give ye status reports on how they defeat their enemies. Knowledge is better than nothing, and will help ye prepare."

Ishtar sighed. "Fine. Do you have a father in mind for your future bride? Or will Baalim do?"

"Nay, I find Marduk more finely formed and of richer lineage than Baalim."

"Marduk? Who is Marduk?" Ishtar asked intrigued. She preferred Baalim. Baal was one of the common words for god. The Canaanites had baals for every locality and terrain. A god for a river, a god for a mountain, a god for a town, etc, etc. His name inferred that he was the god of the gods which tickled Ishtar. Elohim's name meant God of the gods, referring to all the Nephilim who claimed to be gods and paraded themselves as such. Elohim was the Creator of the Nephilim as much as the Creator of the whole universe. Baalim's arrogance with the creation of his own name always delighted her.

Loki turned away from her, the black cavern of her mouth and throat reminded him of a grave. His gaze slid over some approaching men who hauled trees behind them. The men walked by, showing reverence to their goddess-mother before nailing the trees to stand upright in and around the pigs roasting. Their future brides giggled with delight as they decorated the trees with silver and gold in preparation for the night's festivities. He could imagine the sight of the gold and silver reflecting the fires of the pits while everyone feasted and danced. Now, they stood hacked down by the will of the gods to serve in the orgies that would eventually take place below their boughs.

Caleb let out a heavy, weary sigh.

Loki's eye darted to Caleb and kept a vigilant perusal of Caleb's boredom of the festivities. Ishtar had to keep touching his arm to get his attention.

Blocking Ishtar from hearing, Loki whispered to Caleb, "Ye should visit the Israelites. It is as a breath of fresh air, and ye will be greatly intrigued."

SIX WEEKS LATER...

Loki meandered through a ravine. Towering black cliffs rose on either side of him. It was a great place to hide, and a great place to be trapped. The path he trod had been beaten down by hundreds of thousands of Hebrews. It would have taken them a very long time to walk through the narrow path. Only five or so would be able to walk shoulder to shoulder, but the cliffs rose at least fifty feet overhead and provided much needed shade from the desert sun. The tunneled path seemed to suck in cool air that would hover over a large lake. Loki could smell it. The water smelled like freshwater, perfect for drinking.

He closed his eyes and tried to imagine what it would have been like to walk this path with the presence of Elohim over him, guiding him. In the daytime, the cloud of Elohim would have made the walkway cool and refreshing, yet at night, when the desert turned cold, Elohim's pillar of fire would have warmed the black rock and given a warm hearth feel. It was perfect. Elohim was perfect. Elohim was good.

Loki had often walked among the Hebrews. Elohim had never struck him down. *Moshe* (Moses/Ah-Mose) had never told him to leave. So he followed. He witnessed. He observed Elohim's deliverance of his people.

Loki stretched his hand out, allowing his fingertips to rub the porous black cliff wall. It left his hand slightly dusty, yet moistened from the humidity in the air. The cool air off the upcoming lake blew gently along his face, lifting his burnished copper waves in undulating patterns. Inhaling, it seemed as if the cool, crisp air could cleanse all that he had just witnessed. It seemed a paradise compared to the dusty, sun baked city he had just left.

The black cliffs began to widen, and the dirt below slowly turned to black sand. Loki took one last turn, and the cliffs ended to reveal the Hebrew encampment. It sat on the other side of the crystalline turquoise water, made even more brilliant contrasted by the black cliffs and sand. The cliffs surrounded the lake and the encampment, hiding them from the world. It was an intimate setting. A perfect location for Elohim to reveal himself to his select few, his chosen race. Loki couldn't help but feel special that he was allowed to experience this. But he was not the only stranger, some Egyptians had come, some who believed in Elohim and had chosen to become one with Elohim's chosen and serve Elohim as well. Perhaps, that's why no one bothered him, no one knew if he was one of those. He certainly didn't look like any of the Hebrews. Loki's anger had evaporated when he realized this. Elohim had chosen his people, yet anyone who bonded with his people, denied their own religion and rituals, and became one with them, then they were treated and seen as a Jew. They fell under Elohim's covenant when they denied all else and partook of all the commandments of Elohim. Loki remembered when his anger had shifted into intrigue. These people, these Jews, were already the testimony of Elohim and his fulfillment of promises, his continuing covenant with those who obeyed and served him. Loki had a feeling that the Hebrews would be used by Elohim to make his wishes and commands obvious to all those wishing to join in with the covenant.

There were about six hundred thousand men, besides their women and children, who had settled on the black sand on the opposing side of the lake. They stood motionless outside their tents, waiting, their eyes pointing to the heavens. Loki waited. Something was about to happen. The sun slipped behind the mountains and twilight fell. Bird chirping could be heard, then the sound of wind picked up. Loki's hair began to move. Screeching quail flew over the cliff from behind him and soared straight to the Israelites who were waiting for them. The quail quickly landed all about them on tents, the sand... anything standing. The men quickly scooped them up. The birds didn't fight them, never tried to leave, but unselfishly sacrificed themselves in a staggering fashion of peaceful submission.

Small fires in cooking pits slowly began dotting the encampment. Women pitted quail carcasses and patiently waited for them to cook while their men told stories of Elohim's grandeur, their trials in Egypt as slaves, and the Promised Land that was yet to come. Children dodged amongst them in their games while young girls saw to the wounded and elderly.

The Israelites had been attacked by the Amalekites on their travels, but Elohim had blessed them with victory. Loki had watched the battle from a distance. The Amalekites were a tribe descended from the Nephilim, so their enemy had been stronger than they. The Nephilim had seen the wondrous watering rock Elohim had provided for his chosen people. The black rock spouted water and followed the Hebrews wherever they traveled, always ready to quench their thirst. In a desert situation, a rock that poured forth living water would be the difference between life and death.

One quail separated itself from the others at the encampment. It flew straight up, then down to land on Loki's shoulder. The bird stared at him a long time, then slowly walked sideways till it was against his neck. Cooing, the little quail nuzzled Loki's neck. A tremor ran through him. His eyes grew moist.

Loki slowly walked into the cool lake, washing off all the hot desert sand and sticky sweat that coated his body. Keeping his shoulders above the water, he treaded across, making sure his little friend stayed warm and dry. Once at the encampment, he looked for an empty fire pit, but a kind-eyed old man grabbed his arm and offered for him to use their fire pit. The quail hopped down his arm and went to stand beside the pit, ready to sacrifice himself to nourish Loki. Loki hardened his heart and killed it. After pitting Elohim's gift, he joined the other men who had moved on to their next recounting of Elohim's goodness.

"Ah, it was so bitter, so bitter. We could not drink from it. Why would we drink from it? To save ourselves? Three days. Three days we had gone without water in the desert. What was to become of us? We followed Elohim, and he led us to water that could not be drunk. We thought... Would have been better to have stayed in Egypt. Yes, yes, that is what we thought. Elohim provided several times, but if he did not keep providing, what good would it be to us? What were we to do? Go back to Egypt? Die in the desert? My wife could no longer walk. My children foamed at the mouth, their little bodies barely moving, their eyes not even recognizing their own father. We grumbled. We complained. And then Moshe took a piece of wood and tossed it into the water. Said to drink. Was he insane? What were we to do? We tried." The man paused, smiling, a light beginning to beam from his eye. "Yes, we tried. Why not, eh? What would we lose by obeying the man Elohim spoke to? And what do you think we found? Yes, yes, the water had become sweet." His toothy grin stretched from ear to ear. "Sweet water.

Wondrously sweet water. I still remember it. Then Moshe gave us one of Elohim's laws. Said we would be tested. Yes, he said we would be tested." He leaned in, challenging everyone, hinting that there was more testing to come.

The same man, apparently the tale teller of the bunch, continued, "Adonai, our God, then gave laws and rules of life, and he's started the testing already. Some have already failed. We must obey. Elohim wants to be obeyed. If we collect more than one day of manna, it rots. But if we collect two days of manna the last morn before the Sabbath, it stays good. For Elohim wants us not to work on the seventh day, the day of rest, the holy day, the day ADONAI chose for us to show our obedience to him. Moshe said, 'If you listen carefully to the voice of Adonai your God, do what he considers right.'" He leaned in for drama and lowered his voice, "'Do what He considers right' not we ourselves, but Adonai. 'Pay attention to his *mitzvot* (commandments) and observe his laws.' And Adonai promised that he would heal us, for he is the Great Healer."

A younger man with a somber face, who had just recently wed, asked, "And do you remember the *mitzvot* already given?"

Crinkling eyes gazed at Loki before responding, "I believe our guest can answer that. He listens. He thinks. He takes everything in and ponders them."

Loki nodded sagely, "To believe in Elohim, and that he created all things. To not believe in anything else other than Elohim. To believe in Elohim's Oneness. To fear Elohim. To love Elohim. Not to pursue the passions of our heart and stray after our own eyes." Loki paused, reflecting back to Ishtar. Had he wanted a wife from her loins because of her beauty? He shook his head, driving out his own question, reviewing the tale of *Ya'akov* (Jacob) and Rachel.

"Oy, we shall be tested," the tale giver repeated.

The somber young man sat up. "How can those things be tested? How does Elohim know what is in the heart of man?"

"By the greatest way of all, by watching our obedience to his commands. The heart is fickle, but our actions say more of our heart than our words do. Words are easy to say, and emotions are easy to sway."

Loki sat up himself. "But, what is the heart, without conviction? Without love? What if he just obeys the laws and loves Elohim not?"

"Eli, your sad tonight. Why is that?" the tale teller asked.

The young somber man sighed heavily. "My wife obeys me not. I tell her one thing, and she argues with me. Thinks she knows a better way. Keeps trying to find ways to strengthen her argument and rational. Prove me wrong. Prove she knows what's best. I don't feel respected. She loves me well at night, but her actions in the day grieve me, makes me wonder if she loves me so well just to ease her own heart and desires. Using me to make her feel better about herself. Reveling in my love. Glorifying in it. Ecstatic to know my love, but when the sun rises, so does her disobedience."

The tale teller nodded his head. "So you understand. Respect is more important in the showing of love. For the husband, and for the wife. If there is only respect on one side, it is lopsided. Earthly passions and romantic emotions fade quickly, but respect lasts. It is the stronger of the others. It shows the heart more." He turned his head to Loki. "If there is only respect, then there is still love. Not all the love a groom would want, but enough to know it's real, not born of selfishness from what the groom can give the bride. Elohim wants more, yearns for more as Eli does. But Eli doubts his wife's love because it is so shallow. She loves herself more than she loves her husband. She revels in his continuing openness and ability to give her what she needs while she denies him what he needs - respect. How is that love? Does she love him only to make her life less dreary? To ignite her own heart? To feel well loved? These are selfish reasons. This is not true love, not sacrificial love, not respectful love. Do I want my children to only hug me? Forbid it not, but I want their obedience." He grinned. "And their hugs. But what are their hugs if they obey me not? If they respect not my wishes? If they only obey the rules that they want to obey and do all else that pleases them?" He shook his head. "No, it would grieve my heart, and one day, I would not even call them my child, even if they still used my name."

Loki sat back. Reflecting upon all that had been said and his former life. The night grew quiet as the campees slowly turned in for the night. One by one, each fire pit was extinguished.

Eli's wife came and knelt down in front of him. She was very beautiful, and her action seemed respectful. Loki wondered if Eli had been fair.

She raised one hand and caressed Eli's face, love shone from her eyes. "I love you, Eli. I don't think that I could live without you. You take care of me, love me, and listen to all my woes. When you love me, I feel like I've reached Elohim's paradise itself. You are the only one who truly cares about me."

Loki knelt back farther, so she wouldn't be able to see him in the flickering light.

She leaned forward and kissed Eli. The entire area was now empty. Loki knew she thought she was alone with her husband.

"Come, my husband. I need you. I need your love. I need it to fill my heart and heal it." She kissed from his lips, down to his strong jaw, and nibbled down his neck before she lovingly clasped his hand to bring him back to their tent. "Come, I need to feel you. I need to feel you deep inside me." She stood, holding her hand out, and waited for his reaction.

Eli slowly stood and took one step towards her. A smile leapt to her face. He paused. "Did you move the bed as I asked?"

His wife rolled her eyes. "Eli, you know I like it when Martha wakes us up in the morning. I love her chatter. It's so perky, and I hear all the gossip that happened the day before." She stood on her tiptoes. "It doesn't really bother you, does it? You still love me?"

Eli gave her a half smile and let her pull him towards their tent. He sent a sad, heart wrenched look to Loki as he passed by. Apparently, it did bother him.

Loki extinguished the fire and walked to the center of the encampment. The tents he passed were elegant and beautiful. Egyptian silks and cotton in vibrant hues were used for their tent dwellings. The Egyptians had given them many items to get them to leave after the plague of the first born. The Angel of Death had killed all the first born if they didn't have a lamb's blood covering their doorposts. Such a harsh payment for disobedience, but the Hebrews were now quite wealthy from all their labors as slaves. Gold lanterns could be seen, slowly being extinguished throughout the encampment.

Loki moved towards the tabernacle. Elohim had given instructions on how it was to be built - well, erected. It consisted mainly of acacia wood poles and hanging fabric for walls. It was rectangular and partitioned into three chambers. At the back was where the Arc of the Testimony resided in the Most Holy of the

Holy areas. Loki preferred to sleep near that end of the tabernacle.

As he drew nigh, his heart thundered. Elohim, as usual, was in residence. Above the scarlet, purple, and blue walls of the tabernacle, a tall pillar of fire swirled up into the stars. The night was black, but where the flames shot through the clouds, it created a dark sunset in the matching scarlet, purple, and blue shades.

Loki paused. It had been too long since he had beheld this sight. The flame pillar rose higher than even he could see, and from time to time, it almost seemed that a face would be molded by the flames, but it was always gone so quickly that it made you doubt you saw anything. But one thing was sure, whenever Loki drew near, he felt like Elohim was watching him from within that flame pillar. He was spellbound, with an intensity that he did not believe could ever be matched.

Loki walked up to the side of the tent and laid down. The smell of roses assailed him. Why it always smelled of roses here, he didn't know, but it pleasantly rolled back the stench of mashed humanity coming from the encampment. The heavy rose perfume, that normally pervaded the entire encampment during the day, dissipated and was replaced with a strong smell of lavender. Loki felt his emotions ease, his stress lift, and a calm settle over him. He had heard that lavender had that effect, but the way the fire pillar heightened its intensity revealed that Elohim was aiding his children to sleep. It made him think of how the aunts would tell bedtime stories to him and Thor to get them to fall asleep. Loki smiled and drifted off.

Movement woke him the following morning. The dew was still on the ground. It was so dense that it reminded him of snow. Loki felt someone watching him. He quickly hopped up and turned around. Elohim's glory beamed from the midst of a cloud pillar that had replaced the fire one. The clouds were a pale powder blue, but a bright light, as if a ray of the sun, glowed within it. If he wasn't mistaken, wet drops were in the clouds, which reflected the light and made the entire cloud appear speckled with diamonds. It was breathtaking.

A hand fell onto his shoulder. "Don't forget to take two days worth of manna. *Shabbat* (Sabbath) begins at twilight. Manna will not come on Shabbat."

Loki smiled at the elderly man. His body was so frail, he

seemed made of corn husk. Loki glanced around. Everyone was staring hungrily at the dew on the ground. They just stood there, waiting.

Slowly the dew evaporated, and thin flakes of bread lay in its place. Without care or concern, each Hebrew stooped down and picked up what they needed before returning to their tents. Loki knelt down and gathered his own breakfast. The bread was simple but satisfying. He put enough to feed himself for the seventh day of the week in a satchel and began walking back to where he met the others the night before. It wasn't long before he noted the lines of people forming at various tents. He stopped at one. "Why do you stand in line?"

"Moshe no longer judges every case. Many judges and leaders have been selected from among us to decide cases, and Moshe only judges the ones that cannot be easily decided. It is much easier this way."

Loki nodded his head, seeing the wisdom in it. He wondered what Moshe was doing then.

"Friend."

Loki turned to find Eli standing in front of him. Loki nodded. "Friend."

"I am waiting, hoping, that my wife will come to love me as I do her. My mother told me that I should divorce her for her rebellious and disobedient ways, but I... I long to see her return my love. To show her love by respecting my wishes, honoring me with her obedience, and delighting in the fruit of our union. She needs my love. I will be patient and giving of my love and guidance." He lowered his voice, "But, if at the end of her days on earth, if she still has not respected me as her husband and learned to obey my commands, I will not claim her. For I will not have her falsehoods, disobedience, and selfish ways destroying my heaven." Eli curtly nodded his head and walked away.

Loki thought Eli loving, but just.

He turned and spent the day wandering the encampment and listening to the tales of the patriarchs. He waited for twilight. There was something in the air that bespoke of change. Loki was pleased that he had arrived in time for whatever was about to take place.

At twilight, the shofar blew, sending shivers down Loki's being. There was a heightened expectation in the air that could be tasted. Energy zang in the air, igniting him.

MOSHE.

Everyone froze. The voice was coming from the mountain. It was not human. It was deep, and caused a timber deep within the soul, a stirring of the spirit. It was a compelling voice. There was something about it that made you want to drop to your knees and obey everything it bespoke. Awe and reverence flowed forth from the most secret and ancient of places within the heart.

As everyone turned to face the mountain, Moshe walked forward, alone, and stopped at its base. Dark storm clouds swirled above its peak. Then Elohim's voice spoke again.

HERE IS WHAT YOU ARE TO SAY TO THE HOUSEHOLD OF YA'AKOV, TO TELL THE PEOPLE OF ISRA'EL: YOU HAVE SEEN WHAT I DID TO THE EGYPTIANS, AND HOW I CARRIED YOU ON EAGLES' WINGS AND BROUGHT YOU TO MYSELF. NOW IF YOU WILL PAY CAREFUL ATTENTION TO WHAT I SAY AND KEEP MY COVENANT, THEN YOU WILL BE MY OWN TREASURE FROM AMONG ALL THE PEOPLES, FOR ALL THE EARTH IS MINE AND YOU WILL BE A KINGDOM OF *COHANIM* (priests) FOR ME, A NATION SET APART.

Moshe turned and walked back to the people to speak with them. To tell them what Elohim had said, but they had already heard. Everyone quickly agreed to obey Elohim fully and to keep his covenant. They had replied as one, "Everything ADONAI has said, we will do."

Moshe returned to speak with Elohim and tell of their response.

SEE, I AM COMING TO YOU IN A THICK CLOUD, SO THAT THE PEOPLE WILL BE ABLE TO HEAR WHEN I SPEAK WITH YOU AND ALSO TO TRUST IN YOU FOREVER. GO TO THE PEOPLE; TODAY AND TOMORROW SEPARATE THEM FOR ME BY HAVING THEM WASH THEIR CLOTHING; AND PREPARE FOR THE THIRD DAY. FOR ON THE THIRD DAY, ADONAI WILL COME DOWN ON MOUNT SINAI BEFORE THE EYES OF ALL THE PEOPLE. YOU ARE TO SET LIMITS FOR THE PEOPLE ALL AROUND; AND SAY 'BE CAREFUL NOT TO GO UP ON THE MOUNTAIN OR EVEN TOUCH ITS BASE; WHOEVER TOUCHES THE MOUNTAIN WILL SURELY BE PUT TO DEATH. NO HAND IS TO TOUCH HIM; FOR

HE MUST BE STONED OR SHOT BY ARROWS; NEITHER ANIMAL NOR HUMANS WILL BE ALLOWED TO LIVE.' WHEN THE *SHOFAR* SOUNDS THEY MAY GO UP ON THE MOUNTAIN.

Loki turned and immediately walked to the lake to cleanse himself. He was not alone. Many were scrambling to cleanse themselves as ADONAI had requested. Loki thought of flying to the other side to be more alone, but he didn't want to give himself away as being something more than mortal. He did not want to be set apart.

When he did get to the water. He dove in, deep enough that he wouldn't be able to be seen, and swam to the other side. Standing on the soft, black sand, he let out a prayer to Elohim to hear his requests to be made clean. He fully immersed himself for several moments and arose a new creation. He felt a sense of renewal, rebirth, and a fresh start. Gone were trials and temptations of Odin's court. Gone were the mistakes of his youth. Gone were the sad and painful memories that haunted him. He praised Elohim.

Jubilantly, he swam back to the encampment, considering on whether or not he wanted to return to the men he had met the night before. He yearned to hear more tales. He hadn't been able to witness everything. There were holes in his knowledge of Elohim.

He closed his eyes briefly to revel in the fresh, clean feeling possessing him. He bumped into someone. Loki popped open his eyes and began profusely apologizing before stuttering to silence. Moshe stared at him. He had run into Moshe. Everyone watched.

Moshe's eyes enlarged, taking in Loki's supernaturally lit eyes. He quickly looked up and down Loki's warrior frame, towering height, and luminescent skin. Even Loki's burnished copper hair seemed alive, like glowing embers embedded deep within each hair shaft. Moshe nodded his head respectfully. "Welcome."

Loki nodded respectfully in return, but chose not to speak. If anyone could throw him out, it would be Moshe.

Moshe continued his perusal of Loki. Loki stood stiffly: he had not changed out of his former clothes. He wore a golden torc around his neck, a simple cloth that hung from his hips, and most of his skin was bare. Moshe's eyes caught on Loki's tattoos. He couldn't seem to be able to tear his eyes away from them. "What does it say?"

Loki swallowed. "These were forced upon me as a child." He pointed to the encircling tattoos on his upper arms. "They speak of my allegiance to Odin."

Moshe's eyebrows rose. "Well, I see you have cleansed yourself. Would you like a new robe? I believe one can be found for you." Moshe motioned with his head and Y'hoshua (Joshua) left immediately. Moshe took Loki's right arm and moved it to look at the tattoo still not explained. "And this one?"

The tattoo took up most of the tender flesh on the inside of Loki's lower arm. Something that would be seen by the wearer whenever he would reach for something. "It is a symbol I created to remind me that I serve Elohim."

"Is it his name in your language?" Moshe asked intrigued.

"Nay. I would be killed for doing so. It is a private compact between me and Elohim and serves as a constant reminder," Loki spoke submissively.

Moshe's eyes sparkled. "I think I can identify some with your plight. Being torn by how one's raised and.... Never mind. We shall not speak of it."

Y'hoshua returned and handed Moshe a long white robe. Moshe in turn handed it to Loki. "I welcome you. We have fought some of your brethren already. Perhaps, ADONAI has sent you to help even the score. If you turn from your previous ways and obey ADONAI's commands, you will be our brother, for Yehovah invites all to be redeemed and restored. He sees the heart and the heart's true motivations. One cannot fool Him. Even if one chooses to decieve themself."

Moshe walked on, leaving behind a very curious Y'hoshua. It was the comment that Moshe made on the battles against the weaker Nephilim tribes. Realization dawned on who Loki was and prompted him to speak, "What is your lineage?"

"Second generation," Loki answered.

Y'hoshua's eyes widened. "How old are you?"

"Let's just say... since before the flood," Loki answered.

Y'hoshua blinked several times. "Have you much experience fighting your brethren?"

Loki nodded. "Thor and I took it upon ourselves to hunt down those who abused mortals. Since the flood, Thor has taken residence with the redeemed and runs with the Judge and Executioner of the half-breeds who violate the laws of Elohim now."

"Are you Loki?" Y'hoshua asked reverently.

Loki nodded slowly, not knowing if his invitation would be rescinded.

Y'hoshua held out his hand. "I am honored. I have heard whispers of all three of you since before I could walk. We must talk. Soon. I must attend Moshe, but we will talk. I have much to ask you."

Loki held out his hand and accepted the offer of friendship. Loki was surprised at the strength in Y'hoshua's grasp. This mortal would be one to be reckoned with. Smiling, Y'hoshua squeezed extra hard, then let go to follow Moshe. Loki was left standing alone, holding a long white robe which he quickly put on before heading to Eli's fire pit.

"You see? You see? If you obey me fully and keep my covenant. It's a stipulation. We cannot just love him, we must obey him fully and keep his covenant. What is love without obedience? What is love without respect? It is shallow. Self-serving. Selfish. It is about the receiver, not the giver."

The tale teller had already started his commentary for the night. Eli sat quietly, still grieved, his eyes watching his wife from afar as she flitted amongst the women gossiping and laughing.

"Reverence. I speak of reverence. If you truly love someone, you reverence them. You want to make them happy. You choose their happiness over yours. It is a sacrifice. It is sacrificial love." The tale teller's wife squatted behind her husband to hug him from behind. She kissed the back of his neck and whispered something in his ear. He laughed. "My children do not want to go to bed. She has come to ask for help. I shall return shortly." He stood and departed with her.

Loki slowly looked over to Eli. His besotted look gave him away, but his wife never acknowledged him. She was currently showing her enthusiasm for some of the gold bowls that someone had collected from an Egyptian. Loki didn't speak.

It was thirty minutes later when the tale teller returned. He looked exhausted. His children must be rambunctious indeed, Loki mused. His wife quickly followed, sitting down amidst the men. Her husband didn't shew her away, but welcomed her gladly. She first offered him his portion of manna, then began to eat hers before nestling deep into his side.

Eli glanced over the married couple. The tale teller had wrapped his arms around his wife and whispered something in her ear as he pointed up to the stars above. They both looked fully content. Eli winced and sought out a view of his wife again.

"Don't be afraid, Avram. I am your protector; your reward will be great. Look up at the sky, and count the stars - if you can count them! Your descendants will be that many. Know this for certain: your descendants will be foreigners in a land that is not theirs. They will be slaves and held in oppression there four hundred years. But I will also judge that nation, the one that makes them slaves. Afterwards, they will leave with many possessions. As for you, you will join your ancestors in peace and be buried at a good old age. Only in the fourth generation will your descendants come back here, because only then will the Emori be ripe for punishment."

Eli faced them once again. His face etched with grief concerning his wife. "And soon afterwards ADONAI gave the covenant of circumcision. A carving in the flesh that would show our bodies belonging to him." Eli looked down at Loki's tattoo. "And he warned, that if his covenant was not obeyed fully, each person would be cut off because he had broken the covenant." Eli sat quietly for many minutes before standing, "I will seek out my wife since she will not seek me. Shabbat Shalom."

The tale teller's wife leaned forward. "She is young, Eli. Deep in her heart, she will treasure that you seek her out. If not now, one day, when she has time to ponder your love and devotion."

Eli gave a half-smile before nodding and leaving. That was Loki's cue to leave. He walked back to where he slept. Excitement grew within him. Three days. On the third morn, Elohim had promised to speak to his children again. Loki couldn't wait.

Before sunrise on the third morn, thunder and lightning rocked the encampment. A fierce storm, that did not rain, swirled above the mountain. It was an unusual storm, unlike anything anyone had ever seen. The cloud did not appear dark, but a vibrant sapphire blue. Light blue lightning bolts streaked out, scaring many.

Loki rose from his sleeping position. He quickly glanced back to where the flaming pillar should be, above the Most Holy of Holies, but it was not there. Elohim had moved. The energy in the air could not be contained. Every hair on his entire body, stood up, straining away from his skin, made alive by whatever swirled upon the mountain.

A loud trumpet sounded, making everyone tremble. Then a great ball of fire fell down from the heavens and stopped right above the summit. It was so hot, it was white and tinted blue. Loki knew that the hottest stars in the universe were white and blue. It seemed as if they all should be scorched. The heat was so intense, his skin wanted to melt off his bones and pool in submission to the entity that had increased itself. Black smoke surrounded the peak as if unable to endure the magnitude of what came close to resting upon it.

Loki blinked several times because he could not believe what he thought he saw. At the very top, where the bright white and blue flame burned, a path had begun, and was slowly snaking down the cliff in a pathway that a human could walk upon. The most breathtaking aspect of the footpath was that it was pure sapphire. It looked like millions of sapphires had been pulverized and gelled into one pathway, a pathway leading to Elohim. But what was confusing was that no one was to approach the mountain, so why would there be a path?

Moshe had walked up to the mountain to watch everything first hand. Y'hoshua stood to his right, Aaron to his left. The sapphire river flowed all the way down and touched the sandals of Moshe's feet. It did not touch the sandals of those beside him - only Moshe. Moshe obeyed and followed it up to the top.

Everyone below quaked and trembled. Even Loki.

I AM ADONAI YOUR GOD, WHO BROUGHT YOU OUT OF THE LAND OF EGYPT, OUT OF THE ABODE OF BONDAGE.

Lightning flashed in a rampage. Terror reigned below. Many fainted.

YOU ARE TO HAVE NO OTHER GODS BEFORE ME.

Loki dropped to his knees.

YOU ARE NOT TO MAKE FOR YOURSELVES A CARVED IMAGE OR ANY KIND OF REPRESENTATION OF ANYTHING IN HEAVEN ABOVE, ON THE EARTH BENEATH OR IN THE WATER BELOW THE SHORELINE. YOU ARE NOT TO BOW DOWN TO THEM OR SERVE THEM; FOR I, ADONAI YOUR GOD, AM A JEALOUS GOD, PUNISHING THE CHILDREN FOR THE SINS OF THE PARENTS TO THE THIRD AND

FOURTH GENERATION OF THOSE WHO HATE ME, BUT DISPLAYING GRACE TO THE THOUSANDTH GENERATION OF THOSE WHO LOVE ME AND OBEY MY *MITZVOT* (COMMANDMENTS).

A growl of thunder sounded for several long minutes, as if to emphasize the importance of loving Elohim and keeping his commandments.

YOU ARE NOT TO USE LIGHTLY THE NAME OF ADONAI YOUR GOD, BECAUSE ADONAI WILL NOT LEAVE UNPUNISHED SOMEONE WHO USES HIS NAME LIGHTLY. REMEMBER THE DAY, SHABBAT, TO SET IT APART FOR GOD. YOU HAVE SIX DAYS TO LABOR AND DO ALL YOUR WORK, BUT THE SEVENTH DAY IS A SHABBAT FOR ADONAI YOUR GOD. ON IT, YOU ARE NOT TO DO ANY KIND OF WORK - NOT YOU, YOUR SON OR YOUR DAUGHTER, NOT YOUR MALE OR FEMALE SERVANT, NOT YOUR LIVESTOCK, AND NOT THE FOREIGNER STAYING WITH YOU INSIDE THE GATES OF YOUR PROPERTY. FOR IN SIX DAYS ADONAI MADE HEAVEN AND EARTH, THE SEA AND EVERYTHING IN THEM, BUT ON THE SEVENTH DAY HE RESTED. THIS IS WHY ADONAI BLESSED THE DAY, SHABBAT, AND SEPARATED IT FOR HIMSELF.

Lightning flashes circled the top of the mountain, illuminating it in an awe-inspiring ethereal light that made it appear supernatural.

HONOR YOUR FATHER AND MOTHER, SO THAT YOU MAY LIVE LONG IN THE LAND WHICH ADONAI YOUR GOD IS GIVING YOU.

DO NOT MURDER.

DO NOT COMMIT ADULTERY.

DO NOT STEAL.

DO NOT LIE ABOUT YOUR NEIGHBOR.

DO NOT ENVY YOUR NEIGHBOR'S HOUSE; DO NOT COVET YOUR NEIGHBOR'S WIFE, NOR HIS MALE SERVANT, NOR HIS FEMALE SERVANT, NOR HIS OX, NOR HIS DONKEY, NOR ANYTHING THAT IS YOUR NEIGHBOR'S."

Everyone witnessed the thunderings, the lightning flashes, the sound of the trumpet, and the mountain smoking. They became so fearful that they moved to hide from the presence of Elohim. When Moshe descended from the mount, they clambered to him, begging him to speak with Adonai alone. They feared for their life. Loki couldn't believe their reaction.

Moshe turned towards them. "Do not fear; for Adonai has come to test you, and that his fear may be before you, so that you may not sin, for sin is defined as the breaking of Elohim's laws."

Loki nodded. This was fear to create a reverential love, an obedient love. Eli's love was not winning over his wife. But Elohim was teaching his people to respect him, to fear him, and to love him. Without reverential fear, many would never obey his commands. Already, many were shying away from Elohim's greatness for their own measure of comfort. A warrior served no matter the comfort level of his assigned duty. A wife who respected and reverenced her husband served and obeyed him no matter her own comfort and rationalizations. Obeying Elohim's commands would truly be the test of the heart.

Loki shook his head. Elohim was striking fear because he loved his people. This was for restoration. The angels had been kicked out of the heavenly dimension for breaking the Kingdom of Heaven's laws. Adam and Eve had been kicked out of the heavenly dimension for breaking Elohim's laws. Anyone who broke the Kingdom of Heaven's laws would not be permitted to remain within the Kingdom of Heaven on earth. It was the consequence of rebellion. Breaking laws was rebellion and showed a rebellious heart. And Elohim knew the heart. He knew if someone broke a law by accident or the heat of the moment, or if they broke a law because they rationalized why they could discard it.

Saddened, Moshe returned to the sapphire path and rejoined Elohim.

"YOU HAVE SEEN THAT I HAVE TALKED WITH YOU FROM HEAVEN. YOU SHALL NOT MAKE ANYTHING TO BE WITH ME."

*

"You shall not make anything to be with me. What does that mean? I do not understand this." The tale teller scratched his chin in befuddlement.

Eli shook his head. Everyone was still stunned from all that they had seen and heard that day. Elohim had expounded on the first ten commandments he had given, then had begun giving rules for how they were to live amongst each other. Apparently, it was how the judges and leaders were to judge the people. Were there to be no kings? Was Elohim to be their only king? Were they not to need anyone but judges to police them? Were men to behave so well that nothing more would be needed?

They had all stood waiting for Moshe to return to them. Loki was glad that he had spotted his friends, and they had come to kneel with him throughout the giving of Elohim's rules.

When Moshe finally returned to the encampment, he had asked if the Israelites would heed the words of Elohim. Together, everyone replied, "All the words which *ADONAI* has said, we will do."

Moshe immediately sat down at the main judging table where he worked and began writing down all the laws and rules Elohim had given. He worked on it throughout the night and built an altar to *ADONAI* on the morn. He had Aaron and Y'hoshua help him erect twelve pillars around the altar for the twelve tribes of Israel. Shortly thereafter, he bid the young men and children to fetch oxen to be burnt on that altar. He drained the oxen of their blood and speckled half the blood onto the altar. He rose before the people and read out loud the laws and rules of Elohim that he had written through the night. It became the Book of the Covenant. When Moshe had finished, all the people replied, "All that *ADONAI* has said, we will do, and be obedient."

Happily, Moshe took the remaining blood and sprinkled it on the people and said, "This is the blood of the covenant which *ADONAI* has made with you according to all these words."

With over a million people present, it took a long time for Moshe to sprinkle blood on everyone. It took the remainder of the week, and Moshe burnt a new offering each morning before reading through the Book of the Covenant again. Loki, Eli, and the tale teller were able to be sprinkled on the first day, and they spent their evenings discussing the laws and their days listening to Moshe read them aloud again.

Loki lounged back and popped his quail meal into his mouth. Amazingly, he didn't need that much food while he was here. Usually, he was ravenous, but here, one small quail satisfied him till the morning.

"You shall not make anything to be with me." The tale teller scratched his head. "You shall not make anything to be with me."

Loki paused. "Most gods have accomplices... wives, mothers, councils..."

The tale teller hooted his laughter for a long time. "A wife to Elohim the Creator? A council for Elohim? A mother of Elohim? A mother of *ADONAI*? A mother of God? Who would say such a thing? Who would believe such a thing?"

Loki smiled. "'Tis the only thing I could think of."

"Ahhh." The tale teller leaned back and gazed up at the stars. "At least you have a thought. I, myself, have none. But, but I see what you say. If someone was to be with someone, then they are placed as high as that other entity. Is that what you say? How Isis was the wife of Osiris, yet she resurrected him long enough to have a child by him. Then Isis became the mother of Horus, the god who reigned on earth. She became the mother of god. But who would ever say that a woman was the mother of Elohim? And who would make that mother equal to Elohim?"

"I know not. 'Twas only an idea," Loki repeated.

"But an idea it was," the tale teller mused.

Loki sat up. It seemed that Moshe, Aaron, and the elders were approaching the mountain. "What are they doing?"

Eli stood up and strained to see. "Moshe is taking the seventy nobles of Israel up the mountain."

Loki stood up as well. "Come. Come with me." Loki led Eli and the tale teller up to the beginning of the sapphire pathway. Loki wanted to walk up that path with every ounce of his being, but he feared to do so. Would Elohim become angered? Apparently, the nobles were allowed to go, but why no one else?

Loki squatted down and held out his hand to the sapphire road. Its clarity was like that of the heavens. No dirt or rock marred its perfection. Loki wondered if he could touch it. He was not mortal like the others, an angel's blood flowed in his veins. Would his body be able to touch it and live? Would Elohim allow him to go unpunished?

"Look the nobles have not gone far," Eli pointed out.

Loki stood. Moshe had left them just beyond Elohim's cloud cover and had walked on without them. Loki stepped back from the sapphire road, repentance blossomed within his heart. Quickly, he returned to their fire pit.

The glory of Elohim rested on top of the mountain for six days. Moshe waited twenty feet above the nobles. The cloud that rested on the summit resembled a consuming pure, white flame. On the seventh day, shabbat, *ADONAI* called out to Moshe, and Moshe approached the consuming fire and disappeared within its midst.

For the next forty days and forty nights, Moshe stayed within the midst of Elohim's consuming presence. Lightning and thunder threatened the campsite, but most people did not hear Elohim's voice. Loki was able to make it out and repeated it to his two friends. What grieved Loki's heart, was that after the first entire day and night that Moshe was gone, the people began to be bored. They became restless. They searched for things to do, things to gossip about, things to make them laugh. But Eli, the tale teller, and several others stayed reverently around the campfire listening for Loki's words. With Loki's heightened hearing, these few were blessed. But the more everyone else went about their daily activities, the more difficult it became for Loki to hear Elohim's voice. They were a fierce distraction. Each day, Loki and his friends moved closer to the mountain, each day becoming more and more bold.

To Loki's shock, only a few days after Moshe disappeared, Aaron and the nobles left their privileged position and returned to the people, but they did not force the Israelites to await Elohim's new laws, nor did they stop them from cavorting about from morning to night. Without Moshe, the people did as they pleased. It became evermore increasingly difficult to hear the words of Elohim with the commotions caused by the Israelites. They were becoming their own stumbling blocks to hearing from Elohim.

On the thirty-eighth day, Y'hoshua motioned for Loki and his friends to approach him. Loki was excited. He took his first step onto the sapphire path and felt a warm, shimmering sensation slowly travel up his legs and throughout his body. With each reverential step, he breathed in the cloud that surrounded him; it smelled of roses and frankincense. Y'hoshua was fit within a crevice of the mountain. When Loki walked into it, he understood why Y'hoshua chose to remain there. The voice of Elohim could be heard clearly, and the noise of the encampment was blocked out. Loki would not need to speak what he heard anymore, everyone would be able to hear.

It seemed intimate being there. Completely obscured by darkness, Elohim's mighty voice quaking around him. It sent tremors through Loki's spirit. He felt connected. He felt one with Elohim.

"TELL THE PEOPLE OF ISRA'EL, 'YOU ARE TO OBSERVE MY SHABBATS; FOR THIS IS A SIGN BETWEEN ME AND YOU THROUGH ALL YOUR GENERATIONS; SO THAT YOU WILL KNOW THAT I AM ADONAI, WHO SETS YOU APART FOR ME. THEREFORE YOU ARE TO KEEP MY SHABBAT, BECAUSE IT IS SET APART FOR YOU. EVERYONE WHO TREATS IT AS ORDINARY MUST BE PUT TO DEATH; FOR WHOEVER DOES ANY WORK ON IT IS TO BE CUT OFF FROM HIS PEOPLE. ON SIX DAYS WORK WILL GET DONE; BUT THE SEVENTH DAY IS SHABBAT, FOR COMPLETE REST, SET APART FOR ADONAI. WHOEVER DOES ANY WORK ON THE DAY OF SHABBAT MUST BE PUT TO DEATH. THE PEOPLE OF ISRA'EL ARE TO KEEP THE SHABBAT, TO OBSERVE SHABBAT THROUGH ALL THEIR GENERATIONS AS A PERPETUAL COVENANT. IT IS A SIGN BETWEEN ME AND THE PEOPLE OF ISRA'EL FOREVER; FOR IN SIX DAYS ADONAI MADE HEAVEN AND EARTH BUT ON THE SEVENTH DAY HE STOPPED WORKING AND RESTED.'"

Silence enveloped them.

Y'hoshua whispered, "I believe he's done for the day. You may all stay here and sleep as I do."

All but Loki stood up to leave, each mentioned their wife and children. None wanted them to worry what had become of them. They promised to return in the morning. But they did not. And Elohim spoke not again.

"Put to death for not keeping the seventh day holy," Y'hoshua whispered.

Loki tilted his head. "One day in heaven is a thousand on Earth. No one cursed is permitted to live the whole day, that is why Adam died at age 930 from the day of his rebellion and expulsion from the heavenly dimensions. Eventual death is not so unjust, Y'hoshua. In his mercy, Elohim permits those cursed and in rebellion to live up to 120 years. It is Elohim's spirit which animates your flesh, so the removal of his spirit extinguishes that life. You breathe at His bequest. Consider the word 'kill' along those lines, and ye will see

Elohim's loving justice for what it is - just. His holy spirit will only be housed in unholiness and endure a rebellious heart and soul for so long."

Moshe arrived into Y'hoshua's crevice the next afternoon. It was still pitch black inside. "Loki?"

"Aye," Loki replied, surprised that Moshe knew he was there.

"*ADONAI* wishes you to have this." Moshe dropped a bracelet made of the black stone of the mountain into his hand. "I must return now." Moshe turned and left.

Loki stood and walked outside so that he could look at what had been given to him. It was a bracelet. There were ten squares of black stone, from the mountain, held together by hematite. On each stone square was one of the ten commandments that Elohim had given. The inscription was made of the sapphire path material. It would last for thousands of years. Loki dropped to his knees, kissed the bracelet, and allowed large tear drops to roll down his cheeks.

Loki quickly fastened the bracelet onto his wrist and held it out for Y'hoshua to examine. "It looks to last an eternity."

Y'hoshua smiled. "Perhaps *ADONAI* has a purpose for you that will last throughout eternity."

Loki grinned. "Perhaps, just till the end of the world, or my life."

"Whichever it is, seems to be a long time to me." Y'hoshua laughed.

Loki grew somber. "Aye, a long time. A very long time to stay loyal."

Y'hoshua stopped laughing. "What say you?"

"Temptations fall on us all. T'would be a very long time to fight me flesh."

Y'hoshua didn't reply, but the seriousness of not breaking Elohim's commands for thousands of years was weighty. It was a big undertaking. It would call for immense fortitude.

Y'hoshua stilled as a revelation came upon him. "It will be a constant reminder of your marriage to Elohim."

Loki looked surprised. "Marriage?"

Y'hoshua nodded. "The ten commandments are our portion of our marriage contract with Elohim, to be his bride and wife. In our culture, a husband and wife write out the expectations and requirements we ask of the spouse. These are his. What he requires of his wife. How we are to show our respect and what is required for Him to bestow His name, His mark, upon us, calling us His." He shook his head, coming fully out of revelation, and clapped Loki's back. "Do you hear that? It seems the quail gathering is quite loud tonight."

Loki turned to the noise coming from the encampment. There was yelling from the masses. Loud banging. Instruments playing. And lots of singing. He didn't think what was occurring had anything to do with the quail Elohim sent each night.

Loki moved over to the edge of the cliff and looked down. A large bonfire burnt near the base of the mountain. Aaron stood near some piles of golden bowls, cups, and jewelry. Loki's eyes swept the encampment. Women were cooking a feast. Children were helping their fathers kill oxen and cattle. Why were they eating their cattle? The quail would come at twilight.

Loki watched mesmerized. To his back, he could feel the presence of Elohim, and down below him, he could see the activities of the camp. It was a horrifying sight. He saw many sitting and lying around Aaron, worshiping the god of the star Reifan, the god the wife of Joseph worshiped, the daughter of the Priest of On. They worshiped the god they worshiped in Egypt while they ruled in splendour. Joseph had never worshiped anyone but Elohim, but his descendats who ruled after him had done so to appease the Egyptian masses. His stomach twisted. For it was Elohim who had favored Joseph to rule over Egypt, but it was his descendants' syncretism that had landed them back into slavery and imprisonment. Repulsion gnawed at his insides.

"It sounds to be preparations for war. Why else would they run around so feverishly?"

Loki murmured, "No. No, it isn't war."

Y'hoshua kept asking Loki what he could see or hear. To tell him exactly what they were doing. Loki refused to answer.

Hours crept by. Darkness descended.

The silence from above was deafening.

The revelries below repulsive.

Loki could see what the Israeli were doing. The entire encampment had bedecked itself in brightly colored silks of violet, fuschia, yellow, and orange. The pit fires bathed everything in a warm orange light. Children ran rampant. Adults feasted, sang, and became drunk. Women, wearing sheer veils, danced before the men, igniting their lusts. Drums beat out a sexually base rhythm as the masses moved in hordes to the base of the mount where Aaron stood beside a golden calf.

Loki couldn't believe his eyes. They had created a golden calf, Apis, the Egyptian sun god. On the golden calf's head sat a sun disk between its horns, representing his mother, Hathor, who had been born from a sun ray. Apis was a fertility god, yet also connected to the Egyptian pharaoh as a protector after death. Thus the golden calf also represented resurrection and the renewal of life for those worthy of an afterlife. Bulls were symbols of strength and fertility and manifested the leader's courageous heart, virility, fighting spirit, and great strength.

Loki watched as the golden calf was lifted by strong men and led through the encampment. Men bowed down to it. Women stroked their hair over it, kissed it, and pled for strong sons to be born to them. Jewelry, flowers, and wreaths were thrown onto the golden calf, many catching on its horns and its sun disk. As the golden calf passed, the women who had once stroked the bull for fertility, ran to various men for their prayers to be fulfilled. Loki leaned back, stepping away from the cliff as orgies began below.

Moshe turned the corner and halted before them. "ADONAI says that the people have become corrupt."

Y'hoshua murmured, "No, there is a noise of war in the camp. They must be scared."

Moshe's eyes flashed fire. "It is not the noise of the shout of victory, nor the noise of the cry of defeat, but the sound of singing I hear." He quickly stepped around them and continued down.

Loki couldn't help but stare at the two large stone slabs that Moshe carried. From where he followed, he could read the ten commandments written on them. The inscription went all the way through; he wondered how Moshe was able to do that unless..... unless it wasn't Moshe but the finger of Elohim that had written it. Moshe stopped just above the golden calf. He raged. No one heard him. The singing and dancing continued. Y'hoshua blew his shofar. The encampment slowly settled and turned to face Moshe. Moshe's blazing eyes hunted out Aaron. Aaron was responsible. Aaron had been left in charge. Elohim had made Aaron his High Priest, and this is what he had done. He had allowed them to get out of control. Slavery no longer filled the Hebrews' days and exhausted them into their beds early. With nothing to do, their idle hands had made idols, their pure bodies and hearts had been polluted.

Aaron ran up to his brother. "Don't be angry, Moshe. These people you left me with are prone to evil. They carry evil in their hearts as surely as Elohim carries goodness in his. They asked me to do this. They were sure you were dead. That your relationship with *ADONAI* had killed you. They wanted to worship a god they could see, feel, touch."

Moshe looked incredulously at Aaron. Did they not see, feel, and touch the manna they woke to each morning? The quail that flew to them each night? Did they not see and hear the thunder and lightning on top of the mount? Did they not hear Elohim's voice when He spoke?

Loki said, "They have allowed their own carnal desires and past traditions and teachings to block the voice of Elohim. Not even I could hear. I had to approach the mountain to hear Elohim."

Moshe shook in his rage. His voice bellowed supernaturally throughout the encampment, "Whoever is for *ADONAI* come to me!"

Eli, the tale teller, and the ones who had spent most of their time with Loki approached. They were of the tribe of Levi. Loki could tell that all the Levites rallied to Moshe. Moshe spoke to them, "Each of you, put his sword on his side; and go up and down the camp, from gate to gate; and every man is to kill his own kinsman, his own friend and his own neighbor."

The Levites nodded solemnly and went out to do *ADONAI'S* bidding. When they returned, three thousand had died. Moshe told them, "You have consecrated yourselves today to *ADONAI*, because every one of you has been against his own son and against his own kinsman, in order to bring a blessing on yourselves today."

Loki knew that what had transpired before him was extremely harsh, but he also realized just how seriously Elohim took obedience. Not everyone who committed a sin died, just three thousand out of a million.

Moshe turned to the people and said, "I will now go up to Elohim and beg his forgiveness. I will try to atone for those who have broken his commandments yet remain alive." He took a few steps, paused, and turned back around. "Listen. Listen for his answer this time."

It took Moshe hours to reach the summit. Everyone remained silent and motionless. Elohim's answer was finally heard. Fear spread throughout the encampment. Loki vowed obedience.

THOSE WHO HAVE SINNED AGAINST ME ARE THE ONES I WILL BLOT OUT OF MY BOOK. NOW GO AND LEAD THE PEOPLE TO THE PLACE I TOLD YOU ABOUT; MY ANGEL, YEHOVAH-ANGEL, WILL GO AHEAD OF YOU. NEVERTHELESS, THE TIME FOR PUNISHMENT WILL COME; AND THEN I WILL PUNISH THEM FOR THEIR SIN.

NINEVEH

Caleb leaned back and relaxed. This was his favorite religious holiday. Everyone was laughing, women were cooking, children were decorating. It was the eve of Tammuz's birthday celebration. His mother, Ishtar, was already showing in her pregnancy. She still hadn't met with Marduk yet. He thought she'd seek him out directly for Loki's alliance, but since he had not yet returned, she must not be taking him seriously.

Ishtar, representing the Queen of Heaven, sat down beside him. She was dressed in a deep emerald green veil and had painted her lips red. A wreath of red and green adorned her head. She reached out her hand to Caleb. "My son. How are you?"

Caleb, happier than normal since his mother had modestly covered herself, replied, "Wonderful. And you? How is the babe?"

"Our yule is doing well." She patted her belly affectionately. "Do you miss your father?"

Caleb let out a long sigh. "I was hoping he would be here for the festival."

Ishtar squeezed his hand. "So was I."

The winter solstice celebration was the highlight of each year. The wind was cool, the nights had grown long, and leisurely activities had increased. It was a more peaceful time. People stayed at home and warmed themselves at their hearth and waited for the spring to resurrect outdoor activities. Women shivered and dressed modestly. Ishtar, though, with her furnace-like temperature as all

Nephilim had, only dressed more modestly for the winter solstice celebrations because she was representing her virtuous state of the immaculate conception of the sun.

They sat at a high table on the balcony of Ishtar's Temple so that they could overlook the festivities. Down below, men led wild boars through the streets. Their wives would soon be cooking them. Everyone always had ham for the day's feast in honor of how Tammuz died: a fatal wound from the tusk of a boar when Tammuz was forty. The boar would be sacrificed first thing on the morn, and everyone would dine on it over the next few days.

As darkness fell, little candles were lit. A single flame winked from each window, welcoming in the birth of the sun which would take place sometime during the night. Caleb knew his mother preferred the spring equinox festivities and only did what she had to for the winter solstice celebration.

Glancing over the citizenry, Caleb noticed a head of burnished copper. He squeezed his mother's hand. "I do believe Loki has returned."

Ishtar quickly stood and motioned him up to their banqueting table. Priestesses scrambled, searching for extra gold plates and utensils to place for the newcomer. Ishtar quickly turned to them and said, "Tell the king, I will dine only with gods this eve. Loki will take his place beside me." The priestesses bowed and dismissed themselves.

Loki, dressed in a long white robe that completely covered him, walked over and kissed Ishtar's hand before taking his seat. "I see I came at an opportune time."

"Like you didn't know." Ishtar giggled.

"Know what?" Loki asked.

"Please, Loki. Everyone celebrates the winter solstice. You knew exactly what you were doing," Ishtar chastised.

"Actually, I've been with the Hebrews, and they do nay acknowledge such feasts and festivities. They only worship Elohim, not the birth of the sun," Loki stated.

Ishtar gave him a baleful look.

"They do nay set their calendar to the sun, but to the moon, so they do nay even know when the equinoxes and solstices are." Loki looked around himself. "This be quite different from the winter solstice celebrations in the north." Loki examined Ishtar's five month pregnant belly. "Even different from the Babylonian winter solstice celebration."

Ishtar tilted her head defiantly. "I like what I like. I wish to give birth at the spring equinox rather than the winter solstice. This is only a commemoration of when I gave birth to the sun."

Loki chuckled. "Really, ye gave birth to the sun?"

Ishtar bristled.

"Spout yer foolishness to the gullible, but do nay speak thus in my presence." Loki glanced around. "It's been over forty years. Where is my betrothed?"

Ishtar turned disdainful eyes in his direction. "Where is your great news that begets you a betrothed?"

"Have ye even met with Marduk?" Loki demanded.

"No. He's quite the charmer apparently. Can't seem to make it here to see me," Ishtar placated. It was humbling being denied, but she had an uncanny notion that Loki could read minds anyway, so she decided not to lie just in case.

"That burns doesn't it," Loki purred. "Go to him."

Ishtar's lips grew grim and her back stiffened. "And what news do you have for me?"

"I'd run for the hills if I were ye," Loki murmured. "When do we eat? I'm starving."

Caleb leaned forward, his red robe contrasting brightly against Ishtar's green. "The food will be served shortly now that darkness has fallen."

Loki nodded. He watched the citizens below, most dressed in red or green, as they moved banqueting tables and began placing food down. To the right of the open square, at the base of Ishtar's Temple, stood a twenty foot tree. It had been hammered down to stand securely on top of the brick flooring. "At home, we do nay cut down the trees, but go to them."

Caleb perked up. He had never traveled and was quite intrigued on how different people celebrated the equinoxes and solstices.

"Well, you live out in the woods, not in grand cities made of stone, so why would you?" Ishtar commented contemptuously.

Trying to cover for his mother's rudeness, Caleb cut in, "What else is different?"

Loki watched as a steaming platter of ham, honey, and raisins was placed in front of him. "Do ye have anything other than ham?"

"Ham is the choice of the gods. Would you offend them?" Caleb asked.

"Aye, I would. May I have something else please?" Loki answered.

Caleb motioned to the priestesses to bring something else for Loki to eat. Ishtar's eyes narrowed, but she didn't say a word.

The feasting had begun in the square below. Loki could feel a searing look periodically from an ornately dressed man with a gold crown on his head. Loki could only presume that the man was the slighted king whose chair and place he had taken.

Caleb tried to get his attention back. "Do the Norsemen not eat pig?"

Loki nodded. "Aye, aye they do. I no longer do. Elohim says it's not good for the body, and I only have one to last for thousands of years." Loki winked. "I need to be keeping it in top form for as long as I can."

Ishtar's eyebrow rose. "You mean to say that you obey Elohim?"

"Ye mean to say that ye think it wise not to listen to the Creator of yer body on his instructions on how to keep yer body at its peak health and form?" Loki smiled. "Ye may nay go into battle, relying on yer sexual wiles, but I am a warrior, and I am wise enough to listen to the Creator's instructions. I have no desire to float about as a demon."

Caleb frowned, then motioned for the priestesses to bring him some figs, milk, and chicken as they had done for Loki. He pushed away his ham.

Ishtar squirmed, trying to think of a new conversation. "What are your winter solstice celebrations like?"

"They hang red apples on evergreens with mistletoe on top. Mistletoe is seen as sacred to them - a plant of the gods, and then they kill their yule, an infant babe, to appease the sun god so that he will be reborn." Loki waved to the citizens who had finished feasting and moved on to decorating the large tree with gold and silver. "The Northmen are more earthy, not so wealthy in gold and silver. Red apples do for decorations, but they do tie small candles to the tree and light it. Of course, they do nay have windows like ye all do."

Ishtar, flattered by his comments on her town's wealth, smiled and squeezed Caleb's hand. "Our yule will be born at Easter. Do your people celebrate Easter?"

Loki's eyes slowly shifted towards Caleb. "Our yule? Yer the father?"

Caleb grimaced then laughed. "Surely not, she's my mother."

Ishtar rolled her eyes. "If he was the father, he would be dead. Remember? The chosen father of the yule is sacrificed and fed to me."

"Ah, yes." Loki turned his attention back to the revelers down below. A few of the banqueting tables had been pushed together to make a stage. A beautiful woman, that resembled Ishtar, sat on a dais. Harps were brought out, and musicians began their songs to celebrate the coming birth of Tammuz, the incarnation of the sun.

"That's an interesting bracelet," Ishtar mused as she scathingly took in the bracelet Moshe had given Loki.

"Aye, 'twas a gift," Loki replied.

"Is it just me, or does it resonate power?" she hedged.

"Actually, it was given to me by Moshe. It has Elohim's ten commandments inscribed on it," Loki answered.

Ishtar snorted derisively. "You are a fool to wear it."

"I am wise to wear it. Would ye have me hide far away from the leaders? Or sit in and listen to their war plans?" Loki chided.

Caleb stared intently at the bracelet. "What does it say?"

Loki watched Caleb for a very long time before giving a few commandments. "He commands them not to have any other god. He tells them that he is a jealous god. He forbids fornication and adultery. He commands to set apart the seventh day - to make it a holy day, to show their dedication and covenant only to him." Loki looked over to Ishtar. "He forbids murder... which I presume includes human sacrifice."

Ishtar raised her hand and spoke haughtily, "Quiet. The play begins."

Caleb turned to the play about to begin. A large pillow had been placed under the woman's veils to make her look pregnant. The revelers had returned to the banqueting tables and waited for the orator to take his position and speak.

"Behold the Queen of Heaven! Behold she, who births the Great Mediator. The Sun who vanquishes our foe, that hateful

Creator god who plagued us with the flood."

The actress immediately began writhing in pain and screaming her anguish.

"Behold she, who endures the great pains of childbirth, another curse from the god who hates us."

The actress slowly enacted the birth of a baby, then held a naked doll to her bosom as if to breastfeed. The doll had a round, gold plate attached to the back of its head to represent it being the sun god. A large, red cross was painted on the gold disc, representing the cakes of heaven made at his resurrection in the spring.

"Behold the babe, born of immaculate conception, born to subdue the enemies of our gods, born to subdue the god who would have us perish."

Four men quickly stood and hefted the dais upon their shoulders. They began carrying the actress and her babe throughout the square. The citizens broke out in a lively tune commemorating their salvation at the birth of the sun. When the actress and babe passed by, they reached out to bless and kiss them.

"Hmm," Loki mused.

"Didn't you like it?" Caleb asked.

"I've never seen a winter solstice without presents," Loki murmured.

Caleb smiled. "Oh, that comes tomorrow. Mother will lay out the gifts under the tree before the sunrise so they know that the Mother of God has blessed them yet again. Do you have presents?"

"Aye, the winter stag god, the god of the hunt, is led about by eight flying reindeer to deliver presents to all the children who have been good that year," Loki explained.

"Flying reindeer? What are reindeer?" Caleb asked excitedly.

"They're like deer," Loki answered.

Caleb turned to Ishtar. "Mother, isn't that clever? You fly at Easter, why don't you fly and deliver the presents tonight?"

Disdain dripped from Ishtar's tone, "You want me to walk through the front door of everyone who lives in Nineveh and give them a present? The priestesses help me with the tree."

"Actually, he enters by the smoke hole above the fire pit," Loki interjected.

"He gets smoky? Does he ever land on the fire? Get burnt? No, absolutely not." She threw Loki an annoyed look. "We are more civilized here."

"He is known to be all-knowing, even of the sins and deeds of the children, and all-powerful. What are ye here? Just a woman who births a babe?" Loki mocked.

"I am known to be the Mother of God!" Ishtar quaked in her wrath. Her eyes bulged. Her incredible beauty transformed to a mask of hate. "Now tell me what you know. We have waited long enough. Have the Hebrews entered Canaan?"

Loki sat back relaxed. "Aye."

Ishtar mocked Loki's accent. "Aye? And?"

"They have taken Yericho." Loki plopped his feet upon Ishtar's table. Caleb's eyes widened. Loki was disrespecting Ishtar greatly.

"Yericho? That great fortress? How did they do it? What is their weakness?" Ishtar implored.

"I want my betrothed," Loki bartered.

Ishtar sat quietly for a long time. "Fine. I will seek out Marduk as soon as this babe is born. Happy?"

Loki leaned in and whispered conspiratorially, "First, the commander of Elohim's angelic army came to Y'hoshua to aid him."

Ishtar squeaked, jumped up and stomped around the table. "An angel? How can I compete with that? But not just an angel, an entire angelic army? Led by Elohim's commander?" Ishtar smacked the table. It overturned and flew food everywhere. The revelers froze at the base of her temple.

Loki planted his fingertips along his jaw, enjoying Ishtar's rant. "The angelic army did not just kill those in Yericho."

Ishtar spun towards him, giving him her full attention. Caleb sat, open mouthed. Elohim's angelic army was involved in the reclaiming of the chosen's Promised Land.

"Nay. Yericho was made into the stronghold it was known for. There was no way any mortal could get into that city. Unlike us, who could just fly in. Nay. Elohim had the fighting men of Israel march around the city once a day for six days. Seven *cohanim*, priests, went with them, blowing *shofars*, ram's horns, as trumpets before the Arc of the Covenant."

"Arc?" Ishtar asked.

"A box of sorts that holds holy objects given to the Israelites by Elohim."

Ishtar narrowed her eyes. Caleb could only guess she was thinking of stealing it.

"Aye, well, on the seventh day, shabbat, the men and cohanim marched about Yericho again. But this time, when they finished, the cohanim let out one long shofar blow. The soldiers shouted. Then the commander of the angelic army let out a loud trumpet blow and the angelic army rushed down and broke down the walls of Yericho."

Petrified eyes scoured the walls of Nineveh. Ishtar whispered, "The angels knocked down the walls?"

"Crushed them." Loki paused. "Then the Israeli soldiers rushed in and killed everyone - man, woman, child, livestock... everything. They burnt the corpses and all the remains of the town... back to the dust that it had once been."

Ishtar slowly blinked several times. Her mind was racing. Her fear growing.

Loki smiled. "It's worse. They are led by Yehovah-Army-Commander, Yehovah-Angel, Yehovah-Man. The promised Messiah, Son of God, who will restore mortals from the curse. He shows himself now in an angelic form as He guides them in the recovering and restoration from their fallenness. Similiar to the preparations of the oncoming War of the Messiah, if ye ask me."

"They must have a weakness. Everyone has a weakness." She pierced Loki with a devastated look, lacking hope. "Surely, you know something."

They did have a weakness. Elohim said that they would be tested. Would it be Loki's fault if they became unworthy? Would Elohim hold Loki responsible? No, no he didn't think so. Elohim said they would be tested. If the chosen fell, it would be by their own doing only. "They must obey Elohim's laws and commands."

Ishtar spoke perplexed, "I don't understand."

"It is not the angels ye have to fight. In order to defeat the chosen, ye must have them break Elohim's laws." When Loki saw that she still was not grasping his advice, he gave her an example. "After Elohim gave the chosen the ten commandments, and they entered into a covenant with him, he held them accountable. Once they enter into covenant with Him, they are accountable, Ishtar. When Moshe went up to speak with Elohim..."

Caleb gasped in wonder. "Elohim spoke with a mortal?"

Loki nodded quickly before continuing, "He was gone for forty days. The Israelites got antsy. They built a golden calf with a sun disc to worship because they wanted to see something solid. Elohim was much angered. Thousands were killed for their disobedience. He let many live who had broken the covenant, but Elohim had vowed that they would not enter heaven because of it. When they reached Canaan, the spies were so scared of the Nephilim tribes that they feared entering and fought Y'hoshua on entering and warring with you. Elohim became angry. He forced them to wander the desert for forty years, until all the fighting men had died, and a new generation had risen. Not only were they not able to enter heaven, but they were not able to enter their Promised Land. Elohim is a jealous god. He demands respect and obedience, and he punishes severely those who break the covenant. He divorces them. No longer protects nor provides for them."

"Divorces them right away?" Caleb asked.

"Not always. Sometimes after a very long time. After his patience and mercy have dried up."

"So, we must get the chosen to break the covenant." Ishtar nodded her head, fully realizing the task ahead of her. "You said they were not allowed to fornicate? I'm good at that, that shouldn't be a problem. Bend their knees to another god?"

Loki nodded his head. "Not even participate in any festivities worshiping other gods."

"No orgies? No feast days to gods? No partaking of any fun. That will probably be the easiest. It is very difficult to stop oneself from joining in the party when the festive mood is high." Ishtar laughed. "No bacon? Ham? Boar roasts? Eh, Loki?"

Loki nodded.

"So we are to pollute them. Whore them to other gods. Yes, this I think can easily be done." Ishtar laughed and clapped her hands jubilantly.

Loki stood to leave.

"Loki. There are more rules? More laws?" she asked.

Loki nodded slowly. "More than I can memorize."

"Then bring me a copy of these rules and laws to Babylon. That is where Marduk is, isn't it? No, no, I will still be pregnant. You will have to bring it here. You will have to trust me concerning your betrothed."

Loki glared at Ishtar.

"Surely, it will take longer than five months for the Hebrews to defeat all of us. Come now, Loki. There is time. I will reward, as I have promised. Have I ever turned down mating with a god?" Ishtar continued coquettishly, "I've even offered myself to you several times. I'd prefer to do so now."

Loki curtly nodded. "I will await my betrothed. Good day." Loki flew straight up and over the walls distancing himself as quickly as he could. He had forgotten what day it was. His world was blending with the chosen. He spent most of his time with Y'hoshua. He flew as quickly as he could, passing many winter solstice celebrations until finally reaching the outskirts of the encampment.

When he landed, he saw a well with many camels. As he walked closer, he could make out a traveling caravan. The very weak blooded Nephilim spoke with some of the Hebrews encamped nearby.

"Who is the baal of this well? I would not want to offend him as I am sure you are aware," a small giant of seven feet asked.

"The baal of this well? I'm sorry, but I don't understand your meaning. Do you mean the owner?" the Hebrew replied.

"No, the divine being, the spirit who presides here," the giant answered.

The Hebrew laughed. "Oh, I don't know. I wasn't aware that there was a deity for the well."

The Nephilim descendant looked at him perplexed. "But every stream, mountain, locality and well has a baal over it. What of the master or chief baal of the land? Do you not fear him?"

"Oh, I didn't know the customs of this land. Am I offending you? I didn't mean to be so rude," the Hebrew said sheepishly, looking over the giant's seven foot height.

"You should be most respectful to the baals. They give you power. Some make your women fertile, others give you protection from roaming bandits, all of them give you power of something else," the giant explained.

"Well, our baal travels with us, protects us," the Hebrew offered.

"Truly? How marvelous. But I would be careful if I were you. Yericho's baal is most fearsome. He could possibly crush yours."

The Hebrew smiled brightly. "Our baal already defeated their baal. The entire city has been laid to waste. Our baal is most strong. He led us out of Egypt, even killing the pharaoh in the Red Sea when he chased us down to imprison us."

"I have heard of you and your baal. You are the Apiru."

"Is that what you call us? Apiru?" the Hebrew asked.

The giant knelt down on one knee. "Pray. Pray to your baal to bless me. Please. Let us be friends."

The Hebrew stood confused on what to do. He quickly bowed his head and prayed, "Lord, my Baal, bless this... Nephilim... for his kind words and deeds to your children and followers. May you guide his footsteps and guard his back."

Happily, the giant jumped up and took the Hebrew by the arm. "Now, come and dine with me to seal the blessing." The Nephilim led him into a tent and to a small altar where two candles lit an image of the Mother Goddess and her Sun feeding at her breast. "It is the winter solstice. We shall pray to my baal so that she will bless your wife with sons. Come, my children are already feasting out by the tree. Come, it is a most joyous night, and my baal will bless you with a gift by morning for your devotion."

Loki watched the man trying to act like an ambassador, trying to make friends with a Nephilim living in the land they were to conquer. With a grieved heart, Loki turned to walk back to Y'hoshua. The Hebrew looked to fall without Ishtar's schemes. Sooner than he would have thought. It pained him greatly. He would tell Y'hoshua. These were Y'hoshua's men. What a laughingstock, the Hebrew was making of Elohim's greatness. Did the Hebrew not think to hold himself separate as Elohim commanded? Was making friends and allies more important than consecration to YHVH?

951 BC, JERUSALEM

Caleb stared at all the dignitaries and ambassadors seated around him. He and his mother had watched the activities of the chosen of Elohim through the centuries and had continued to be amazed. Ishtar was most intrigued with Deborah, that Elohim would use a woman as he had, but his mother had lusted after

Samson. She had heard tales of him on her way to find Marduk and had pursued him relentlessly, but when she found him, he only had eyes for Delilah - a mortal. Samson had spurned Ishtar's advances, and she had run away to lick her wounds, never taking the time to find Marduk. Then the kings had risen. First Saul and then David. She watched in fascination, tried to entice David as well, but was spurned. She still spoke of how he danced around the arc naked. Her jealousy rising when tales of Bathsheeba's beauty circulated Nineveh. But now, now was Solomon.

Caleb had been sent to speak with Solomon - the new object of Ishtar's desire. She wanted to make one of Elohim's men choose her instead. It was rumored that Solomon had spoken to Elohim twice, and that Elohim had granted him his one request - to be wise. Solomon's empire had grown, his wealth could no longer be counted, and he had pleasured himself well. He broke Elohim's laws and married foreign princesses for political alliances. Ishtar knew that this king would be the one to fall to her.

The dark chamber was lit by bronze candelabras and incensed with a heavy floral musk that was mysteriously masculine. Solomon sat at the head of the table arrayed in a gold dusted purple robe. Five amethysts sat on his golden crown, and two dangled from his ears. He looked to be in his late thirties but could have been older due to his lack of exposure to the sun. He was a genteel man, an indoor man. He had strawberry blonde hair and a rosy complexion accented with black eyes. It was an intriguing mixture. His skin shone with oils, and he moved with an air of decisiveness that impressed.

The entire room was bedecked with brightly clad foreigners, all vying for his attention. Egyptians, Hittites, Aryans, Persians, Greeks, Ethiopians and more cloistered around him in their most impressive native garbs and finery. A tiger, caged to the corner of the room, roared, causing most of the visitors to tremble. Solomon only smiled. Elephants could be heard outside where a moving zoo had been brought for his amusement.

Caleb leaned forward. There was one seat empty between Solomon and himself, but somehow he knew that he was not to sit in it. The empty seat was treated with reverence, and Caleb wondered if one of Solomon's wives were to join the all male company. Just as the roasted boar, grapes, figs, raisons, and wine were placed upon the table, the seat was filled by a man with long waves of burnished copper hair. Supernaturally lit eyes, that swirled orange, red and green flecks in a molten brown pool, turned towards him.

"Caleb."

"Still occupying yourself with the Hebrews?" Caleb returned.

"Yer mother still wanting what she cannot have?" Loki quipped.

Solomon turned to the two Nephilim. "Is he one like you, Loki?"

"Aye, but not such a strong lineage. He is one da away from aging." Loki grabbed a little bit of everything except for the ham for his consumption. "He is Ishtar's son with Madai ben Japheth ben Noah."

"Ah, post flood then. What brings you to my table? Elohim has given me much wisdom, but I wonder at it in comparison to those who have lived so long," Solomon charmed.

Caleb leaned back. Solomon spoke eloquently and humbly, but his eyes were proud. Wise, but perhaps not such an excellent actor. "My mother, the great Ishtar, would like to have an official meeting with you."

"Ye mean an official laying with," Loki muttered. "She wants a babe from yer loins."

Solomon laughed. "Ah yes, so many do."

"I do nae ken why they call ye wise," Loki joked. "Seven hundred wives and three hundred concubines doesnae sound so wise to me."

Caleb's eyes grew enormous. "Do you have children by them all?"

Loki grunted. "Nay, his timing with their moon flows isn't too great."

Solomon smiled. "I have many beds to visit."

"Who is your heir?" Caleb asked.

"Rehoboam, first son of Naamah," Solomon answered.

Loki chided, "Son of an Ammonite."

Solomon barely sighed before replying kindly, "The Ammonites are descendants of Lot, kin to the Israelites. And what do I have to squabble about? My father David was a descendent of a mixed marriage between an Israeli and a Moabitess, an even farther relation than that having to go all the way back to Terah."

"And exactly how does yer marriage to the daughter of pharaoh not counteract the commands of Elohim concerning intermarriage?" Loki asked bluntly.

"Why through Joseph, who was married to an Egyptian himself, a daughter of the Priest of On. We already have Egyptians in our blood."

Loki leaned over and whispered to Caleb, "Elohim commanded 'You shall not intermarry with them, nor they with you. Surely they will turn away your hearts after their gods.' And that is what they did. Wait and see fer yerself. We will be going to the temple when the meal is over."

Caleb began to wonder if Ishtar would want Solomon since he didn't seem like such a challenge after all, but just in case, he decided to pursue the reason his mother had sent him, as detestable as it was. "King Solomon, will you accept a meeting with my mother?"

Loki muttered under his breath, "Why not, every other woman has already been there."

Caleb shot Loki a nasty look while smiling politely at Solomon.

"Ishtar. I have heard tales of her grand beauty. I have not taken... met a female Nephilim yet, especially one as powerful, sensual, and of such a strong lineage as your mother. I would be most humbled to accept her gracious offer," Solomon bequeathed. "Mayhaps, she will give me a son who would never age as you do. Someone who could reign Isra-el forever." An odd glint came into Solomon's eyes as he considered that thought.

Caleb grinned, that would be a feat Ishtar would love to accomplish. Her son sitting on the throne of Elohim's chosen. Leading his people.... away.

Loki grumbled, "Nothing new under the sun."

Solomon's head jerked. "What was that you said?"

Loki cleared his throat and threw back the rest of his wine. "Nothing new under the sun."

Solomon grinned. "Nothing new under the sun. I like that. Yes, I like that indeed." Solomon stood up and held out his hands to his guests. "Come, for it is shabbat, the Lord's day, let us make our obeisance. My wives await."

Solomon led all the men out to a hill on the eastern side of Jerusalem. Donkeys waited just outside the palace to transport the royal dignitaries. Solomon's wives arrayed in their finest apparel could be seen encircling an altar on the Mount of Olives, or as Loki called it, the Mount of Corruption.

Loki began quoting from memory, "ADONAI said to Moshe, 'Speak to the people of Isra'el; tell them, 'I am ADONAI your God. You are not to engage in the activities found in the land of Egypt, where you used to live; and you are not to engage in the activities found in the land of Canaan, where I am bringing you; nor are you to live by their laws. You are to obey my rulings and laws and live accordingly; I am ADONAI your God. You are to observe my laws and rulings; if a person does them, he will have life through them; I am ADONAI.'"

As the caravan of dignitaries approached, Caleb could make out stone images of the Moabite god Chemosh, the Sidonian goddess Ashtoreth, and the Ammonite god Molech. A large altar rose amidst them, a high place for sacrifices.

Loki shook his head and continued his diatribe, "You are not to make yourselves any idols; erect a carved statue or a standing stone, or place any carved stone anywhere in your land in order to bow down to it. I am ADONAI your God."

When Solomon arrived, he walked up to each idol and lit incense to them. When he approached Molech, he paused, then went and stood by a small idol. It was the bust of Ishtar - the famed bust that had been sent throughout the world. A priest approached Solomon's side and handed him a golden wreath. Solomon took the wreath and crowned Ishtar, naming her the MLK, the Milcom, the deified king of the Israelites. Caleb paused. Was that a sign that she would be the mother of the next king of Isra-el? Solomon turned and gave him a sly glance before nodding his head in anticipation of their families' merger.

Loki growled low in his throat. "Do not make yourselves unclean by any of these things, because all the nations which I am expelling ahead of you are defiled with them. The land has become unclean, and this is why I am punishing it - the land itself will vomit out its inhabitants. But you are to keep my laws and rulings and not engage in any of these disgusting practices, neither the citizen nor the foreigner living with you; for the people of the land have committed all these abominations, and the land is now defiled. If you make the land unclean, it will vomit you out too, just as it is vomiting out the nation that were there before you. For those who engage in any of these disgusting practices, whoever they may be, will be cut off from their people. So keep my charge not to follow any of these abominable customs that others before you have followed and thus defile yourselves by doing them. I am ADONAI your God."

Caleb snorted, "They don't seem to be so obedient, do they? These are Elohim's chosen?"

Solomon nodded to the priests standing behind the idols. They brought out a sacred bull. He waited while they slashed its throat and sprinkled its blood over Solomon's wives, who began immediately chanting and singing praises to their gods. Instruments began to play, and the masses began dancing around the torch lit high place. The royal dignitaries approached and kissed the feet of their idols, praying incessantly to them as the women began to strip in their rapture. The priests pushed the slaughtered bull onto the altar and lit it on fire. The women screeched an unholy pitch, sending chills down Caleb's back. Solomon nodded to the priests one last time before turning and walking towards Elohim's temple.

Caleb stood watching as the priests threw three children onto the burning sacrifice. Their cries were drowned out by the screeching of the women. Caleb was stunned. "They are no different."

Loki referenced yet another Scripture, "Here are the laws and rulings you are to observe and obey in the land ADONAI, the God of your ancestors, has given you to possess as long as you live on earth. You must destroy all the places where the nations you are dispossessing served their gods, whether on high mountains, on hills, or under some leafy tree. Break down their altars, smash their standing-stones to pieces, burn up their sacred poles completely and cut down the carved images of their gods. Exterminate their name from that place. For you are not to worship ADONAI your God this way."

Loki and Caleb watched the priests take the burnt meat of the children, cut it into pieces, put it into bowls, and serve it to Solomon's wives. Loki turned and beckoned for Caleb to follow.

As they trudged down the hill, the revelries lessened but never diminished fully. The sacrificial bonfire blazed the night sky into a deep purple, and lit up the gold on Elohim's temple. Some of the Hebrews had followed Solomon when he left, but many remained behind with his wives and concubines.

When they were far enough away to speak easily, Caleb said, "I honestly had hope. I've never... Ishtar's festivities have always sickened my stomach. I've been intrigued with the Hebrews, had hope that they were different, but they are not, are they?"

Loki faced Caleb. "They were. They have bad spells, but nothing like this until Solomon polluted himself with pleasure and married for politics. Elohim warned that intermarrying would lead his children astray, and it has. Solomon once had such a passion for Elohim, then his heart was turned away by his wives. It is the flesh they fight against in order to serve Elohim. It is the selfish desires and whims that intrigue them and their own rationalizations that allows them to find reasons to do as their heart wills. Listen to what has been told them. 'When ADONAI your God has cut off ahead of you the nations you are entering in order to dispossess, and when you have dispossessed them and are living in their land; be careful, after they have been destroyed ahead of you, not to be trapped into following them; so that you inquire after their gods and ask, 'How did these nations serve their gods? I want to do the same.' You must not do this to ADONAI your God! For they have done to their gods all the abominations that ADONAI hates! They even burn up their sons and daughters in the fire for their gods! Everything I am commanding you, you are to take care to do. Do not add to it or subtract from it."

Loki led Caleb back through Jerusalem and up to Elohim's temple. In the daytime, its painfully white marble facade was blinding, and its golden pillars dazzled from afar. Now, at night, it beckoned like a cool resting place in the midst of a desert. The building, as a whole, was shaped as a rectangle, with a ninety foot length and thirty foot width. On either side of the main entry, soaring double white pillars with golden tops reached up sixty-seven feet. It faced east, where the sun would rise and catch the reflection of the sunrise beautifully. Directly in front of the entry steps was a fifteen foot bronze bowl filled with water, and over to the side of it was a raised altar for sacrifices.

Loki leaned in. "The temple was constructed and sanctified as Elohim ordained, but it's..."

Caleb moved to the left, so he could peer inside. The Lebanon cedar doors had been left open. It was dark inside but a few candelabras gave light within. It appeared to have three chambers, each perfectly aligned, but Caleb couldn't see into the third. He could barely make anything out, and Solomon was nowhere to be seen.

Music drifted up from Jerusalem, and Caleb turned to see Solomon's wives dancing up to Elohim's temple. Jewish men and women joined them in their revelries as the High Priest and Solomon exited out of the temple. First, two oxen were offered as a burnt sacrifice. Then Solomon stepped up to the water-filled bronze bowl and jumped in, arising fully drenched. His twelve most favored wives followed him in and began cavorting with him.

Solomon spoke loudly for all to hear, "So God, our baal, created man in his own image, in the image of baal he created him; male and female he created them. God blessed them and said to them, 'Be fruitful and increase in number; fill the earth and subdue it. Rule over the fish of the sea and the birds of the air and over every living creature that moves on the ground.' For this reason a man will leave his father and mother and be united to his wife." Solomon grabbed one of his wives playfully. "And they will become one flesh. The man and his wife were both naked, and they felt no shame. And God said it was good." Solomon laughed as he and his twelve most favored wives stripped off all their remaining clothes. The royal dignitaries, Jews, and the rest of Solomon's women stripped naked and danced before the altar as Solomon worked at being fruitful and multiplying.

Loki turned his back. "It is time to leave."

760 BC, NINEVEH

A hot desert wind blew through Caleb's dark chestnut curls, rustling them playfully, and leaving them disarrayed. His characteristic surliness was at an all time high. Something wasn't right. He couldn't put his finger on it. But an oppressive weight burdened him, filling him with anguish, desolation, and frustration. A comment that Loki had said still haunted him. "Nothing new under the sun."

Caleb was already beginning to forget how old he was. Everything fused together without change. His mother's antics still irritated him. The festivities still repulsed him. He had gone to war, battled amongst the greats, but shortly afterwards, he felt despondent again. Always wondering what to do next. He had visited the Greek scholars, the Egyptian medicine men, the Persian Magi, and he still felt empty.

He had followed as Ishtar advised, and given as many of his sons to Nineveh as he could, but his sons aged. It grieved him to watch them die. Ishtar advised him to drown himself in sexual pleasures, but again he felt empty when he awoke, used, and restless. Love was Ishtar's response. He had tried, but there just seemed to be something within him that wouldn't allow him to. He didn't know if it was fear of them dying on him, as his sons did, or something else. He did know that he felt less miserable the more he pulled away from humanity. They were fleeting while he was not.

Caleb had next taken on large building projects but after a decade, that bored him too. He had learned many instruments, only to create the most soul wrenching songs imaginable. The music that came from him was tear jerking. What did that say about him? He hid behind a peaceful facade, always acting as if he was in charge of his surroundings, and always bored with the activities going on around him. He didn't want people to know how his spirit cried, and that is what happened when he wrote and played instruments - his emotions became imprinted on his sleeve for all to witness.

Caleb walked to the balcony and looked down upon mighty Nineveh. He saw women working in their gardens, men selling wares in the streets, children stealing from travelers, and soldiers drawing blood from their comrades in mock fights to the death. No one seemed to smile. Looking to the left, he saw men walk up the steps to Ishtar's Temple, stopping at the prostitute level to pay a priestess to have sex with them. The men lusted, the women obeyed. Neither looked happy. Why would they? If the men were happy with their wives, if their needs were being met, if they felt respected and cherished at home, would they be seeking out temple prostitutes? It seemed to Caleb that it was an aching loneliness, an excruciating lack of love that drove men to seek out such short, shallow displays of love, love that had to be bought since it was not given.

Caleb turned, resting his back against the wall, and gazed

into his own bedchamber. It was filled with countless treasures, wealth, and the most luxurious items. His bed was made of down feathers. Lavish scarves in royal blue and black hid all the brick walls, and gold was sculpted into his ceiling with royal blue plaster to create an intriguing array of swirls. Off to the side was an entire garden of exotic flowers and plants which hid and shaded a pool for him to swim in. The whole room was dark, cool and humid - a delightful respite to the hot, arid desert outside his balcony that the citizens toiled in all day. But he was still displeased. It wasn't that he disliked his abode, it was that he had nothing of importance to do with his life or his time.

Caleb balled his fists in frustration and allowed his anger to shake his arms. He was so bored! Why couldn't he find something worthy to do? To spend his life doing? Why couldn't he find happiness? He searched for reasons to like his life, to enjoy his many years on this planet, but to no avail. The only thing that kept him from taking his life was imagining how much worse it would be floating about as a demon. At least food and the seasons gave him some break from the ongoing mundane boring existence he was doomed to.

"Caleb."

Caleb swirled around and took in the tall handsome man before him. He had sapphire eyes and dark chestnut, wavy hair. His eyes were crinkled in the corners from laughter, and currently twinkled while gazing at his son.

"Father." Caleb ran up and hugged him. He loved traveling with his father, but his dad rarely allowed him to join. "I am so glad you have come. What have you been up to? How long will you be staying?"

Madai laughed heartily and tussled Caleb's hair. "This and that." He winked.

Caleb gave him a disdainful look. "More information will be needed."

Caleb was quite interested. His father used to hunt with Nimrod before the great king had gone missing. On their first trip, Caleb and his father had traveled through Egypt before heading south. They hunted every animal the tribal chiefs spoke of, especially the ones the mortals feared: lions, elephants, rhinos, hippos, crocodiles, saber tooth tigers and mammoths. When they had run out of land, they sailed to an icy plateau and traversed it, seeing some of the cutest animals. He still chuckled when he remembered their small velvet bodies of black and white. Penguins, he thought his father had called them.

On their second trip, they had headed east and found tigers and elephants. The scenery had been breathtaking with the highest mountains imaginable and the deadliest jungles. They continued their path till the land ended again, and then they sailed, searching out whales, sharks, and other creatures under the sea. But where had his father been this time?

His father, slowly stripping, walked over to his son's pool and dove in. Caleb decided to be patient. The pool was the first place he went after returning from a trip in the desert. His father would talk when he was ready.

After swimming several laps, Madai walked to the shallow end and leapt onto the ledge, allowing his legs to continue dangling in the cool water. "I went up to the Northmen, and they invited me to sail to a new land." Madai held out his hands to encompass everything around him. "Almost as big as our land mass, but it's not connected to us at all. Some of them had walked to it on ice in the deep of winter. They said that at certain times, the stars became streaked and stayed streaked. The sky glows unusual colors at night. They appear rippled and glow ethereally."

"What colors?" Caleb interrupted.

"Pink, orange, purple, turquoise, green, mint, yellow, red... Any color imaginable, and it stands out beautifully against the black sky. It's breathtaking. Then we sailed, and sailed, and sailed. I didn't think we would ever reach it. It took months to get there. We saw stranger sea creatures than what you saw in the east. We landed in the cold northern regions. They stayed for only a short while, but I took off south on my own. I found two mountain ranges, one almost nothing but hills, but the ones farther out west had nice waterfalls. I killed some bear, mountain lions, and what they call buffalo. I'll try to draw you a picture of them. I found many Nephilim living in the main river valley in the northern half. They were in the midst of battling one another, so I decided to get involved." Madai sent his son a sheepish grin. "I don't know why they were fighting though. Afterwards, I headed south and found black Nephilim."

"Black?" Caleb smiled, here was something new.

"Yes, black. As dark as your mother's heart." Madai winked. Caleb chuckled.

"Then I moved south and found that other Nephilim had been visiting the natives. Apparently, the mortals saw the Nephilim as gods there, as they do here, because they made statues of them and worshiped them. Some, get this, even floated over on cane rafts. From the looks of it, they were of Osiris and Egyptian, looked just like his boats. Oh, you should see the snakes they have there. Now, they were scary. They called them anacondas and boa constrictors. They were giant snakes that could easily swallow a Nephilim whole." Madai shivered with distaste. "You know how I hate snakes. Then I moved farther south and found true beauty. The waterfalls were amazing, the jungles were perilous, and the mountains breathtaking. You should really take time to visit it."

"Well, I would have gone with you if you had informed me that you were leaving again. But still, that took hundreds of years?"

"Well, that's a lot to walk. You know I don't fly. Then I decided to do a bit of sailing on my own and headed west. Found a few more islands. Another large land mass. Then walked back through the east that we visited," Madai explained.

"Oh, I see, is that all?" Caleb asked sardonically.

"I didn't find Nimrod. Where do you think he went? If he died, there would have been something big - a funeral or celebration, but there's been nothing. It's as if he grew tired of living and disappeared to explore the world on his own. Oh, I did find the Amazons. They've moved to the southern land mass of that new place. They're on an island that you can only get to through an underwater passage. They're right smack in the deadliest area of the jungle, surrounded by those nasty anacondas. You'd think females would stay away from snakes."

Caleb quirked an eyebrow and held his tongue, but his curiosity got the better of him. "And how long did you stay there?"

"Well now, don't be acting like that with your father. I had to be a gentleman. They hadn't been visited by a male Nephilim for a very long time. The queen was a most gracious host. How could I be rude?"

"Madai?" Ishtar called from Caleb's bedchamber.

Madai sent Caleb a scornful look. He whispered, "How did she know I was here?" He motioned for Caleb to throw him a blanket to cover himself with.

After becoming modest, he responded, "Just washing off the desert sand."

Ishtar seductively swished through the jungle vegetation, slowly revealing her beauty. Her flaxen hair glinted in the sunlight, and her emerald eyes mesmerized. Too late, Caleb realized that his mother was nude. "Mother, go put a robe on!"

Ishtar cocked her head, her eyes stayed on Madai. "Your father has seen me thus before. It will not be a shock to him."

"It is a disgusting shock to me. I do not want to see you thus, and I don't want anyone to see you thus in my chambers!" Caleb yelled, his face turning red with wrath.

Ishtar pursed her lips and drank in Madai's form. Her voice lowered seductively, "Would you like me to serve you in your bath, Madai?"

Madai replied caustically, "I'd like you to allow me and my son to catch up. Alone."

"Yes... *our* son."

Caleb went back to his chamber and found the robe she had left on his floor. He returned and wrapped it around her. Ishtar pouted. "And do I presume too much that you will dine with me tonight and allow us to catch up... alone?"

Madai sighed. "I don't know."

Ishtar jerked as if she had been slapped.

"I've changed Ishtar."

Caleb turned intrigued.

"What mean you?" she quizzed.

"I mean that if I seek a loving embrace, I will seek it from one of the virgins you force to lay with strangers. At least I can ease them with their first time rather than let the repulsive, lust hounds you let in there rip through them violently."

Ishtar's lips squeezed together into a fine line. Caleb had done that often himself, feeling pity for them.

Madai rose, keeping himself covered. "Anyway, you know I like to explore the new, not the old." He watched Ishtar's eyes flash with rage. "Or the well-used."

Ishtar quaked. Caleb lowered his head. He didn't think his father needed to be mean, but then he didn't know a lot of what had happened between them. Perhaps, in his own way, he was just getting even. Caleb knew his mother, he wouldn't be surprised if she had slept around during their affair. It would actually make sense if his father had left because of that very reason. Then again, Ishtar was coming on way too strong. It was revolting and screamed desperate. Without saying a word, she turned and left the room.

"Ishtar," Madai called. She froze, just barely out of sight and waited.

He continued solemnly, "We will never lie together again. That is over between us."

She stiffly walked out.

Caleb turned to his father. "You should be careful. She is still more powerful than you."

Madai gave his son a long, level look. "Would you ever lie with a woman like your mother?"

Caleb knew that he wouldn't. "But you did once."

"That was before. She may be more powerful, but she is not older than me. I was her first, and you were her first child. You know how fertile she is," Madai explained.

Caleb had never heard the story, and he wanted to. "Tell me what happened between you two."

"At first, she feared giving herself to any man. She saw how females were treated - like property - and she refused to be seen as such. She was always a thinker, a schemer. She wanted glory, power, and reverence. At first, she built her independence and warrior skills. She was a sight to behold back then. Does she ever battle anymore? Hunt?"

Caleb shook his head.

Madai nodded for awhile before continuing, "She quickly realized the power her beauty gave her. Men would do anything to be in her presence. She used that, knowing that as soon as she gave herself to one of them, she would lose much of her power and desire. Everyone wanted to be her mate, everyone wanted to be her first. Her intelligence, beauty and virginity was a heady package. But she did not want to be any man's possession."

"Why did she choose you?"

Madai shrugged his shoulders. "I know not. I think it was because I didn't act like I wanted her. Perhaps, it was because I bested her on the hunting ground and the battlefield. But she gave herself to me. I felt honored. She was faithful throughout her pregnancy and decades afterwards as I was to her, but then she met Nimrod, the mightiest hunter of them all, the king of the world. He was the best of everything: intelligence, architect, artist, musician, hunter, warrior, leader, lover. She had to have him. She wanted to be his queen, the queen of the entire known mortal world. She saw the children he gave to mortals and wanted powerful children as well. You know, I am much weaker than Nimrod in my Nephilim ancestry. My father's wife lacked the height and many of the visible traits of Nephilim as you and I both do."

"So she slept with Nimrod, and you left her," Caleb surmised.

"No. Nimrod would not have her. Nimrod slept with many, many females, but he was wise enough not to sleep with the lover of a good friend; especially, a woman who wanted to use him to become more powerful herself, or assert herself as his queen. Nimrod was wise. Wise men do not allow the lusts of the flesh to complicate politics, business, nor friendships. Eternity is a long time to make a cherished friend an enemy."

Caleb nodded. Yes, Nimrod sounded like a wise man. He chuckled. "Mother tried to have a son with Solomon."

Madai turned shocked. "Tried? Solomon turned her down? Well, he was proclaimed to be the wisest mortal that ever lived." He broke out laughing.

Caleb remained quiet. He didn't have good thoughts towards Solomon. He agreed with Loki, Solomon wasn't that wise. If Elohim had spoken with him and opened the door for a personal relationship, Caleb would have obeyed his commandments. But then, he had lived a lot longer than Solomon. Maybe he shouldn't be so hard on him. "Solomon didn't turn her down; she became barren."

"Elohim closed her womb?" Madai asked reverently; he paused a whole minute before continuing, "I have heard tales in my last travels that Elohim ordained three Cities of Refuge to be built for redeemed Nephilim, but I do not know where they are."

"What mean you by redeemed?" Caleb asked intrigued.

"Those that obey his commandments and serve only Him."

"What commandments?" Caleb questioned.

"Well, normal ones of purity and holines, then the three Nephilim commandments: Do not allow mortals to worship you as a god. Do not use humans as food or drink their blood. Do not mate nor breed with a mortal. Furthermore, all redeemed Nephilim will be executed if they refuse their duty of Kinsman Redeemer by the Day of Atonement. Elohim decreed that the closest relative be responsible for eliminating the Nephilim committing atrocities against mankind."

Caleb suddenly realized that his mother had never told him about this. In fact, she made him almost as guilty as she was. "How long have you known of the laws?"

"All my life." Madai paused. "Your mother never told you?" Sorrow etched his face. "It is why she barely leaves Nineveh. She fears Tagas, a first generation Nephilim who presides as the Judge and Executioner of our race. I am so sorry, my son. I thought for sure she would have told you. But I just found out myself about the three cities. Apparently, many have flocked there, found their Nephilim spouse, and raise their Nephilim children. They await to fight in the War of the Messiah that Elohim has planned in completion of the full restoration. They hide from the mortal world."

Loud wailing was heard below. Caleb turned perplexed, breaking out of his father's conversation. Why were the masses wailing? He rushed to the balcony and looked down. A lone man was walking the streets. He wore a long dirty robe, and his hair was matted by grease. The citizens were lined up on either side of the street, lying on their stomachs, and throwing dust and ashes into their hair. They wore sackcloth. Why weren't they wearing their finest like normal? What in the world was going on? Who was this man?

The stranger yelled out, his voice carrying as if a trumpet were mystically attached to his vocal cords, "Forty more days and Nineveh will be overthrown for her wicked and vile ways. Elohim proclaims it. Her unlawfullness will be wiped from the earth."

Madai stood aghast. "It is a prophet of Elohim. Nineveh is being called to repent. And the people are repenting."

Of course the people were repenting. They had all heard stories of Elohim and his greatness. They had all seen Ishtar's fears and heard the tales from traveling caravans about the god of the Israelites. They knew what happened to Yericho. They were being given a chance to repent? Elohim was providing them an escape from destruction?

Madai grabbed Caleb's hand. "Let us put on sackcloth and repent as well. Elohim will forgive, but we must obey."

Something irrevocable happened within Caleb at that moment. Something had clicked, something had snapped. He shook. His whole body trembled. He had been sinning his entire life, and he hadn't even known it. Realizations came slamming down upon him. Things Loki had said suddenly made sense, the entire world made sense. It was as if he had been blind his entire life, but he could see clearly now. The veils of deception had fallen away. No, not veils, scales of deception, because they had completely blinded him. Deception by she who had raised him, molded his world, and taught him what to believe and why. And now, Elohim was giving him a chance, a chance to repent, a time to turn to ADONAI.

Caleb clutched Madai's hand and rushed down to the street. They rent their clothes, rolled in the dust, and poured ashes on their dark brown hair. Still clutching hands, father and son cried out to Elohim in anguish for forgiveness. They repented for their unlawfullness. Rising up on one knee, they vowed to Elohim their future obedience to his will.

Happiness surged through Caleb like a lightning bolt striking a fuse. An inexplicable joy flooded his entire being, and all his frustrations lifted from his shoulders. A tranquillity settled over his spirit that he could only deem was peace, something he had never experienced. It felt like his insides were glowing and shooting out bright light through his every pore. Tears ran down his cheeks and disabled him from speaking.

"Don't you dare bow down to Elohim!" Ishtar yelled.

Caleb felt a wash of warm, sticky liquid splash over him. Horrified, he turned to find his mother standing over his beheaded father, her bloody scimitar still clutched in her hand. Tears coursed down her face, as she lifted her fearful and anguished eyes to her son. "Get up."

Caleb stumbled back. His heart pounded. The whole world slowed down. A pain grew in his lungs, and he realized he had stopped breathing. Taking a gasp, he stood as she commanded. Minutes passed as he stared at his mother. Sobs wracked her body. She slowly held out her hand to him for compassion, for strength, and for solidarity. He turned and fled.

761 BC, JERUSALEM

Caleb leaned over the scroll made of stretched animal skin. It was halfway covered with Hebrew symbols. Everything had to be perfect. Not one flaw could exist. The word of Elohim could not be altered in any way. He took his feather and returned it to the clay ink pot. Stretching to ease his back, he looked all around him. It was the same, yet so very different. The Temple was brilliant and cleaned to perfection. Not one unsanctified hand touched it. The priests seemed lenient with him, often mentioning his lineage under Noah, often asking him questions on previous centuries. They probed into his visit with Solomon, and how the Canaanites reacted to Elohim's help in conquering the Promised Land. It was a peaceful time, a spiritual oasis. He had never been happier. He had never had such joy and mirth. He had never regretted his decision.

One of his delights was visiting the Mystic's School. The elder mystics taught the young seers how to grow in their mysticism without breaking any Torah laws. Seers had great natural spiritual abilities, but they could grow their spirit-man in mysticism to see into the other dimensions and realms. Enoch, Elijah, and Ezekiel were some of the great mystics of YHVH. Some had even entered the heavenly dimensions to prophesy what was or is to come. Caleb especially loved it when Loki was there, for he would read the thoughts of their mystic travels first hand and then tell him.

The elderly prophet, Zechariah, waved from the temple, then hobbled to Caleb's side. His withered skin and frail appearance caused fear to traipse down Caleb's spine each time a strong gust of desert air swept through the temple's courtyard. His flowing white robe was tied securely at his waist by a scarlet sash that seemed to constantly get underfoot. A cone-like white cloth encircled his head and covered the back of his neck to protect it from the scorching sun. To his right, helping him along, was a much younger man who wore a long purple robe and multi-colored sash.

Caleb had seen the younger man before but had never spoken to him. He was always sitting in the frankincense chamber writing. What he wrote was not shared with many. Caleb stood up and helped Zechariah sit down, keeping a hand on him in case he blew away. "Coming out to warm your bones, my friend?"

"Yes, yes, but nothing seems to warm them anymore. I want you to meet Isaiah." Zechariah pointed out the younger man beside him.

Isaiah nodded his head solemnly. His ragged, black, uncut hair fell in front of his matching black eyes. Oddly, he had a dark swarthy appearance for spending so much time in doors.

"Ah, frankincense boy," Caleb joked.

Isaiah's serious stare unnerved Caleb. It seemed to carry the weight of the world and a hidden sorrow etched deep within. When he didn't speak, Caleb cleared his throat and tried to be a little less playful. "Are you a prophet as well?"

Zechariah took on a bit of a perplexed expression. "He's definitely a mystic. Receives many visions and dreams. They seem to trouble him greatly, but writing them down helps." He paused before revealing, "He has traveled to the heavenly dimensions."

Caleb was fond of the elderly prophet. It was under his tutelage that King Uzziah of Y'hudah had become a strong leader of Elohim. At only sixteen, Uzziah had taken the throne, then strengthened Israel back to one of its most prosperous times since Solomon. He was a virile and decisive ruler, full of a balanced wisdom that gave his people a respite and haven in the midst of tumultuous reigns. His achievements had reached far and wide, even being recounted by Egyptian pharaohs. Unlike Solomon, Uzziah had continually done right in the sight of Elohim. He was known to be a faithful servant of YHVH. Even now, he was not sitting idle. Caleb could hear the king's skilled warriors constructing machines for the corner defenses of Jerusalem. These structures would be able to hurl large stones at the enemy and protect his archers during an attack. He did not take his peace for granted and guarded against the possibility of a future assault. Caleb hoped his fame would not cause his peers to fear Y'hudah's growing power and strength.

"I, ah, I thought you might be of some assistance to our Isaiah, Caleb," Zechariah continued. "He sees many things. I have read some, but he even fears to show me some of them. I know not what to do. No, I often know not what to do for him. He is often grieved. Holds things in. It is not natural. It is not good. You have lived long, Caleb. You have seen many things that once grieved you. Perhaps, you can help. Yes, perhaps you can help. Aid him in letting go of the visions and dreams once he's scribed them, for surely there is nothing he can do about them. No, no, it seems some things he has seen, is even before your time, Caleb, so nothing can be done. But 'tis a record. For what reason, I know not, only Elohim knows."

Caleb nodded. "I will do all I can." He tried to give Isaiah a compassionate look, but it was not returned. No, Isaiah just stared at him. It wasn't the normal stare he received from the priests who knew what he was. Zechariah and Uzziah had decided that only the mystical Levites would know Caleb's background. The same had been decided for Loki when he passed through.

Isaiah's stare was not scared or awed. It was knowing. As if he was familiar with the sight of angels, and Caleb was only a weak mortalized version that didn't merit much of his attention. It was not a rude stare, but one that hid a knowledge that a mortal was not to know, knowledge that purported the man into another realm as if he could see both the spiritual and physical at once. His solemnness, made everyone near him gravely serious and wonder what Isaiah had seen.

Fear tingled down Caleb's spine. "So what do you do for fun?"

"I meditate on the Word of Yehovah. Just one verse. And eventually it opens up into a revelation. Where all my spirit goes, I do not always know. Nor if I be in body or not."

Caleb's voice dropped an octave. "What have you seen? What do you know?"

Isaiah's eyes never moved, his face never changed. "I am ADONAI's servant."

Both Zecharaiah and Caleb waited for more, but nothing else was said. Zechariah rolled his head around wearily and stood to leave. "Stay with Caleb this afternoon and through shabbat. Perhaps you will be allowed a rest from ADONAI's work, Isaiah. I believe ADONAI knows you need it."

Zechariah hobbled off, leaving the other two behind. Caleb didn't exactly know what to do or say. Isaiah just kept staring at him in a way that made Caleb's soul uncomfortable. What was going on inside that seer's mind? Or perhaps the question should be, what had this mystic seen that had disconnected him from this world and haunted his spirit so.

Caleb decided not to push. Isaiah may already feel pushed

to open up about the things he'd seen, and if he wasn't willing to tell Zechariah, how could Caleb compete with that? Caleb turned back to his scroll, pushing his long sapphire robe and white sash behind him to make sure he didn't get any ink on them. He should have veiled his head because the sun was scorching his flesh, but he loved the feeling of the wind shifting his hair. He picked up his quill and began again. He was still in Exodus. He wrote 'Do not make for yourself an idol in the form of anything in heaven above or on the earth beneath or in the waters below. Do not bow down to them or worship them; for I, ADONAI your God, am a jealous God, punishing the children for the sin of the fathers to the third and fourth generation of those who hate me.'

"He is a jealous God, a very jealous God - something to always remember."

Caleb glanced back up to Isaiah who continued his solemn stare. Only a few moments passed before Isaiah began again.

"ADONAI will have compassion on Y'akov. He will continue to choose Isra'el and plant them in his land. Foreigners will join and become one with them, uniting with the house of Y'akov, and ADONAI will take them as his chosen. Yet the grave that hovers around you waits for your coming, it rouses the spirits of the departed, waiting to greet you to the bosom from which you sprang. Once rulers and leaders of this world, they are brought low, a shade not even seen by men. Man will say that you and your kind have become weak, as we are; you have become like us, if not weaker than us. How the loftiest of you have fallen. Cast down by Elohim's own will and trampled by those that obey Elohim's commands, for they will have power and authority over you. Once man stared at you in awe and pondered all the things you have seen, soon man will not even know you existed. To most men, not seers, you will be nothing but a chill that runs up their spine in the middle of the night. Man is laid in a tomb when he dies, but you will be released from yours to wander the earth a vagabond till the day of judgment. You are covered with your slain, dragged down by the mortal corpses you have collected, and Elohim will wipe your kind from the face of the earth till only the righteous remain to serve him. For you were never to have inhabited this realm, and your wicked brethren will never be mentioned again."

Caleb's joy evaporated. Was this a prophecy? Had he just

received his first prophecy? Or was Isaiah just speaking on things he'd seen? Things from the past and things of the future. Nothing particularly about Nephilim. Isaiah's sorrowful eyes drank him in. A glimmer of horror had flickered within them for a moment or two, but now they were back to being soul-ripping inconsolable. His despondence was contagious, and Caleb could feel his own spirit falling mournfully into a dark unfathomable desolate region. Isaiah's eyelids fluttered down for only a moment as he seemed to try to regain his inner strength, but a crestfallen look had taken residence on his normally placid expression. Dejected, he turned and walked back to the temple.

Caleb breathed deeply. He had always wanted to have the gifts of a seer, but now he was grateful he didn't. What could one say to such a one as he?

751 BC, JERUSALEM

Clattering was heard in the temple. Caleb jumped, almost spilling ink all over his robe. No priest would cause such calamity in Elohim's house. Caleb quickly ran into the temple but had to stop for his eyes to adjust. It took precious moments, and the only thing that Caleb could make out was Isaiah saying, "Uzziah, no!"

Caleb blinked several times. What was Uzziah doing? In the last few years, his pride in his own righteousness had soared. He had begun moving about the temple as if he was a Levite priest. Not too many people said anything because he had acted as righteously as a priest through most of his life, yet it was against Elohim's laws. What were the priests to do? It was Uzziah who had kept his citizens in reverence to ADONAI.

Finally, the darkened chamber became visible. Uzziah was standing at the altar of incense. He turned a disdainful look towards Isaiah. "I am Elohim's king. I have served him well. Surely, I am as a priest in his eyes. What king has served so righteously before me, obeying his every command and law?"

The High Priest stood at the entrance to the Most Holy of Holies. "Uzziah, you will break his laws now if you do this."

"Are you saying that you are better than me?" Uzziah questioned.

The Hight Priest looked down. "No, of course not. You have been a righteous king before ADONAI our God."

Uzziah curtly nodded and ignited the incense. "I will pray now for our people. A prayer from a king to his God. I have kept Him in my palace, and now He, in return, has allowed me into His." Uzziah walked to the base of the steps leading to the Most Holy of Holies and laid down prostrate to worship Elohim.

No one moved. No one said anything. Uzziah finished and slowly rose. Gazing down at his hands, he gasped. Slight bumps that looked akin to water blisters appeared, they were barely a lighter shade than his natural skin.

Grief stricken, the High Priest spoke, "Leprosy. Elohim does not abide your pride."

Isaiah spoke from his corner of the incense chamber, "Elohim does not abide disobedience to his rules, commands, and laws. No matter how much good you have done for him. Above all else, Elohim demands respect and obedience."

It felt like the floor fell away underneath Caleb's feet.

Isaiah turned to face Caleb. "Above all else, Elohim demands respect and obedience. No matter how righteous the service, no matter how close the relationship, remember Moshe, remember David, remember that there are no exceptions. Remember, Caleb. Elohim does not make exceptions to the rules for disobedience. You would be wise to remember this for your future, and the loved ones of your future."

Caleb nodded his head. Yes, he would remember this lesson.

740 BC, JERUSALEM

Caleb exited out of Uzziah's bedchamber. It had been a long illness, and he was finally at rest. Although struck with leprosy, he had repented right away and did right in the sight of ADONAI till his death. Caleb hoped his son would be righteous as well. He shuddered, remembering the atrocities Solomon had committed in the temple.

Darkness consumed the palace. It was near three in the morning, and those awake were mourning the loss of such a great king. Only the candles in the king's bedchamber were lit. The rest of the palace was pitch black. Caleb made his way in the dark and avoided the lamenting citizens on the floor. He didn't need to see to know what they were doing. He had done it before. They were rending their clothes, lying prostrate on the floor, throwing dust on their hair, and crying for their lost sovereign.

A commotion was heard outside, and the palace door was swung open. Caleb heard leather sandals slapping the stone floor in a fast rhythm. Suddenly, a man plowed into him. Caleb, barely able to see the man, grabbed his shoulders to keep both of them from falling. The man's shoulders heaved, sweat coursed down his body. "The king has just died. What is it my friend?"

Rasping breaths met Caleb's question, and the man sank to his knees. "Then there is to be no help?"

"Help for what?" Caleb remained calm, trying to soothe the man to talk rationally and with clarity.

"The Assyrians. The Assyrians have invaded the northern tribes. Reuben. Gad. And Manasseh." The man clung to Caleb, his rasping turned into sobbing.

"They repented not. Amos and Hosea warned them. They continued to disobey Elohim's commands," Caleb pointed out. "Elohim commanded, 'Do not make yourselves unclean by any of these things, because all the nations which I am expelling ahead of you are defiled with them. The land has become unclean, and this is why I am punishing it - the land itself will vomit out its inhabitants. But you are to keep my laws and rulings and not engage in any of these disgusting practices, neither the citizen nor the foreigner living with you; for the people of the land have committed all these abominations, and the land is now defiled. If you make the land unclean, it will vomit you out too, just as it is vomiting out the nation that was there before you. For those who engage in any of these disgusting practices, whoever they may be, will be cut off from their people. So keep my charge not to follow any of these abominable customs that others before you have followed and thus defile yourselves by doing them. I am ADONAI your God.'" Caleb pulled the man up. "Surely ADONAI thought that Elijah and Elisha would have made an impact. Such great prophets to the northern tribes, yet still..."

The soldier grabbed Caleb's legs tightly and begged, "Please, please aid them. You know not what they do."

"Caleb."

Caleb looked up. He could see a tall outline, but still the darkness was too much to be certain.

"Come."

Disengaging himself from the soldier, Caleb followed the man out of the palace. The moon reigned down brightly and revealed Loki's stern countenance.

Loki's eyes glowed like molten lava swirling in a face of anguish. "Your mother is leading the troops with Pulu. She has been plotting her revenge for twenty years and is the most blood thirsty I have ever seen her. She takes her wrath out against Elohim and his prophets for taking away Madai and you." In despair, Loki shook his head. "Elohim warned that they would be vomited from their Promised Land, but your mother... 'Tis much worse than it needs to be. Come, see what you can do for the fallen of Elohim's chosen."

Caleb nodded and followed Loki. After leaving the populace of Jerusalem, Loki grasped Caleb and flew off to the north. The desert below slowly turned to lush vegetation. When smoke made flying difficult, Loki landed. They walked by burnt houses, devastated crops, and empty sheds. Not a single mortal was to be seen.

After an hour of walking, they saw a large bonfire. The closer they came, the quicker they realized they had reached the largest town of Manasseh. Beside the bonfire was a staked man. The flames brightly lit his features, revealing that his skin had been flayed off. Next to him, his skin had been stretched out, and highlighted, so all the townsmen would see.

"Intimidation. They told the villagers that if they surrendered, they would not be killed." Loki paused, sighed, then brushed his long copper waves behind his back. His robe was stained and dirty; he didn't look like he had been taking care of himself.

"And did they?" Caleb asked.

Loki nodded. He walked to the northwest corner of town and pointed out thousands of footprints. Some had been dragged. Others pulled to the side, where signs of struggle could be found. Loki met Caleb's eyes. "Rape."

Caleb immediately began walking, and Loki fell in line beside him. Hours passed and the sun rose. Devastated towns and homes dotted the landscape with nary a mortal left alive. By the time the sun had reached its zenith, sounds of war could be heard. Loki and Caleb took off running.

At the top of the hill, they could see the carnage below. One town had decided not to surrender. Arcing swords glinted in the sunlight, blood sprayed the countryside, mortal grunts and moans echoed through the valley. It was a bloodbath. They were too late to be of any help.

Loki grabbed Caleb's arm and pointed to the right. Caleb looked. Ishtar was floating above the mortals, beheading all who came within her grasp. She looked like an avenging angel. Her sword reached out in a graceful line as she danced above in ballet moves, sliding her sword through mortal butter. When she swirled high above, actually taking joy in her task, Caleb saw an illuminated bundle strapped to her back. The second time she swirled, he identified the bundle as a baby.

"Is that me betrothed?" Loki asked.

"I, I don't know. It could be fathered by Marduk... or someone else." Caleb stammered. He didn't dare go near his mother at the moment. She was deeply immersed within the battle, and the last time he had seen her, she had beheaded his father. His gut twisted and indecision bloomed, but a passionate need to take Ishtar's child away from her took hold of him. Desiring to raise the baby, how Caleb wished he had been raised, took firm root within his heart.

"If she is me betrothed, I will take her now," Loki announced.

"No. No, that wouldn't be right. She'd feel like you were her father. I'm her brother. If it's even a girl. I will raise her up to worship Elohim," Caleb vowed.

"Ishtar would never allow you to take her away from her. Whether boy or girl, that child has power," Loki argued. "You are not Ishtar's equal, but I am her better. I can take the child away."

"No. Ishtar wants me back, and if she sees you, she will flee somewhere neither of us will find her."

Loki paused. What Caleb said was true. The child was powerful. Ishtar would never let him take it away once she saw him, and she had. She had just turned and looked straight at both of them. Her eyes narrowed. Loki flew backwards and disappeared.

Ishtar, garbed in purple and gold armor, floated to Caleb. Never once did she take her eyes off him. Hovering slowly, she lowered herself to the ground. "My eldest son."

Caleb bowed his head. "Mother."

Ishtar smiled. A small glimmer of hope sparked in her eye.

"My sibling seems to be in the midst of a battle. I don't think that is very safe. Let me care for her while you lead your troops," Caleb said softly. "She looks amazingly beautiful. Almost your spitting image. You must be proud. I know I am just by looking at her. May I hold her?"

Ishtar debated his request. Neither moved. Finally, she asked, "And will you be returning to Nineveh when our empire is secured?"

"Into empire building are you?" Caleb teased.

Ishtar's eyes shimmered. She was on the verge of tears. "Marduk used me for our daughter. He cares nothing for me and seeks Raechev for his own purposes."

Caleb frowned. Perhaps she would have wanted Loki's aid in protecting his betrothed. "Well, she is our light, our love, and our joy. I will guard her with my life."

Her back slowly stiffened. "I cannot have you worshiping Elohim in my city." She paused, noticing Caleb's emotional withdrawal. "I will not make you do anything you do not want to do, but I must have your solidarity. I must have you at least attend the festivities. You know how important it is for there to be no sign of discord amongst the ruling gods, or the citizenry will become unruly."

Caleb took his time answering. He wanted her aware of how firmly he still served Elohim. Caleb slowly nodded. "I will attend the festivities. Now, may I hold my baby sister?"

Ishtar smiled, rushed into his arms, and sobbed his name. Her tears broke the hardened shell he had erected around his heart. She was evil. He would never be able to get the image of her bathed in his father's blood out of his mind. Yet, at the same time, he felt sorry for her. The entity she hated the most, was the entity she needed the most.

After twenty minutes, Ishtar disengaged herself from Caleb's arms and removed her daughter from the satchel strapped to her back.

When the cooing bundle of illumination was placed in his arms, love, like he had never experienced, wracked Caleb's body. Raechev's glittering emerald eyes, ethereally glowing skin, and flaxen baby hair marked her strong Nephilim parentage. Her rosy, cupid's mouth broke into laughter when she spotted her older brother. She quickly grasped Caleb's beard and yanked hard, stunning him into a facial expression that made her cry out with glee. She yanked again, and his heart shifted.

This was the reason he was alive. Raechev had become his purpose. Along with her, each time her new eyes would take in the world, his eyes would be cleansed from all the unholy things he had seen. Her innocence would birth an innocence within him. He was being reborn and would experience life for the first time just as she would. Raechev was the one being, he had been created to love.

In his heart, he vowed to Elohim that he would raise her to serve and obey him, and only him. A warm burning in his chest spread throughout his entire body. Lifting her to kiss her lips, he was surprised when she gave him an intelligent yet bemused, scornful look. Her face scrunched up, as if she was about to cry, then broke out laughing. She reached up and laid her hand against his cheek. Caleb sighed. So this was love. It seemed he had waited a lifetime.

Her face calmed into an angelic peaceful state as she lovingly gazed up at him. Then she picked up her hand and smacked Caleb in the face. She burst out laughing.

Interesting, Caleb mused. Very interesting.

668 BC, NINEVEH

Caleb had let his hair grow out too long. It would get in his way hunting. He had resumed Assyrian dress while in Nineveh to appease his mother. There were no commands regarding that, so he wanted to let her win the little battles that would not affect his obedience to Elohim. Priestesses currently worked on his beard. They were curled into tight ringlets that fell eight inches past his chin. His long hair was being curled into tight ringlets as well and fell twelve inches past his shoulders.

A priestess's cool fingers brushed his leg suggestively as she wove the leather sandal straps up his calf. He shot her a disdainful look, and she immediately became professional again. Caleb realized that he probably should have put a tunic on to cover his chest, but it was exceptionally hot, and the leather and weapons made him hot enough without silken tunics getting in the way.

It had been seventy-two years since he'd left Jerusalem. Raechev had grown up being holy before Elohim. Caleb winced. Well, almost. She needed to kill her mother in order to obey Elohim's law of Kinsman Redeemer. He had considered doing it himself, but he knew how much Raechev loved her mother. Raechev wasn't blind to Ishtar's atrocious ways, but Ishtar doted on her daughter, and Raechev felt fully loved. He worried that if he killed Ishtar, Raechev would turn her back on Elohim and himself.

Raechev was a powerful and amazing warrior. Caleb had never been a warrior, nor enjoyed it. He knew that his skills would not ensure a victory against Ishtar, but Raechev would. Not only was Raechev more supernaturally powerful than her mother, she was also a much more skilled combatant. It was only Raechev's will that was needed to slay Ishtar; Ishtar would have no hope in a battle against her daughter.

Caleb stood and stretched when the priestesses finally backed away from him. He wore only a leather girdle about his waist and a purple kilt with reflective coins. When the priestesses tried to attach his weapons, he turned and walked out the door. He needed to get away with his thoughts for just a few minutes. He left his bedchamber, walked down a tall hallway with Assyrian victories etched into it, and made his way to the back gardens. Stepping out, he inhaled deeply. Roses, lilies, and jasmine competed with the smell of incense. He moved away from the beige brick wall and immersed himself completely in the most dense area of vegetation. The shade cooled the scorching Assyrian sun and led him down a well known path that ended at a barred window.

Caleb stared into the black shadows of the prison and reflected upon his time spent where he stood now. Every day, he had come and talked to the prisoner, glad the lush vegetation shielded him from prying eyes. For only a moment, Caleb closed his eyes and envisioned the pale prisoner who, in the beginning, had been filled with such hate, but who left filled with love and compassion. King Manasseh of Y'hudah reminded Caleb a bit of himself, yet Manasseh had committed more sins than even Caleb had considered.

Manasseh had become king when he was twelve. He quickly

began rebuilding the altars and high places to foreign gods his father Hezekiah had torn down. The king, himself, carved wooden images of the zodiac and bent down to worship them, astral projecting and communing with other worldly beings. He then carved wooden images of fallen angels who visited him, placed them in Elohim's temple, and built altars to them there so that he could commune with them in the firmament dimension. And still his sins grew. He used angel guides to give him wisdom, and performed as a fortune teller for Elohim's priests. He encouraged witchcraft and sorcery throughout all of Y'huda, seducing Elohim's mystics to turn and speak with spirits not from Elohim. Then he did the worst, he sacrificed his own sons in witchcraft ceremonies that called for human sacrifice.

Caleb shivered. Elohim had sent the prophet Nahum to Manasseh, but the king would not listen.

Caleb remembered how Manasseh arrived. He had been pulled along with a hook through his nose. When he stumbled, the hook ripped through his flesh, so by the time Manasseh arrived in Nineveh, his nose was shredded. His cartilage could be seen amidst the flapping strips of skin, and his legs and arms were encased with bronze shackles. At first, he had been led to Babylon, so Assyria could boast her victory before he was led to Nineveh for Ishtar to gloat. He spent weeks in each main Assyrian town so that everyone who had lost loved ones to the YEHOVAH-ANGEL could join in the victory. The Assyrians still whispered of that fateful night, when Sennachareb was encamped around Jerusalem, and an angel came down and slaughtered one hundred and eighty-five thousand soldiers. But Elohim had done that for Hezekiah who had shattered all the idols in his nation, not for Manasseh, who practiced the occult.

It was here, in this cell, that Caleb kept quoting the Torah to Manasseh. At first, Caleb could barely stand to look at the king, it seemed as if hundreds of spirits stared out through Manasseh's vacant eyes. Caleb was positive he had been possessed at some point during all his witchcraft and sorceries. Caleb wouldn't have been surprised if Manasseh's angel guide had originally claimed to have been sent from Elohim to guide him. That would have made sense after what Elohim's angel had done for his father Hezekiah. The angel guide would have helped him know things only a seer would know, making it appear that he was blessed of Elohim. Then year by year, the angel's seductions would turn more and more toward the occult, whispering in Manasseh's ears that all his seers were to be used of Elohim, not just the ones who obeyed Elohim.

He remembered Manasseh recited the tale of Elohim asking Abraham to sacrifice his only son Isaac, and that he had many sons, so it was not such a great sacrifice. This was his excuse for sacrificing his own sons. Caleb could easily imagine the rationalizing and reasoning used that made many fall away from Elohim's commands - because that was the whole point. Elohim demanded obedience, so Elohim's enemies only had to persuade the redeemed that there were exceptions, that certain reasons sufficed for a little turning away here, a little turning away there.

Caleb leaned up against the beige brick wall and let his memories consume him. Manasseh had repented of his sins in Nineveh's prison. He had begged to be freed from his spirit guides. He had asked for an exorcism, and Caleb had complied. Caleb shivered at the memory of that night. So many had entered and taken possession of Elohim's chosen. Such a mockery to Elohim. Such a powerful way to cause deviations. But Manasseh had repented, had been exorcised, and miraculously had been freed by Assyria to go home. Then, he crushed all idols and altars and became a righteous servant of Elohim. He spent his days rebuilding the outer wall, fortifying his cities, and stationing military commanders throughout his realm. On shabbat, he worked at cleaning out the temple and bringing it back to its previous glory.

Loki had just written to Ishtar, keeping up his part of the bargain for Raechev's betrothal, telling of Manasseh's turn to righteousness and how he made sure the priests sacrificed many thank offerings to ADONAI. Loki wrote that Manasseh constantly encouraged all of the Hebrews to worship and serve only Elohim, forbidding all forms of idolatry. But within the homes, Loki saw trees decorated with gold and silver at the spring equinox and winter solstice. He witnessed the women baking bread to the Queen of Heaven and heard young girls crying for Tammuz's resurrection. Ishtar was soothed. Although the king had repented, the people had not. They still clung to the traditions and festivals of the pagans. Polytheism reigned in Elohim's land.

A strong gust of wind blew the trees, and Loki dropped to the ground beside him. His eyes were fearful, his breaths short and quick. "Where is she? Raechev? Is she safe?"

Caleb's brow creased in confusion. "Of course, she's safe. Why wouldn't she be safe?"

"'Tis the Day of Atonement. Tagas is on the rampage. He just killed Marduk." Loki leaned over, clutching his side and winced from pain. "I must go to her. We must protect her this day."

"No. She's not ready yet. I'll protect her."

"She's seventy-two!" Loki yelled.

"That's a babe compared to you and I!" Caleb yelled back. He knew of the betrothal. He knew Loki had been patient thus far, but Caleb could not, no he would not, live without his baby sister.....yet. He needed her. He couldn't imagine life without her. "Give her at least a century, Loki. Surely, that's not too much to ask."

Loki's eyes flamed in a way that had fear shooting through Caleb. "Ye cannae protect her from Tagas. Ye cannae even protect her from herself. Of the three of us, ye are the weakest, and I am the strongest. Yer requests are irrational."

Caleb gulped. "Loki, I know her. She's not ready, and if you stalk around her today, she will get suspicious of the betrothal and possibly run."

Loki straightened, his voice dropped to a threatening tone, "She doesnae ken we are betrothed?"

Now Caleb was the one out of breath, but from fear not exhaustion. "She is like her mother. She yearns for independence, equality, and freedom. She chafes at her mother's requests and barely deems to acknowledge my own. She will run."

"Yer parenting skills lack greatly, Caleb. I thought more highly of ye than that. It sounds like ye allow her to walk all over ya. I see I should have raised her meself."

Caleb hardened his heart. "Whatever the past, I love her well and know her well. She will ask questions if she spots you guarding her today, and when she discovers the truth, she will run."

"Caleb, I begin to wonder if she's not ready, or if ye be the one not ready. Ya could have killed Ishtar, but ye fear Raechev's reaction too much to do so. Do nay use her warrior skills as an excuse. Ishtar's mortal side is still mortal and easily killed with poison." Loki stepped close to Caleb and whispered, "If we were married, I could perform the act of Kinsman Redeemer for her, and

I would nay hesitate to do so."

Caleb stared at Loki, who in turn stared back. Loki's stance was threatening, and Caleb knew that Loki was powerful enough to do whatever he wanted. The fact that he was even taking the time to argue, spoke volumes of a Nephilim who could easily bend things to his will.

Loki spoke, giving his vow, "I will give her a century. Ye will tell her of our betrothal within a year from now although that deceitful Ishtar should have done so herself when Raechev was but a child." Loki paused, allowing Caleb to understand how Loki saw Caleb as well for never telling Raechev. She should have been told at a very early age, knowing what was expected of her. It was how things were done. One did not promise a betrothal before a child's birth and then never tell her, allowing her to imagine she had a choice. It was completely unfair to both of the betrothed, making both their lives more difficult when their lives became one. "I will guard her today, but she will nay ken. I have many tricks that would cloak me that ye ken nothing of. After the Day of Atonement ends, I will depart."

Caleb nodded in agreement. He would have twenty-eight more years with her. He left to find Raechev, she had to know immediately that Tagas had just executed her father.

641 BC, JERUSALEM

Caleb led Raechev down a dusty path towards Jerusalem. It had been ninety-nine years since he'd left. His heart weighed him down heavier with each step into Y'hudah. The idolatrous ways were back. Why was it so difficult for them to obey? Did Elohim have to constantly punish them to remind them of his existence?

The golden dust pounded up from his sandals as he drew closer to the Mount of Olives. Memories flooded him of Solomon and his wives. Would the temple be desecrated as well? His hope faltered with each town he passed. The rolling hills spotted with trees were all his eyes could see now. A swelling rise of gold earth and sparse vegetation. If grass attempted to grow, it camouflaged itself as dry golden husks of what it should have been. Rocks and small pebbles crept into Caleb's sandals, causing him to yearn to end his journey on the mortal path and take up with his brothers in the Cities of Refuge.

"I have never seen you so sad, Caleb."

Caleb tried to smile at his baby sister. Compassion shone in her glittering emerald eyes. She was so beautiful. Her flaxen hair glinted in the sun, making it appear that she wore a diamond sheer veil. Her luminescent skin was accented with deep peach lips and high cheekbones. She was only 5'6" and could blend into the populace if they covered everything on her, but she needed her eyes, and they would always give away her Nephilim lineage. "You should have seen Y'hudah under Uzziah when he was still righteous. If you could see the comparisons, you would be sad as well."

Raechev nodded then pointed her head towards an Asherah pole. "Yes, I didn't expect to find them here."

Caleb looked to where she motioned. A tree, still rooted in the earth, had been chopped down to its post and carved into Ishtar's feminine form. The fact that it was still rooted, let everyone know that it was well tended by the locals to keep it from sprouting limbs and leaves. On the wooden goddess's head were two horns as ears and a phallus pointing straight up. The goddess herself was nude. It was crude and spoke so much on so many things. Being carved from a living tree, represented the mother goddess being the tree of life, but also a mockery of the woman choosing the Serpent (Black Sun) over Elohim's command (not to eat of the fruit of good and evil). The woman had chosen knowledge and to better herself to a position higher and closer to Elohim. The phallus on her head represented her refusal to be submissive to her husband and her openness to beget children with angels. The carving down of a living tree also represented how mankind had desecrated what Elohim had made, and the purpose for why it was made, to bear fruit and nourish his children. These idols blended into the natural landscape, making it appear as if the gods and goddesses were always present, always watching, and always growing. They were a part of the land itself.

Caleb sighed, clutched Raechev's hand, and pulled her onwards. They were at the base of the Mount of Olives and would be able to see Jerusalem when they reached the top. Raechev squeezed his hand and did not comment.

Caleb's long flowing royal blue robe and white sash dragged in the dirt. He had returned to wearing the clothes he had worn when studying at the temple. As usual, he had left his hair free of a turban, but he had chopped it at his shoulders and let it hang raggedly. Luckily, his dark brown waves, hid how uneven it was.

Raechev pulled at his hand for him to stop. "Should I use the dirt to dust my face?" Sometimes, before entering towns, Raechev would use the land's dirt to darken her skin and make her appear more mortal. Her silk mint green robe softened her marble skin and deepened her emerald eyes. Her features were like a saving oasis in the harsh desert climate. Caleb needed that now, more than anything else. He shook his head and pulled her on.

Chanting echoed down the mount, pitting Caleb's stomach for what he would find at Loki's so nicknamed Mount of Corruption. Oh, how he longed to go to the Cities of Refuge, but his love for Raechev outweighed it. He was supposed to give her to Loki sometime next year. His time was running out. He could go to the cities then, he thought, but deep down he didn't really believe he would. He didn't see him ever giving up his sister. Elohim had given her to him. No match made by Ishtar should stand.

Caleb reached the top of the mount and froze. Elohim's High Priest stood before a shrine erected to several baals, one being Baalim and another Ishtar. The High Priest was bedecked in his ceremonial clothes. He wore a long flowing white robe with a gold surcoat over that. His breastplate consisted of twelve gems and was affixed to his chest. Upon his head was a gold sash that tied a white, pouffy hat to the top of his head. Several priests wearing the colors of Elohim surrounded him. The blue represented the heavens and the spirit, the scarlet represented the earth and mortal clay, and the purple represented the joining of the two, the merging of spirit and mortality. Elohim breathed his spirit into man and gave him life. They had bodies of dust with a spirit given to them from their heavenly father.

"Oh Baal, our great Baal. Come and visit us again," the High Priest intoned, as he lit incense on an altar. "Speak to us through your seers. Give us wisdom from ages past, and tell us of our future. We pray to you, oh, Mother of the Heavens, Mother of Baal, and embodiment of our moon, who sheds her light on her children, guiding them in their most darkest nights. Come to us, oh Baal, god of the sun and bring us your consorts so that we may worship them as well." Two priests stepped up and added more incense which the High Priest quickly lit. "Oh Molech, god of the sun, have compassion on us for we offer our first fruits. We offer our most loved. We offer our firstborn sons."

Firstborn sons? Elohim was to be given the first born sons. They were to be taught to be the most righteous of all men. To study Torah thoroughly. What were they doing with the firstborn Elohim had proclaimed to be his own?

Just past him, deep in the valley, drums began to beat strongly. Caleb grabbed Raechev's hand and pulled her to the cliff's edge. The High Priest yelled behind them, "Oh to all the host in heaven, watch us now as we sacrifice our offerings to you!"

A jagged outcropping gave Caleb and Raechev a spectacular view of the temple on the next mount over, but down in the valley, the Valley of Gehenna, the masses were dancing. Loud drums and clanging timbrels beat and drowned the sounds of the dancing Hebrews as they circled around a large bronze statue. Molech. The protecting father god of the Ammonites, the descendants of Lot.

Molech rose sixty feet into the air. The idol had no legs, but started at its waist and moved upward. It's body was that of a human, but the head of a bull, and its arms were outstretched as if to receive something. Surrounding the large statue of Molech, were six smaller brass ones, with hands held out straight in front, creating an altar before them. On each of the smaller ones, various fowl and animals were being burnt to death, but it appeared that the seventh, the soaring one, was reserved only for humans.

Men moved in and out of Molech's belly, feeding the fire, causing the flames to rise higher and higher. They constantly kept checking the outstretched arms, and when the hands and arms had begun to glow red from the heat, they finally shut the belly door and moved a large brass stand up to the red-glowing hands. One by one, a firstborn son was raised from one priest, to the next, till it finally reached the top, and was laid into Molech's hands. The babe's face wrenched in agonizing pain as its skin began melting off. Blood dripped down, baptizing the priests and dancers beneath. The babe's cries of anguish were drowned out by the drums and activities below.

Twelve, unclad seers pushed their way to the base of the idol.

They began dancing in violent gesticulations as they circled their god, hoping to be splattered by the blood of the sacrificed firstborns. Down below, two priests with protective metal on their hands, grabbed chains and pulled. The chains lifted the arms of Molech, causing the babe to slide down with its melted skin into the open mouth of Molech. Quickly, the priests raised the next firstborn to be offered.

Caleb and Raechev gaped in horror. They lost count of how many children were being sacrificed. Raechev beat her own chest in agony each time a babe got stuck on an unheated part of Molech's arm, its skin ripping as the priests kept jerking the chains to get the babe to fall into Molech's mouth.

The dancing seers began cutting their bodies with knives and lancets, begging Molech for a vision to prophesy. One by one, they began prophesying, ranting and raving as if possessed.

Tears streamed down Raechev's cheek. A gentle hand wiped them away.

A soft-spoken voice murmured, "Is it necessary for her to witness this, Caleb?"

Raechev turned and gazed up into the most exotic eyes she had ever seen. They were fire agate gems. The irises had a swirl pattern of deep gold, orange, red, and green specs. In the midst of the pupils were the same colors but speckled in black depths. Long waves of burnished copper hair blew gently in the breeze, over freckled shoulders and tattooed arms. His eyes held so much intelligence that Raechev became mesmerized.

"No. It is not necessary. We were shocked is all to find such an abhorrent practice being performed by the Hebrews. Raechev has never been to Jerusalem. I thought it wise she visited before she turned a century," Caleb answered. He didn't like Loki's affect on Raechev. She just stood there, staring at him.

Loki lifted the back of his hand and caressed Raechev's cheek. She smiled. Loki smiled back. "Ah yes, she's not yet a century. But soon." He glided the back of his hand down her neck, shoulder, and arm before tenderly holding her hand. He nodded with his head, and she followed. They began the descent to the valley below.

Caleb had no choice but to follow. He knew Loki's honor enough that he would keep to his vow, but Raechev's reaction terrified him. She hadn't looked his way yet. She hadn't asked him if Loki could be trusted, and she hadn't asked his permission to hold hands with a male!

Raechev's eyes slowly gazed down Loki's body, then traveled back up. Her features showed intrigue. "Where are you from?"

Loki had just returned from hunting for his children. He still wore his gold torc around his neck and upper arms, but the only other thing he wore was a white leather kilt that hung low on his hips. "North."

A becoming peach blush crept up Raechev's face as her eyes fell once again to study his physique. He was ripped in a way that you could see his every muscle move as it sensually glided underneath his ethereally glowing skin. There was no doubt that he was a Nephilim. "How old are you?"

Loki shrugged his shoulders and smiled. It was good that she was asking questions. He gave her a flirtatious smile. "I never thought to count the years before the flood."

Raechev's eyes enlarged. "I've never met someone who survived the flood." Her eyes began shifting quickly, questions popping in her head as excitement bloomed. She had always wanted to know what the world was like before the flood.

Loki patted her hand. "Later. I will answer all yer questions later." Loki jerked his head back to get Caleb's attention. "They're making repairs on the Temple of Elohim. Ye willnae like what ye see when we approach."

They had just arrived at the outer wall of the temple. Caleb would have found out in only seconds what Loki was referring to. Raechev jerked, then quickly looked around herself and behind her. She had been so entranced with Loki, she hadn't even noticed they had walked through Jerusalem. Caleb didn't like this at all.

Once they passed the outer wall, Caleb halted. Just outside the main entry into the Temple of Elohim stood two idols, chariots of the sun. He had never seen an idol inside Elohim's Temple before. Bile rose, he worked not to vomit.

Loki lowered his voice, "They have misplaced part of the Torah. They do not even have the Book of Deuteronomy, but I was here when Nahum hid it so that the Assyrians would not take or destroy it if they prevailed." Keeping Raechev's hand, Loki entered the temple. Caleb followed.

The walls were made of Lebanon cedar aged to the darkest of

browns. Ornate gold patterns of the Tree of Life rose in columns on both sides of the walls. At the base of each column was a winged lion, and above was a thick ribbon of gold trim that rose to the ceiling. Overhead, large wood beams crossed in perfect squares and showcased gold patterns within them. The whole temple was dark wood and gold.

Loki walked through the first vestibule and entered the second. He approached the steps leading to the Most Holy of Holies and its ornate gold door, but veered to the right and stopped in front of the wood paneling at the side of the steps.

Lit candelabras flickered romantic firelight over his features. Loki tenderly caressed Raechev's hand. "Ye saw among them detestable images and idols of wood and stone, of silver and gold." He lowered his lips and tenderly kissed Raechev's inner wrist. She inhaled the scent of him. He whispered, "Break down their altars, smash their sacred stones, and burn their Asherah poles in the fire; cut down their idols of their gods and wipe out their names from those places."

Loki kicked his heel into the wood, smashing it to pieces. He leaned down once more, stopping to inhale Raechev's warm fig smell before kissing her more intimately. Raechev jerked at first, unfamiliar with his intrusion into her mouth, but then tentatively began kissing him back. After a few minutes, he raised his head. Joy danced in his eyes. Raechev blushed. He spoke loud enough for Caleb to hear. "Soon."

Caleb watched Loki leave the temple, then turned to inspect his sister. Apparently their marriage wouldn't be too tedious on her. He walked over to the wood splinters on the floor and bent down. Raechev held her fingers to her lips and stared after Loki.

"He was so handsome, Caleb. And he knows the Torah so well. Who is he?"

Caleb reached inside the hole Loki had made and pulled out a scroll of Deuteronomy. "That was your betrothed."

Raechev blinked several times. She was as he was, emotionally drained from all they had seen that day. He took her hand. She was still pliable from Loki's charms. "Come, let us take and present this to the king. Remind him of Elohim's laws."

The meeting with the king had gone better than Caleb hoped. Josiah had begun a religious reformation based on the Book of the

Law. Caleb's heart had softened when he realized how much of the Torah the Hebrews had been missing. How could you not go astray when you didn't read directly from the Torah? When people spoke from sketchy memories of what they thought a priest had said decades before. Words of men were not to be trusted. Human reasoning often altered the meanings and true messages of the Torah to fit selfish wants and desires.

Josiah had immediately burnt down the chariots of the sun standing outside the main entry to Elohim's temple. He destroyed every altar, Asherah pole, and shrine to foreign gods. He removed every idolatrous priest who had aided in burning incense to other gods or sacrificed unto them, and to make sure no child of Elohim was ever forced to pass through the fires of Molech, he defiled and brought down every structure in the Valley of Gehenna. Caleb could often hear Josiah muttering underneath his breath, "Do not intermarry with them. Do not give your daughters to their sons or take their daughters for your sons, For they will turn your sons away from following me to serve other gods, and ADONAI your God's anger will burn against you and will quickly destroy you. This is what you are to do to them: Break down their altars, smash their sacred stones, cut down their Asherah poles and burn their idols in fire. For you are a people holy to ADONAI your God. ADONAI your God has chosen you out of all the peoples on the face of the earth to be his people, his treasured possession."

522 BC, BABYLON

Caleb stared up at the magnificent gate named after his mother. It reached up forty feet and was topped with four crenelated towers. Upon it, archers and spearmen stood watching the thoroughfare down below. Sweat trickled down his spine and pooled in the small of his back. It was suffocatingly hot, and the looming structure seemed about to smother him. How a gate could smother, he didn't know, but it just seemed like it could. As if everything he had run from, he would never escape. Everywhere he turned he saw his mother, witnessed pagan festivities, and inhaled incense to idols.

He tried breathing deeply to steady his chaotic mind and

irrational emotions. Closing his eyes, he focused on his last thought. Irrational emotion. Were any emotions rational?

"Do you think it would have worked?"

Caleb glanced down at his sister and shrugged his shoulders.

"It's pretty impressive. Marduk didn't spare any expense, but he could have put her image on it."

"Perhaps, he doesn't want people to remember he did it to woo a woman back," Caleb snapped.

Raechev paused, unfamiliar with his reaction. "Sort of gives it away, calling it Ishtar's Gate though."

"A name can easily be changed; the edifice cannot," Caleb answered. He inwardly shook off his foreboding to admire the structure before him. Marduk had used thousands of mud bricks to create an interior gate which dwarfed the outer one. Both were completely covered with a deep blue glaze and decorated with inlayed gold. Various colors of glaze depicted bulls, lions, dragons and palm trees. A connecting inner passage, made up of arches, connected the two gates. Overall, it represented the strength and power of the Babylonians.

A camel caravan sped by Caleb, causing him to move quickly out of the way. Babylon's great processional way led from the palace and great temples, in the middle of the city, to the outer edge of its suburbs. It was highly trafficked and therefore highly dangerous. He clasped onto Raechev's elbow and nudged her forward. He wanted to find a decent place to spend the night before darkness fell.

"One, only one. The darkness here settles too deeply within my spirit."

Raechev raised her eyebrows. "But we'll come back?"

Caleb gave a curt nod.

"I say Zurvan then."

Caleb's brow furrowed. Why Zurvan? Albeit, Zurvan did allow mortals to worship him, but he wasn't violent. He was a scholarly, scientist type. His head resembled a lion. He had large white angelic wings, female breasts and male genitalia. Some said he was a sterile hermaphrodite while others said he was genderless. He spent most of his time studying the universe, the Nephilim body, and the mortal body. Some of his experiments and breeding programs weren't.... kind, but he was extraordinarily gentle mannered. Rumors had swept the Nephilim world that without sexual relations, he had created a two headed Nephilim - one purely good, the other purely evil. "Well, he shouldn't be too difficult to find. They say he walks around with a crown and plays with a flame in his hand when he thinks."

"And of course, the small lion head," Raechev chirped in.

"Yes, that as well."

Caleb continued hauling Raechev through the crowded thoroughfare. Soldiers walked on walls that rose high on either side of them. It would be a deadly place for an army to be caught, but the bottom eight feet was covered with the same gold and blue glaze decorations like Ishtar's Gate. It was beautiful, but stifling hot. The walls did not allow any breeze off the Euphrates River, and pedestrians moved shoulder to shoulder to their destinations.

A loud crashing could be heard ahead of them. Pedestrians scrambled, causing a small riot at the end of the processional way. Caleb tightened his clutch on Raechev. These were the times, he wished they could fly. Plowing forward as mortals crushed against them, trying to escape whatever was making all the raucous, Caleb almost swore. He hated structures like this. He felt trapped, like a mouse caught in a maze with no light shining forth the way out. He saw death, death in the unknown world around him. Answers being just out of grasp, eluding him. He hated being blind, especially when so many could float above the maze and see the maze objectively, but his view was subjective - his view was hampered by man's constructions.

A deep lowing sounded. It seemed like the lowing of oxen, but the pitch was so deep, it shook the earth and trembled the road.

"What is that?"

It was definitely the sound of some animal, and if Caleb guessed correctly, it was something that should not be inside a city's walls. Protectively encasing Raechev, Caleb surged ahead and finally broke into the central square.

A rheem thrashed madly about in a brick enclosure. Mortals futilely attempted to close a wooden gate to trap it within. Rheems were formidable creatures, wild oxen of elephant proportions. Its sleek white fur and pink skin added to its glorious visage, but it's sharp pointy reddish horns struck fear in hearts. When its head was down, no one could get near a rheem. The horns pointed out in an almost perfect "v" on top of its head and stretched a good six to eight feet. A Nephilim had a chance in combat, but not mortals.

The beast let out another long low, then jerked its head, sending ten mortals smashing into the brick wall, their bones audibly breaking in pieces. More mortals rose to the challenge, and the rheem lowered its black eyes in challenge.

"Shhhh. Now, now."

Caleb's spine stiffened. He knew that voice. Quickly turning to Raechev, he leaned in to whisper, "Go ahead and find some lodgings at Ishtar's Temple. I'll catch up soon. I want to help them. They shouldn't have attempted this."

Raechev snorted, "I'd be more help than you."

"Just," Caleb paused and stemmed his fear, "just please go and do this. Please, Raechev."

Raechev paused long enough to take him seriously, then nodded and left.

Caleb turned and walked into the quiet stall. Loki stood stroking the tamed beast. Raechev was over a hundred, but he wasn't willing to give her up yet. He just couldn't.

"I saw her."

Caleb nodded as he walked to Loki. "She feels responsible for all the mortal deaths and wishes to go on a crusade to redeem the deaths caused by her negligence of Elohim's commands."

Loki's eyebrow rose.

"She only plans on killing Nephilim who are killing mortals. She seeks redemption, atonement."

Loki's stroking hand slowed on the rheem's long nose. Without looking up at Caleb, he nodded. "I'll wait. Take one trip, then return."

A deep inhalation eased Caleb's fear of losing Raechev. He couldn't help but like Loki. If nothing else, he was a patient male.

"Ye should stay with the Levites. She would enjoy that, and ye probably miss their torahing."

"Why do they stay?" Caleb asked.

Loki sighed. "I will stay for as long as they do." He paused. "The Persians are different than the Babylonians. They are more accepting. Within their empire, with their conquered peoples, they allow each civilization to practice their own religion."

Caleb's stern voice matched his eyes. "They should return to the Promised Land. It is where Elohim wants them. They enjoy these pagan streets and grand cities more than they should."

"Loki?" a frail voice called from an upper window.

Loki and Caleb looked up. A wrinkled, kind faced magi waved down to them. He was missing most of his teeth, but an ornate mitre sat upon his head. The white silk cap had a gold embroidered base and rose seven inches before tapering off into two separate pieces of cloth, one for the front, and one for the back. Each cloth was a gently rounded pyramid, reaching another seven inches or so above the man's head. Stitched onto the front was a red sun and lion.

Caleb wrinkled his nose. "Interesting hat."

Loki grinned. "Typical pagan fascination with genitalia. The woman encircling the head, and the phallus breaking... or thrusting... through it." He laughed.

"I'm coming," Loki replied to the elderly man who smiled and moved back into the upper chamber out of sight. Loki shot a bemused glance to Caleb. "Ye should come and see what is transpiring."

Caleb's brow furrowed, but he turned and followed when Loki departed.

"These Magi, these occultists, have been projecting to the stars and communicating with those who live there, and asking the Hebrews about their god."

"Elohim?" Caleb's voice dripped unbelief.

"Aye. Some knew Dani'el, known here as Belt'shatzar, when they were babes. They knew of his great seer gifts. His mysticism surpassed those of the Babylonian magicians and enchanters while never once breaking Elohim's laws concerning the occult. Dani'el was made the provincial ruler of Babylon and was placed in charge of all the occultists. He then appointed other righteous Jews as administrators over the smaller provinces so that he could stay at the royal court. The king kept having dreams and visions, and only Dani'el could interpret them, but he always gave the credit to Elohim. Eventually, N'vukhadnetzar began giving praise to Elohim, the God of the gods, the Lord of kings, and the revealer of mysteries."

Caleb's eyes never strayed from Loki's. "And the occultists followed suit?"

Loki smiled. "Not yet. Jealousy reigned through most of them. They had been displaced. When N'vukhadnetzar built a golden image of Ishtar as the Queen of Heaven and the Mother of the God of Light, he demanded his citizens to bow down and worship it, but the righteous Jews appointed by Dani'el did not. The magi quickly reported it to the king who condemned Daniel's co-horts to be sacrificed in a fiery furnace. Then those same children, the children of the magi, watched Hananyah, Misha'el, and 'Azaryah, known here as Shadrakh, Meishakh and 'Aved-N'go get tossed into the fiery furnace and survive. A transfigured Dani'el, reflecting the glory of Yehovah, came and walked in the fire with them. Dani'el's transfiguration, being a gateway created into the Kingdom of Heaven on Earth, extended to the other three, saving their physical lives. For the spiritual realms are more real than the physical realms. Then the wise men and their children began noticing the power of Elohim, for now it was more than just the interpretations of dreams - it had conquered fire and death."

"And N'vukhadnetzar's reaction?"

A half-smile crept over Loki's lips. "He decreed that anyone who spoke against the Hebrew god would be cut into pieces in fear this god's wrath would fall on him."

"Always looking out for the most important," Caleb muttered.

"'Tis the way of kings. But he did not go unscathed. Elohim turned N'vukhadnetzar into a beast before the wise men's eyes until he praised Elohim. Elohim wanted the king to know that he did not hold the fate of the Jews in his hands, that Elohim did. When N'vukhadnetzar repented and praised Elohim, he was restored to his original appearance. When his son Belshatzar took the throne, he began a great feast with his concubines to worship their many idols, but he used the golden cups from Elohim's temple." Loki turned purposefully towards Caleb and stopped walking. "Elohim's finger wrote a message to the king on the wall." Loki smiled. "A visible, enormous, cloud-like hand. Dani'el was sent for, and you know what Elohim wrote?"

Throat parched and breathing constricted, Caleb shook his head.

"M'ne! M'ne! T'kel ufarsin.'" M'ne (Elohim has counted up your kingdom and brought it to an end). T'kel (you are weighed upon the balance-scale and come up short). Ufarsin' (your kingdom has been divided and given to the Medes and Persians). "That very night, the king of the Medes killed Belshatzar in his bed."

Caleb exhaled.

"And the wise men, the great magi of Babylon, tried yet again to rise above the Jewish mystics who served and acknowledged only Elohim. They went to the new king and influenced him to make a decree to prove the citizenship now loyal to him. The citizens would do this by bowing down and worshiping only the king for an entire month, no other gods were to be worshiped. And if they did, they would be seen as traitors and thrown into the lion's den."

"And did Dani'el stand firm?" Caleb asked.

"Aye, and Elohim delivered his seer yet again. Angels were sent. They kept the lions' mouths closed and sang them to sleep. When Daryavesh the Mede saw Daniel's baal deliver him, he killed all the magi conspirators in that same lion's den, and decreed for everyone in the kingdom to fear and reverence the baal of Dani'el. So the kingdom reverences Elohim, but the citizens see him as just one baal among many. The only wise men left were those who liked Dani'el. It's been rather peaceful and easy for the Jews since. King Daryavesh died, and Koresh the Persian took the throne, nothing changed much. Until now."

"Now?"

"A new king named Daryavesh came to the throne this past year. He says that the Persian baal, Ahura Mazda, chose him to usurp the false son of Koresh who had stolen the throne."

"He sees Elohim as being an enemy baal?" Caleb guessed.

"Nay. He sees the baal of the Jews as being the Persian Ahura Mazda."

"What?" Caleb's question turned sarcastically hostile.

"Elohim means the God of the gods. Hebrews respectfully say Adonai, Lord, instead of saying the real name. It is not illogical to believe that a polytheist would connect one of their gods with similar qualities of Elohim to Elohim, especially one who has shown such great power." Loki tried to soothe Caleb's alarm. "He has asked his occultists to learn all that they can from the Hebrews about their god, but the Levites have become close lipped in fear of losing their place amongst the Jews. Can you imagine if the magi became as throughly versed on Elohim's commands as the Levites?

There are some Hebrews who share knowledge with the occultists, but they are tricked into doing so. The magi come as beggars to Jewish street vendors while others listen in to the women and men telling stories to their children."

"So they are learning? Are they mixing Elohim with Ahura Mazda?"

Loki sighed. "I'm still trying to figure things out meself. Ahura Mazda does take on more and more of Elohim's characteristics, but most of it is gleaned from the stars."

"The stars?" Caleb probed.

"Elohim said, 'Let there be lights in the dome of the sky to divide the day from the night; let them be for signs, seasons, days and years; and let them be for lights in the dome of the sky to give light to the earth'; and that is how it was." Loki paused, "Elohim created constellations as signs, they tell the story of Elohim and the messiah. This is what the occultists are researching, they are studying the stars and piecing together the story of Elohim so that they can create a deception."

Dumbfounded Caleb shook his head. "Is that even possible?"

"Aye. 'tis one reason why everyone is accountable. The signs, the testament of Elohim, is painted each night in the heavens. Everyone must choose between the savior born of a virgin or the serpent." Loki jerked his head towards the upper room. "Come and observe."

Caleb looked back at the peasants and noblemen moving about. Most wore long flowing robes with square, flat-topped hats. Gold and gems glinted off nobles who were carried on elevated chairs by their servants. Temple prostitutes swayed erotically to entice offerings to their deities, and one lone Levite walked carefully through the masses trying not to allow himself to be touched by the unclean pagans. He rose his voice and called out to Loki. Loki moved to his side, nodded several times, then returned to Caleb. He whispered, "The Levite says one copy of each of the prophets has been stolen. Two copies of Isaiah." Loki continued on, and Caleb followed.

They walked up a narrow staircase and stopped just outside an ornately carved golden door. A large eye enclosed within a triangle was etched into a gold star. The eye stared straight at them, unnerving Caleb. Above the door read *Praise be to the name of God for ever and ever; wisdom and power are his. We praise, exalt, and glorify the King of Heaven because everything he does is right and his ways are just. And lo to those who walk in pride, for he who is able to humble may one day humble you.*

Loki leaned in and whispered, "Do not disclose your allegiance. These are the sons and grandsons of the magi who stood against Dani'el. Those fathers are dead. And there is a new king who wants the occult trinity as the one and only Supreme Being. They commune with other worldly beings to grow in power, and to become more powerful than Dani'el ever was. Out of fear for their lives, they do not say Ahura Mazda. They simply say god as if no one in the city worships a plethora of gods. This offends no one and protects them. It also causes much confusion... and of course, deception."

"But Elohim..."

"Caleb, these are nay Hebrews. These are nay Elohim's chosen. These be outsiders. Do ye see them obeying all the commands of Elohim? Nay, they dinnae. I have told them all. They only pick and choose what laws they want to adhere to. They think they are nay important, that Elohim only wants to be acknowledged, loved, and worshiped. They care nothing for obedience nor respect. They are trying to please all the gods, including themselves."

Singing could be heard from inside. Loki opened the door, and Caleb could make out the seers' words. "He changes times and seasons; he sets up kings and deposes them. He gives wisdom to the wise and knowledge to the discerning. He reveals deep and hidden things; he knows what lies in darkness, and yet light dwells within him. We praise and thank you, O God, Father and King of Heaven."

The room was pitch black due to all the windows being covered up, but candles were lit sporadically throughout the room, and enflamed, glittering diamonds were embedded into the ceiling. Caleb gasped. Right above his head was the entire planisphere of the heavens, including its corresponding zodiac signs. It was magnificent. Once his vision became used to the darkness, he could see several men in long purple robes lying on their backs in the middle of the floor. All wore long gold chains and had mitres lying near their heads. A few more men, similarly attired, sat with scrolls, ink, and quills. Some were reading Hebrew scrolls, others waited with blank scrolls to write down decisions made by those studying the planisphere above them.

Loki leaned in. "Daniel was awarded purple robes and gold chains for his interpretations. They wear the same."

"And themselves," Caleb muttered as he took in the gold wall hangings. They had various images of suns, winged sun discs, eyes within triangles, and rays of the sun surrounding a pagan god's head which appeared like a crown.

"The virgin seems important," one of the elders spoke while pointing to the Virgo constellation. "See how she bounces the god-made-man on her knee? Yet she continues to appear a virgin. She must have stayed a virgin."

"Impregnated by the King of the Heavens himself?" another magi asked.

"Well, she is the Mother of the Savior God who fights the Serpent." His finger shifted over to the constellation Draco. Do you think the Savior God hasn't been born yet? Wouldn't we have known? Wouldn't Dani'el have said?"

"According to Isaiah the prophet, he hasn't come yet. And somewhere I read that the temple has to be rebuilt and a new power, that we know not of, will overtake Jerusalem," the magi who leaned over the Hebrew scrolls answered. Apparently, this is where the missing books of the prophets had been carted off to.

"We already have a Queen of the Heavens, a Mother of God," another seer spoke up.

"Yes, but this one is a virgin. A real virgin," the first wise man spoke.

Snorts of derision could be heard throughout the room. Then a quiet, young man with unusual golden hair spoke up. "She needs not have a name. We shall just call her the Virgin Mother. It would ease the populace with the king's decree. Then each person can decide for themself which goddess they are really acknowledging. We do it with Ahura Mazda, most just calling him God, we can do it with the Virgin Mother as well." His voice slowly died as everyone soaked in his compromise. "This is good. The king only wants men to worship the whole trinity, so the women can worship and pray to the Virgin Mother."

"And which goddess will you claim as the Virgin Mother?" Loki asked.

The golden haired seer laid quietly for a long time, then answered, "No one. She has not yet come into being. I will watch the Virgin Mother's constellation for a sign when she or her Savior son will be born."

"I do not think he will live that long, and these men are a dying breed," Loki whispered to Caleb. "The King has decreed that all priests are to be celibate and only serve Ahura Mazda."

The eldest seer sighed. "This will work. We will make the feast days of the sun god's birth and resurrection the most prominent in our year. At the winter solstice, we will celebrate the birth of the sun and at the Festival of Ishtar, we will celebrate his resurrection. Yes, that will appease the masses."

"So the son of the Virgin Mother shall be Mithras? The Lord of Heavenly Light? The Lord of Truth? The God of the Sun? The Victorious Light over the Serpent, the Baal of Darkness?" a seer asked, ready to pen their decisions into a clean scroll.

"Perhaps, Mitra?" The golden haired seer asked. "The Persian god of light. The ancient Aryan deity. A Nephilim of great powers."

"Perhaps, Lucciferri. The Light Bringer. Venus. The Morning Star," Loki purred.

The golden haired seer turned and looked up at Loki. "Perhaps, Luciferia, Venus, our Morning Star, would make a better Virgin Mother. She is female. The savior is to be male, not female."

An uncomfortable silence fell over the room.

The golden haired seer spoke again. "We will need to begin establishing the new image of Mithras to coincide with the constellations. He's represented as a lion as in Leo and a sacrificial lamb in Aries. And Pisces. All the fish that follow the lamb who gives them an outpouring of some heavenly water." He sighed wearily.

"Yes, all twelve zodiacs aid in teaching us this great mystery. Why not thirteen? Why not ten? Why not nineteen?" an overwhelmed seer asked.

"I prefer the heavenly bull, Taurus. Perhaps, we should focus on the bull since the Hebrews are shepherds and not cattlemen. It is one of our god's images, so I think we shall cling to it. Our people will not understand a lamb. The fish reek of the Phoencian and Philistine gods. The lion makes people think of Zurvan or the sphynx in Egypt, but the bull has always been sacred to our people.

We should focus on the bull." The golden haired boy stared at the stars above, slowly roaming over them all. "What began in water will end in fire, but in between will be the suffering Savior who bleeds for the sins of mankind."

"And all, whether knowing or unknowing, prepare fer the final battle between the forces of light and those of darkness," Loki whispered.

A sitting scribe glanced at Loki. "But the virtuous, who obey the teachings of the priesthood, will take their place among the Illuminati, the Spirits of Light, and be saved while the disobedient ones will be cast into Hades with the fallen angels. The Final Judgment comes upon us all."

Loki smiled sardonically. "So I must obey yer decrees to be saved?"

The golden haired seer inspected Loki, then pointed up to Capricornus. It was a strange constellation with the head of a goat that slowly turned into a fish. One of the stars was called 'the cut off.'"

Loki glanced over Capricornus. "What do ye think?"

"I'd like to think that the evil of the goat is cut off to make a fish, the follower of the Lamb, but something makes me feel like that is what I want to believe."

"Decide for yourself, but what I see is a mixture. A person who mingles the ways of both the evil goat and a fish, the follower of the Lamb. I see the person who mixes pagan religions with Elohim's as being cut off himself. Do ye see how the Capricornus' back is to the entire message? The creature doesn't study the signs. He chooses ignorance to continue in his disobedience."

The elderly seer who had asked Loki to come, now rebuked him. "Loki, we speak in love here. We worship a God of love not one of punishment."

Loki glanced to Caleb.

The golden haired seer continued to study Loki and moved his finger to the constellation Andromeda. "And her? Why is the Bride of the Lamb chained?"

Loki glanced quickly to know which one he was pointing to. A woman with a fish coming into her side was chained to a cliff waiting for a sea monster to devour her. "She is manacled by man-made methods to a rock. Apparently man's philosophies, interpretations and rationalizations will cause her death. She is to be the Bride of the Lamb not the Bride of Man, but as a whole, she stopped listening to the Lamb and let men set her up to die."

A knock was heard on the door, and a seer quickly moved to open it. A servant-type male came in and bowed to the eldest seer. "Father, the mass is ready."

The eldest seer nodded and motioned for the servant to kiss his golden ring, recognizing his status as one of the king's wise men. Each seer rose and moved into a circle. The golden haired one spoke, "Loki and his friend bring our numbers to fourteen. Only twelve can partake."

The eldest seer smiled kindly. "Love, my brother. They shall watch. Loki does not partake of blood and flesh as we do."

Caleb's stomach tightened unbearably while the servant laid out small round clumps of grilled flesh and twelve cups filled with blood. He knew that many of the priests and priestesses drank and ate of sacrificed humans, but he was a bit startled that these men in front of him would do so. The small clumps of flesh had a cross slashed into them resembling the cakes made to the Queen of Heaven, the Virgin Mother.

"I have seen enough," Caleb communicated to Loki.

"My friend is concerned 'bout his sister wandering the streets alone. We will go and look for her if ye dinnae mind," Loki spoke benevolently.

The eldest seer smiled and nodded. "Ah yes. A wise older brother. Feel free to join us on the Lord's Day for our weekly fellowship in worshiping God."

Caleb's brow furrowed, but he didn't say anything. He smiled and nodded before turning and following Loki out.

"They've chosen the sun god, Mithras. They meet and worship him on the day dedicated to him, first day of the week, the Sun's day."

324 BC, BABYLON

A strong smell of Indian incense permeated the room. The most feared Macedonian officers sat about, but they were hard to discern in the cloudy smoke. Loki couldn't help but wonder if it was on purpose. If they tried to hide their whispers of treason from their great lord.

Dark wooden grates blocked the sunlight, making it appear dark. They were encircled with images of Babylonian kings killing fierce creatures with their bare hands. The walls were covered with the blue glaze Babylon was famous for, and thick foliage lined the perimeter. All of the men sat on the outer edge of a square table formation. Eyes darted to the right and to the left. No one placed their back to another.

High above on a dais, yet still a part of the square, sat Alexander the Great. He was an odd persona with long, curly dirty-blond hair that had been teased to stand out like a lion's mane. Unlike his peers, he was clean shaven, which revealed an unnatural twist in his neck, forcing his head upward at an angle. It was quite unnerving, even for a Nephilim. Added to this, he had one brown eye and one blue, both feminine and dewy which seemed odd with his very short, stocky frame and leather tanned features. He was covered in scars, making his natural ruddy skin more uneven.

Loki shivered. Alexander's neck seemed wider than his extremely square jaw, and with the way it was cocked, it seemed that Alexander was looking at him. Maybe this was one of the ways he controlled his subordinates - his disconcerting tilted head and disdain filled eyes constantly hunting out whispers of treason. It was impossible, but Loki felt like Alexander was constantly looking at him, but each time he looked up, Alexander's eye was on someone else.

A deep gravelly voice spoke roughly. "Lyre."

Suddenly an eunuch was standing behind Alexander, playing the requested instrument. It's sweet stringed melody eased the conversation to a lull. The palpable tension of the room lessened.

Loki had learned that neither of Alexander's wives came to the meals. His last wife, being an excellent choice - Stateira, was a princess, the daughter of Darius III of Persia. His first wife, Roxana, not of any royal lineage, seemed a jealous sort that only intensified Alexander's own paranoia and rages. It was his best friend and only confident, Hephaestion, that presided with him at the dais. Some had joked that it was Hephaestion's height that created the bond between them, for he was the only man that Alexander could look upon without straining his neck to see. Sadness speared through Loki. How much of Alexander's deformity drove him to prove himself to his peers?

Alexander's hand lifted and beckoned someone from Loki's area to approach. Everyone began cautiously glancing around. With his neck skewed, no one could really tell who Alexander was looking at, and no one wanted to offend him.

"Red," that same gravelly voice thundered throughout the room. "My mother has hair that color. She is descended from Aeacus, a direct son of Zeus and the grandfather of Achilles. Come and tell me of your family. No need to bow to me; I can see your ancestry in your eyes. We are family."

Loki nodded and walked up to the dais. He wouldn't lie down prostrate as Alexander had begun making inferiors do when approaching their superiors even if Alexander would have demanded it. He'd probably fly above his head and then disappear out the window if Alexander demanded his pride be pampered. Yes, he and his generals had conquered what they knew of the world, but they didn't know how much world was out there.

As soon as Loki sat, freshly squeezed oranges mixed with sugar was added to Alexander's wine. Alexander pointed to Loki's cup to be filled as well. "Mother tells me I'm the son of Zeus. An oracle in Egypt said I was the sun god Ammon. What think you?"

"There is only Elohim. The divine beings who mated with mortals were only his disobedient servants," Loki replied firmly.

Alexander's cup froze on its way to his lips. "You call Zeus a disobedient servant?" He turned his whole upper body towards Loki to clearly look him in the eyes.

Loki shuddered. His one blue eye seemed to glow in contrast to his dark brown eye - both stood out strangely. His delicate eyes were framed by lush, exotic eyelashes and set amidst a war-ravaged ugly face. His neck's deformity forced his one blue eye to be the most prominent feature, drowning most else out, and his voice was harsh and gravelly as if the neck's deformity stretched his vocal chords unnaturally, making it painful for him to speak. "Anyone who allows himself to be worshiped as a god is disobedient."

Alexander continued his stare for many moments, then quickly resumed his normal pose to keep a watchful eye on his supposed loyal generals. "Do you know of my mother?"

"Olympias, she calls herself now? Aye, I ken of her, though I have nay met her. She's a devout member of a mystery cult - the orgiastic snake-worshiping cult of Dionysis."

"That is where they met, my father and mother. They were both initiated the same night into the mysteries of Cabeiri at the Sanctuary of the Great Gods, on the island of Samothrace. They both received dreams." Alexander's voice quieted, and he quit speaking for a whole minute before continuing, "Hephaestus also joined the Dionysian mystery cult, but he never sleeps with snakes." Alexander shivered. "My mother always slept with them. Every night, I can still feel them slithering over me. I hated those snakes. I still do. Hephaestus eases me."

"Yer father married a woman who partook of such rituals?" Loki asked amused. It seemed unusual for such a proud man to marry a woman who enjoyed orgies.

"After they met, my mother never joined in the orgies. She only partook of the first night when she communed with the spirits of the underworld, so there were no men involved. It was just her and the spirits. She still speaks to them. She became one of their concubines." Alexander paused, his eyes shot to two generals whispering between themselves. When the two men noticed Alexander's attention, they quickly separated and refilled their goblets. "My father greatly valued the knowledge she gained from her spirit-lovers. What do you think of mystery cults?"

"I think anything done in secret is not to be respected. Trying to gain respect by fear is cowardly, and that is what secret cults do. They instill fear in those excluded. True power and great respect is won by those who dinnae hide their actions from those around them."

Alexander kept his eyes on his generals. "There is a mystery cult here, Mithraism. The soldiers have become very fond of it. No snakes involved." Alexander chuckled. "It is of the great Ahura Mazda and his son Mithras and the son's Virgin Mother. It pleases the philosophical side of our Macedonian souls. The great enemy is a demon who tries to corrupt the soul of man away from righteousness and greatness."

"It is based on the Jews' religion. Elohim beat fear in the hearts of the Babylonian, Mede, and Persian kings before yer arrival. N'vukhadnetzar was turned into a beast for claiming to be a god and refusing to praise Elohim; three Jewish seers were cast into a fiery furnace for refusing to worship the king as god and came out unscathed; another king saw an enlarged hand write him a prophecy that his death and kingdom were over, he died that very night; and it goes on and on. The seers who put Mithraism together witnessed these accounts. They saw Elohim's power fer themselves. They stole copies of the Jewish prophets' scrolls and filled in the holes with the tale found in the constellations," Loki spoke reverently. "But it is still pagan."

"You mean the drinking of blood and eating of flesh? I do not prefer these things, nor human sacrifice. Enough life is lost in battle, and all men and women are needed for soldiering and creating soldiers. In the services I attend, I drink red wine and eat bread as the famed cakes of heaven with little crosses on it." Alexander leaned back and allowed his back to relax against the throne. "While I was still in Macedonia, wondering how to defeat the Asians, I had a dream. A priest approached me in a purple robe, white linen, and a golden headdress with the words 'Holy unto YHVH'. The priest told me to boldly cross the sea to Persia, and God would direct my armies and give me dominion over Persia." Alexander drank from his goblet before continuing, "When I went to Jerusalem, that very priest from my dream, approached me, so I reverenced this god in front of my entire army. They were shocked and surprised until I told them of my dream. Then, the priest, Jaddua, took me to their temple and showed me a scroll of their seer Dan'el. In Dan'el's writings, he had predicted my rise to power and victories, including the manner in which I had already conquered Tyre - using the rubble of a mainland city to build a bride to destroy the island fortress."

Alexander's brow furrowed. "But the High Priest does not normally wear such clothes that he approached me in. He said that he only wore that because he was told to wear all his finery to greet me in a dream." Alexander finished his orange wine and refilled his cup. "Mithraic priests wear garb like that." Alexander threw back the contents in his cup and quickly refilled his cup again. "After I sacrificed to the god of the Jews, I swore to them that I would allow them to keep to their ancestral laws."

Loki whispered, "A wise choice. Wiser than the rulers here who had to learn the hard way to reverence Elohim."

Alexander thoughtfully murmured, "Elohim. God of the

gods."

Loki slyly looked at Alexander, whose eyes were studying the beautiful wood beamed and gold dotted ceiling. A young, exceptionally beautiful eunuch with obsidian eyes and hair stood quietly behind him. The youth's, Bagoas's, huge almond shaped eyes adored Alexander. There were rumors. There were always rumors especially with men of power, but Loki had not seen anything to indicate a relationship had formed. Alexander was known to be a man of extraordinary self-control when it came to pleasures of the body. He had a harem and two wives, but rarely frequented them. He had become great friends with Darius's mother Sisygambis - a very unusual characteristic for a Greek or Macedonian man. The Persians whispered of the oddness that women were never allowed to attend the feasts. They were always locked up behind doors, but that was the Macedonian and Greek way. Women were seen as nothing more than beasts and property. They were good for procreating, but the greatest Greek philosophers degraded them to stirring the base nature of a man, turning him into a lustful beast. Women were never to be trusted, never to be allowed anywhere a man needed to think logically, and never allowed somewhere where her distraction would be harmful to a man's decision making. The Greeks and Macedonians believed that only true love could be expressed with another man, sexually or in friendship. "Where is Hephaestion?"

Alexander stirred, "He feels ill this night. He rarely becomes ill. It should pass by morning. I do miss his presence." Alexander gave a wane smile. "You know I could never defeat him in wrestling. He has these strong thighs that he used to flip me to my defeat. With my neck, I could never see his move coming." Alexander inhaled deeply. "I don't know if anyone else could defeat me. I knew that most of their father's told the other sons to always let me win, but Hephaestion would not. I respected him for that."

"As is well understandable," Loki conceded.

"But even more so, when I saw him deny our tutor." Alexander turned and faced Loki. "Hephaestion is the most beautiful male I have ever seen. You should have seen him when we were youths. He had many offers, but accepted none."

Loki's stomach turned. He abhorred pederasty, the love of boys, the relationship between an adult man and an adolescent boy outside his immediate family. Philosophers debated it, all saying that a chaste relationship that instilled a spiritual love was the highest form of love on earth, but oftentimes in Athens, the love turned carnal. When the boy began to grow whiskers, the relationship would end. "I was unaware that Aristotle was a lover of boys."

"Socrates favored chaste pederastic relationships, but Plato's *Symposium* and *Phaedrus* seemed to elevate it to something more divine, more spiritual, and more appealing to the Greek masses who carnalized it. Plato wrote of Socrates' pederasty, 'that it is given by the gods and is the best and noblest of all the forms that possession by a god can take, but it is lessened if made sexual. If made sexual, then it is often damaging and shameful to the boy. The adult man turns predator.' He wrote, 'Do wolves love lambs? That's how lovers befriend a boy.'"

"And Aristotle?" Loki probed.

"Was vague. But overall thought it fine for it to turn sexual if the younger desires it, but not if he is induced to do so. Aristotle often quoted Plato to me. He would say, 'Think Alexander, think on the great Plato's words. If there were only some way of contriving that a state or an army should be made up of lovers and their loves, they would be the very best governors of their own city, abstaining from all dishonor and emulating one another in honor; and it is scarcely an exaggeration to say that when fighting at each other's side, although a mere handful, they would overcome the world.'"

"Yet there would be no sons. No heirs to rule that world." Loki philosophized, since it seemed that is what Alexander esteemed.

Alexander squinted. "It is perfect. Mithraism. It incorporates all of Plato's theories but allows room for Aristotle's as well. Plato doesn't believe in a god, but he believes that one should teach the masses to believe in a god, much like Ahura Mazda. Plato wrote that the best methods to extinguish undesired sexual liaisons and flames of passion is to associate pederasty as unclean, unholy, and shameful so that no one would dispute them, for who would dispute good and evil if evil is often damaging to another individual." Alexander tapped his fingers several times. "And yet, within the fraternity of Mithraism, where only men may trod, the father priests would be able to take male youths under their wings and train them spiritually. Pederasty could easily continue for those who wish it, but no one would know, for it is a secret assembly, a mystery cult. To the outside world, every sinful infraction would be punished. The masses would be taught as Plato's *Republic* prescribes. Yet within, we would build a spiritual fraternity that could overcome the world." Alexander grew quiet. "I was named the sun god in Egypt, and now I learn that Mithraism centers on the son of Ahura Mazda, the representative sun god, also symbolized as a lion as I am. We are both crowned with gold about our heads. The women could stay at home or worship the Virgin Mother." Alexander snorted derisively. "That would make my mother deliriously happy. She would think I'm honoring her."

Loki pursed his lips. "Isnae she the one who has believed in ye the most?"

Alexander guffawed. "She believes in her spirit guides. I am just the way to her own power. I am her pawn in her war on the world of men. I am to complete the destiny promised by her spirits." Alexander's eyes scanned the room. "I do not like being without Hephaestion. Sometimes, I feel the eyes of her spirits on me. Often they are invisible, but sometimes they possess ravens to warn me that they are watching, and that I should heed my mother. Have you seen spirits possessing a bird.... or even another human before?"

Loki nodded.

"Would you be truthful if I asked you to be my eyes and ears this eve? Between Hephaestion and myself, we keep an excellent grasp on the whispers of those who claim to serve and obey me. But I am alone tonight." Alexander grew somber. "His wife nurses him."

Alexander and Hephaestion had once been referred to as 'one soul abiding in two bodies' by Aristotle. They were now brothers through their marriages to Darius and Sisygambis' daughters. Loki heard that they wanted their sons to grow up together as cousins, and that if something were to happen to Alexander's sons, Hephaestion's son would rule. Loki noticed Alexander's tense muscles. His eyes, barely stopped scanning the generals, as if waiting for an attack. Loki had heard that Alexander was becoming ever more paranoid that his generals would try to assassinate him. They were tired of warring. They wanted to rule.

Hephaestion often sat at Alexander's right side, eating from his plate, and drinking from his cup. In fact, he always ate a little of everything on Alexander's plate and drank from his wine before Alexander did. Hephaestion wouldn't allow his friend to eat till he was sure it had not been poisoned. Loki wondered if Alexander blamed himself for his friend's sickness.

Alexander whispered, "He is closer than a brother to me. I could never trust a brother. Hephaestion seeks not my throne. I value him as I value my own life." Alexander paused and drank more wine. "You know how I knew I could trust him? When he respected me enough to defeat me, and when he chose our friendship over Aristotle's offer. Do you know what being Aristotle's lover would have done for him? In all but my blood relation to the king, he would have surpassed me. He would have been the most favored in every way."

"And did you decline Aristotle's offer?"

Alexander stilled.

Loki waited.

"Hephaestion favored Plato. Thought it could only be damaging to the youth. He abhorred the practice." Alexander rose, making it very difficult to look him in the eyes since his neck twisted grotesquely up. Loki rose to make it easy for Alexander to keep eye contact. "He is the Jonathan to my David. Yes, I've heard the tales of the Hebrew kings." His eyes squinted again. "Walk me to my chambers, brother."

Loki followed him out, and servants quickly scrambled to attention. Bagoas's frantic attempts to stay close to Alexander was almost comic. What a feat for a eunuch to be chosen as Alexander's boy lover, but Alexander did not spare him a look. Instead, Alexander demanded wine be brought to his chamber, and that no one be permitted entry.

When they reached Alexander's door. He paused and turned to Loki, motioning everyone else to leave. After they were alone, Alexander asked, "What do you think of Elohim's seers?"

Loki shrugged. "They are always correct."

Alexander squinted again. "But... our seers are often wrong. My mother's spirits are sometimes wrong."

Loki grinned. "Is this what yer Greek philosophers taught ye? To believe in spirits and religion? Don't they attempt to rationalize such things away?"

"Do not play me for a fool, brother. I have witnessed too much."

Loki stood amused. So, the kings of logic had not blinded a son of a seer. Olympias was an evil witch for sure, but a strong seer nonetheless. "And do ye listen to her spirits or yer own?"

"Neither. I am not my father. And her spirits never aided him to conquer Persia."

"But ye listened to a dream."

"Yes," Alexander conceded. "Which appears of Mithraism, yet was used by Elohim's servants. The God of the gods. Do you suppose it is the same god? Or do you suppose, the God of the gods knows what all dreams are given by all gods?"

"There is only one. Elohim."

"To us," Alexander cut in, "but perhaps, not to mortals."

Loki folded his arms over his chest and leaned against the door frame. "Do ye believe ye were fathered by Zeus?"

Alexander intently examined Loki. "You remind me of Hephaestion." He smiled. "Philip and his father both have physical deformities as do I. It gave my father peace knowing that I was his. He never trusted my mother, and except for birthing me, as his fourth wife, she didn't stand to gain power in his kingdom. I often wondered if she brewed a love potion. They were both miserably married."

Loki nodded.

"Loki, is it possible for Elohim's seers to be wrong? Have you ever known of Elohim's prophets being wrong?"

Loki dropped his head. "I have been on this earth since before the flood, and I can attest that Elohim's prophets have never been wrong. Why does this concern ye so?"

"Elohim's High Priest showed me Dani'el's scroll. It weighs upon me. It states 'in the first year of Darius the Mede, even I, stood to confirm and to strengthen him. And now will I shew thee the truth. Behold, there shall stand up yet three kings in Persia; and the fourth shall be far richer than they all: and by his strength through his riches he shall stir up all against the realm of Grecia. And a mighty king shall stand up, that shall rule with great dominion, and do according to his will. And when he shall stand up, his kingdom shall be broken, and shall be divided toward the four winds of heaven; and not to his posterity, nor according to his dominion which he ruled: for his kingdom shall be plucked up, even for others beside those. And the king of the south shall be strong, and one of his princes; and he shall be strong above him, and have dominion; his dominion shall be a great dominion. And in the end of years they shall join themselves together; for the king's daughter of the south shall come to the king of the north to make an agreement: but she shall not retain the power of the arm; neither shall he stand, nor his arm: but she shall be given up,'"

Loki nodded. "I am familiar with this prophecy, and Dani'el is a seer of Elohim who would never be wrong."

"My empire will die with me? It will be divided into four?"

"If Elohim decrees, so shall it be."

"Then if my empire will not stand after my death, the only glory to be achieved is how wide it is spread."

124 BC, PACIFIC OCEAN

Caleb closed his eyes and inhaled the thick sea-coated air. He had lost count of how long they had been sailing the vast ocean west of their home, but it soothed his soul. Their traveling had brought back too many bad memories, and here in this blessed emptiness, humanity was forgotten.

Salty sea-spray drenched him, and he could feel the oncoming storm in the currents rocking their small vessel. It had been a long time since he'd encountered a fierce ocean storm, but anything void of humans was delightful. He had wanted to forget all he had witnessed in the last two hundred years. At first, he simply wanted to take Raechev on a hunting expedition like his father had done with him. She of course wanted to find every evil Nephilim and put them to death. When he saw what they were doing, he was always more than willing to help her, but what pained his soul the most was that oftentimes, the mortals continued as they had done before. Their people's traditions, no matter how vile, had been so deeply entrenched into their psyche that they were unable to see it for what it truly was. Their hearts had deemed it necessary for their existence.

Sharp gusts of wind whipped through his hair, causing it to lash his face painfully. He could feel the raft rise high and knew the ocean swells were increasing to a terrible pitch. He didn't need to see it with his own eyes, he could feel it in the very way the air churned and vibrated around and deep within.

The clouds had blocked out the brilliant stars hours ago, so all they did was wait for the storm, but Caleb's soul was already there. His mind drifted back to another storm he and Raechev had witnessed shortly after leaving Babylon. He remembered a storm that had brewed along the coast of Greece, hampering a military expedition. The Acadian cult had called for the poor to bring their babes and toddlers to be sacrificed. And what shocked Caleb, was that they did. In this first instance, there was no Nephilim demanding a human tribute, but the humans were doing it themselves. The priests smashed the babes' skulls, then handed them back to their parents, who laid the corpse on their idol's outstretched arms. If any parent or relatives cried, the sacrifice would have been voided, so a strange silence engulfed the area, the loudest sound being that of the babe's skull being crushed. Three hundred. Three hundred babes were sacrificed for that expedition. After several prayers to the idol, and the fulfillment of the blood demand for the spell to work, each babe was hand tossed into a fire pit. The only evidence of sorrow that could be seen, was the small grave markers made by the parents, thanking their sons and daughters for sacrificing their lives to have their prayers answered in defeating their enemies.

A year later in Carthage, when Agathocles defeated the Carthagians, the Carthagian nobles believed that they had displeased the gods by using low-born children in their sacrifice, so they strove to make amends by sacrificing two hundred noble-born babes. The mothers of the nobles were not able to obey the law against weeping, so the priests called for drums to be beaten to drown out their cries. In the zeal to appease the gods, an additional hundred babes were butchered in an attempt to override how many had been sacrificed by their enemies.

He and Raechev had run into human sacrifice so many times in Greece, they had begun to realize that the Greeks sacrificed more than the Babylonians and Assyrians. What also drove the numbers up in Greece was the secrecy involved in the Elysian mystery cults, for if anyone witnessed a service or ceremony, who was not in the cult, would become a sacrifice themself. The penalty ignited curious youths, which led to greater numbers being sacrificed. At the temple of Zeus on Mount Lykaion, Caleb heard rumors of ghastly sacrifices being performed nearby by a people who were older than the moon. Who murdered, dismembered, then communally ate the child at the very tip of the mountain.

Lightning streaked the skies and thunder deafened the ear. The storm was approaching fast.

"Shall I fasten you to the raft?"

Caleb opened his eyes. An ocean swell rose over a hundred feet above him. Raechev sat, playfully dipping one of her ethereally glowing legs in and out of the black churning water.

"They're beginning to peak."

Unlike Raechev, Caleb could not stay indefinitely underwater. He could not hold his breath like her, and he didn't have the strength to fight the ocean if the storm lasted for days. And of course, neither of them could fly to safety.

Caleb nodded, and Raechev crawled over the wooden raft to tie him with leather bonds to the structure. Raechev's main concern would be to keep whatever side he was on, air born. He could hold his breath for five minutes, but that was it. If they were capsized, she would need to swim to the surface and flip him before he drowned.

"If it continues to worsen, I'm going to tie myself to the raft, but not snug like you. I just don't want to lose the raft in the dark storm. I'll give myself a good thirty feet of pull though, so I won't get hurt by the raft itself."

Caleb nodded. It was a wise choice. If she got stabbed by any of the smaller wooden poles in the raft, they'd both be lost. Caleb laid back and felt her small, agile hands cord leather bonds around him, tying him securely. The rain pounded on his face and competed against the sea spray each time they crested a wave.

The thunder boomed consistently, and lightning jagged through the sky. Because of his closed eyelids, the light show created a bloody visual of zig zagging capillaries. The thunder took on the sound of pounding drums, and his black and red haze triggered its own memories. Bonfires blazed in the blackest of nights. His skin crawled. Evil could be felt everywhere. He was back on the Malabar Coast of India.

Two Theyyam dancers whirled in delicate moves around a fire. The male was completely covered in blood red paint. Black holes were painted around his eyes, and dark red creases aged him and gave him a demonic look. Silver curling fangs protruded from each side of his mouth, stretching halfway back to his ears. Upon his head sat an elaborate golden crown with red fur sprouting from the top. A six inch red jaw decoration circled his head and connected to the crown. Large silver discs stood on either side of his neck. What slowed his movements, was the five foot head piece made of bamboo, decorated in red, orange and yellow. He looked twice his height with a face of a demon. His body was painted to make it appear that he had red leathery skin aged a millennia.

The female's face was delicately painted in orange, red, and yellow with the same black holes for eyes and silver horns protruding from the mouth. She had a smaller headdress, shaped like a star that closely encircled her head. Her body had been painted a golden metal shade as if she was a statue of a goddess herself in one of their shrines. She had a small skirt, that barely covered her, made of coconut bark and leaves, painted in the matching golden metal shade. Her arms and legs were weighted down with bracelets and anklets.

Their bodies mimicked the quickening drum beats till they were in a frenzied state, and positioned directly in front of the shrine of the deity they were calling up. Some of the deities were dead heroes or powerful ancestors while others were trapped terrestrial spirits who had been attached to megaliths and released only for ritual. Either way, it was willful demonic possession for divination purposes. As soon as the spirits had begun to possess the mortals, Raechev had tugged his arm to leave. There was no point for them to be there. There was no Nephilim to be killed, and the mortals were asking for a spirit of divination to possess one of their own, to tell them their future, to give counsel to their problems, and to resolve minor community disputes.

Their gasping breaths of pain still sounded in his ears. The spirits were entering. Eyes fluttered uncontrollably as their eyes rolled back. A low multiple-voiced entity pressed upon the vocal chords to talk from their fleshly prison.

"Do you think I could fly if I jumped in?"

Caleb whipped his eyes open. "What?"

Raechev pointed to a tornado swirling on the surface of the water. "Do you think that if I leapt into the tornado, I would get to taste the freedom of flying? The exhilaration? The power?" She turned sparkling eyes to her brother. "Don't you think it would be fun?"

"Terrifying. I think it would be terrifying."

Raechev pouted her lips. "So boring, Caleb."

Caleb grunted. "You hate losing control, and in there you wouldn't have it. You'd be at its mercy."

"But don't you think it would be romantic? For something else, something bigger, or stronger than you to take control of you?"

"You are a very strange female. And no you wouldn't like it. I believe you don't like it when male Nephilim try to force their way with you."

Raechev grimaced and slapped her foot upon the ocean wave. "That's not what I'm talking about. I'm talking about....love."

"Love?"

"Don't mock me, Caleb!"

"I just can't believe my baby sister would say such a thing. I think the storm's getting to you." Or all the death they'd seen crossing Asia.

"I've heard tales of great loves that were stronger than..."

Caleb wished he could sit up. It wasn't like Raechev to ponder love and romance, and she had just turned her face away from him. "What's brought this on?"

"I can't stop thinking of that wife. The one who died with her husband at the gigantic wall."

"Oh." Caleb remembered, but for a different reason. He feared that he would die if he ever lost Raechev. He commiserated with the wife.

While passing through central Asia, the eastern tribes had been building a stone and lime fortress. The huge wall stretched fifteen hundred miles along the western portion of their lands to keep out invaders. But as was customary throughout Asia, each new building, bridge, and temple was dedicated by human sacrifice - to appease the spirits living in the area and to ask them to protect the structure. Some even believed that if the structure was attacked, the spirit of the slain would rise as an immortal bodyguard.

Unfortunately, the Great Wall of China required many human sacrifices. It's light grey and white lime stones gleamed from amidst fog covered hills. Its width allowed for over ten people to walk shoulder to shoulder. Battlement structures and gateways allowed sleeping quarters for garrisons which could also be used as signal towers if a section of the wall was attacked. It was a monumental feat beaten from the blood, sweat, and tears of criminals, commoners and soldiers alike. Most of the criminals became the human sacrifices, but when there weren't enough, the holy men dipped into the commoners. In case the workers came under attack during construction, the soldiers were never sacrificed. Each wall segment had its own sacrifices, no segment went undedicated or spiritually unprotected.

Thousands of commoners were sacrificed. After toiling for months in its construction, several were chosen to give their last breath and drops of blood for it. In one instance, a wife willingly clung to her husband who was to be sacrificed. She cried that she couldn't live without him, that her heart would die, and there would be no purpose for her life. Her sacrifice to join her husband did not spare another. So they died together. Brick by brick sealed together in death. Caleb could still see the way their fingers caressed each other's between the bricks, the wife singing her husband's favorite song till their enclosure sealed them off from everyone. He often wondered how long she had been able to sing.

It was their activities at the wall which had led them to some Jews who had wandered to China. After their wall's segment was finished, he and Raechev visited the Hebrew community nestled deep within the Southern Song Dynasty.

Caleb opened his eyes. His sister still hadn't talked yet. She sat stiffly on the raft, straining up to see over the crest of the waves.

"Do you see something?"

"It's another volcanic island," she said plainly.

"Do you want to swim us there till the storm ends?"

"I want to swim us away."

"Not every volcanic island is filled with head hunters, Raechev. This one could be deserted for all we know."

"An image of Pele is carved into the side of the volcano. I can see a procession of tribal people fighting their way up to the top."

Well, Caleb guessed they wouldn't be going there. Apparently, they were trying to pacify their goddess with a human sacrifice at the top of her volcano. They probably thought her anger was causing the storm, or that she needed a blood sacrifice to gain enough power to end it, or fight off whatever spirit was causing the storm.

Even here, in the midst of a vast ocean, in the midst of a storm, they couldn't get away from mankind's foolishness and depravity. He needed to protect his baby sister. She was changing before his eyes. She teased when she hurt and toughened herself when her heart was at risk. Her sweet, innocent spirit was constantly being chipped away, scarred, yet strengthened by its scabs. He feared that those scabs, though protective when the wound heals, would one day eliminate her tenderness altogether. If more and more scabs formed, she'd never get them all off, and she'd lose feeling there for the rest of her life. She wasn't even a thousand years yet. She was barely five centuries. What would she be like in a thousand years? Two thousand? She barely laughed now-a-days. And her question on the tornado? On love? Was she craving new adventures? Was she bored with life already? Was risking her life, the surge of adrenaline, the only thing that made her feel?

She needed to laugh, to have some frivolous, light hearted fun. "Raechev, we should head south. There's a large land mass with the cutest little black and white creatures I've ever seen. My dad showed them to me. They call them penguins." And no humans lived there.

Her eyes stayed glued to the volcano.

He waited several minutes then twisted to get a better look at her. "Raechev."

She slowly turned vacant eyes to him.

"Penguins? Cute little creatures?"

"I... don't... understand... humans."

"Raechev, Sweetie, not all humans are bad. It's the priests who are leading them astray. Many love their spouses and children well," Caleb soothed.

She slowly cocked her head to one side and raised both eyebrows.

Caleb flinched. Penguins. He had to get her away from mankind, death, and human sacrifice. He needed to get her away from evil spirits and Nephilim as well. Antarctica was the perfect answer - as long as they didn't run into any killer whales. Together, they could handle a polar bear.

Caleb gave up the argument for mortals. Even the Jews seemed to have trouble with loyalty sometimes, and she had not witnessed their strength and obedience in the earlier days. She had never met David, Uzziah, Isaiah, Samuel, or many others. She was born when Elohim had begun to fulfill his prophet's prophecies for their punishment if they continued to practice the feasts and festivals of the pagans.

It was probably Australia that had done Raechev in. The aboriginal mothers ate their first born in order to obtain more children. In droughts, the Kaura tribe ate all new born children for sustenance. And on the Island of Yam, they had been served finely chopped man-meat mixed with crocodile-meat. Luckily, the chief fell ill from it before Raechev and Caleb had eaten - keeping them from unknowingly breaking Elohim's commands. The chief explained that the mixture always made them ill, but the purpose of eating it was to make the 'heart come strong inside.'

Then the Wotjobaluk tribe had a couple who struck their new-born's head against an elder child's shoulder till the new-born was dead. Then they fed the babe's muscle-flesh to that older sibling so that he would become stronger. Caleb had tried to lighten the mood by snapping his teeth towards Raechev's biceps, but she was not amused.

They were informed that human flesh-eating was a sign of respect for the dead, and that at funerals, everyone received a portion of the body fat depending on how close in relation they were to the deceased. But at the same time, they also ate their enemies' hands and feet, growling and angry-faced, to show their contempt for the person.

All in all, Raechev just kept muttering under her breath that she didn't understand. It seemed like they really enjoyed cannibalism and were quick to kill loved ones for other loved ones. She thought it was gross to eat mortals even though many Nephilim saw mortals as nothing but beasts of the field, animals. But the thought of eating another Nephilim? She couldn't even imagine it. Caleb never knew what to say to her. He had difficulty too with mortals eating mortals. He supposed he could do it if he was starving, and they were already dead. But to kill them and then eat them? To eat his own wife? His own healthy child? Or to kill a healthy child in hopes it makes the weaker one stronger? He would have killed his mother if she would have killed Raechev and fed her to him in hopes that his Nephilim strengths would grow. Raechev's happiness affected the very beating of his heart; she gave him a purpose here on earth; and she was the individual who made him smile, love, and laugh. He couldn't think, wouldn't allow himself to think, of the time when Loki would find them. When she would fall into a rapturous love like she craved - an all-consuming love that would shatter the very life from his being.

A small hand caressed his cheek.

"This is not from the storm, Caleb."

Caleb opened his eyes to see his bluish tinted tears. As always, his tears were speckled with small sapphires.

"I love you." She checked to see if the leather straps were still holding firm. "Try not to drown."

He could not stop his vision from blurring as his silent tears increased and watered the face he loved to an unrecognizable blur. She laid down, curled up beside him, and rested her head on his shoulder. Her small hand patted the rhythm of his heart on top of his chest to soothe him. It slowly began working. The tears subsided, and Caleb stared above at the towering storm swells arching menacingly around them. He felt safe.

68 BC, HISPANIA

A tall, stately man stood at the crossroads staring up at a statue of Alexander the Great. His stern, chiseled face was weathered by the sun, yet accented with bright grey, grief-stricken eyes. His shoulders were stiff yet dejected. A red toga draped his form and was covered with a cloak made of bear fur that fastened with a large gold Roman coin.

He stood out amongst his surroundings, the only splash of color in a barren world. Snow drifted from dark grey clouds and covered the frozen mud roads. Drab grey and wood structures lined the streets, hiding any green foliage that would have been able to be seen. And there stood a striking man who seemed the only living entity in existence. His dark brown hair moving in the wind, was the only indication that he was not a statue himself.

Something about the man drew Caleb. Perhaps it was his stateliness, perhaps his grief tinged with despair, but Caleb felt compelled to speak with him. As he approached, the man threw a cautionary glance, scrutinized his impressive attire, then curtly nodded in acceptance before returning to his perusal of the statue. After drawing up alongside the man, Caleb began inspecting the statue of Alexander whose deformed neck forced his face to tilt upwards. It was a lesson to all soldiers who gazed upon him. Even with a physical deformity, a man could conquer the world. No physical or emotional barrier could stop a man who chose to fulfill his destiny. Only a man himself, would be the cause of his own downfall and weakness.

"I am thirty-two. At thirty-two, Alexander had conquered the known world."

Caleb took in the man's rich wardrobe. "You must be of some importance to wear such gold coins."

Displeasure crossed the man's face. "Quaestor of Hispania Ulterior. Under Antistius Vetus."

Caleb knew that in the Roman Republic a quaestor was elected by the soldiers. He was a trusted and respected man who oversaw the treasury and financial affairs of the army, the officers, and all the state of governance. "Alexander commanded an army he was given at birth, with a mission failed by his father, but you were honored with your position by the great respect the soldiers have for you."

The man drew his silver grey eyes from the statue. His assessing gaze was bold and thorough. "What do you call yourself? And from whom do you hail?"

"Caleb. I am a traveler of the world."

"Is that so. I too have traveled extensively but done so in the confines of the Roman army, serving the Republic. Of what kingdom are you?"

"One I am sure, you are unaware of." Caleb smiled.

The man, amused, allowed one side of his chiseled lips to curve up. He nodded.

"And where did a Roman attain such height?" Caleb asked.

The man quirked one eyebrow. "My family claims descent from Lulus, the son of the Trojan prince Aeneas, the son of the goddess Venus. And your height and magnificent eyes?"

Caleb chuckled. "My family claims descent from the goddess Ishtar. Do you believe we are children of gods?"

The man turned back to look at Alexander. "He claimed descent from Zeus, the Roman Jupiter, but then worshiped Mithras at the end of his life." The man's shoulders slightly curved forward. "I believe that my family is tall and marries tall women. I believe we are who we make ourselves to be, but I have not done so well thus far."

Caleb glanced around the crossroads and the seemingly deserted government square. "Is your tall wife here? My sister would love to speak with another female, it's been quite some time since she's had feminine companionship."

"Cornelia passed last year, along with my most beloved aunt Julia. Cornelia was proud when I had been elected military tribune. She always wanted me safe in Roman politics and off the battlefield. She would always say, 'Gaius Julius Caesar get off the battlefield, my love, there you cannot protect your back from your enemies like you can in Roman politics." Julius chuckled. "You should have witnessed her fear when I was sent to end Spartacus' rebellion."

"Spartacus?"

"A gladiator who freed other gladiators to revolt against Rome and their Roman masters."

Caleb returned his attention to Alexander's statue as Julius had done. Without even looking at Julius, Caleb could sense the deep grief and whirling mind of the man. Caleb began circling things Julius had said, trying to understand the complex man who had riveted his attention. "Did you say that Alexander had begun to worship Mithras?"

Julius' face grew even more contemplative. "Yes, it is one thing that has lingered. He was so wise. He knew how to forge men together, to make them so strong as to conquer the world. He understood the power of mixing politics and religion." Julius turned and faced Caleb. "Come."

Caleb followed the long strides of the quaestor out of the town and into the woods. Here some evergreens gave color to the white blanketed landscape. They entered the forest along a well-trod path.

"I have a few things in common with Alexander. My father died when I was sixteen, and I had to give up my betrothal to my first love and marry a patrician's daughter to fulfill the requirements of my family. I was to be the new Flamen Dialis, the high priest of

Jupiter. The previous one had been killed for partaking in my Uncle Marius' civil wars to control the army and the republic. Marrying Cornelia was one of the best decisions I made. She watched politics closely, quite unusual for a female, but she understood me. I should listen to her again and request a discharge so that I may return to Roman politics."

"So you are a high priest of Jupiter."

"But not for long."

Caleb was surprised. Julius Caesar was going to give up the Roman gods just like Alexander gave up the Greek gods? Caleb didn't quite understand why either would do that since it was common for rulers to claim descent from their gods. Religiously, it gave them divine right to do whatever they wanted with their kingdoms. They were worshiped by their citizens. But one thing had already struck him about this somber man. He was a thinker. He was logical. And he had decided there was something to attain.

They entered a long cave that had candles flickering at the end. As they approached, Caleb spotted an eye encased within a triangle with sun rays beaming from around it. He saw images of bulls and a sun. Above the candles, carved into the stone, was an image of the god Mithras with sun ray's shooting out from his head. He was surrounded by images identifying the twelve zodiac constellations. All wore the same sun ray's shooting from their heads.

"Mithras was the Persian god of light. Alexander adopted him as the one true god while in Babylon. He was known for his bull-like strength, his great knowledge, and his bravery in battle. Mithra represents power and goodness and promises a reward after death for those who withstand evil. Death is honorable if fighting to overcome any form of darkness. He is the perfect god for soldiers." Julius turned to face Caleb. "Have you read Plato's *The Republic*?"

Caleb shook his head.

Julius nodded. "You should read it one day, but it is too masterful for me to explain in a cave." He moved to a darkened corner and brought up some wine skins and poured some into two cups. "This will help keep us warm."

"You keep wine here?"

Julius nodded. "We partake of bread and wine in a ceremony on the first day of each week, the day given to worship the sun god."

Caleb accepted the wine and moved about the chamber trying to take in a few more of the etchings. One was of a man slitting the neck of a bull.

Julius walked up behind him. "Mithras is said to have captured and killed the sacred bull. This sacred blood became the spring of everlasting life here on earth."

"I'm concerned on one point though. Doesn't the name Mithras bear a striking resemblance to Melek who was known as being the king of the netherworld?"

Julius laughed. "You think the sun god is the ruler of Hades? Impossible. The sun shines above the earth, not below it."

"The lesser light to rule the night," Caleb murmured.

"You refer to the stars? The stars guide us. Guides the sailors, guides the military's movement to its outposts, lights our way at night. An army would be lost without them. The sun is harsh. Its light finds and illuminates every flaw of man. They are both good and both need to be studied. Both are of the heavens."

"So you will follow Alexander's footsteps and take up Mithraism?"

Julius sat down on the ground, leaned back along the cave wall, and rested his head. "Yes, but I am also intrigued with the Druids. What Alexander hoped to accomplish with Mithraism, the Celts have already done. I will learn from both."

"What is so enchanting of the Celts? Aren't they considered barbarians to the Romans?" Caleb waited.

"Rumors of Gaul spread throughout my outpost. I wish to study them myself. Rome has an empire, luxuries unknown to most cultures, and a stoned city that awes any visitor. What do the Celts have? Trees? Homes made of twigs? Yet they are bound in a way that have proven them unconquerable. They mastered what Plato philosophized. 'If there were only some way of contriving that a state or an army should be made up of lovers and their loves, they would be the very best governors of their own city, abstaining from all dishonor and emulating one another in honor; and it is scarcely an exaggeration to say that when fighting at each other's side, although a mere handful, they would overcome the world.'"

"The Celts kill any man who loves another man and any woman who is unchaste. How does that fit with Plato?" Caleb asked.

"It is their religion that binds them, not pederasty. The Celts are a superstitious people full of magical observances and are easily controlled by their priests, the Druids, who also oversee the social laws as well. Their religious leaders are also the government leaders, they are one and the same. The Celts are awed by the Druids quasi-scientific nature about natural phenomena, knowledge of the heavens, and their use of magic. They keep their power through sacerdotal organization - only the Druids and a privileged class are permitted to know such things. They confined learning, further entrenching a deep level of respect for the intellectual supremacy and religious awe of the Druid priest structure which is the sovereign power over all the Celtic tribes, socially, politically, and religiously."

"What are they priests of?"

"The sun. They are great astronomers. They have some other gods, but centrally worship the sun and its divine power and believe in the immortality of the soul." Julius took a long sip of wine and sat thinking.

Caleb squirmed. He didn't like Julius' probing thoughts. Using acts of supernatural power to awe the masses into compliance? To keep intellectual knowledge to only a small caste to keep the masses humble and submissive? It was about power, control, manipulation - the very definition of witchcraft.

"I heard they have colleges all over Gaul. Very disciplined. The crowds flock to the Druids to witness the powers of the Druidic order. One Roman said that it is not the tribal chiefs who command their people, but Druids, and chiefs are merely servant administrators of the druids' persuasion.

34 AD, JERUSALEM

It had been six hundred and seventy-five years since Caleb had tread the cobblestones of Jerusalem. The city was in chaos. Jews were pitted against Jews. Brothers against sisters. Sons against fathers. All yelling of a Yeshua being the promised Mashiach, the Messiah.

The Levites were dressed appropriately. The activities in the temple seemed to be as Elohim decreed. The people appeared righteous, many wearing scrolls of scripture on their foreheads and hands. Roman soldiers were not allowed to bring idols into the temple or desecrate it in anyway. Overall, the Jews seemed to be in a righteous place with their heavenly Father, but a seething cauldron of hate and condemnation swirled around him ready to erupt. It was such a malevolent spirit that Caleb felt fear wrap his insides. What was wrong?

"There is so much power here."

Caleb turned to Raechev. "Power?"

"Pockets of power. It's as if.... I can't explain it. Every once in a while I feel as if I just walked through a pocket of pure unadulterated power. Righteous power. Terrifying power."

"Does it feel evil?"

Raechev shook her head. "But it terrifies me. Its holy. Too holy. I don't know if my spirit can contend with it. It fills me more than I can handle - the fullness of it makes my spirit burgeon to shatter into a million bits. In my mind, I have a vision of pure, white light surrounding me. It overwhelms me." She turned her face to him. "Don't you feel it?"

Caleb shook his head. "What I feel is heavy, oppressive, and amplified beyond reason."

"Whoever this Yeshua is, he had great righteous power."

And something that provoked evil to a high degree, Caleb mused. A kid slammed into Caleb's back in his frantic race to get closer to the temple. A woman called out to him. "Reuben, where are you going?"

Without stopping, the boy yelled behind him. "The Sanhedrin are questioning a Follower of the Way. They say it is Stephen!"

The woman dropped her basket and ran after the boy. One by one everyone in the street began running towards the temple. Caleb grabbed Raechev's hand and ran with the crowds. Was this a new cult? Another false religion tearing apart Elohim's chosen from his bosom?

When they approached the quickly gathering crowd, Caleb shouldered his way to the front, clinging to Raechev. A young man in his early twenties stood peacefully in the midst of stony faced black-garbed men. The hatred poured off the black sepulchers and rolled into the crowd, igniting a frenzy. And still the man seemed serene. His dark brown eyes held love and an indefinable sparkle that tickled Caleb's spirit. Caleb yearned to get closer to him. There was something unique about the mortal's spirit that he had never encountered. It drew him.

Raechev clasped his hand. "What is it? He's more than mortal, but not one of us."

Twenty men dressed head to toe in flowing black robes created a semi-circle around the man as he continued his speech. None of the men in black stopped him from speaking, and the serene man's calming voice spoke in love.

"This Moshe, whom they rejected, saying, 'Who made you ruler and judge? Is the very one whom Elohim sent as both ruler and deliverer. This man led them out, performing miracles and signs in Egypt, at the Red Sea and in the wilderness for forty years. This is the Moshe who said to the people of Isra'el, 'God will raise up a prophet like me from among your brothers.' This Moshe is the man whom Elohim spoke with personally, whom was given the commands of ADONAI, and whom was given living words to pass on to us.

"But our fathers did not want to obey him. On the contrary, they rejected him and in their hearts turned back to Egypt. That was when they made an idol in the shape of a calf and offered a sacrifice to it and held a celebration in honor of the sun god. So Elohim turned away from them and gave them over to worship the sun, moon, and stars - as has been written in the book of the prophets: 'People of Isra'el, it was not to me that you offered slaughtered animals and sacrifices for forty years in the wilderness! No, you carried the tabernacle of Molekh and the star of your god Reifan. Therefore, I will send you into exile beyond Babylon.'

"You stiff-necked people! Your hearts are still uncircumcised! You continually oppose the *Ruach HaKodesh* (Holy Spirit)! You do the same things your fathers did! Which of the prophets did your fathers not persecute? They killed those who told in advance about the coming of the *Righteous One*, and now you have become his betrayers and murderers! You! Who received the Law - but do not keep it!"

An evil gnashing of teeth began behind the black robed men and soon the black robed men were gnashing their teeth as well. Their fury struck fear in Caleb's heart. He had witnessed a prophet's anger before, but this was different.

"Things are much changed, little brother."

Loki stood beside Raechev. Caleb's fear rose, but his curiosity took control.

"Who are the black robes? Are they prophets?"

"They are the blind who put themselves above the Walking Torah."

"What?" Caleb asked.

"In their zest to bring the Messiah, religious elders have formed and created their own laws in order to make sure no Hebrew broke Elohim's laws, but these laws have become about the law itself and not the reason for the law. They want the Messiah to come and kick the Romans out. They want to rule the world with Messiah. They have become religious, pious, proud, condemning, and full of hatred. They enforce their man-made decrees and burden the people who have become steeped into a religious spirit that glorifies the self. They have made religion itself an idol."

The serene man made eye contact with Loki. A brief moment of acknowledgment passed between them, causing questions to spring into Caleb's mind. "Who are the Followers of the Way, and who are the Sanhedrin?"

"Followers of the Way are those who follow Yeshua who called himself The Way, The Truth, and The Life. He was the living Torah. For the Torah became flesh and lived amongst its people. Some heard and followed, others rejected, preferring the religious spirit and traditions taught to them by their parents and grandparents. The men in black are the Sanhedrin. They are sticklers to all the man-made laws."

"Was? Did you meet this Yeshua?" Raechev asked.

"His flesh no longer walks this earth." For the first time, Loki ripped his gaze away from Stephen to look at Raechev. "And yes."

Raechev opened her mouth to ask another question, but Loki quickly placed his fingers over her lips to hush her and glanced up to the heavens.

"Look!" Stephen exclaimed and pointed in the direction that Loki was looking. His face shone like an angel's. "I see heaven opened and the Son of Man standing at the right hand of Elohim!"

Screeching ripped from the crowds. The masses covered their ears, yelled to drown him out, and charged him. Pushing and pulling, they dragged him out of the city. Loki pulled Raechev into a protective embrace and muscled his way to the front of the mob.

Caleb forced his own way.

Raechev whispered up to Loki, "It is apparent you have feelings for this mortal. Will you not protect him? The crowd yearns for his blood. Do you fear betraying what you are to them? Surely it is a small cost to save your friend." She watched as several people picked up large rocks, so large they needed both hands to hold it above their heads. They threw them at Stephen. The rocks slashed his skin. Stephen did not fight. "Loki! Help him!"

"Nay."

Raechev turned to Loki. "You are not the male I hoped you to be."

Loki turned vacant eyes onto her. "We are nay longer to meddle in mortal affairs. If something is to happen, it will be by the power of Elohim."

"Power?" Raechev whispered.

"Aye. Power, Raechev. The Lamb raised people from the dead. He raised himself from the dead. He would not permit me to defend him from his enemies. It would have been a simple task for me, and ye ken that, but he said that Elohim commanded his death."

Stephen dropped to his knees, still staring up into the heavens. A smile of joy beamed from his lips, and love shone from his eyes. Arms reaching up, his lips moved silently in adulation of whatever he saw.

Loki glared at a short, well-dressed man with beady eyes who protected the cloaks of the stoners. He leaned away from Raechev and spit contemptuously into the dirt.

"Sanhedrin?" Caleb asked.

"Worse. Pharisee. They search for loopholes within ADONAI's laws, then create new man-made laws to help people get out of whatever of Elohim's laws that displeases them. They are a manipulator of laws to serve the people's own desires. That one is called Sha'ul. His spirit is filled with murderous hate. Can you not smell the stench of his pride from here?"

"ADONAI Yeshua! Receive my spirit!" Stephen yelled. "ADONAI! Don't hold this sin against them!"

"Ah, following the same words of the Lamb himself," Loki murmured.

Stephen drifted into a deep sleep and moved no more.

"Do you think he will be raised from the dead?" Raechev asked.

Loki frowned. "I dinnae ken. 'Tis according to the purposes of Elohim. Come, the disciples will want to know."

Caleb's spirit fell. He didn't know much about this Yeshua, whether he was a false Messiah or not, but the mortal's spirit had been changed in a way that made Caleb believe.

Loki weaved in and out of the crowds masterfully, bringing them to a small wooden door that could barely be seen in the poor section of town. Loki pounded on the door.

The door swung open and a strapping man with light brown eyes and dark wavy brown hair gasped. He dropped to his knees, raised his hands to heaven and began exorcising Loki away from him. "Leave, you unclean spirit! You vile demon in the flesh! Spawn of Ha-Satan!"

One elegant eyebrow rose, but Loki's eyes burned with hatred. "Stephen be dead. Stoned. Protect yerself. I wouldnae want the Lamb's prophecy to go unfilled." Loki slammed the door and began muttering under his breath, "What do ye ken of commitment ya walking clay pot? Ye live only a few years. Yer struggle against the flesh is nothing compared to the longevity of which we fight. Ye think that now that ye have been filled with the Ruach HaKodesh, ye are above me?"

Loki was babbling too much nonsense for Caleb to keep up, but what seemed of the most import was the time frame of one of Yeshua's prophecies. "What prophecy?"

Loki growled. "That Peter would be the rock, the foundation, upon which the Messiah, the Son of Man, would build his community, and the gates of Sh'ol would not overcome it. He gave him the keys of the Kingdom of Heaven. That whatever he prohibited on earth would be prohibited in heaven, and whatever he permitted on earth would be permitted in heaven."

Caleb and Raechev both froze. Their jaws dropped wide open. Peter would decide what was prohibited and permitted in heaven? And he thought even the redeemed Nephilim were unclean demons and spawns of Ha-Satan?

80 AD, ROME

It was a city of stone. Stone and blood. Caleb's stomach curled. He walked down the thoroughfare heading towards the towering structure in front of him. Men jostled him, all trying to get inside before the activities began. He could hear men hawking their wares on the edges of the streets, politicians debating as they marched to the Colosseum, and courtesans flirting as they flitted by. The marriageable women were under lock and key at home. This was a man's world. And it was frightening.

Caleb forbade Raechev joining him. Romans took after the Greeks in the way they treated their women. Pure women, seeking marriage and family, were not educated nor allowed out of the house. On rare occasions, they joined their husband, but most men never risked it. Between male predators and their own need for control, the women were safe guarded. Only the courtesans were permitted to walk about with the men. The well-paid prostitutes visited the library, debated with politicians, and rubbed shoulders with men in the public square. And today, they joined the men in the grand opening games of the Colosseum.

Caleb had bypassed Rome and Athens many times. These two cities portrayed themselves as the most educated and intelligent in the world. They philosophized, debated, and rationalized the world and their religions. They said they were a society of the mind, of logic, and of intellect. Caleb had to admit that their cities were nice, but were they really better than Egypt, Babylon, or Assyria? He didn't see beautiful towns on mountain peaks, hanging gardens in a desert, nor a light house that could be seen across the entire Mediterranean Sea. It was stone. A city of stone and death. He didn't see beautiful artwork. He didn't hear elegant music, and he didn't like not being able to walk a city with his sister because every man would assume she was a courtesan.

The golden rays of the sunrise lit the yellow stone facade, and a cool breeze enticingly swept around him. He wondered how long he could enjoy such things. With the stupefying heat and masses he would be enthronged in today, he didn't envisage much leisure. A few Roman soldiers could be spotted moving in small companies as the hordes moved into the oval stone structure - he could only assume the soldiers were there to hold rioting at bay. The bottom level was the tallest, with arches reaching up twenty feet. Then, on top of that, three shorter levels rose one above the other. Smaller arched windows with statues loomed magnificently on the two middle levels which served as hallways. Men stopped to kiss the feet of a colossus statue - a man with sun rays shooting from his head. It appeared that the face of the man had changed, and below was inscribed Nero Invictus.

As Caleb entered, his heart sank. Debauchery was everywhere. He was glad the marriageable women were not allowed to witness such things. Caleb knew that when the women of an empire fell into moral decay, the whole empire was lost. Men seemed to need women to assist them in morality. A man's mind was a scary place sometimes and often disobedient to his own heart and longings. Lustful thoughts, a need for control, and testosterone were damaging even to himself. A woman softened a man, listened to him, and loved him. Although a man's body drove him to shameful desires, his heart was often hurt if his body reigned. Logically, Romans strove to understand the Greek philosophers. They sought to think intellectually and enjoy themselves physically, but leaving the heart and spirit out changed a man to something more akin to an intelligent beast of the field.

Caleb turned his head away from an elderly man paying for the pleasures of a young boy. To Caleb, pederasty was one of the worst things Greek philosophers advocated. Of course, what was happening here was only the physical side of pederasty for these were mere catamites - male youth prostitutes. Caleb didn't like philosophy. It chose man's rational over Elohim's commands and discernment. It placed humans as gods and able to make decisions on and about the gods and their religions. It was a treacherous path they followed.

Caleb picked up an orange and some bread before entering the arena. He had considered the wine but decided against it. He didn't think today was a day to dull his senses. He had finally come to see what the supposed best civilization of the world was. He wanted to witness it in all its glory.

Caleb hadn't come as prepared as others. Most of the fifty thousand spectators sat on pillows, trying to avoid the stiffness that sitting on stone benches would lead to. The arena rose level upon level so that all would be able to see the activities below. Above them some fabric had been pulled along wooden poles to help give shade to those sweltering in the heat. To the left of Caleb was a section reserved for the senate and beside them was a box set aside for the emperor and his closest friends. In front was an oval sand pit with twelve phallus statues pointing to the heavens in an inner oval ring. Phallus statues were common features of sun god worshipers.

Normally, phallus statues were placed at religious circles where orgies were to take place. Caleb began to have doubts on whether he should have attended. It was mostly men with only a hundred or so courtesans and catamites. He quickly got up and chose a seat near an exit asking himself if he truly wanted to witness what was about to happen, but his curiosity kept him there. This was the country that was conquering the world. He should know what they were like. He couldn't imagine Julius Caesar joining in with an orgy, but Caesar had just chosen to follow the sun god Mithras when Caleb had met him. Perhaps, he had changed.....greatly. Then again, things altered over centuries. Mankind had a way of making something beautiful, perverted.

Horns blew, making Caleb jump, and he watched a robust man with a red wig walk to the center of the arena.

"Emperor Caesar Vespasian Augustus had this new amphitheater erected with the spoils of war."

A loud applause swept the colosseum, and Emperor Titus stood and bowed. His father Vespasian had begun the arena in 72 AD but had died before it was finished.

"Jewish hands built this."

Caleb turned to find Loki standing beside him. His face was somber, but hatred burned in his eyes, igniting them to molten fury.

"Raechev is not here, is she?"

"She is just outside the city," Caleb answered. "Why would Jews build such a thing?" Caleb's eyes ran over the phallus statues. The Jews had become overly righteous, they would never have built something pagan.

"No choice. Ten years ago Titus cleaned out the temple and razed it to the ground. The surviving Jews were enslaved and sold in Rome." Loki's eyes roamed the arena. He bent over and spit. "Elohim's temple and chosen people paid for this grotesque mortuary."

"Mortuary?"

Loki's eyes flashed to Caleb's face for only an instant. "You will see. Much death will occur here. Spiritual, physical, and moral." He stared ahead as the red wigged man left the arena. "These, the civilized of the world, have come to conquer the barbarians." He paused for a few moments. "The Celtic chief Vercingetorix surrendered to Julius Caesar. After imprisonment and a parade through Rome, he and his family were sacrificed to Mithras."

Caleb watched in building horror as twelve hundred men from conquered territories were escorted out onto the sand pit. Collectively, the crowd hushed. Caleb could hear lions, tigers, bears, and elephants. His eyes scanned the perimeters, but he saw nothing. Shadows moved from gated archways. The hair on Caleb's arms stood up.

A square of sand dropped - a hidden trapdoor. Several men fell into a black hole and a rhinoceros stormed up, thrashing its horn wildly about. Men fled, then turned to attack. Although weaponless, they had quickly realized that they were being given unto their deaths. With each minute that passed, a new trapdoor opened. It made the men jumpy, not knowing if the ground beneath their feet would suddenly drop beneath them. After twelve trapdoors opened, the archway gates clanged wide to release lions, tigers and bears. Caleb's jaw dropped.

Crowds cheered. Wine spilt. Blood flew. Animals and men fell in death. It took over an hour, maybe two. Caleb lost track of time. The once golden sands had become red, saturated by the blood of Rome's enemies.

"Roman gods have always been placated with blood. During the Second Punic war, hundreds were buried alive under the Forum Boarium."

Caleb motioned to a section of the audience where three hundred Jewish men sat. "How can they watch this?"

Sad eyes lifted to the men, then returned to the field of blood where workers were clearing some of the carnage. "They are to see what their hands have built. What the riches of their temple have been used for. Then, they will be the last to die today."

Caleb was glad Raechev wasn't there, and he was glad that Loki hadn't mentioned their betrothal. Did Loki not care anymore?

He seemed different. Harder. Sterner. Darker. Before in Jerusalem, he seemed distracted. More interested in Yeshua and his disciples than Raechev and their impending marriage.

Caleb contemplated the nurturing benefit of females. Caleb had been protected by Raechev. Although a warrior, her loving side was obvious, but something he didn't bring up because he knew it would irritate her. In a patriarchal world, Raechev could become quite defensive of her warrior abilities. Did Loki need Raechev? It had been thousands of years since Loki had a wife to walk the world with. He had no sister or any other family that Caleb knew of. He leaned back to get a better look at Loki's stone face. Caleb wanted a helpmate, he wanted his own wife, but his heart refused to leave Raechev. She had been denied entrance into the Cities of Refuge for redeemed Nephilim. He would not be able to live in peace, worrying about his sister. Loki trotted the globe, not seeking refuge. Would that work? Could Loki be her protector?

Twenty girls and ten young boys were led out to the sands. Wild animals followed them. Some of the women cried; some were stone faced; some moved sensuously. Each animal-wrangler helped their animal position themselves, so the women and boys could have sex with them. Caleb lurched forward and vomited. He jumped up and tried to shut out the egging on of the male spectators. Caleb grabbed Loki's arm. "Let's go.

Loki shook his head. "I will stay and witness the deaths of the Jews. I will share their grief."

Caleb stared at Loki's icy eyes before turning and leaving. All around him, men were paying for the services of the courtesans and catamites - pleasuring themselves in front of everyone. He retched again. How could the sight of animals rutting with women and boys stimulate anyone? Caleb turned his head as one man bent another man in front of him for penetration. Caleb dropped his food and ran.

Once the crowds had dissipated, Caleb dropped to the ground. Lying crumbled on the dirty street, Caleb breathed in fresh gulps of air. He felt dirty. Stained. Feared he would never be clean again, or be able to forget the sights he had seen. These were the 'civilized' people taking over society? The world narrowed. His vision tunneled. His memory blurred, and tears ran down his cheeks.

The sun's shadows on the wall facing him shifted. Hours were passing, but Caleb could not go home to Raechev. What would he say to her? What could he tell her? He didn't want her to know anything of it, of these Roman pigs. These unclean beasts who called themselves intelligent but stupidly hurt themselves.

"Isis. We call to thee, Isis," a voice intruded into Caleb's thoughts.

Darkness had fallen. The street was still deserted, but candlelight gleamed from a temple in front of him. It was a temple dedicated to Isis. He had known that Rome stole religions, cultures, philosophies and everything they found amusing from more advanced cultures. They altered it a bit then called it their own. He wondered if the ritual inside was a combination of Rome's bloody culture and Isis', or if it had stayed true to its origin.

He snorted. Rome. The land of butcherers and thieves. Their republic had been built on Plato's *The Republic*. They conquered and enslaved every civilization they could find, stealing the best of each culture and molded it to meet the needs of their blood-thirsty, depraved race.

A young Roman mother stood in front of the priestess of Isis. The young mother wore a covering over her head, signifying that she was a married or marriageable woman. She looked about nervously as if she feared being caught outside the house. She quickly laid the baby down on a stone altar on the far side of the room. "Please. Ask Isis if I will gain my husband's love again. Ask her if my lying with a servant will be forgiven."

The priestess looked down at the babe. "Is this the babe of the infidelity?"

The young mother nodded her head. "My husband was away serving in the army. I became lonely."

"What of the servant?" the priestess asked.

"He's been sold to the colosseum. My husband is searching for a replacement now."

The priestess nodded sagely. "You know what our mother thirsts for?"

The young mother nodded.

Caleb sat enraptured.

"She will reveal your future with the sacrifice. This is not a love spell, but a conjuration of our mother's spirit."

"I only ask for the truth... And guidance on how to win my

husband's love back. I had a friend who's love potion went horribly wrong."

The priestess slid out of view and began singing an Egyptian chant that had been put to a Roman tune. She slowly reappeared, holding a sacrificial dagger in her right hand. With her left hand, she caressed the child, then plunged the dagger down with the right. Caleb's vision dropped with her hand, till his head was cradled in his hands, his eyes closed tight.

"Caleb?"

Caleb lifted his eyes and met Loki's. "You searched for me?"

Loki shook his head. "I walk these streets and pray to Elohim. It's my mourning ritual."

"For Rome?"

Loki looked confused. "Nay, fer me friends."

Caleb frowned. "What friends?"

Loki jerked his head towards a long torch. It was unusual for night-torches in the ancient world. A tall metal pole stood attached to the wall. Stretched out from the pole was a metal arm that held a six foot metal casing with something burning in it. The six-foot-burning-substance lit the entire block like a bonfire. Upon closer inspection, Caleb could see the form of a man bathed in tar.

Abruptly standing, Caleb gasped. "Who is that?"

"That is me friend Lucius. He is a Follower of the Way. What the Greeks call 'Christian' now. In Hebrew it would be 'Messianic.' *Christ* is the Greek word for *Messiah*."

Caleb stared. Had he ever witnessed so much hatred in a race before? So much love for death and carnage?

"His wife and daughter are farther down," Loki murmured. "Would ye care to join me? They were loving, Elohim filled people. I would cherish the opportunity to share their tale with ye."

Caleb noticed the respect gleaming from Loki's eyes. "I would greatly enjoy hearing any tales of Elohim's righteous, especially those who survived in a world like this."

Loki stood and drifted off. "There are thirty-three lighting the city tonight."

Caleb followed. "Why?"

Loki paused, his eyes averted. "Because there's nothing new under the sun." He motioned sideways and took off down another street, leading away from the torched Followers of the Way. He walked in silence, bypassing rich marble homes, poor wooden apartments that stunk of disease and death, and then out past the city limits. Crossing over the Tiber on a simple bridge, he walked up to the top of Vatican Hill, in the original Etruscan town of Vaticum. A large phallus statue stood erect in the middle of a large circular bricked path. Behind that, men in long flowing purple and golden robes dodged in and out of a temple.

"Look familiar?"

It took Caleb a long time to place the strange garments with the cone shaped mitres. "Mithraists from Babylon?"

"Mithra, the Protector of the Faithful and Guide to the Souls. Since Alexander the Great adopted the religion, most empire-building warriors have followed suit. Nero wanted to be a member. He also wanted to be worshiped as the sun god Mithras himself, but the pope kept rejecting him until he proved himself."

"Blaming the Followers of the Way for the fire."

"While Nero lived, the pope reigned from Vatican Hill and permitted Nero to be a figure head pope. Nero was permitted to administer the sacraments to his cult brothers on the Lord's Day, Sunday." Loki leaned back against the statue. "Everybody wants to replace the glory of Alexander the Great."

"So he began killing Followers of the Way?"

"Of course. They wouldnae worship him as a god. Did ye see his statue near the entrance to the colosseum? He had on the solar crown as all Mithras deities and saints do."

"Yes, I remember that from Babylon. I also remember the Mithraist, Julius Caesar, taking communion with bread and wine," Caleb said.

"Aye. They use wine and bread with lots of chanting, bells, candles, incense, and divine water fer spiritual healing. They follow specific rules, and Mithras grants them immortal life. Nero, and succeeding emperors, have affixed titles to their name to legitimize their claims of divine right rule - similar to the pharaohs. They use words like *Dias* for devout, *Felix* for blessed, and *Invictus* for invincible. For Mithra is *Sol Invictus* - the Invincible Sun."

"And the Followers of the Way are killed for not worshiping the emperor as the son of a god?"

"Aye. Just like in Babylon," Loki confirmed. "Like I said, nothing new under the sun.

"Nothing new under the sun," Caleb whispered.

80 AD, DANUBE BASIN, ROMAN ARMY

Caleb leaned forward. Two soldiers were whispering about the Mithraic Mystery Cult as they stumbled along in the dark. Caleb kept to the side, interested himself on exactly what was going on in these rituals. He had overheard from the blond soldier that they were having mass at midnight. The brunette soldier was being initiated.

"There are seven ranks: *Corax* (raven), *Nymphus* (bride), *Miles* (soldier), *Leo* (lion), *Perses* (Persian), *Heliodromus* (sun-courier), and *Pater* (father). You will enter as a *Corax* and work your way up to *Leo* like me," the blond explained.

"I heard that Romans were.... free with themselves" the brunette stated.

"I don't know of Rome, but the soldiers would never be so," the blond answered.

Caleb kept behind the black barked trees and registered the difference of the Mithraic cults. It wasn't surprising that the soldiers would be more pious. The Roman army took soldiers from its conquered people, and the Germans and Gauls were known for killing any woman who was unfaithful to her husband before and after the marriage. Even the male tribal soldiers were careful not to sleep with Roman women brought to the forts for their pleasure. They learned quickly what sexually transmitted diseases did to their body, and how it weakened them in battle.

The soldiers came from Brittain to Germania to Gaul and were not known to respect Romans. More and more commanders were from nonRoman stock, and the son of a Spanish tax collector had recently taken the seat of emperor. Rome had a way of poisoning a person, and the soldiers heard tales of debauchery, drunkenness, and laziness. At first Rome was to be feared, but now nonRomans smirked at them. Adult men paying for sex with boys? Citizens who didn't work but lived off the work of others? Men who never soldiered, watching thousands die in arenas for entertainment? The Germans didn't see them as men and didn't see any reason to respect them. Any German soldier would have loved to go hand to hand combat with one of the Roman citizens who lazed away all day gloating off the victories of others.

The soldiers ducked into a craggy cave opening, and Caleb followed. It was almost pitch black inside, but flickering lights could be seen ahead in another chamber of the cave. The moisture in the air made Caleb's robe stick to him, and he tried to make sure his sandals didn't stick in the mud. A bull's moan sounded from the lighted chamber, and Caleb wondered just how much of the Babylonian ways were kept by these men.

The soldiers entered the lit cavern, and Caleb walked up to the cut-away door and peered inside. It was a long vertical tunnel in front of him. Along both sides of the cave walls were reclining couches where many men sat in silence. Most wore long red robes without *mitres*, but Caleb could see that the men near the end wore purple robes with gold chains and tall cone-shaped *mitres* on their heads. Only the religious elders wore the *mitres*.

A pedestal-like altar stood at the far end with an image of Mithras slitting the throat of a bull. It was behind this altar that a completely black bull stood. The purple robed priests were pushing it up the altar so that its neck hung over the steps below where the brunette soldier had been ushered to kneel. The bull bellowed in outrage, and a soldier asked, "Father, do you need assistance?"

The priest jerked his head negatively, then raised his voice. "Welcome, my sons and brothers. We have gathered this eve to initiate a new son into our ranks, a soldier that has welcomed the call of the *Sol Invictus*, the Invincible Sun."

Two priests in gold robes began passing a platter of bread and cups filled with wine. Each soldier took one, and passed the rest down.

The chief priest spoke, "Let us bond together again, my brothers, and remember Mithras' great sacrifice and resurrection. For like him, we will physically die, be placed in the rock, and then triumph over death to live once again. But we must command our own bodies, we must restrain our sensual lusts with our self-control if we are to be like the son of god himself. For Mithras sacrificed himself to redeem mankind, and now has the power to dispense mercy and grant immortality. We prepare for the Day of Judgment and the final battle between the forces of good and evil."

A red-headed soldier, sitting near the end, stood up and walked out. He walked right past Caleb but didn't act like he had seen him. He grabbed a leather strap with glittering shards in it and swung it in front of him to hit himself in the back. He jerked in pain, his eyes widened, he gasped, then tore the strap out of his back and repeated. The man began mumbling to himself over and over again, "Mithras forgive me."

"Do you wish to be reborn into Mithras? To be one of his devout followers?"

The brunette nodded. "I do."

"Do you forsake all other gods but Mithras, his father and Virgin Mother?"

The brunette nodded. "I do."

"Do you vow to fight your beastly nature and never speak of our proceedings and beliefs?"

The brunette nodded. "I do."

"Then so be it." The priest slashed the neck of the bull, raining blood down onto the head of the initiate. "I baptize you in the name of Mithras, his father Ahura Mazda, and the Virgin Mother. You are a new divine creature, and you must never forget who you belong to. Arise, for you are now a Soldier of the Lord."

273 AD, VATICAN HILL

Caleb and Raechev elbowed their way through the crowds. Thousands of people held lit candles and sang songs to Mithras. He was having a flashback to his own mother's festivals celebrating the birth of the sun god. Normally though, it was celebrated at the winter solstice on December 21st, but Emperor Aurelain had legally marked December 25th as the official birthday of Mithras.

The pope stood high above everyone on a balcony looking down at his children. Midnight was dawning and the annual mass would soon begin.

Raechev huffed, trying to lift her hood to be able to see better. She was agitated that no woman was allowed to attend. The Mithraic Mystery Cult stood firm on its decision that women were not allowed to participate. When Caleb had offered for Raechev to check out what the women were doing at the temple dedicated to the Virgin Mother, she had just rolled her eyes and muttered something about male chauvinism.

Caleb edged closer to Raechev to enjoy her warmer body temperature. It was snowing, and yet these religious adherents remained standing in the black of night, freezing their arses to commemorate the birth of their god. He almost didn't get Raechev past the guards. Roman soldiers dressed in red military robes surrounded the perimeter to keep women and nonmembers out. Luckily, Caleb had called a name or two of the men inside the circle, and the soldiers thought they belonged.

"Males are such idiots," Raechev muttered.

Caleb tried not to chuckle. He didn't want to egg her further into her male pessimism.

She grabbed his arm and kept moving about, searching.

"Stop pulling me. We're here."

Her lips moved about as if trying to decide what to say, then spoke quietly, "Do you think Loki's here? He always seems to be in the thick of things."

Caleb's heart sank.

"Today is the birth day of our Grand Deliverer, the Sun-God, and Great Mediatorial Divinity. Birthed from the Queen of Heaven herself, our Virgin Mother, who has given us the greatest gift, The Protector of the Empire, Mithras. Likewise this morn, may we participate in gift giving to our loved ones in memory of the divine gift to mankind."

Another priest brought up a platter of Cakes of Heaven, of course it had the cross imprinted into it, just like the Cakes of Heaven for the Festival of Ishtar. "As a special blessing to you all, I, Mithras' representative in Rome, will present each of you with the sacraments."

Caleb grabbed Raechev's arm and began directing her away from the balcony.

"Where are we going?"

"Away. He'll place it in your mouth and on your tongue. Your lips are too feminine."

They wheedled their way through the soldiers and finally made it back over the bridge to Rome. As they passed homes, they noticed the gold and silver decorated fir trees. Some already had presents laying at their base while others didn't. It wasn't surprising to see the old customs since Rome was notorious for stealing and embracing all the other culture's religions. The only religions they didn't embrace was Judaism and Followers of the Way which taught monotheism and morality. Romans didn't like morality. They loved gladiatorial games, hedonism and things Caleb didn't want entering his mind tonight.... or ever.

"Where do you think Loki will want to live?"

Caleb jerked out of his thoughts. "He seems a bit of a roamer."

She beamed a smile up to her brother. "Like me."

"Not quite like you. He seems to stay with the Levites and Judeans. Actually, come to think of it, he seems to be closely staying with the Followers of the Way."

"Hmm, that could be a problem. I don't much like hanging out with humans."

"Not to mention that he won't like you fighting. He'll want you pregnant soon, I'd guess. He mentioned a child when mother was negotiating the deal of your betrothal and conception. He chose your father on purpose."

Raechev's face became blank. "I suppose he's waited a long time for me. A wife of his own."

Caleb didn't mention that he wouldn't mind a wife of his own, but had a feeling he wouldn't find any redeemed, female Nephilim left alive. "He's had a mistress and three children already."

Raechev faltered in her steps. "He's been with a female?"

Caleb decided not to point out that he had as well. "It was before the flood."

"Did she die in the flood?"

"Before, murdered by a witch," he said cautiously.

"And his children? Are they still alive?"

"I think the daughter, who he searches for."

Raechev turned hopeful eyes to Caleb. "Maybe she's your helpmate."

Caleb's gaze swung quickly to his sister's. His gut twisted. That was something he'd never thought of.

Raechev huffed and moved farther up the street. Anger became palpable on her face. "So I'm not that special? He's had a family before. That's why he doesn't really care isn't it? Maybe he really just wants his wife back."

Caleb shook his head confused. What was going on with Raechev? "What wife?"

"The one killed by a witch, Caleb! The mother of his beloved children! The true love that he lost!"

Caleb's jaw dropped. She was jealous? "He never married her. She was a mistress. You are the only female he's wanted to marry. That makes you special. He has lived over four thousand years and not taken a wife waiting for you!" Caleb clamped his mouth shut. What was he doing? He didn't want Raechev to leave him and marry Loki. Elohim had given Raechev to him, not Loki. Loki already had known a female's real love, and the love of children. Caleb wanted to know what it would be like to be a father. He deserved his chance with a family. Why should Loki get two families and steal Caleb's only one.

Raechev's bottom lip quivered. "But he doesn't want me. Why else would he wait so long to find and marry me?"

Caleb's heart twisted. "He promised me a hundred years with you. He wanted you while you were still a babe to raise himself. Then he wanted you when you first met him in Jerusalem, but he promised me that he'd wait till you were a hundred before taking you as a wife."

"But where is he? I am over a hundred, Caleb."

"Raechev..."

"Don't. We have seen him different times. He's always too engrossed with the Jews or Yeshua or these fledgling Messianics. These mortals interest him more than I do. He chooses them over me time and time again."

Caleb didn't know what to say. It was true, and her pride was stung. He whispered, "You are his betrothed."

"And either of us could lose our mortal flesh any day. He plays games with my heart."

"But you don't really know him. How could you love him?" Caleb asked.

"I, I don't love him. It's just that I think about him as my husband, the father of my children. I see happy families, and I wonder what it would be like. He's my betrothed. So I think of him in that role." She sniffed.

"You've idealized him into the man you think he is, not knowing whether or not he will be that man. That's a very dangerous thing to do, Raechev. No one can live up to romantic idealizations."

"But..."

"Raechev, it's one thing if you knew him really well, but something else to concoct his personality, wit, intentions..."

"Intentions? I thought we were betrothed! But then I guess his actions say that he doesn't really care, don't they? Well, I don't care either. It's just, it's just a romantic season." She turned on her heel and marched off.

Caleb's eyes widened when Loki showed up beside her. He slowly wrapped an arm around her waist and planted a hand on her hip. She grabbed his hand, twisted in the opposite direction, and threw him over her shoulder. He hit the opposing wall and fell to the ground. After staring at her in shock for a few moments, he burst out laughing.

When she heard his laughter, she stopped and looked back at her assailant. "Loki?"

"Love."

She ran towards him and knelt down to see if she had wounded him.

His eyes were mischievous. "Are ye trying to excite me lass? Cause I must say I'm feeling very much alive." He lowered his eyelids. "Now that I've received your sweet and gentle ministrations."

She glared at him. "I can be sweet and gentle, but apparently I don't know my betrothed's touch from a stranger's, and whose fault is that?"

"Do ye want to ken me touch better, lass?" Loki reached out and caressed her face. She kept her eyes cast down. "Are ye ready for me touch?"

"In the middle of the street?" Caleb complained, reminding them of his presence.

Raechev rose quickly and moved away. Doubt flickered in her eyes.

"Beloved, are ye ready fer me?"

She didn't respond but began pacing back and forth between Loki and Caleb.

"We dinnae need any witnesses. Just Elohim. All ye have to do is come with me tonight. I can fly us somewhere beautiful."

Raechev paused. "You can fly?"

"Raechev," Caleb spoke her name solemnly. Was this it? Was he about to lose his sister forever?

Raechev turned and inspected Caleb then turned back to Loki. "And if I'm not ready?"

"Then, we'll wait," Loki answered.

Raechev's lips firmed into a straight line and her nostrils flared. She walked up to him and yelled, "Like you even care!" Then she slapped him hard before turning on her heel, scurrying off.

Loki continued leaning against the wall, holding his face. "She likes it rough?" He looked a bit dazed and confused, then glanced over to Caleb. "She is aware of the betrothal and doesn't fight to get out of it?"

Caleb nodded. He wasn't going to help Loki. He'd had a mistress; he should understand women more than that. Raechev wanted to be chased. She wanted to be pursued by him. She wanted him to fight for her. She was a warrior, and she wanted to feel important, loved, and cherished. He wasn't wooing her - at least on a consistent basis.

Raechev popped in from the alleyway. "Trickster."

"Trickster? Yer mother, brother, and I made a legal contract fer our betrothal. There has been no trickery." He threw a look at Caleb. "On my part."

"Oh, a legal contract. How foolish of me. What female wouldn't want such an impersonal bid for her love?"

Loki's eyebrow quirked up.

Raechev's face blazed red. "I mean, no one really knows whose side you're on. How can anyone trust you?"

Loki stood up slowly and swaggered towards her. "Such an impersonal bid? Sounds like someone wants to be romanced." His grin covered his whole face. "A little kissing under the stars, a little poetry at a waterfall, a lot of snuggling in the Alps."

"Stop. Don't come any closer, Loki."

Loki continued, a sparkle lighting his eyes brightly.

Raechev began backing away. "I'm serious!"

"So am I."

Raechev's eyes widened. She turned and sped away. Loki chased her out of sight.

Caleb remained where he stood, listening to their laughter echo off the buildings that enclosed him - the buildings that became walls of separation.

312 AD, TRIER, GERMANY

Loki lounged back into a luxurious red velvet couch and checked out his surroundings. He had been quite impressed with the capital of Rome north of the Alps. Trier sat on the beautiful wine covered hills of the Moselle River, a safe distance from the Rhine. It boasted the largest bathing complex in the empire, able to serve thousands. Trier had a pleasing arena for gladiatorial games for those who were interested; however, Loki was not, but the arena was small yet safe, making the fighting much more personal than in Rome.

He much preferred Germania to that of Italy. The grass was green, the breeze cool, the wilderness soothing to his soul. The black gate was impressive and kept out any and all undesirables. It led into a beautiful dark grey stone town nestled in the mysteriously romantic black forests of Germania. Currently, he sat in Constantine's throne room which was always prepared for his officers and legionnaires to dine and relax. Trier had even been nicknamed the City of Constantine due to all of Constantine's constructions while his father Flavius Constantius sat upon the imperial throne.

Constantine's palace was a massive brick structure completely covered in marble, except for the ceiling which was an intricate pattern of black wood beams. The structure was shaped as a long rectangle and had two levels of windows on each ninety foot wall. The windows were above the height of men to keep everyone safe in case there was an attack. At one end was an apse, where Constantine and his mother sat. The apse was elevated so that those residing there would be able to see all below. The room, as a whole, gave an overwhelming sense of spaciousness and freedom, yet of being watched.

Many changes had occurred in the Roman Empire. The emperors were no longer Roman, and the Roman army was mostly made up of conquered tribes. Foreigners who rose within the ranks of the military guided the empire. Diocletian solidified Mithraism firmly as the army's religion and officially proclaimed Mithra, *Sol Invictus*, as "Protector of the Empire." He hunted down every Messianic he could find to kill in the arenas. His hatred for the Followers of the Way was ferocious. Diocletian, a Bosnian, searched for some symbol of unity to unite the empire, and although Mithraism united the soldiers, women and male civilians were often excluded. Mithra was seen as the god of the army, and each emperor took his throne by the all-powerful, unconquerable sun, *Sol Invictus*.

Flavius Constantius, a Serbian and Constantine's father, took the throne next and ruled from Trier. Constantine's mother, Helena, had been collected by his father as a concubine while fighting in Asia Minor. She was a low born commoner who had been called a stable maid by many. She was a devoted worshiper of Ishtar, the Queen of Heaven and Virgin Mother, and never balked at being excluded from Mithraism. Although never legally married, many nobles saw a problem with Flavius Constantius' common-law marriage, so he divorced her and married a suitable woman to rule the empire with. Constantine stayed loyal to his mother Helena, bringing her to each new post the army sent him.

Helena sat meekly on a purple reclining couch along the wall behind her son. She rubbed the icon of her goddess gently. Her lips moved in a prayerful way, making Loki wonder as to what she was asking of the goddess Ishtar. She seemed a sweet, gentle woman, and Loki had never heard of her being unfaithful to her husband, but he didn't know what she had been like before she was married. Worshipers of Ishtar weren't known for keeping their virginity.

It was obvious that Constantine had a great respect for his mother and took after her in his religious devotions. He was known to be an avid worshiper of Mithra. He believed in the celibacy of Mithraic priests and chose a moral path, warning his soldiers away from debauchery and drunkenness. Loki mused that his time spent amongst the tribesmen of Germania, and away from promiscuous Rome, had left an indelible imprint on his character. He sought out Druids to speak with and respected self-discipline.

A soldier walked up to Loki and halted. "Caesar would like to speak with you."

Loki looked over to the mesmerizing and intelligent black eyes of Constantine. They sparkled in intensity, making his darkly tanned face seem pale in comparison. Loki stood and followed the soldier up to the throne. Constantine was an august and virile man, his mind as scary as his finely tuned body for war. Even sitting, Loki could see his grand height and confident composure. This emperor was a man to watch.

Constantine brushed his black wavy bangs out of his eyesight and motioned for a red reclining couch to be brought for Loki. Loki sat and waited while servants piled grapes, bread, and wine onto a standing platter for him to eat.

"I hear that you speak with many Christians. Are you a Christian yourself?" Constantine's voice was deep and commanding. He spoke with a calculating air that made everyone pause before answering, knowing that he would weigh every syllable uttered and note any facial reaction to help him discern the truth of what the man spoke.

"I am very aware of them, me lord. They intrigue me, and I study them," Loki answered.

Constantine's face didn't alter. "When I served under Aurelian as his bodyguard I came across a few myself. Intriguing people."

Loki didn't know what to say. Although Constantine had stopped the persecution of Messianics in his provinces, he had been the right hand of Diocletian for many years.

"Before the Great Persecution, I was able to speak often with one of their philosophers. Their monotheistic belief appealed to me. It's simplicity, it's wholesomeness, it's strong commands to live morally." Constantine popped a grape into his mouth. "Rome used to be feared. Known for its hard working citizens, its self-discipline, and it's military might. Now, the conquered rule the conqueror. Romans don't work, they receive free food and bloody entertainment while waiting for their sexually disease infested bodies to die. Who respects them?"

Loki chose not to speak. He definitely no longer respected Romans. After Pax Romana, there wasn't anything left to respect.

"They have become a burden to the world. The world pays for their welfare. They are a mockery of a great empire, and I will no longer pay for their gross laziness." Constantine sipped from his wine goblet. "Your thoughts?"

"I prefer Messianic Jewish morality, me lord. It makes strong, productive citizens."

Constantine nodded. "As Mithraism makes strong, disciplined soldiers. The tainting of pederasty in the Roman branch I could do without though. But how does that affect the women?"

Constantine shot a backwards glance at his mother. "I attended various lectures of Lactantius, a known Christian scholar of Latin, and grew to respect him greatly. At that time Diocletian was forcing me to stay at court with him." His eyes lowered sadly. "And then there was the great oracle of Apollo, the Roman sun god, the Persian form of Mithras. Diocletian, a strong adherent of Mithraism, sent a messenger to the oracle of Apollo to inquire of the Christians. You know what the oracle was? Universal persecution of Christians. The court approved, and the Great Persecution began. Churches and scriptures were burned, treasures seized, leaders imprisoned, and all Christians ousted from government rankings. Not to mention the arenas. Mithras, the sun god, wanted every Christian destroyed or killed."

"Are you not an avid follower of Mithras as well?" Loki asked confused, but noted how Constantine kept using the Greek term.

"I am Sol Invictus... But these Christians, you should have seen them die in the arenas. They had so much peace, so much bravery. How they faced their death... They were soldiers in their own right. It made me think, yearn, that my legionnaires could have such peace when they faced death. Women and men. Weak civilians. Their spirits were of Sparta in obedience to their god." A cunning glean shone from Constantine's eye. "Can you imagine trained soldiers with that kind of spiritual valor?"

"But Yeshua, their christ, instructed them to love their enemies, not kill them."

Constantine shrugged his shoulders. "But if their Peter said it was okay, it would be okay. They would believe and follow blindly."

"Excuse me?"

"Peter, Yeshua's disciple, whom he gave the keys to the kingdom of heaven. Peter became christ's representative on earth. Yeshua said that whatever Peter permitted and prohibited on earth would be permitted and prohibited in heaven; therefore, if the christ's representative on earth said the Christians should war, then they would overlook their christ's teaching."

A strong pit of unease began rolling in Loki's stomach. Yes, Constantine was wise, more wise than what Loki liked mortals to be. This form of philosophy would not work with Jews who forbade taking a small piece of scripture out of its context - taking one sentence and annihilating all the rest of the scriptures' teachings, but Graeco-Roman philosophers thrived on debate like this. There was already strife amongst Messianic Gentiles on this issue - those who saw the Scriptures as a whole, and those who took a few sentences of Paul's writings to live as hedonistically as the Romans. Loki's fears rose as he thought of how weak humans were, but he couldn't be unfair. There were some amazingly strong humans, and he hoped that enough would stay obedient to all of the Lamb's teachings, or they would become nothing different than any other religion.

Loki considered explaining the truth of what the Lamb had meant in his comment to Peter. The Lamb had asked his disciples who they thought he was. Peter had said the 'Messiah, the son of the living God.' The Lamb's response was that no one on Earth had revealed that to Peter, but Elohim himself. It was by revelation of YHVH. The Lamb was referencing revelation by YHVH as being the rock/foundation of his sons of God community, as the Keys to the Kingdom of Heaven on Earth, and with the maturity of the sons of God in the Last Day would bring full restoration from the effects of the curse, and those who matured to be sons of God would be returned to full dominion over the Earth and its heaven as YHVH had made Adam to do. For man would even judge angels, but not until his maturity into a son of God.

Constantine's eyes shifted to a messenger and noble to the right, whispering amongst themselves. "They mock me, call me a son of a harlot."

Loki pulled back his memories of following the Lamb, then paused just long enough to wonder at Helena's worship of Ishtar before she became Flavius' mistress. He shrugged it off because it wasn't really important. Constantine was worried. The rebellious uprisings and enforced political suicides had shifted the public's opinion of Constantine's right to rule. He had lost his source of legitimacy to rule the empire, and he needed a new one. Just two years ago, orators had been sent out to proclaim that Constantine was the rightful ruler by an ancestral connection to a third century emperor and could not be removed by someone without ancestral ties. It wasn't enough. Rome was more religious than that.

The empire had been ruled by a religious ideology of a Tetrarchy with twin dynasties, one to rule the east, and the other to rule the west. Caesar Augustus was over the twin caesars, patterned after

Jupiter and Hercules. The idea of having only one caesar rubbed the populace the wrong way, so Constantine had sent out orators throughout the empire to declare that he had been granted a divine vision by Apollo, the Roman sun god. He appealed to the Roman commoners by choosing Apollo, the counterpart of Mithras' image of being the sun god, especially since Mithras was for the select few, being a mystery cult of the army. As the poet Virgil had foretold, an emperor had been anointed victory, sole rulership, long health, and the "rule of the whole world." Constantine quickly changed the coinage of the western empire to depict himself as Augustus Caesar. He included Apollo's divine sun rays shooting from his head, to show the sun god's favor. The masses applauded.

In reaction, Constantine's main opposition, who still ruled Italy, made a move to embrace the love of the masses by officially decreeing religious toleration, even supporting the Christian community in electing a new Bishop of Rome, Eusebius. But this was not enough, and Rome was constantly filling with military in preparation for war with Constantine.

Loki glanced at the scrolls Constantine had been reading. They were Julius Caesar's comments on the Celts, the Druids, and their powerful priests. Priests who ruled all things secular. They had kept knowledge to only a select few, which forced the less educated to simply follow the dictates of the educated ones. In Julius' commentary, this form of exclusive religion, with the masses seeing the priests over tribal chiefs, was the strongest form of citizenry he had witnessed. The combination of the priests having a connection to the gods and being more educated than all others, grew a reverential, obedient fear from both chiefs and tribesmen.

Constantine stood abruptly, a hush fell over the crowds. "It is time to go to Rome."

Several advisors and generals stood to talk, all wanting to caution him against beginning another civil war. Maxentius had already lost his lands in Africa, and the populaces were turning against him. They believed that it was only a matter of time before Rome would fall to Constantine's rulership.

Constantine rose his arm, and all talking ceased. "We will leave in the morn. Make preparations."

Constantine and Helena's soothsayers stood up quickly, pleading against such an action. They warned that in their sacrifices, unfavorable omens were found in marching against Rome.

Constantine raised his arm once again, and they quieted. He glanced over to the leader of their Mithraic cult long enough for all soldiers to understand his meaning. "I'm being guided by the sun god himself in this. I will not allow weaker gods to tell me what to do. I am a Soldier of the Lord and remember who I serve. He has promised victory."

Loki watched as all soldiers bowed their heads in submission, then quickly left to prepare for the army's departure.

Loki followed the army, wondering what would happen when they got to Rome. Only the first few cities put up a fight. Eventually, Maxentius called his army back to Rome and prepared for a siege. Italy welcomed Constantine with open arms. Turin was a turning point in Loki's eyes. Constantine seemed to change there, he became brooding, darker, and malevolent. Loki couldn't wait to leave, Turin was one of the most occultic towns in the world, and the dark spiritual forces at work there taxed Loki greatly.

The masses flowing in and out of Rome began taunting Maxentius that Constantine truly was Sol Invictus, and appointed by the divine sun god as his orators had claimed. By the time they reached Rome, all the bridges had been destroyed. Constantine set up camp. He had left Trier with only a quarter of his troops, less than half of what resided in Rome.

It was high noon, and Loki stood amongst the soldiers waiting for Constantine's orders. Surprisingly, Maxentius had led his army out of Rome for a battlefield confrontation. It was rumored that he had received a prophecy from his soothsayers that Rome's enemies would die that very day. Both sides claimed victory from the gods.

Forty thousand soldiers stood waiting for Constantine. Their blood red robes matched Constantine's tent, but not Constantine himself. The young emperor walked out in full battle armor and a purple tunic representing his imperial status. Two simply clad men in brown tunics followed him out and stood behind him. Loki pulled out to the side where he could be seen and etched an image of a fish in the ground. Both men standing behind Constantine noticed and drew an image of the fish as well. Loki's eyebrows rose. These were Followers of the Way? The emblem of the fish was the symbol of Messianics and it was how they secretly let others know who they were.

Constantine rose his head and spoke loud and clear to his soldiers. "Last night I had a dream. A shining angel, a divine messenger, told me to mark your shields with the sign of god."

The soldiers stilled. Which god was he referring to? Their god? Mithras, the god of the army? The god they swore obedience to?

Loki wandered what the mark would be. A fish? A solar deity representing Mithras? It just didn't seem right to him. The Lamb was a man of peace and love not war. He didn't even try to defend himself when he was crucified, yet healed the soldier who was escorting him to his enemies.

Constantine pointed up to the sun. "Look! I see the mark yet again, and above it, the words 'Conquer by This'." All the soldiers looked up at the sun and quickly looked back down again in pain. They blinked uncontrollably.

One of the men standing behind Constantine yelled, "I am Eusebius, Bishop of Rome, it is a vision from god! Constantine tell us what you see!"

Constantine remained staring at the sun, unblinking. "It is a solar halo around an X."

Eusebius yelled, "It is the mark of christ!"

Loki staggered back. That was not the mark of the Jewish christ (messiah). Followers of the Way used fishes. An X inside a sun was an ancient occult symbol representing the Black Sun - the true enemy of Elohim. It represented Mithra, the son in the occult trinity. It was used by the Druids, the ancient Egyptians, Amerindians, Wiccans.... Loki's eyes grew even wider and his chest compressed. Constantine was out to conquer the world. Eusebius had either turned or syncretized religions in pursuit of political advancement. Eusebius yelled again, "It is a twisted cross!"

Rolls of hatred poured out of Loki. The swastika. Only the enemy of Yeshua would use the image of a cross as an image of victory. The Lamb's death was seen as a victory by witches not Followers of the way. Resurrection was seen as the symbol of victory. Witches still celebrated the death of Yeshua.

Loki growled. Twisted cross indeed.

Constantine spoke calmly to his soldiers, "Go and draw the image on your shields, but make the X out of swords, for you are in the Army of the Lord. When we are victorious, we will partake of mass on the venerable day of the sun, for worship."

321 AD, ROME

Loki descended the dark staircase, carrying a torch. On either side of him stacks of skulls and bones had been plastered to the walls. These were where the poorer residents remained. His eye caught a small fish etched into one of the empty plaster areas facing the left hallway. Loki turned left as directed and continued further into the catacombs.

The heat from his flaming torch intensified the coldness of the dank air moving within the underground tunnels, causing his hairs to rise. It was a creepy place to meet, but Loki couldn't fight the Follower of the Way's reasons. He ducked his head and passed an elevated slab with a corpse that had barely begun to deteriorate. The stench was appalling and reminded him of pigs being slaughtered. Skulls and bones had been used to construct an arch and pillow for the recently deceased. He wondered if the man was special or if this was the place where all bodies were laid until the bones were able to be taken apart and plastered to other walls.

A low chant-like song could be heard ahead of him and his torch flickered, momentarily bathing him in darkness. The mysterious skulls, representing lives ended, glowed a dark orangish-red as the light from his torch shone brighter, but the movement of the flames soon cast them in shadows reminiscent of the flames of hell itself. He breathed deeply and continued on, refusing to allow the spooky environment from deterring him. It was shabbat, and he yearned for fellowship with other Torah observers. For his own spiritual health, he needed to see others who held firm for Elohim.

The same year Constantine took Rome, he proclaimed that he was a follower of the one true god. Convenient how he used a general term and did not specify which god. In the next year, he had created the Edict of Milan which gave toleration and equality for all cults and religions; however, anyone who observed the seventh day as holy instead of the first day, the 'venerable day of the sun for worship,' was actively persecuted and forced to go underground. It was a direct attack against Messianic Jews who had continued worshiping Elohim on the seventh day as Elohim had commanded.

Loki's shoulder brushed up against some skulls, so he bunched them up to keep from getting burned from the torch or brushing against the dead. The passageways were about eight feet tall and three feet wide with corpses of varying degrees of decomposition. Most were lined up like long shelves which occasionally had an arm dangling down. He stopped at another staircase realizing that this was the fourth level he was entering. As he descended, he did the math in his head and quickly realized that there was about sixty-five feet of corpses lying between him and the surface. He shivered. The lower he went, the more it felt like the burial niches in the walls were enclosing in on him, suffocating him with the most recent decompositions. The corpses were crammed into a sixteen inch to five foot rectangular hole and tightly bound in linen. Some had slabs covering them with their name, age, and day of death while others had artistic frescoes painted on or above their setting.

Loki could now hear distinct voices up ahead. From what he could see, they had settled into a twenty foot side chamber separated for a noble family. A small fire burnt on the stone floor bathing the room in a flickering orange light.

"Here, I have a copy of the new decree. It reads, 'On the venerable day of the sun let the magistrates, and the people residing in cities rest, let all workshops be closed. In the country, however, persons engaged in agriculture may freely and lawfully continue their pursuits.'"

Whispers circulated and heads shook.

A woman in blue spoke up, "Eusebius has said that since the christ was resurrected on the first day of the week then we should commemorate the first day."

A legionnaire disagreed, "God blessed the seventh day. He established the seventh as the day for humans to receive physical and spiritual redemption and rejuvenation. Yeshua was physically dead for three days fighting for our spiritual redemption. When He was done, his physical body was resurrected. He fought OVER the seventh day, the blessed day for healing. Yeshua didn't bless a new day. All the disciples continued observance of the seventh day. We should stand firm on what YHVH has commanded."

Loki agreed with the legionnaire. Yeshua was sacrificed as the Lamb right before Passover and because so many Jewish festivals coincided at this unique time, shabbat lasted for three whole days, the same three days Yeshua rested in the ground and spiritually redeemed the mortals.

The woman in blue spoke again, "But Yeshua healed people on shabbat, so would it be so bad for us to work on shabbat and then worship him on the first day? How long can we fight Rome? All we have to do is align with the other religions, and we won't be persecuted."

A soldier stood up. "Align with other religions? Do you hear yourself? Mix our religion with paganism to keep from being persecuted? Yeshua healed on shabbat, it was a sabbatical act and obedient to the Law. The Levites worked twice as hard on shabbat for the spiritual redemption of the Israelites. Yeshua healed and redeemed people physically and spiritually on shabbat, he was in full alignment with Torah. If he didn't, if he was so pious and selfish to obey the man-made laws and leave people hurting and unrestored on shabbat, then he would be breaking the Law as the religious elders were doing. Don't you see? Look at what Constantine is doing."

The legionnaire rested his hand on the younger soldier to quiet him. "Eusebius has become political and reasons against the scriptures for his own purposes." He shot the woman in blue a look. "He has aligned with the Mithraists, which we as soldiers are very familiar with. Constantine has always been an avid follower of Mithras and seems to be combining the two religions. He uses Yeshua's words of Peter holding the keys of the kingdom to change Yeshua's teaching and the observance of Torah. He excommunicates anyone who defies his decisions and claims Yeshua appointed him as divine ruler. He has told his soldiers that Yeshua is just another form of Mithra, and that they are really the same god but with a different name, similar to Apollo and Mithra."

Loki moved into the room and settled down beside an ornately carved corinthian pillar. Few nodded to him, others were too engrossed in the conversation.

The legionnaire continued, "Eusebius has now decreed that Yeshua was born on Mithras' birthday, December 25th, and resurrected on the Festival of Ishtar. He continues to align all polytheistic religions into one claiming it's monotheism. I have traveled the empire, and I can tell you that these holidays are pagan.

Eusebius has even adopted the forty days of lent leading up to the spring equinox that the followers of Tammuz do that Jeremiah condemned."

Loki murmured, "Elohim gave the feasts and festivals that he wants his children to commemorate. And in the way he wants it. The obedient are his children. They are not to be grafted out for obedience. Anyone can be grafted in if they turn from other religions and follow how Elohim desires to be followed. Stand firm, or yer lampstand will be removed." Loki looked at the woman in blue. "Ye should re-read John the Beloved's revelation... the warning to the believers."

563 AD, INVERNESS, SCOTLAND

The tree speckled landscape in its various shades of deep green was breathtaking against the royal blue loch at the mountain's base. Caleb inhaled the moist imbued air, cleansing himself internally. He forgot the wet wool agitating his skin, his sore feet from walking, and Raechev's near death experience the night before. She had been fighting a much stronger Nephilim than she had anticipated. One that could fly, something she didn't have much experience with. To the praise of Elohim, Loki had appeared out of nowhere and took out Raechev's prey. Of course that didn't make Raechev happy, and she now refused to speak with him, so here he was alone, to meet with Loki.

Caleb had a nagging suspicion that Loki watched over his betrothed much more now than he did before. Loki had been watching the Jews, but they'd been flung far and wide throughout the empire. Perhaps keeping up on them had become too daunting, but Raechev only saw herself coming in second place for Loki's devotion which chafed at her female pride.

Clouds began dissipating on the mount, and Loki's burnished copper ringlets could be seen blowing in the breeze. He stood in traditional Celtic garb. His gold torcs and arm bands secured his ancient position, and his tattoos spoke of his past, but the bracelet with the ten commandments inscribed upon them told a different tale. Caleb could feel Loki's burning stare and wondered who was going to whom.

"Where's Raechev?"

"She didn't appreciate you taking over her fight and doesn't want to see you."

"She was losing. Her life was in danger hence my future was in danger. There is no shame in a female allowing her male to protect her. If I wasn't a better warrior, how would she respect me? How would I be her protector and provider? Elohim didn't make the male to be the female's helpmate, and no self-respecting male would watch his female die while he stood by and watched."

"Do you no longer wish to speak?"

Caleb turned to the left and headed towards the grey fortress along the loch. The massive structure didn't have many windows, just a few small slits for archers to shoot from. A small town was enclosed within the castle's protective outer walls, and Caleb wondered if his kilt would be seen as friend or foe. As he walked up to the wooden doors, Loki appeared beside him, startling him.

Caleb wanted to know if Loki had been following Raechev. "Why are you in Scotland?"

"I'm often in Scotland."

Caleb shot him a curious glance. "I thought you followed the Judeans."

"I have many interests."

"Like the tales of wolf men who roam the hills at night?"

Loki turned an empty stare onto Caleb yet continued walking ahead. "King Brude's Druid is ill. Come. Columba has sent him something to heal him."

Caleb's brow furrowed. Constantine's Roman Catholic Church had spread far and wide throughout the empire. The term catholic had always made him raise his eyebrows for the word itself meant 'according to the whole/general/universal' and many of its sacraments and theologies were a blending of all pagan beliefs, feasts, and celebrations. While he and Raechev were in Ireland, they had discovered that the Druid schools had been converted to monasteries and theological institutions. It left a very unsettled feeling in the pit of Caleb's stomach when he remembered his talk with Julius Caesar.

When they had visited Clonard Abbey, situated on the River Boyne, Caleb was surprised that all learning was in Latin and excluded the masses from knowing exactly what the scriptures actually said. The nontheologians had no choice but to blindly believe whatever they were told by their priests, they had no check system, and it presented a very controlled environment. Anyone who asked too many questions was excommunicated and barred from heaven to suffer the fires of hell. Three thousand souls studied at the Clonard monastery, and twelve of them became known as the Twelve Apostles of Ireland. Columba was one of these. He was a monk and later ordained a priest.

"Columba? The same Columba said to be a descendant of the Irish high kings?"

"And now a Gaelic missionary monk, dubbed the Dove of the Church," Loki continued.

"Dove of the Church. Couldn't be the same monk. Just a few years ago, Columba had a fight with his teacher over a psalter that led to the Battle of Cul Dreimhne where many men died. How could someone like that be called the Dove of the Church? It must be someone else."

"He exiled himself to Scotland, vowing to make a new convert for each man killed in the battle."

"But I thought the Catholics didn't fight their attackers because the messiah said to love your enemy?"

Loki paused, turning to meet Caleb's gaze. His ethereally glowing skin was heightened by the dew drops glistening on his bare chest. "Do not confuse the word catholic with Followers of The Way. Catholic means according to the whole, the general, the universal. Do not confuse that term with Christian or with the Lamb's church for Catholics do not obey the Jewish Messiah at all, but their pope who blends all religions into one. That is why it is the universal church or the general church. It combines the universal pagan beliefs with monotheism. It leads Followers of the Way away from Torah and Elohim's commands."

Caleb wished he had followed Yeshua while he was alive. He didn't know whether or not Yeshua was who Loki seemed to believe he was, but Loki's devotion to Yeshua raised many questions in Caleb's mind. Who was this Yeshua? Caleb greatly respected Loki. He was the most intelligent entity Caleb had ever met, and yet he was careful to obey Elohim. He wondered if Loki would ever sit down and tell him of all what Yeshua said or did, but Loki always seemed burdened with one thing or another, so he left him alone.

Loki turned and headed into the small town. He passed several grey stone buildings before turning onto a path that led back out of the town and into a copse of trees. Gaelic chanting could be heard, raising the hairs on Caleb's neck. Where was Loki taking him?

In the center of the trees was a small megalith circle with several brown robed figures. Hoods hung over their faces, hiding their eyes and identity, but Caleb knew that he had entered a Druid ring. In the center lay a sickened man, his eyes bulged from his emaciated form. Outside the ring stood four warriors painted blue and dressed in leather straps and kilts. Every man had tattoos covering their body, signifying their ownership by Odin.

At the head of the sickened man, was a man who wore a white robe and stood a regal warrior. By his bearing, Caleb assumed that this was the king.

"Christ is my Druid."

Loki's head tilted to the side wondering why the king would say such a thing.

Caleb marveled at the men in front of him. These had stood firm against the Roman Empire. They had not been forced into the Catholic church by Rome's conquest.

"Their Saint Patrick had much magick in him. He even controlled the snakes. Perhaps, so does Columba," the king spoke to all. "Columba says that christ is his Druid. He has magical relics that show his power. He wrote that this is one of them. Lift Druid Broichan up. He must drink the water I pour over this white stone."

Something felt unnatural, and Caleb's peace fled. He had seen and heard of magical relics before, but mostly they had been created by sorcerers and seers who spoke to fallen angels who gave them occult knowledge. He watched as the priest was raised and forced to drink the water. Nothing happened. The king stood for a few minutes waiting, then shook his head and beckoned his warriors to follow him back to town.

Loki motioned for Caleb to follow as well. Caleb had no desire to return to the town; the whole place was filled with a darkness that unnerved him. He and Loki ate a late supper and spoke of Raechev throughout the night. Periodically, Loki would wander away when wolves howled at the moon, only to return and resume the conversation as if he had never left. It baffled Caleb. Loki slowly turned the conversation to what was occurring in Scotland.

"These 'Celtic Saints' send magical relics to Druids, kings, and chieftains. It started because the commoners had magic relics, so when the missionaries spoke to them, they'd show their supernatural power that their gods had given them. The monks left, not able to show power as well. Eventually, the monks returned with magical relics of their own. It worked. The Scotsmen followed the monks who had pagan druid powers."

Caleb look confused. "What did these Catholic ministers do?"

Loki looked at Caleb for a long time, then stood and walked out. No wolves had howled, so Caleb followed. While passing through the town's square, Caleb noted that the sickly priest in white was healthy again and walking about showing everyone the magical white stone that had healed him. Without speaking, Loki walked by him and out of the town. When they were out of eyesight, Loki grabbed Caleb's forearm and flew towards the stars. Shocked, Caleb tried to keep track of where they were flying. He loved the feeling of soaring through the air, but hated that he had no control over where he was going. If Loki wanted to, he could drop him, and Caleb could be horribly maimed for the rest of his life. Caleb slowed his breathing and prepared his body just in case Loki let go.

They descended into a copse of trees near a dimly lit monastery. It had been constructed over the remains of one of the Druid schools which were passing into extinction. Many Celts moved in and out of the structures, talking with brown robed monks. Caleb stilled. Loki paused. Caleb turned his head to look again at the monk who had just passed him. His head was illuminated by an encircling supernatural celestial light that shone out like a crown. Caleb shivered. They were walking images of Mithraism. Every Mithraic image had a crown of light about their head, a solar ring.

Caleb looked questioningly at Loki.

"It's not so strange here. Druids used Imbas Forosnai, illumination between the hands, to discover hidden things. These Catholic monks are relating to their fellow Celts that they will give them hidden truths of the universe."

Caleb moved to the first small structure. It was a small stone room separate from the monastery. A line of Celts waited outside. When Caleb leaned into the doorway, he saw a monk standing on one leg, with one arm extended, and one eye closed. He balanced himself in the middle of the room. A Celt sat at his feet. The monk was cursing the ungodly person plaguing the man who had come to the monk complaining. Shocked, Caleb left quickly. "Cursing?"

"Yeshua would never instruct anyone to curse someone else, especially by magical incantations. A method left by the Fomorians."

Caleb shot him a confused look, never having heard of the Fomorians. Loki shrugged his shoulders and jerked his head to the next structure. Caleb sent him a leery look, worried what he would find there.

The line was even longer for this small structure. Caleb passed many Celts who threw him stony glares. Inside a monk sat on a cot, and a Celt knelt before him, begging him to divine whether or not his wife was committing adultery and what he should do about it if she was. The monk nodded and held out his hand. Another monk gave him a cup. The sitting monk drank the potion and quickly fell into a trance-like state. From the monk's torpid state, he began to roar and then speak in short bursts of rhymes. After ten minutes, the monk returned to his natural state, blinked several times, and asked the Celt if his questions had been answered. The Celt nodded sadly and left to be replaced by another man with questions.

"Trance-utterance is common with fortune tellers. How could those following YHVH possibly say that it is okay?"

Loki backed out of the room. "They say it is a spiritual gift. The gift of prophecy."

Caleb walked to the next building. "Do they know nothing of pagan ways to understand that they are calling occult activities of YHVH? It is a gift given by spirit divination and possession, not by Elohim."

"They are not testing the spirits," Loki answered sadly.

Stopping just outside the next doorway, he looked over to Loki. "Just tell me what's going on inside."

"Healing."

"With magical relics like the white stone?"

"Some."

Disgusted, Caleb nodded. "I'm almost scared to walk into the monastery."

Loki turned and pushed open the dark oak doors. Heavy

incense floated out and tantalized Caleb's entrance. It held a wet, cloying scent that tickled his nose and made him think of cloves being burnt. He had to squint to make anything out. The darkness hid most of the dark, grey stone walls. Wooden pews lined both sides of the wall, and a wooden altar and crucifix stood at the front. In the front right corner a minister levitated as he prayed.

The levitating monk slowly opened his eyes and smiled. Gently descending to the floor, he stood up and walked towards them. He had a kind, gentle face and was most gracious when he had been disturbed during his prayers. "May I help you?"

"We were wishing to speak with Saint Columba," Loki said.

"Oh, he would love to speak with you, but right now his angel is ministering to him." The monk blinked slowly and smiled wider. "He is such a blessed saint. The Lord has gifted him with communication with the angels themselves." He sighed deeply. "I'm sure that he will be able to answer any question that you have about our Lord. Is there something I can do for you in the meantime?"

Loki measured his word choice. "The great goddess Dana, the mother of the Irish gods, has always been helpful to me. I do not believe that I could turn away from her benevolence in worshiping only our Lord."

Caleb froze, trying not to show his surprise.

The monk's head tilted, and he nodded sagely. "Ah, a common problem which really isn't one. For our Virgin Mother is the Mother of God. Dana is just a heathen form of her, so you would not really be turning away from her. Here we offer prayers to Mary, the Mother of God. If it ails you so, just say Virgin Mother rather than Dana when you come here to pray. As you have seen, our lord is stronger than all the gods worshiped locally." He moved to the far back corner of the sanctuary to stand in front of a megalith that had been carved into a statue of Saint Brigit. "The Irish Dana is more widely known as the goddess Brigit throughout all Celtic peoples. You may bow and pray to her here. We have made her a saint and worthy to receive your prayers."

Loki's solemn gaze met Caleb's before he walked out. Once outside, he turned and faced Caleb. "Everything of the occult is a counterfeit for what Elohim established. The line between mysticism and the occult is thin. If you keep the commands and laws of Elohim, they will safeguard a mystic from crossing over into the occult. Paul explains the importance of keeping Torah in Romans for this very reason, but the gentiles, not liking being under Messianic Jews, do not understand how the laws of YHVH safeguard His children. They do not understand the spiritual realm, nor do they understand how things done in the physical realm affect the spiritual realm. The spiritual realm is more real than the physical, but the curse has blinded them too much. Logically, it makes no sense in keeping some of the Torah laws, but that is because they do not see how it affects their soul and weakens them. Nor do they understand that YHVH's blessings and curses last for all eternity, and there are curses for breaking Torah, Elohim's laws. Aye, the Word of YHVH promises a curse to fall upon the chosen, the children of YHVH, if they fail to keep their end of the covenant. They do not heed the warnings in John the Beloved's Revelation.

JULY 15, 1099 AD, JERUSALEM

Dust and sweat swirled, then dripped down Loki's neck and back. He could hear the pounding on the outer walls. See the golden dust puff above the battlements. Deep male guttural shouts and curses reigned from outside. The walls shook.

He stood, eyes wide.

Disbelief confounded him.

Standing in the midst of the gold colored cobblestones of Jerusalem's streets, Muslims and Jews alike ran for cover or for war. Women and children screamed, hovering just inside synagogues for protection. Men stood shoulder to shoulder at the weakest area of the wall where the invaders would enter. They stared, a mix of fear and hatred burning from their eyes. Occasionally, a darted look towards their loved ones could be seen, but most stared ahead, preparing for the breach and inevitable death.

Constantine's army had come to Jerusalem.

The pope promised that, as a reward, anyone who fought in the Crusades would spend a shorter time in Purgatory. This was not in their Bible, but how would they know that? Julius had been wise. Only a small percentage could read and write in Latin. None of the masses would know if what the pope said or promised was true.

Fights amongst popes and kings had been overcome when Pope Urban II pointed out a common enemy, and they bonded together to take possession of Jerusalem.

The Catholic "universal' church had started a strong persecution against the Jews which had never let up, but it had reached its zenith when the Crusaders began their march to the Holy Land. They condemned Jews as Christ-killers, telling them to convert or die. In the Rhine Valley alone, twelve thousand Jews had been massacred. And now, they were here. Pounding on the walls of Jerusalem.

They didn't know that Elohim would bless those who blessed the Jews and curse those who cursed them. Hadn't they had proof through the last thousand years? Europe was the armpit of the world. Their masses were illiterate. They lived according to foolish superstitions, even scared to take a bath. They were the ignorant, blindly following their religious and political leaders.

A loud crack sounded. A jagged line appeared in the wall. Men wet themselves.

Loki took a deep breath. Would any be spared? Would the Crusaders kill everyone like they did on the march here?

His mind swirled. He had seen too much, witnessed too much. This was Jerusalem. He could see David, Solomon, Uzziah, Isaiah and Jeremiah as they walked the streets. He saw Yeshua preaching love and forgiveness, commanding his followers to love their enemies. How could these Crusaders call themselves soldiers of Yeshua when they didn't follow his commands? They obeyed their petty popes over their christ's own teaching. They obeyed a pope over Elohim. If there was ever a time that Loki knew that Mithraism was the Catholic church, it was now. Killing the Jews? John had prophesied that Jews were required for Yeshua's return. If anything, the extinction of the Jews would be a devil's wish, not Elohim's.

Gold colored bricks fell. An opening cracked forth.

Jerusalem's defenders began losing ground. Shouts erupted that they could not stand against the Crusaders. That all was lost. They had heard of the massacres of their people and knew that no Jew would survive. Jewish defenders slowly began backing away, as more and more bricks fell to the ground in front of them. Many turned, running to their synagogues to prepare for death as they had sent their wives, mothers, sisters, and daughters to do.

Loki couldn't blame them. From what he'd seen, no Jewish survivors would be left. The Catholics had an insatiable thirst for Jewish blood.

A last pound sounded, and men yelled in victory. Loki shivered. The wall crumbled before him. Chain-metaled soldiers rushed in. Only the skin of their faces could be seen, every ounce was protected by metal. They wore white surcoats with a large red cross made of swords. They hacked their way through the line of mortal flesh in front of them. Blood spewed in all directions.

Loki backed up and turned towards the synagogue he prayed at. He would spend his remaining time with the Jews there. He had heard what the Lamb had said, he remembered the promise for his own kind, but his spirit was heavy, his soul burdened. He didn't think he could watch humanity any longer.

He could hear another portion of the outer wall cave in. More shouts of victory screamed above the death rattle of those dying around him. He wondered why he wasn't being struck down. He was dressed similarly to the Jews.

Walking up to the ancient synagogue, Loki could see the men, women and children huddled together. Some prayed, others canted Torah portions.

A large red cross on white flashed in front of him. The synagogue doors were slammed shut and locked. Torches were tossed into windows, then sealed. Screams sounded. Franks surrounded the synagogue, raised their Crusader cross shields and sang 'Christ, We Adore Thee!' The door shook. Men pounded on the walls. The synagogue went up in flames. No one escaped. The stench of burning flesh stung Loki's senses.

1743, PALATINATE, GERMANY

Caleb's finger ran over the old parchment. Sir Thomas More's 'Utopia' was already over two hundred years old. He had heard many mortals discussing it but had never taken the time to read it. Raechev was the historical researcher and often pulled him into rooms selling ancient scrolls and famous writings. With the invention of the printing press, more and more books were readily available, and the scriptures had even been translated into the language of the masses, so they could understand for themselves. Factions had risen, wars had broken out, and some were fleeing to the colonies across the Atlantic to get away from religious persecution.

Caleb carefully turned the dusty page. His eyes roamed over the old text, taking in as much as he could while standing in the store. The Holy Roman Empire had been broken down into small canons and had been hurt the worst in the battle between Catholicism and the sweeping Protestant storm. The Protestants fought many false teachings of Catholicism, but Caleb didn't think that they knew what they were fighting against. It appeared the top echelon of Catholics did.

His finger paused over one of Sir Thomas More's sentences. "There is one chief and principal God, only Mithra."

Caleb sighed. Sir Thomas More was known for being a pious Catholic, one who, when received power by Henry VIII, used it to burn Lutherans at the stake. Catholics saw him as a devout follower, and he was hailed for killing anyone who opposed the pope's interpretations and decrees. It was religious tyranny. Death to all those who disagreed. If anyone doubted who Catholics truly worshiped, Sir Thomas More left no doubt in his book. Caleb had often wondered if the masses knew who they were being led to worship. Such general terms like God and Virgin Mother were constantly used.

Looking up, Caleb moved to the window overlooking the rushing Alpine river. It's frothy joy to reach the next town was a constant reminder that this was only one stop of many. The old German cobbled streets were damp from rain. Three-storied structures towered above them, jetting out, and appearing to be ready to fall onto pedestrians below. Picturesque windows, with vibrant flower boxes, accented the white plaster and black timber frame houses, while charming rounded, stone bridges connected neighbors to neighbors.

He had to admit his lack of fondness for the century's clothing. There was too much of it, and society's modesty forced him to cover his overly heated body from head to foot. Sweeping his eyes back to Raechev, he took in the racks of wooden book shelves filled with scrolls and old hand-written books. Raechev wasn't fond of the printing press and veered away from stores that primarily sold them. No, she wanted the original works, crafted by the writer's own hand. She had already created her own personal library, buying items and preserving them through the centuries.

Her gown was form fitting in the bodice, then stood straight out at her hips, eighteen inches on either side. She chose muted colors to help her invisibility and powdered her face to look fashionably dull. She didn't need to look paler, just not ethereal. Her hair sat on top of her head and was hidden by a large straw hat that shadowed her eyes. Leaning sideways, she took one stockinged foot out of her leather boot to scratch the back of her other calf. Caleb smiled. She became so engrossed in her books that she wouldn't have known if someone was watching her.

Today, she wore a creme and flaxen threaded gown with delicate lace edging her bodice, neckline, and sleeves. An extra piece of fabric was attached to her shoulders and flowed down her backside, further hiding her form from the world. Her face scrunched up in confusion. "Did you know Moshe?"

Caleb's eyebrows rose. "The ten commandments, Moshe?" She pulled her lips into her mouth and pressed down on them. "Mmh, hmm."

"No, but Loki did."

A frown further creased her brow, then flickered back to her original confused expression. "Did you know of Moshe performing magicks?" Her eyes never left the book she was looking at.

Caleb walked up and tilted the book to see its cover. Two slabs of wood had been covered with thinly stretched animal skin and dyed a dark brown. It was fastened together by two large black leather straps attached by brass tacks. On the front cover was a Judaic emblem and the words, *Sixth Book of Moses, authored by Moses.* "Moshe only wrote five books. The five books of Law that prohibited practicing magicks."

"Well this here has spells to perform the same miracles in the Bible, has Talmudic magic names, words... incantations to control weather and people... and instructs how to contact dead Christian religious figures for guidance."

"It's a grimoire. Put it down." Caleb's eyes flew to the window looking out at the German town. A large Amish family wearing all black passed by. Something drew him. He walked to the window and searched for them. They were heading to the ships to take them to Philadelphia. Under one of the son's arms was the *Sixth Book of Moses*. Caleb's heart constricted. Protestants were seeing the name of Moses and thinking the writings were of Elohim. It was a masterful deception. A grimoire with a saint's name? A grimoire was a textbook of magic used for invoking fallen angels and demons, divination and accessing magical powers.

"And Shlomo?"

Caleb turned back to his sister. She held a blood-red leather book with iron decorations up in front of her. On it was written, *The Greater Key of Solomon*. "What does it say?"

"Umm, it lists angels and demons, gives astrological correspondences, instructs on casting charms and spells, mixing medicines, creating talismans, and summoning unearthly entities. Demons." She popped her head up. "Do you think Shlomo actually wrote this?"

Caleb didn't know the answer to that one. Shlomo got involved in things he never should have. He broke so many of Elohim's laws that Caleb didn't think he would put it past him, but knowing how Shlomo's wives had turned his heart against Elohim, Caleb couldn't trust any advice given by him.

When he didn't answer, Raechev opened the book and began reading a portion. "Concerning Sacrifices To The Spirits, And How They Should Be Made. In many operations it is necessary to make some sort of sacrifice unto the Demons, and in various ways. Sometimes white animals are sacrificed to the good Spirits and black to the evil. Such sacrifices consist of the blood and sometimes of the flesh. They who sacrifice animals, of whatsoever kind they be, should select those which are virgin, as being more agreeable unto the Spirits, and rendering them more obedient."

"Stop, Raechev. No matter who wrote it, it's a grimoire. Do not align yourself with anyone who willingly breaks Elohim's laws. Solomon was weak. He rationalized his way out of Elohim's commands that prohibited intermarriage with those who refuse to release their pagan traditions. It led to his dark fall into sin, idolatry, and occultism. Do not be like him. Do not rationalize your way out of Elohim's law. There are consequences."

CHAPTER 1:
THE DAY OF THE DEAD, THE ISLAND OF SHADES, & THE EVER-LIVING ONES

MEXICO CITY, MEXICO

REBECCA ELLEN KURTZ

MEXICO CITY, MEXICO
CONTINENT: NORTH AMERICA

Caleb's stomach growled. It slightly distracted him from the stifling heat and rivulets of sweat coursing down his back to wet the top of his slacks. He hated hot climates. Swiping his heavy, dark chestnut brown hair over his shoulder, he was finally able to get a small breeze to cool his neck. He didn't know why, but the back of his neck always sweated the most.

Mia turned her deeply exotic black eyes to him. "Want to get that cut off?"

Caleb's brow furrowed in indecision. He looked at Mia's own sweating neck, her swinging bob allowed her to continue looking feminine even though her hair was hacked up to the base of her hairline. Her fragile Asian neck was bared. He nodded.

She took off, expecting him to follow. Not as easy a task as he thought it would be. She was slight of build and agile, easily moving in and out of the masses of Mexico City. He lumbered his massive six foot five frame above the much shorter Mexicans. His sapphire eyes and pale skin screamed gringo, but his chest span kept Mexicans from throwing sarcastic comments his way. As agile as he was, Mia's body was much better at slithering through the crowds.

His stomach growled again.

Desiring a second breakfast, he wanted to search out a eatery, but he didn't dare take his eyes off Mia. He was never fond of plane food and didn't like Mia's constant caustic remarks to the amount of food he ate. After arriving early that morn, they had quickly found a suitable hotel and planned their first research trip. At the hotel, he had bought beige slacks and a white tank top that he foresaw wearing daily with this heat. He'd probably need to buy a few more before they left for Palenque.

A tiny hand grasped his bulky wrist and yanked him right. Stumbling a bit, Caleb gained his balance and realized he was standing in a barber shop. Mia released him quickly and plunked down into a chair. Her unique blue chunks still framed her face, but the royal blue hair dye was beginning to fade.

"How can I help you?"

Caleb's attention spun to the short man in front of him. "I need it cut off. Not shaved, but short."

The barber led him to a chair, sat him down, and threw a plastic cape around him. Caleb's stomach growled loudly.

Mia's eyebrow lifted, before meeting Caleb's gaze in the mirror. She shrugged and walked out.

"Hey, wait!" Caleb bellowed.

The barber pushed Caleb down hard. "She'll return, senor. Women always return. I have a lot to cut. Stay still."

Caleb grunted. Women didn't always return. Raechev never returned. And Mia? Mia wasn't one to return, but he knew she was exhausted and wouldn't be checking out of the hotel without him. Anyways, she didn't have the money for their trip.

Caleb closed his eyes and tried to relax. The sound of the scissors clipping near his ears, caused him to ponder how his life had changed, and how he needed to cut away the sadness of the past he had lost. Raechev was happy now. He would be an uncle soon. Granted, Nimrod's passing wasn't a good change. Caleb had become quite attached to him in the short amount of time he had known him. And the girls? Mia, Stacey and Samantha? They were a pleasing distraction, and Mia was a balm for his sister's abandonment. In so many ways, they were similar.

Something fell on his hands, and Caleb's eyes sprung open. A large bag sat in his lap. Mia held a drink in her hand. Food? She had brought him food? She pushed the drink into his hand and returned to her seat in the waiting area. He watched her. As soon as she sat down, her eyes darted to him, then darted away.

Caleb paused. He had noticed her inspecting him from time to time on their flight from Monaco. She always seemed to be watching for differences - trying to note his inhumane qualities. Whenever he caught her doing it, he just shirked it off. If he was mortal and was given a guardian that wasn't quite human, he'd probably be doing some inspecting himself. It would only be natural.

Caleb opened the bag to find a green burrito filled with beans and cheese. Well, he guessed she knew what to expect from his bodily secretions. There were ten. Ten burritos. He attacked with relish.

By the time he had finished his second breakfast, the barber was ready to shave his beard. Caleb paused to look at himself in the mirror. His hair had never been this short before. He looked.... modern. His hair was extremely short on the sides and back, but his wavy bangs were longer and partially fell over one eye. With sweat, they'd probably droop fully into his vision. Maybe he should get that whacked as well.

"I like it."

He shot a look back at Mia. She gazed directly into his eyes.

For all his lack of humanity, she never appeared alarmed or in fear of him. If she liked it, then maybe he'd keep it. A truce of sorts. He nodded and leaned his head back for the shaving to begin.

It wasn't long before he and Mia were out on the street again. He had to admit the short cut was cool and made his head feel a lot lighter. Mexico City was a diverse city, not surprising since it was the most populated city in the world. It was a mix of breathtaking skyscrapers and dust covered shacks, both set beautifully in front of a blue mountain range. Within a short distance, some lived in opulence while others fed themselves from dumpsters.

Periodically, Mia would glance about searching for something. Her eyes always alert.

"Are you scared?"

She shot him a threatening look. "Mexico City is one of the main cities for sex trafficking. If I see something of it, I will try to rescue the girls."

Caleb jerked in surprise. He would think that she would be scared of sex trafficking and keep away from it, not risk herself to help others. "Is that our plan for the day?"

She stopped, turned, and stared hard at him. "You're not going to try to stop me?"

Caleb shook his head. "I'd help you."

She tilted her head to the side and stretched out her hand. Perplexed, Caleb returned the gesture, and they shook on their partnership. Caleb didn't know if it was for the day or for their overall mission together.

"Do you have a lead?"

She shook her head. "I wasn't planning on coming here, remember? I didn't even know if we'd be staying in town. Didn't have time to do any homework."

Caleb winced. She hadn't demanded, but he hadn't given any information either. He paused, taking in that last thought. She hadn't fought his decisions nor demanded to know them. It just seemed odd compared to her surly attitude towards men in general. Caleb's mind ran over the past few weeks and quickly realized that she hadn't really been the one making the decisions. Sam had. Stacey and Mia made comments, but they both primarily let Sam take the lead.

Mia shrugged. "In these situations, Stacey and I just normally walk around until we see something. Sometimes we ask where the prostitutes are, but often we can find them just by walking around."

"Sam doesn't help?"

Without looking back, Mia answered as she headed to a more historic area of the city. "This is what Stace and I do when we're waiting on Sam to finally arrive, so we can get on to the project of why we're even in that part of the world."

"So, I'm Sam in this situation?"

"No." Mia stopped, turned around and faced him directly. "You're actually here."

Caleb absorbed what all that statement entailed. So did Stace and Mia often feel like they were waiting on Sam? Did they feel that their leader was gone most of the time? Were they more followers than leaders?

She turned in a full circle before moving down a street to the right. They were no longer in the downtown area. Modern buildings had turned into rambling stone structures echoing of times past. She paused at a statue of an angel.

Her head jerked to the right, peering behind the statue, before fleeing to her next destination. A convention was being held in the large rambling hotel of beige stone. She jerked her head for Caleb to follow.

Caleb didn't know if she had seen anything or was just curious, but he followed her into the hotel. Outside, posters advertised a great prophet of god who could heal with the aid of an angel. It brought back bad memories. He remembered how mortals would pass through large holes in megaliths to be healed by the spirits inhabiting it. The Cult of the Stone was one of the oldest occult religions. Its spirits were able to heal, provide women with fertility, and grant the use of magic. The dead spirits residing in stones were to help the living. The mortal acquiesced to their aid by their willing participation, damning their own souls. Caleb shivered remembering how spirits would incarnate themselves into the children conceived by the women who came to them for fertility. But what did these women expect? That there was no cost? That fallen spirits and angels gave out of the generosity of their hearts?

Caleb followed Mia into the conference and halted. Gold dust and feathers drifted down from above. Mia threw a bewildered look to Caleb.

The man at the podium opened his arms wide and began dreamily telling of how an angel had visited him one night and had begun sharing god's will with him. He, as god's anointed, was able to heal many now with the angel's help, prophesy over anyone needing knowledge concerning their future, and inform them of god's plan. He claimed that the gold dust and angel feathers were god's sign for others to believe and follow his teachings. Beaming, he proclaimed that god's power was being poured out on man, and a new chapter was being written - the End Times were coming. He beckoned others to follow him, learn from him, and if they were blessed by god, then they may just be visited by their own angel.

Mia cast another beseeching look at Caleb before he grabbed her arm and hauled her back outside. As soon as they were out, she spoke, "What was that? I have never heard of such a thing." She shook her head in confusion. "Why would God do cheap theatrical tricks? It just doesn't make sense. That is no where in the Bible!"

"Everything of the occult is a counterfeit for the real. So there is a real. You must look at the source, test the spirits, and inspect the teachings. Remember Moses? YHVH turned his staff into a snake. The magicians in Egypt also turned their staffs into snakes. Sometimes the 'wonder' isn't what is done but the source, reason, and message. Your Messiah did signs, miracles, and wonders and became extremely frustrated because many Jews still did not repent and come back into obedience to YHVH. In his anger, your Messiah said that Nineveh would judge them for they repented without signs, miracles, and wonders. You must look at the message, Mia. Your Messiah did signs, miracles, and wonders, but he taught repentance and obedience. His whole exemplified obedience. That was why he was perfect. He was without sin. He had never broke a law or commandment of YHVH. His life showed he was Truth.

Unfortunately, I didn't hear the man say anything about testing, nor repentence, nor redemption. Everything is about repentance, honoring YHVH's commands, and maturing oneself. Why did you think the god he was speaking of is the God of Abraham, Isaac, and Jacob?"

Saucily, she shook her hair back from her face. "What other God would there be? There is no other God, just one."

"Well, in my lifespan, I have met many Nephilim who have called themselves gods. Spirits have called themselves gods as well as fallen angels. It could be a number of many."

Mia paused, soaking in Caleb's age and comments. "So you're saying that his visiting angel wasn't from my God, but a fallen angel from....."

Caleb knelt down, so she wouldn't have to strain her neck so much. "I'm saying that Elohim commanded his children to test prophets, teachers, and spirits - to recognize which are false. It's not about the wonder, it's about the message. Test the message. Your Jesus warned that anyone who didn't test, but blindly followed false prophets, would be held as responsible as the false one because the Torah explains how to test them. So no believer has an excuse."

"*Your* Jesus?" Mia asked.

"Yes, your Jesus. Jesus came for mortals. His sacrifice didn't extend to the Nephilim," Caleb said bitterly.

"How do you know that?" Mia bugged.

"Because we know," Caleb answered flatly. "Can we move on now?"

Mia waited a while, inspecting Caleb's reaction before shrugging and moving down the street. She continued to wear black leather pants and a black tank top. Caleb could only assume it was because mortals didn't have such a high body temperature. She trudged on, glancing from side to side, but her face revealed that her mind was still distracted with all that had been witnessed. An eerie feeling creeped over Caleb, and he jerked his head to the right to see some people decorating several graves. The Day of the Dead. Or as Catholics preferred to call it, All Saints Day. Various countries celebrated it in different ways. The Celts had celebrated it at Samhain, October 31. When the Catholics couldn't stamp out the pagan celebration, they had created All Hallow's Eve or Hallowmas. They tried to get the Celts to come to church at midnight to pray for the dead instead of partaking of their former tradition. Likewise, in Italy, Romans would fast for three days each spring to protect themselves from malevolent spirits of the dead. Once again, they refused to give up their holiday, so in 609 AD, Pope Boniface IV consecrated the Roman Pantheon to the Virgin Mother. The pope made pagan gods holy, so the citizens could still pray to them.

The cemetery belonged to the Archdiocese of Mexico City. The church loomed largely above them and was magnificent in the setting sun. Not only did it sprawl the entire length of a city block, but two grey stone turrets rose on either side of the main entrance. Caleb guessed that this was one of the older buildings in Mexico City.

Caleb's eyes shifted to Mia who was fighting her way to get inside. He rushed to her side and asked, "Sightseeing stop?"

Mia swung the ancient oak door out and paused long enough to explain, "I need to pray."

Grimacing, Caleb followed her inside. He hated going inside cathedrals - mecca to Mithraism - the great deception.

Inside, the cathedral was astonishing. It's grey stones seemed bleached white. Large striated columns ran up and down the long rectangular room, and darker grey stones were used to decorate the ceiling. Burgundy chairs lined two aisles leading up to the podium where mass would be held later that evening.

Without much of a choice, Caleb sank into one of the chairs a few rows behind Mia. She knelt down on her knees between the rows of chairs and prayed. He really didn't like coming into a cathedral. Granted, they were beautiful, but the deception bothered him too much. A deception so dark and hidden that modern believers were fooled, but in truth, if they actually read their Bible and tested false teachings and prophets, they wouldn't be fooled. So who was really to blame? It wasn't like the old days when only the church workers and nobles could read. Everyone could read now. And with technology? Anyone could do research on the holidays and festivals they celebrated. Really, were there any excuses?

And why didn't anyone research? Because they all relied on pastors who said it really didn't matter. Only if in their heart, they were worshiping the god they thought they were praying to.

Hours passed as she prayed. Caleb's stomach growled.

Caleb couldn't help but wonder what took her so long to pray about.

She finally rose and took the seat next to him. "You didn't have to stay."

Caleb gave a lopsided grin. "I'm your protector, remember?"

Mia's eyes narrowed. She turned away and gazed about the darkened interior. Night had fallen and only candles lit the stone cavern. Priests bustled about preparing for Hallowmas, expecting hordes of people to attend. Finally, she muttered under her breath. "I cannot beat you in a house of God, but I advise you to keep those type of comments to yourself in the future before I make you eat your words."

Caleb couldn't help but quirk a smile.

Her face continued facing in the opposite direction where he could not see it. Her feet dangled like a child's as she took in the changed environment of the cathedral. She was so tiny, her legs didn't even reach the floor.

Sighing, her gaze finally worked itself back around to him. "Don't you love cathedrals. They're so beautiful, and when left alone, you feel closer to God."

Caleb tried not to react to why it was important for her to be left alone. She was a prickly little thing and had no reason to open up to him. It was apparent that she had a distaste for men in general as Raechev had, but Caleb was Raechev's brother. This tiny mortal had no familial cords of affection to breach the chasm between her distaste and a friendship. He knew with Raechev, not to push for her to open up. It was part of the independent streak that she and Raechev had in common.

Mia's eyes had fallen on an elderly woman kneeling in front of a statue of the Madonna and child. Her lips moved in silent, fervent prayer. Mia's head tilted in contemplation. The woman's voice rose, her anguished pleas to Mary to bring her wayward son back into the fold was heart rending. Mia leaned in close and whispered, "I never understood why anyone prays to Mary. She isn't God."

Caleb chose to be kind. He whispered gently, "Behind your doors and your doorposts you have put your pagan symbols. Forsaking me, you uncovered your bed, you climbed into it, and opened it wide; you made a pact with those whose beds you love, and you looked on their nakedness. Whom have you so dreaded and feared that you have been false to me, and have neither remembered me nor pondered this in your hearts? Is it not because I have long been silent that you do not fear me?"

Her breathing slowed but she did not lean back from him. She didn't speak, and Caleb didn't move. Her eyes slowly drifted from his eyes and skimmed over his face, ending on his lips. "What is that from?"

"You do not recognize it?"

Her eyes returned to his. She shook her head no.

"From Isaiah."

"Isaiah?"

Caleb leaned his head even closer, his forehead almost touching hers. "As in prophet of Elohim. His writings are in your Bible."

Mia gulped, dropped her eyes and slowly turned and stood. At the end of the row, she turned. "I suspect your stomach is empty. Let's feed you."

Although the thought of food was tempting, he rather liked the intimate environment that had just been established around them. She seemed more at peace after her trip to a cathedral, so he may just have to have more cathedral stops. She seemed to thaw in what she perceived to be holy chambers. He'd remember that for the future. She stood waiting for him. Her eyes watching him. Curious and intrigued.

Caleb stood, and she quickly walked before him, leaving the cathedral to find the quasi empty square now littered with hundreds of people. Some priests sold relics at tables in preparation for the night, while pedestrians quickly prepared to decorate the graves of their ancestors and friends. Happy little christmas lights crisscrossed above the square, lighting the area festively. Mia walked up to one of the priests at the table and looked over his wares. "What are these for?"

The priest smiled indulgently. "For your protection, my child." He pointed over to some small glass vials with stoppers. "These here are vials of holy water. You may use them to spread over your forehead to keep the evil spirits away from you, and these here..." He pointed to a stone with a cross in it inside a circle. "...are rocks made sacred by the emblem of our Lord which also may be used in protection tonight."

The priests eyes appreciatively took in Mia's slight frame, his smile broadened. "You would be a choice morsel for them." His eyes ran over her leather clad hips and belly button piercing. "It is too bad I do not have a relic to offer you."

Caleb's arm wrapped protectively around Mia's waist. His eyes clashed with the priest's. "I am her protector. She needs nothing else."

Mia jumped out of his protective embrace. "I am his protector. Don't let his brawny look fool you." She rolled her eyes and took off down the street. Caleb had to stretch his legs to catch up with her.

"Don't ever do that again!" she yelled.

"What? Protect you?"

"Touch me. Don't touch me. And I didn't need protecting. He wasn't going to get anywhere near me," she fumed.

"So you knew he was checking you out? A priest? Sworn to celibacy?"

She rolled her eyes. "Everyone knows most priests don't live up to that." Her voice dropped to a menacing growl, "and the Catholic church is known for its pedophiles."

"You will know them by their fruit."

She stopped in her tracks. Her head swiveled around. "You cannot judge all by what a few have done."

"Don't you judge all men by what a few have done?"

Mia's leg whipped around fast and nailed him behind his knees. Caleb fell on his ass, only to stare up at belligerent eyes. He stared back, refusing to take back his assessment. She continued the stare for a few moments before pushing her way back into the crowds.

Hopping up quickly, Caleb rushed after her. Things had started off so well, he shouldn't have said what he had. He knew better than that. Raechev had reacted the same when he had thrown that comment at her, but Raechev had good reason to hate males. Many Nephilim had tried to rape her through the centuries, it's not like Mia...... He paused.

Tripping over Mexican feet in his haste, Caleb finally caught up with her. He reached out and grabbed her elbow. "Have you been raped?"

She swung around, flinging a strong left hook, smacking his jaw hard. His head spun. She was stronger than she looked. This was when Caleb wished he was more than just mortally strong. Swinging his other arm around, he grabbed her other arm and held her steady. "Sorry, okay?"

Anger streamed from her being, her breaths hard and labored. Clenching her teeth, she gritted out, "Don't touch me."

His eyes took on a solemn threat. "Don't run."

She gave one nod, and he released her.

"Can we go back now? I just want to go back to the hotel."

Caleb nodded. He didn't like the holiday that loomed over them. The air already seemed full of enchantments. Although modern Catholics claimed they had sanctified it, it was still an occult festival, and many witches partook of their own rites and rituals. The true occult activities of this eve made Caleb shudder. Witches would call forth to the spirit world, and spirits would appear bodily en masse and join the living. Their immortal soul, the cloud-like terrestrial spirit of a former Nephilim, would incarnate itself into a living body, often causing havoc for the human's life. Adulteries, murders, and occult activities became the night's achievements.

Caleb stumbled into Mia. She had froze at the edge of one of the cemeteries. She stared at small skeleton dolls which had been given clay dresses, bouquets of flowers, hair, and flowered headbands. The pretty outfits hung loosely on rib cages while empty eye sockets and huge teeth grinned from large skulls. She shivered.

Dread overcame Caleb. He had spoken so self-assured to the priest that he would be able to protect Mia, but he didn't really know if he could do that. How do you protect a mortal from possession? Fear blossomed in his stomach and apprehension chilled his blood. Huge, Asian eyes sought out his own. "How old is this holiday?"

"Old." He reached towards her elbow to direct her away, but she swung her gaze back to the cemetery. Many stood at their ancestor's tombs, hoping contact would be allowed from the spirit world. The line was stretched thin between the realms this eve. Caleb couldn't imagine any follower of Elohim consulting familiar spirits. It was expressly forbade in the Torah, but then again, most Christians didn't read their Old Testament, and many pastors didn't speak on the laws of Elohim. And that is what he saw. Supposed followers, reaching out to spirits for guidance, answers, or comfort.

Thousands of candles lit the tombs. Food had been left on

platters. Elderly and young alike whispered to tombstones, hoping to wake the spirit of the loved lost one. Candlelight flickered over Mia's face, casting a romantic glow onto her haunted eyes. She was such a mystery to him. Her life so short, yet so unknown. Caleb whispered, "I'll tell you on our walk back."

Nodding without looking at him, she turned and moved on.

Walking almost close enough to touch her, he spoke of Ulysses' island of Shades - dark cloud-like entities that had once been living souls. "In Elysium, the land of gods and deathless folk, dead warriors wait. They spend their time hymn-singing, studying legends, sacrificing, philosophizing, and waiting. Waiting for their people to call out to them for aid. Waiting to assist their descendants. Waiting to be re-born, to transmigrate into a living body - a willing receptacle."

"Gods and death folk?" Mia asked.

"Great heroes of partially divine nature. Nephilim. The Ever-Living Ones."

Spooked eyes turned up to Caleb. "Would you ever possess someone after you died?"

Caleb shook his head. Mia hesitantly nodded. Caleb's voice dropped, "But I want to tell you more of this for I fear..."

A new intrigue turned Mia's attention back to him. Her face and eyes were open, trusting, believing.

"The tale continues that these mighty dead stayed on islands in the middle of vast oceans. The presence of such mighty and great souls caused such horrific storms, any man who passed near them were killed in its wake. These men were innocent and did not know what they were approaching."

Mia's eyes enlarged. "Like the Bermuda Triangle?"

Caleb paused, refusing to comment. "The warrior angels have trapped them until the final battle... the War of the Messiah, so they cannot harm any more humans than necessary."

"So it's okay?" Mia implored.

"But there is another prison. One hidden that no one can find. It is reported to be guarded by demons, but that is not true. It is guarded by a few redeemed Nephilim who have chained the most evil Nephilim. Entities so evil, that they are not to be released till Elohim commands. One is so beastly, it will force world-wide subjugation like it had before Noah's flood.

Mia's voice whispered, "A beast?"

Caleb nodded. "Rising from the oceans. It's chief guardian, Hel."

Mia stood confused. She patted Caleb's arm. "Perhaps, its time for bed. You're getting people and places confused."

Caleb tried not to chuckle. "Am I?"

CHAPTER 2:

TEMPLE OF THE SKULL

& THE

SUN-SERPENT GOD

PALENQUE, MEXICO

PALENQUE, MEXICO
CONTINENT: NORTH AMERICA

Caleb's backpack hung heavily, making his white tank top meld to his body from sweat. Mia, walking just ahead of him, didn't fare much better. She continued to wear her black leather pants, black tank top, and black boots. He was beginning to wonder if she even had any other choice of clothes.

Lush vegetation surrounded them as they hacked their way along the old Mayan trail. They had decided to enter the ruins as the ancient Mayans would have and not by modern modes of transportation. It reminded him of the old days, when he had traveled with his father and Raechev. The only current complaint he had was that Mia was the one slashing through the vegetation with a machete rather than him. Not that he wanted to sweat more, but her short arms didn't cut too high, so he had to duck a lot when he walked. He hoped she would tire soon, so he could take the lead.

Caleb had to fight not to watch her too closely. His eyes kept drifting to the sheen of sweat that could be seen between her tank top and low riding pants where a blue butterfly was tattooed. In the front, she wore a blue butterfly belly button ring. Once again, he dragged his eyes from her form and glanced at long wooden vines hanging from high trees. He had never been fond of tropical jungles nor the snakes that hid within. The one good thing was how shady it was here. The foliage above kept out all sunlight.

The foothills of the Sierra Oriental de Chiapas in southern Mexico held the great temple and tomb of Pacal, the last ruler of Palenque. No giants had been recorded to be there, but Sam was now interested in the various civilizations who worshiped sun gods. Knowing that Loki was searching for Mithras left Caleb a bit worried. Loki was ruthless, and Sam was an excellent researcher. Between the two of them, they might actually find the underwater prison.

Mia stopped, her chest heaving from exhaustion. "Perhaps, I should go first. Test its strength."

Caleb glanced around her and saw the ancient rickety bridge. The rushing turquoise river below frothed too much to give Caleb any ideas of crossing through its currents. He sighed, doubting the bridge would be able to hold either of their weights. Many wooden planks were missing, but the wooden strings on the sides seemed to be sturdy. Looking back down to the river, he surmised it would only be a twenty foot drop. Luckily, he didn't see any jagged rocks below.

Mia grasped the side rope made of tree vines and took her first step. The bridge groaned under her slight weight. Caleb took a steadying breath. He couldn't see her face but her back was stiff and full of resolve. Reaching out her other hand, she grasped the other rope and brought her second leg onto the bridge. It twisted left. Squatting, she equaled out her weight and balanced out the bridge.

"Maybe we should have taken the modern route," Caleb complained.

"Coward," Mia whispered before taking the next step. She slowly inched one foot ahead of the other, being careful to step over the holes where missing planks gaped. The bridge was about thirty feet long, and Caleb didn't know if it was wise to continue this route, but he knew he couldn't back down. Maybe the bridge could hold Mia, she was almost a third of the way by now. But his weight? Caleb shook his head.

He had to respect her determination and courage.

She glided in her movements, keeping low and the bridge balanced. She had excellent control over her muscles and body. It almost seemed a dance.

The hairs on the back of his neck slowly began to stand. He looked quickly behind him, but saw nothing. Frowning, he turned around to further his scrutiny. Not a single leaf moved. No birds or animals called out. It was eerily still and quiet. Caleb squinted.

"Okay. Your turn," Mia yelled from the other side of the river. Caleb turned back around, now happy to be leaving his side. Sighing, he shook his head and regretted not having the ability to fly. It definitely made his life more difficult. He took his first step. The sun-dried plank cracked. Anger welled. He squashed it. He set his other foot on the bottom rope-binding that held the planks in place. His stomach churned. He knew the bridge would not hold his weight.

"Believe," Mia encouraged, safely ensconced in the jungle on the other side.

"Believe?"

"Believe that you can do it," she expounded.

He gritted his teeth. He was the one who was going to go crashing into the turbulent river below. He tried his second step. The plank held. Caleb breathed, then searched for another sturdy looking plank. Up five planks, one appeared. His legs were long, they would stretch. Balancing on his one leg and using the ropes for balance, he lunged ahead. Judging wrong, he overstepped. His foot fell through another plank. Losing his balance, he fell to the right, and clung fiercely.

Mia giggled.

Scowling, Caleb clawed his way back up.

A twig cracked behind him. Caleb threw another assessing gaze to the area they had just left. Nothing. Pasting a threatening scowl back on his face for Mia's benefit, he measured how far to another sturdy plank. Holding his breath, he lunged. His foot slid between the two planks and under the sturdy one. His body lurched left.

Caleb.

Caleb jerked his head behind him to see who called. The movement caused the bridge to flip, Caleb clung desperately, fighting to maintain his grasp, but the bridge snapped, and Caleb fell crashing into the cold stream below. Turquoise water gobbled his vision as he plunged further than he thought, and struck something jagged, ripping his flesh. Blood spilled into the water. Caleb swatted the blood away from his sight and worked his way back up to the surface.

Breaking through, he gulped in air, filling his lungs with its necessary life sustaining element.

"Here," Mia yelled from the edge.

Caleb turned and saw Mia running towards him. She was shrinking in stature. He turned sideways and realized the current was driving him hard towards the waterfall. Using all his energy, he dove towards Mia. Swimming like a madman, he plowed through the frothing river to reach her. She had positioned herself onto a stone plateau to easily leverage his heavy weight out of the water.

Her hand was stuck out and waving as she called to him.

His lungs and muscles burning, he fought against the current and clasped onto her hand. She dug in her heels and heaved him out of the water. The stone scraped his body savagely and shredded his clothes, but he didn't care. He was tired.

He laid back onto the sun heated stones to warm himself, then froze.

Looking behind Mia's smiling face, a black jaguar stood watching. Its yellow eyes held a haunted look that didn't seem quite human. A cunning intelligence glittered ruthlessly as it perused Mia. Slowly sitting up, Caleb's fear grew when the jaguar didn't once take its eyes from its prey. Its shoulders slowly began bunching together, preparing for its leap.

Caleb tackled Mia, just as the jaguar leapt. Fire slammed through Caleb's body, as the cat's claws raked his back. He roared in pain, flipped, and dove for the cat. The jaguar slashed Caleb's chest before he could tackle it to the ground. He was bleeding profusely, and the cat was strong. Caleb hated cats. Lions, tigers, panthers. He hated them all. Remembering his battles with them in Nineveh's zoological hunting preserve, he searched for a sharp twig. Finding one, he plunged it into its eye. The cat howled in rage. Caleb quickly found a thicker, longer branch and wedged it between its jaws, prying its mouth ever more open till the jawbone popped out of joint. Rolling the cat over, Caleb stood and searched for a rock.

"It's as good as dead," Mia mumbled.

Caleb found a rock near her and stumbled back to the cat. He smashed its head in. Then stood over the cat waiting. Slowly a spirit began exiting. Kali.

Kali dove for Mia, but Caleb beat her. Slamming Mia down on the ground, he covered her fully with his body and clamped a hand over her mouth and nose. Mia instantly began struggling. He released her nose.

"Look. It's Kali. The spirit you released from Angor Wat."

Mia's startled eyes glanced to the demon. Her struggles ended.

Caleb laid still on top of her. If Kali was determined to possess Mia, how was he going to stop it? He couldn't hold Mia like this forever.

Mia's lips were moving beneath his hand.

"What?" Caleb asked.

Mia scowled at him. He cupped his hand, giving her space to move her lips freely, but continued to shield her from possession.

"I still can't breathe."

Realization sunk in, and Caleb moved his body off of hers.

"If you take your hand off my mouth, I promise not to open it."

His eyes searched out Kali, but he couldn't spot her. How was he going to keep Mia safe? He was blessed that Nephilim spirits couldn't possess other Nephilim, but Mia was vulnerable.

"You need to clean your wounds."

A smile tilted his lips. "You'll need to clean my back." He stood and offered his hand to help her rise. Without smiling, she took his proffered arm and hauled herself up. Pushing him back to the river, she forced him to sit on the rock. He dropped his hot feet into the river while she inspected his back.

The remains of his tank top jerked, and he heard her ripping them to shreds till he was bare chested. She used his tattered top to wipe off some of the larger chunks of dirt before rinsing it in the river. Wisely, she wrung the wet shirt over his wounds, letting the water rinse away the dirt without actually rubbing it into torn flesh.

She leaned over his shoulder and inspected his chest. Frowning, she placed her hand over her mouth and spoke. "How long does it take for your kind to heal?"

"My kind? You know I'm half your kind too. More than half actually. I'm only one generation away from aging like a mortal."

"How long?" she persisted.

"Like a mortal."

"Oh, you need stitches then. But don't worry I always keep stuff on me." She couldn't help the grin sounding in her voice. "I still have my backpack."

Unlike him, whose backpack was at the bottom of the river or over the falls by now.

"I'll need to build a fire for sterilization. We might as well find a cave to sleep in tonight."

Caleb looked at the sky above. It was early afternoon. They should be able to make it to Palenque.

She knew he was about to buck her suggestion. "We need to stop the bleeding before you go much further."

Caleb grimaced. He was going to starve. He had all the food

in his backpack. He didn't mind sleeping in caves, he was fond of them. Well, as long as a jaguar wasn't living there already.

"Let me just finish rinsing your wounds, and we'll move on."

She went about her work quietly. Not waiting for a response. He couldn't help but not smell her body's natural scent while she soaked his chest wounds. It was a mixture of sensual amber and exotic pink lotus flowers. He leaned in and sniffed to get a more definitive list. She stiffened but continued working silently. Faint hints of vanilla, creamy sandalwood, praline and musk were swirled into the mixture. It was a confident, passionate smell laced with femininity. With her black clothes and tattoos, he wouldn't guess that she had a girly romantic side. Then again, he was just getting to know her.

"There." She stood up, picked up her back pack, and motioned for him to follow.

Wincing, Caleb stood but faltered. She quickly propped herself under his shoulder, and he leaned his weight on her. His adrenaline rush had ended.

They stumbled through the jungle for about an hour before they found a cave large enough for them to rest in. She quickly sat him down, then moved about building a fire. Once a good flame was established, she hauled out some sewing needles and thread. Caleb didn't think they looked too medical, but he didn't need to be picky. Carefully, she heated the needle tip in the fire, sterilizing it, then approached. Her eyes were tinged with sadness, yet determination held her shoulders stiff.

"How many stitches do you think I'll need?"

Mia gave him one long look, but didn't speak. Bowing her head, she took her first stab. Caleb winced. He was going to need some distraction.

"So, why do always wear black?"

Her eyes met and held his, then she went back to work.

Frustrated, Caleb remained silent and endured the pain. Her cool fingers were soothing on his flesh though. He couldn't imagine how he felt to her. Sam had always called Nimrod a furnace, so he guessed that would be a description, but her fingers were gentle and soft, like a cool breeze caressing a fevered brow.

"I mourn."

Caleb jerked. She had answered. "Who are you mourning?"

"Caleb, what are we doing?"

"We're talking," he answered honestly.

Her rolling of the eyes, let him know that, that was not the answer she was looking for.

"We're distracting me from pain?" he tried again.

"What are we doing here?" She tried to help him understand her question better.

"You didn't think I could make it to Palenque?"

Huffing, she tried again, "Why are we even going to Palenque? Jordan... Tagas hired us to research Caucasoid giants around the world, but now that I know the truth, I know that reason is hogwash. So, why are we even still together?"

"Oh. We hired you girls to keep an eye on your research. Make sure you didn't publicize anything we'd want hidden. Then we discovered that Sam was working for Loki and Marduk."

"Marduk?"

"He's a spirit of a former Nephilim who's possessing Darcy's body," Caleb answered.

"So, Tagas wants to use Sam as bait to get information on Loki and Darcy?" she asked calmly.

He could see her protective nature coming out, her hackles rising. "Well, she's already involved with them. It's why Nimrod's dead, and her life could possibly be put in jeopardy as well. We're now helping her to stay alive and out of trouble."

Mia didn't speak for a long time. She quickly finished up Caleb's chest and moved to his back. It put Caleb in a vulnerable mood. He couldn't see her. Eventually, she spoke, "So why are we going to Palenque?"

"For research," he answered confused.

Her fingers paused on his back. "But we know the truth about your race. What is there to research?"

He suddenly realized just how in the dark Mia really was to what was going on. For her lack of information, she had been amazingly trusting with her life and time. Her words encouraging him to believe he could cross the bridge were not as hypocritical as he first thought. At first, he thought that her lack of trust in men for what a few had done disabled her from the right to tell him to trust the bridge and cross it, but then, she had been trusting him with everything since they'd left Monaco. She was alone in the middle of a jungle. Whether or not she would verbally admit it, she was vulnerable being alone with him.

"We're searching for clues to where Mithras is imprisoned. Just like Loki, but we want to beat him there, so we can keep him from releasing Mithras."

"And none of you know where it is?" she asked.

Caleb paused. It would make sense if Tagas knew, but Caleb didn't think that Tagas knew. He believed that everyone who knew were jailers at the prison. Elohim wouldn't want anyone being able to read Tagas' mind and get to the prison. It was rare, but there were a few Nephilim who could read minds like Tagas could. Loki could. "No."

"So, we're racing to this prison," she reiterated.

"To keep the beasts chained."

"I thought you said Mithras?" she asked perplexed.

"There are many names for what all lies therein," he replied.

She chuckled, "Like Oh-Finely-Honed-Male-Specimen-of-Prowess?"

Caleb's lids lowered.

Mia finished stitching his back. She moved back in front of him, walked to her backpack, and threw him one of her black tank tops. He gave her a quizzical expression. Balling her fists on her waist, she rebuked him, "It is stretchy, and it'll help keep the wound clean." She turned back to her backpack and fished around, till she pulled out a dagger. "I'm going to go catch us dinner. You should probably get some rest, let your body restock its blood."

Caleb sat, engulfed in a strange loneliness that was new to him. He thought of laying back, then realized he'd be lying on his back's stitches. Then he thought of his stomach and grimaced. Heck, how was he to lie down? Sighing, he turned onto his side and tried to make himself comfortable.

Their initial deceptive reasons for hiring the girls were now known, and their mission had changed drastically. He didn't really think there would be anything to find at Palenque, but Sam thought it was a good idea, and no one had given him any other options. His life had changed so much in such a short amount of time. His mind flew back to the alarming news that Marduk had resurrected Dagon. He was continuing his plan to build a strong Nephilim army to fight against Elohim at Armageddon. He didn't know why they even tried. The Nephilim couldn't stop Y'hoshua at Yericho or at any of the other Canaanite towns. Why did they even think they stood a chance? Well, they would have their angels too. That's why.

*

Tiny, fragile fingers poked into his shoulder. Caleb's eyes fluttered open. Mia's large eyes gazed down at him. "Meat's ready."

Grunting, Caleb sat up and yawned. "What are we eating."

"Jaguar."

His eyebrows rose. Was it unkosher to eat an animal that had once been possessed? "The jaguar? The black one?"

Mia nodded while pulling off a big slab of meat from the fire pit she had created. She handed it to him. Caleb ripped off a huge chunk, grease spilling down his chin. He didn't care what he looked like. He was famished. Neither spoke while they ate. She ate little, less than half a leg. Caleb ate the rest.

Mia settled against the far cave wall and watched him. Frustration was prominent on her face. Her fingers twisted in the hem of her tank top.

"Nervous?" he asked.

She threw him a quizzical expression. "About?"

"Sleeping out here in the middle of the jungle with me?" he probed.

She shook her head no. "You don't make me nervous."

That bothered him. "Then what?"

"We're waiting. Again."

Caleb was confused. "It was your idea to sleep in a cave and not continue."

Her head lolled down, her eyes yelling at him. "We're waiting. For answers. What to do. What to seek. Don't you find it frustrating? I feel like I'm always waiting. Waiting for something to happen. Waiting for something bad to occur. Waiting to hear from God. Waiting. Waiting, waiting, waiting on everyone else to make up their mind, so I can go on with my life."

"Waiting for the next assignment," he stated.

"Exactly. I just want to do. Get on with it, you know?" Her

head dropped. "What are we doing after Palenque?"

He didn't know. He felt just about as lost as she did. Did anything really matter what they did? If it was Elohim's will, Loki would open the prison no matter what they did. And if it wasn't Elohim's will? Wouldn't he keep it from happening without the aid of them? Sometimes, Caleb grew tired trying to sort these things out. But he could understand the frustration. Caleb couldn't understand why the Israelites had kept getting pulled back in line, but the Christians weren't.

Caleb decided to be honest. "I don't know."

Her head shot up, anxiety and misery etched on her face.

"But, I have walked these hills before with Raechev, and I will plan a course. I know your life is shorter than ours, but we may know how you feel more than you think we do. One thing that has always helped is knowing that if Elohim wants you to do something, he'll let you know. Until then, enjoy life within the parameters of obedience to his laws. So, we are going to visit some ancient places that were used for sun worship and stop and enjoy ourselves from time to time because we don't exactly know what we're doing, okay?"

"But, there's a race," Mia argued.

"And there's only so much we can do. The fate of the world doesn't rest in our hands."

She gave him a measuring look.

"The only thing you are accountable for is whether or not you obey Elohim's laws and accept Yeshua as the Messiah. Then, if he issues you a personal command, you fulfill it. Has he issued you a personal command?"

Mia shook her head.

"One thing I learned from the prophets is that, knowing the future doesn't mean that you do anything to make that future occur. Too often, someone hears a word from ADONAI, and they race to make it happen, often messing up Elohim's plan because it was taken out of his timing. Do you understand?"

Mia nodded. "Knowing the future, doesn't mean you are the force to make it happen."

Caleb nodded in return. "Knowing the War of the Messiah is coming, doesn't mean that we do things to make it happen sooner... or later. We accept."

"We wait," she mused.

"We wait upon ADONAI." He smiled. "So relax. If there is anything we need to know, we will know. Elohim sends Rapha-el to speak with Tagas if a message needs to be delivered." He grinned from ear to ear. "Hey, hanging with us, you'll be ahead of all the mortals on what's going on in the spiritual realm."

She tilted her head to the side. "Why is it okay for an angel to speak with Tagas and not that prophet we saw in Mexico City?"

Caleb sighed. At least she was paying attention. "We were not gifted with the Holy Spirit as a unique connector to Elohim. Rapha-el has always been the chain of hierarchy for Tagas. Rapha-el rarely is given permission to speak to anyone else. It would be like in the Old Testament when God would speak to Samuel to give messages to his people. Samuel was chosen. Tagas was chosen. This was before the time of the Holy Spirit."

Mia squinted. "I can't imagine living without the Holy Spirit."

Caleb let out a long mournful breath. "I would give anything to know the experience."

She sat quietly, studying him, and he in return studied her. After several moments, she nestled down for the night, pushing her backpack towards her head as a pillow. "So, tomorrow, Palenque."

Caleb nodded and watched her fall asleep. The firelight flickered over her serene face. Without the world wariness, she looked like an innocent child, touched with womanly hints. Her pixie, urchin face housed voluminous, exotic eyes that covered the majority of her countenance, or at least, that's how it appeared. Her pointy chin emphasized her heart-shaped face and her button nose was adorably cute. Caleb had kept wanting to tap it throughout the day. She was so petite, so fragile, yet there was iron in her strength and will. She hadn't shown any fear at all that day, but she had ample reason to.

She began twitching, her eyes moving frantically back and forth beneath her closed eyelids. Her breathing staggered out of her, and her arms began flailing around.

"Let go of me! I won't. I won't do it!"

Caleb leapt across the cavern and woke her up. Slapping his hands off her, she shuffled far away from him and curled up in a frightened ball in a corner of the chamber. Her terrified eyes shook him. Slowly, she calmed her breathing. He felt helpless.

"Sorry."

Caleb shrugged.

"I, I thought you were someone else. It was dark. I couldn't see who it was."

He nodded, deciding not to push her.

She gulped, then ran her eyes over him. "Did I hurt your stitches?"

Caleb shook his head. She still seemed a bit frightened, and he didn't want to make any quick movements.

Her eyes darted around the room, not wanting to look at his silhouette. Eventually, she pushed away from the wall and returned to her sleeping position. "I'm going to get my sleep now. Thank you."

Caleb returned and slouched down against the opposing wall. He whispered, "Anytime."

*

Caleb's stomach was grumbling again. Maybe he should have saved some of the jaguar meat for breakfast, but Mia had thought they were closer to Palenque then what they were.

They broke out of the vegetation and stared at the Mayan ruins in front of them. Two grey stone structures rose majestically out of the jungle. One was a definite step pyramid with ten large steps leading to the temple chamber above. The other was a layer of grey stone chambers, grass covered terrain, then more grey chambers and steps to reveal another level of ancient city ruins with a lookout tower.

"Is that all that's left?" Caleb asked crestfallen. It had once been a magnificent city.

Some laughter jerked his attention to a group of tourists being led up the other side of the main ruins. A breeze blew against his exposed belly. Nervously, he pulled down on Mia's black tank top. "This is improper on me," he complained.

She threw him a cursory glance and shrugged. "It keeps your stitches clean, and it's the only shirt you got for now."

Caleb didn't appreciate the way some kids were pointing at him. Mia's black tank top was stretched tight across his chest and barely covered half his ribs. His torso hung out for the world to gape at, but she didn't seem to mind it very much. His shredded pants didn't help his appearance at all and hung low on his hips. "I look...."

"Gay," Mia murmured.

"Well, I'm not," Caleb fumed.

"You shouldn't let it bother you, Oh-Finely-Honed-Male-Specimen-of-Prowess."

"I can't be gay. I'm a redeemed Nephilim," he expounded.

Mia paused and actually looked at him. "What exactly does that mean anyway?"

Caleb looked down, then straight into her eyes. "It means your virtue is safe with me."

She looked down quickly and dug her boot into the dirt, building puffs of dirt that showered her well polished boots.

When she didn't say anything, Caleb continued. "It means I obey all of Elohim's laws which includes fidelity to my helpmate as well as the law that forbids a relationship with a mortal."

She continued to dig her boot in the dirt. Her face contemplative yet shielded. "And what of friendship?"

"Friendships are good, but if I were to ever copulate with a mortal, I would damn my soul, and Tagas would be sent to kill me."

She paused in her dirt kicking.

"Jordan, Raechev's husband, is Tagas, the Judge and Executioner of the Nephilim race. Nephilim refers to all half-breeds - half being mortal. My sister's husband would be sent to kill me. That would hurt Raechev too much, her husband killing her brother."

Mia continued looking down at her feet, but her tiny fists came up to rest on her lower exposed back.

"So you see, your virtue is safe. If I ever crossed the line with a mortal, I would die and crush my sister's heart."

A faint smile flitted over her face, and Caleb felt a stab of disappointment. She moved off in the direction of the Temple of the Skull. She paused, inspecting the sole surviving stucco decoration. A skull with jutting front teeth was carved in the midst of Mayan symbols. Caleb walked up beside her.

"Is there really anything that you need to know, or do you know everything about this place already? Because I'm not the curious kind. I'm not Sam or Stacey. I don't care about the history or the archeoastronomy."

"No, I just need to look around and see if something clicks with my knowledge, something a mortal wouldn't pick up. Do you want to walk along with me?"

Gazing at the skull, Mia shivered. She shook her head no.

"Is there anything you want to know?"

She shrugged. "Maybe just why. Why come here? What's the connection?"

He tugged her arm and led her around the main ancient ruins. "This was the palace." When they wound around to the other side. Mia paused. On this side, the ruins were more structures and less ruins. Countless steps led up to subterraneous chambers with three stone alters on top. He decided against telling her they were used for human sacrifice. He pointed up to the tower. "There shouldn't be a roof there. It was used for astronomy. The Mayans were deeply devoted."

The ghostly steps rose one-hundred and eighty feet above the ground. She stared unimpressed.

"Across the world, the sun god is often affiliated with the serpent god. Here at Palenque, the Mayans were able to construct the temple pyramid in a way that made the sun's shadow appear to be a snake moving down the staircase to the tomb below."

"Sounds creepy."

Caleb grinned. "Yes, creepy. The last rays of the sun end at the base of the pyramid where a relief is drawn of the God of the Underworld. It is at the winter solstice, that the temple's roof aligns with the sun perfectly. The birth of the sun and serpent god."

"And creepiness continues," she said unamused, as she strode up a few steps and plopped down. She laid back, propping herself up on her arms and welcomed the sun's warming rays.

Caleb followed her up. "Each serpent god's cult around the globe revolves around astronomy. The Mayans had constructed observatories to view stars and planets throughout the year. Their predictions on eclipses are still accurate." Gently he sat down near her, inspecting her upturned face. "They believed that human sacrifice could stop natural catastrophes."

"Poor sacrificees," she muttered.

"Not to them." He leaned in closer. "They believed that the soul of the sacrificed would rise to heaven and become an immortal star in the sky. It's similar to the Egyptian Opening of the Mouth Ritual."

"Am I to be impressed?" she asked disdainfully.

He watched her. The sapphire chunks were fading from her black hair. She seemed at peace with her time of waiting. Bathing in the sun's rays, she closed her eyes and uplifted her face. "It is a Nephilim hope. To be able to ascend to our heavenly ancestors' positions in heaven when our mortal clay is washed away."

Her eyes opened, and she gazed soulfully at him. She didn't speak. She just stared at him as if she could see deeply into his soul. He quirked a sarcastic smile. "You want to know the creepiest of the creepiest?"

She nodded silently.

"The Mayans predicted the end of the age to be December 23, 2012."

She shivered. "End of the age? I was told it was supposed to be the end of the world."

"No, it is actually the End of the Age. And it is. A new age has begun. Everything is changing. It is the End of the Age of the Sun-Serpent god. The age has begun when man will be restored, and some of YHVH's servants will mature to be lords, then kings, then sons of God within the spiritual realm. Full restoration to what they were created to be. The curse, and effects of the curse, all repented away. Things change in the Last Day. You should read your Bible more, Mia."

"So you think Loki will open the prison?"

Caleb shrugged. "It has been prophesied to happen... sometime." He turned searching eyes to her. "Do you not know who the sun and serpent god is?"

She shrugged. "You said the sun god had many names: Saturnalia, Ra, Molech, Mithras, etc, etc..." She paused, wrinkled her brow. "You said it was female... like the Morning Star, Venus, Luciferrie, Lucifer.... Wait... What?"

Caleb heard more chuckling as some tourists passed by. That was it. He yanked off Mia's black tank top. "You think about it."

"I don't think. Stacey and Sam think. It's not what I do."

Bewildered by her statement, he turned back to her. She was staring at his tattoo. The sapphires glittered brilliantly in the bright sunshine.

Mia studied the drawing of the Arc of the Covenant over Caleb's heart. It was a simple drawing, just the silhouette, but the line was fine and thin.... and not ink. "What is it made of?"

"Sapphires."

Her stare continued for quite some time. Caleb didn't know how long it lasted, but she eventually tired of it and returned to her sun bathing pose. Once again, her eyes closed him out.

He felt dismissed. That was annoying.

"I think I'll check things out now. Seems less crowded."

She barely nodded. "Yeah, you do that."

CHAPTER 3:

THE FEATHERED SERPENT SUN GOD

&

THE

MORNING STAR

STREET OF THE DEAD "CALLE DE LOS MUERTOS"

TEOTIHUACAN, MEXICO

TEOTIHUACAN, MEXICO
CONTINENT: NORTH AMERICA

Caleb exited his bath. It had been quite uncomfortable, not being allowed to get his stitches wet. Mia had made sure he promised to obey her instructions before entering the bathroom. He was just happy that they were able to buy him some new clothes at the hotel's lobby downstairs. They were in a touristy area, so it hadn't been difficult for him to find clothes for tall men.

Due to his weakness, Mia decided to rent a small car and drive to the next location, but Caleb was determined to return to hiking soon. He didn't want to run out of places to visit while they waited for orders on what to do next, and he greatly enjoyed backpacking through the jungle. Luckily, Mia was up for the challenge. He could see her as a great hunter in times gone by.

He threw on his new basics, beige slacks and a white tank top, and returned to the bedroom. He had been pleasantly surprised when Mia didn't balk at sharing the same room, but she did have her own bed. Really, what difference was there between a bedroom and a cave in the middle of the jungle? And again, her nightmares had awoken her in the middle of the night. Her eyes flying wide open to Caleb's intense, speculative gaze. She just turned over and went back to sleep. Caleb, however, had stayed up for hours contemplating what had given her the nightmares.

He swept out and found the black clad Mia munching on a breakfast of oranges and toast. She pushed three plates of food towards him. Pancakes, blueberry waffles, an omelet, and some fruit.

"Thought this might last you an hour or so."

Caleb grunted, settled down, and plowed into his food. Halfway through his meal, he realized she was staring at him. "What?"

She tilted her head to the side. "You know, I've always heard that food is the body's fuel, but until I met you, I was never able to visualize coal as food being tossed into a furnace."

Caleb raised his eyebrows. "Glad to be of service."

She shrugged and pulled out a newspaper and began to read. Once again, dismissing him. He was really beginning to hate that. His eyes roamed over her. Her sapphire dyed chunks in her hair had completely dissolved. All her hair was one flat color, black, with a strong blue sheen. His eyes trailed down her neck to her shoulder and then to the tattoo on her lower right arm. It was a scripture verse in a feminine-looking font. *But above all these things put on love, which is the bond of perfection.* On her left lower arm, written in ancient Hebrew symbols was *ADONAI is with you, mighty warrior.*

"Are these your only tattoos? Well, other than the butterfly?"

Mia shook her head. "I have two more on my back."

"Can I see them?" Caleb knew that he may be pushing, but people who got tattoos were saying something with them. Some were private, others for all to see. She stared at him for a while, contemplating his request, before turning her back to him.

She first lowered the top of her tank top. In a vertical rectangle, situated between her shoulder blades, and above her black bra strap, was another verse in feminine font. *...that their hearts may be encouraged, being knit together in love, and attaining to all riches of the full assurance of understanding, to the knowledge of the mystery of God, both of the Father and of Christ, in whom are hidden all the treasures of wisdom and knowledge.*

Shifting to the right, she covered the former area of her back, then pulled up the bottom of her top. In a horizontal pattern directly below her bra strap was another scripture verse in feminine font. *Finally, brethren, whatsoever things are true, whatsoever things are honest, whatsoever things are just, whatsoever things are pure, whatsoever things are lovely, whatsoever things are of good report; if there be any virtue, and if there be any praise, think on these things.*

"Thank you."

Mia quickly jerked down her tank top, refaced the table, and resumed reading the newspaper. Caleb felt dismissed again.

Dumping down the rest of his breakfast, Caleb was ready to move on. The hotel was luxurious, and he had enjoyed the last hot bath that he knew he was going to be getting for a long time. His excitement picked up as he began planning their trip in his head. He smirked. She wouldn't be able to dismiss him so easily in the wilds. What else would there be for her to pay attention to but him? They would take the car as far as the ancient city of Mexico, but from there on. It would just be them pitted against the jungle. Anticipation tingled down his spine.

Standing abruptly, he repacked his new backpack. "Lets get a move on."

Mia slowly rose from her seat, disconnected some electronic device that had been charging, and threw her backpack over her shoulder before standing and waiting for Caleb to finish. Flustered, he began moving quicker. Weren't females supposed to take longer to get ready?

Finally, he led her down to the lobby for the final checkout and ran his eyes over the grand chamber. It's walls were made of black and dark grey stones, the ceiling yawned above of ancient wooden oaks, and the floor was pieced together of dark grey stone slabs. Everywhere he looked, it was either dark brown wood or dark grey stone. It would be gloomy, but for the wide ancient sculptured windows that shone in brilliant desert sunlight.

Finished with necessities, he turned and found Mia waiting near the door. He led her down to their yellow bug with fushia fur interior. Without smiling, she crawled inside and waited for him to drive them to their next destination.

It was an odd feeling for Caleb, being in charge. Raechev had always been in charge. As much as he wished to have said that he had been in charge, now being with Mia, who quietly waited patiently to be led, he came to the realization that Raechev had asserted herself so much that he had pretty much always complied to her wishes. Grimacing, he blamed himself for not putting down his foot on forcing Raechev to kill Ishtar earlier. She could have met Tagas a lot earlier than she did. Maybe he would have found a helpmate himself.

Caleb shifted the car into gear and took off for the ancient city of Teotihuacan. He hoped Mia would be impressed.

"Today, my wee Mia..." He ignored the agitated stab of Mia's eyes. "We shall be visiting Teotihuacan - 'place of those who have the road of the gods.'"

She whipped her hair around her head. "Sounds arrogant. I suppose a Nephilim came up with the name?"

"No, it was named by the mortals in honor of the Nephilim who walked their roads," he replied sweetly. "This city is the foundation for all other Mesoamerican cities and religions."

"All affected by *evil* Nephilim?" She forced a smile onto her face.

Caleb curbed his anger by breathing steadily. "Not all." He turned and gave her a steady gaze. "Some, much worse."

Eventually, she returned his gaze, but only for a moment. She quickly looked back to the view outside the window, and they drove for miles without speaking.

"'Tis also called, 'the place where men became gods,'" he hinted.

Her brow scrunched. "As in... men receiving supernatural strength or knowledge by spirit possession?"

"Some." Caleb nodded. "Teotihuacan is unique. It is a mockery of Elohim's creation. The measurements of its structures are replicas of the earth's measurements. The roads are huge, to be trod by the gods of this earth, made by the copulation of divine beings and worthless dust-born mortals."

Mia raised an eyebrow and responded sarcastically, "Tell me how you really feel."

Caleb glanced quickly at her. "It is not how I feel, but how she feels."

"This elusive sun-serpent god who is actually a female?"

Caleb nodded. "Her worship required brutal human sacrifice regularly. It pleased her that Elohim's created mortals would choose to worship her, who had refused to bow her knee or serve them. In retaliation, she demanded their pathetic lives. She had them cut out their heart, while they still lived, and light it on fire. And they still worshiped her. She saw it as the ultimate victory against Elohim."

Mia rolled down the window. Her short hair whipped around her face.

Caleb looked oddly at her. It was devastatingly hot out.

"I'm cold," she murmured.

He looked down and saw her skin was goose-bumped. It was far from cold. He drove in silence, giving her time to prepare herself for what they would soon witness. It didn't take long before they drove into the tourist packed parking lot. As soon as they parked, she hopped out and grabbed several water bottles to pack into her backpack. Next, she grabbed some bags, that he didn't recognize, and stuffed those into her backpack also. As soon as he locked the car, she threw him a water bottle.

He led her away from the tall tour buses and out to the large road of the gods. Directly in front of them was the Temple of Quetzalcoatl. It loomed majestically above them and was decorated with images of the feathered serpent god, Quetzalcoatl. Caleb tugged Mia's arm to face the main, mile-long street. "Calle de los Muertos."

She shivered.

"Street of the Dead," Caleb translated.

She clasped her tiny hand around his lower arm. Caleb kept himself from jerking in surprise. Moving forward, he led her down the long grey street lined with temples, palaces and platforms. He pointed out the Palace of the Jaguars, the Palace of the Quetzal-butterfly, and the moon pyramid. Each one was a step pyramid, but all served different purposes. It was quite amazing. Out in the middle of the desert was a mile-long grey stone street lined with grey step pyramids. It was something one would only assume would appear in Egypt. But step pyramids did not begin in Egypt, but in Sumeria, the beginning of civilization.

Caleb pointed to the largest pyramid along the street. "That is the Pyramid of the Sun, the third largest pyramid in the world. Its base is only ten feet shorter on each side than the Great Pyramid of Cheops."

Mia released Caleb's arm and slowly spun in a circle. The Pyramid of the Moon was at the farthest end with its own square in front of it. The Pyramid of the Sun lined the Street of the Dead, and the Temple Pyramid of Quetzalcoatl sat at the other far end - the exact opposite end of the Pyramid of the Moon. "The sun, moon, and serpent pyramids are the largest."

"The serpent god studied astronomy and gave the gifts of knowledge to his priests. Each sun god across the world taught arcane knowledge of the universe and how to predict the movement of the stars, eclipses, and catastrophes to its priests whether they be Druids, Egyptians, Persians, or MesoAmericans."

"But aren't the pyramids in Egypt tombs? These seem to be temples," she asked confused.

Caleb grinned. "The pyramids were instruments for transforming the soul after death."

She shot him a confused look.

"For Nephilim. Not for mortals," he answered. "They were gateways to help the Nephilim spirits return to their seat in the heavenly dimensions that their fathers had given up to marry women and live on earth." He flicked a wayward strand of Mia's hair out of her face. She stepped back. Nervously, she grabbed for one of the small bags in her backpack and pulled out an apple and tossed it to Caleb. Caleb grinned. So the bags were full of stashed food for him. Continuing to smile, he bit into the apple. A sparkle danced in his eye.

"Why does the Temple of Quetzalcoatl disturb me so?"

"Many reasons." Caleb began moving down the street again, heading towards the Pyramid of the Moon.

"But wasn't Quetzalcoatl the pale-faced god who established the civilization of the MesoAmericans?" she asked, remembering their first trip to Tiahuanaco where a statue of Quetzalcoatl could be found. It had sun rays shooting from Quetzalcoatl's head like a crown.

"Quetzalcoatl has many attributes and nicknames, Mia." He had noticed that her dainty feet had caught up with him. He stopped, turned, and stared at her. "He was known to be the only sibling to survive the great flood and had to begin his race all over again. After visiting the underworld, he was able to mix his blood, via his penis, with the dusty bones of mortals, to create the race which had been lost. Some legends say he was born of a virgin. Some legends say he killed himself in remorse for a grievous sin. He symbolized death and resurrection."

Mia's child-like eyes soaked in all that he spoke.

"He was the god of the morning star, his twin brother being the evening star, Venus."

"But Venus is a female," Mia interjected.

Caleb barely paused before continuing, "As the morning star, he was called Tlahuizcalpantecuhtli 'Lord of the Star of the Dawn.'"

"Morning Star," Mia murmured.

Caleb nodded. "Mercury and Venus both have been dubbed the Morning Star and the Evening Star. Depends on the Earth and their placement. It changes." He turned around, taking in the great pyramids. "I should walk around a bit. See if I can learn anything."

"I.... I'll come." Mia decided hesitantly.

He waited till he felt her cool, itsy fingers close around his lower arm before moving off in the direction of the Moon Pyramid. When they neared the pyramid, he spied the opening to a tomb. He pointed towards it. "In there were found decapitated bodies of animals and mortals. Not for religious celebrations, but to celebrate state power. The Nephilim were announcing their sacred political power to rule the mortals. It was to cower mortals into submission."

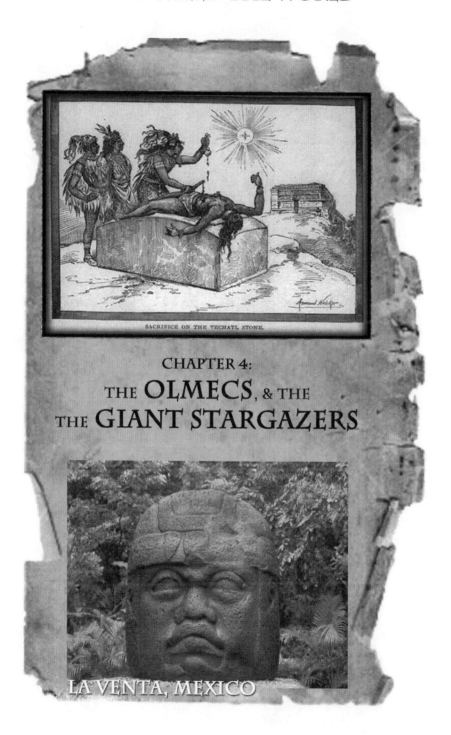

SACRIFICE ON THE TECHATL STONE.

CHAPTER 4:
THE OLMECS, & THE
THE GIANT STARGAZERS

LA VENTA, MEXICO

LA VENTA, MEXICO
CONTINENT: NORTH AMERICA

They had left the car at a rental and took off hiking. Mia made sure they stopped at a grocery store one more time before they left civilization. It wasn't long before the desolate silence of nature once again engulfed them. Caleb looked down at his arms. His skin had darkened considerably and rivaled Mia's. Walking behind her, he checked out her shoulders and was pleased to find them without a sunburn. Most people fried at the ancient city.

His eyes dropped to the large sapphire butterfly, tattooed directly above her low riding leather pants, that just topped her rounded cheeks. Caleb jerked his gaze away and decided to distract himself. "So how come you and Stacey are sisters, considering your Asian, and she's not?"

Caleb waited. After she refused to respond, he thought that maybe it was because the question was too personal. He decided to try again. "Did you like our last stop?"

Again, she did not answer.

He hated being ignored. If he wanted to travel alone, he would have. He loved company. That's why Raechev was such a blessing. Well that, and he had a purpose in life. He had family to love. Someone to take care of. His eyes roamed over Mia's slight build again.

Wincing, he continued on in silence. Waiting had just about killed him before. Waiting to see what Elohim would do. Waiting for the War of the Messiah. Waiting while his mother did despicable things. There wasn't one fond thing that he could remember before Jonah came to Nineveh. Afterwards, he was obsessed with discovering the Torah and watching Elohim interact with his chosen mortal race. Then came Raechev.

Caleb tried to shake his thoughts from his mind. This is why he liked to joke. He didn't want to think on his dark past, and he didn't want to mourn Raechev's abandonment. He tried talking to Mighty Mouse again. "What all did you buy at the grocery store?" When she didn't respond this time, his agitation rose to a new level.

Stomping around her, he placed himself in her way, forcing her to stop.

Surprised, she looked up at him. A white line fell from each of her ears and connected at a small box clipped to her tank top. She quickly pushed a large button on the box. "What?"

"I've been talking to you!"

Mia shrugged. "I was listening to music."

Caleb glared at the little box affixed to her tank top. "What is that?"

"I-Pod Shuffle."

Caleb posed menacingly, his elbows pointed out, his fists resting on his waist. "I'd like to talk."

One slender eyebrow rose on Mia's delicate face. She brushed past him and turned her music back on.

Caleb, deflated, growled in frustration. She had dismissed him again. He spun around and charged ahead of her. He wasn't going to watch her cute backside while she ignored him. He was the male. He would be in charge.

They trekked through the rocky desert clime two days before coming across some gently rolling hills covered in sparse vegetation. Mia kept her iBuds in her ears, and Caleb waited for her iPod to run out of juice. One day, it would.

It wasn't long before the air grew more humid and greenery increased. Within a few hours, they had passed a rock formation and spied a large waterfall cascading down a light grey cliff. Caleb sighed. He needed a bath. He whipped off his tank top and headed straight for the pool of water.

"Hey, you can't go in there," Mia shouted.

Caleb continued. "There are no piranhas in this area. It's fine."

"Stitches. You can't get your stitches wet," Mia reminded him.

He spun around. "I've been sweating, profusely, might I add. I don't see the difference."

She pointed to the pool. "That may have germs."

He growled at her, then shucked the rest of his clothes and dove in. He could hear her mutter under her breath, "Your infection."

The cool water rushed by Caleb's skin like a gentle caress. Ducking his head under the water, all the heat left his body. Why was so much heat trapped in the head, he wondered. He kept most of his body submerged until he felt completely cool and refreshed, then walked to the falls and played in the spray. He turned back, wondering where Mia was. She sat in her black leather trews and boots listening to music. She had to be scorching hot.

"Why don't you come in?"

"Not with you in there."

He saw her do a slight sniff of her person. She knew she had to smell rank like he had. "I told you, your virtue is safe with me."

She threw him a threatening look. "I will not let you see me naked."

"It's not like anything would happen anyway."

Her jaw dropped, and Caleb instantly regretted his choice of words. It sounded like he was insulting her desirability. "I mean... meant..." Ugh, he really didn't know how to get out of that one. "Look, I'll finish up and take a walk. You need a bath. Take one." He grimaced. Now, he just implied that she smelled. "Look, I'm going to go sunbathe and air dry up on top of the cliff. Yell down when I can return." Caleb waded around the bend and left her.

He climbed up the cliff and laid down. His muscles succumbed to the languorous spell of the sun as he drifted off to sleep.

*

"Okay!"

Caleb jerked awake. Grinding the sleepy dust from his eyes with his fists, he sat up to realize that he had just begun to sweat again. He quickly descended the cliff and donned his clothes before looking for Mia. He found her backpack and iPod instead. Curious as to what kind of music she listened to, he put in the iBuds and pushed play. When music didn't begin, he began inspecting the device to discover that the battery had already died. He stood, unamused, before replacing her iPod where he found it. He moved over to a jutting rock, sat down, and waited for her to return.

Within fifteen minutes, Mia, wearing her typical black garb, arrived, and popped in her iBuds. She smiled, pretending to listen to music and pointed in a direction, silently asking which way they were going. Her wet hair clung to her face, and her skin still glistened with water. Caleb snorted, turned, and led the way out.

Hours later, the sun had begun to set. They would need to start looking for somewhere to sleep. Caleb kept a look out for caves or any form of small village where they could bed down, but after two more hours, nothing had been found. They wandered a foot path that wound its way up rocky, dark cliffs fraught with shadowed crevices that sent shivers down Caleb's spine. He didn't like this place.

He turned back and noticed that Mia wasn't wearing her iBuds. Her face was pale in the moonlight, and her eyes didn't hide her unease. She sent him a look notifying him that she wasn't pleased with the path they were on.

Eventually, they came upon a crevice lit by burning candles which had been stuck into the crevices of a carved black stone. It sent chills racing over his skin. The stone was curved perfectly as a skull. Flaming candles had been placed in its mouth, nose, and eye sockets. But on top of the skull, was a pool of blood that flowed over the sides and down its face.

Mia inserted her petite hand into his. He squeezed it and led her away. He thought that one of them would have seen a spirit near an altar like that, but neither had.

The silence drove the eeriness to an extremely uncomfortable level.

"I don't know what to say to you."

Mia's quiet voice surprised Caleb. It was the first time she'd spoken since the pool. She'd thrown him apples and such throughout the day, but no words.

"Anything is fine."

Her hand fluttered in his, but he refused to release it. He would enjoy any form of company she was willing to grant.

"You've lived thousands of years. What could I possibly say that would be of interest to you?"

Caleb gazed down at her honest eyes and mused that she didn't know what a mystery she was to him. There were tons of things she could tell him that he didn't know. Of course, they'd be all about her. She was what piqued his interest.

"I feel dumb compared to you. Naive, ignorant if you will," she continued.

Caleb supposed that's how he felt compared to Loki and Nimrod. Or in comparison to fighting skills, when set beside all his Nephilim friends. "For a mortal, Mia. I believe you can understand me in ways that no other Nephilim could."

She huffed a half-laugh. "Thanks anyway, but I prefer blunt truth."

"That was the blunt truth." He couldn't help but tap her button nose. She jerked back and glared at him. Caleb tightened his hold on her hand. They were finally talking. It only took DAYS! Yet even in silence, he had learned a lot about her. And he liked what he found.

Beginning their walk down the opposite side of the mountain, a tiny village sparkled below. He didn't see any electrical lights, just lights from candles and campfires. It was a poor village, one still living in the past. It would make a good stop.

Mia tugged on his arm. "It's small and close to the altar."

Caleb shrugged, donning one of her common expressions. "I'm sure it'll be okay. Anyway, I want some meat, woman. I'm tired of apples and bean burritos."

He pulled her along to the base of the mountain and through the tiny village. Looking around, he had a sinking suspicion that there were no restaurants. His stomach growled loudly. Grunting, he began searching for the people. Maybe he could find someone who would let him pay them for a meal of meat.

They wandered the dirt packed streets and moved quickly between the clay huts in search of sustenance. Where was everyone? Finally, he spotted a huge bonfire down one of the streets leading out of the village. There were the townspeople. The short women wore cheery grins and stood about in their brightly colored skirts and white peasant blouses. They were barefoot, dirty, and had their hair braided into two braids on either side of their head. The hanging braids seemed almost comical under the conical shaped straw hats they wore. The women stood at the edge of the gathering watching their men dance half-clothed about the bonfire. The men wore loincloths, capes made of feathers, and masks resembling a snake.

"The feathered serpent," Mia whispered, now familiar with the sculptures of the MesoAmerican sun god.

Caleb's furrowed brow took in the activities and then began roving the bonfire's perimeter until he found what he was searching for. A young pre-pubescent girl stood alone, near an isolated hut. She ate a feast laid before her as she watched the festivities. He should take Mia and leave.

"Why is no one eating with the girl?" she whispered.

"Because she is the guest of honor," he explained.

"Like a Bat Mitzvah? A celebration of her becoming a woman?" she asked.

"No. Like a sacrifice to the feathered serpent."

Mia didn't speak for a long time, then she asked menacingly, "As a sexual sacrifice or a death sacrifice?"

Caleb was very aware that Satanists and other occultists practiced sexual sacrifice on children. They would plant themselves in a growing ministry or a church, claiming they had turned from their ways. They were willing participants in their own exorcisms. But then, they would wheedle their way into homes and molest the young children in a sexual sacrifice to their lord. In a way, Ishtar demanded the same thing when she forced each virgin to sacrifice her virginity at one of Ishtar's temples before being given in marriage. He shuddered, considering his own involvement in those situations. But here, this was not the case.

"She is selected, then pampered and fattened up for a year before accepting death. Then the village chooses another."

Mia blinked several times. "Why isn't she running away? Do you think I should bust her out later tonight?"

Caleb grimaced. "They often see it as an honor."

The color drained from Mia's face. "I don't think you should eat any meat here." She turned haunted eyes up to him. "What if it isn't wholly animal? And, and I vote that we find another village to sleep in. A cave would be preferable."

Experimentally, Caleb wrapped a protective arm around Mia's waist. She didn't buck him, so he squeezed a bit to console her before turning her and walking out of the village. He knew that she would not want to sleep anywhere near the town, but it was probably getting close to midnight already. He assumed an hour out of town would be good enough.

They walked in silence and watched the tropical forest yawn out in front of them. Tomorrow, they would return to the shady jungle and continue their search of the Olmecs. Mia didn't know they were searching, but he did. He just hadn't found anything yet. He didn't think it important to let her know that he was striking out on finding a statue or two.

"Are you looking for a cave?"

Caleb laughed. "Yes, I'm looking for a cave, but I want to make sure we're far enough away not to run into the village's shaman. They never live in the village, you know."

Mia grunted but kept walking. She stayed within his protective embrace.

They continued in silence for another forty minutes before Caleb found a small cave. Mia wasn't impressed.

"That's not a cave. It's a crevice."

"It has sides and a roof. It's a cave," Caleb argued.

Mia crossed her arms over her chest. "It's too small."

"It's protection. Now, stay here and build a fire. I'm going to go kill something for us to eat."

Mia grumbled under her breath, "Build a fire outside, cause there's no room inside."

Caleb hid his grin. She was grumbling, but she was still obeying. With the jungle so close, it didn't take him long to find a monkey to eat. He skinned it before returning, just in case she had qualms with eating monkeys. She was still grumbling when he spit the meat over the fire.

"It's gonna be freaking freezing in the crevice tonight. Probably won't sleep a wink."

Caleb snorted. He still preferred her grumbles to her pretend iPod listening.

Breaking out of her bad mood, she asked, "How tough's the meat? Should I tenderize it?" She poked at it. "I think I have something I could bludgeon it with."

Caleb leaned back against the rock wall and demurred, "I'm sure it will be fine. You'll probably only eat the tail anyway."

Mia looked over the meat circumspectly. "It had a tail?"

Caleb pushed his back into the still sun-warmed rock. His stitches had been itching for over a day now. He wanted them out. He tried gently shifting over them to ease the irritation.

"I know what you're doing, and you better stop," Mia accused.

Caleb opened his eyes to see her glaring at him over the stone grill. She knelt there, all surly with him as she cooked his meal. Raechev had never cooked him a meal. She never stooped to such women's work till she married Tagas and then it was too late. She had no skill, and Tagas refused to eat her food. Raechev wouldn't even have known what the word tenderize meant.... well, in connection to cooking.

"I'm just relaxing my muscles with the heat of the rocks."

Mia humphed, but didn't attack again. She kept checking the meat and cutting it down into smaller portions, so it would be cooked thoroughly. He could tell by the way she looked at the meat that she didn't trust keeping it a bit raw like some people liked their steak. Her decisions rolled across her face as she cooked. He could tell that she was going to make sure it was all well done before it hit either of their stomachs.

Mia quietly opened the discussion which had been thrashing about her head. "Why don't the government officials try to stop the sacrifices? Do they not know about them?"

"Oh, they know about them. American journalists don't report on it, but the officials in each of these countries know about it. In Chile, the courts hold 'compulsion by irresistible psychic forces' as legitimate grounds for murder and human sacrifice."

Mia's jaw dropped wide open.

"But to be fair, in Yunguyo, the Mayor did circulate a petition trying to have the lawyers investigate the occurrences more. Make sure spiritual forces were actually possessing people to enact such grievous crimes against humanity."

"Were they doing what they did here?" she questioned softly.

"No. In Peru, they paint the victim's face black and mutilate the body till death. They are sacrificed to the mountain gods." Caleb wondered if the mountain gods were spirits or Nephilim who continued on in their mortal bodies.

"Is it to mountain gods in Chile as well?"

Caleb shook his head. "The Mapuche Indians believe that earthquakes and droughts are punishments from their gods for not performing the required sacrifices. The courts don't even press charges against them when they sacrifice their own children... 'to appease the gods.'"

"And the shamans still drive this superstition?"

Caleb didn't know if it was fair to blame the shamans. Most people made their own choices. Then again, there were still Nephilim floating about.

"I wouldn't say it is all a result of shamans. All throughout Central and South America, tales of blood-sucking demons can be found. It is the shaman cults, who seek them out, driving wooden stakes through the hearts of those they feel responsible."

Overly large eyes rose from the sizzling meat. "Do Nephilim drink blood?"

"The fallen. It is one of Elohim's laws for us. We are never to drink the blood or eat the flesh of mortals."

She whispered, "And you are of the redeemed."

Caleb nodded.

Mia sat up, swiped her hands on her leather pants and motioned for him to take the meat he wanted.

"You know," Mia started, then paused, "you know, to me your blood was almost hotter than I could stand to touch. It reminded me of molten lava."

Caleb nodded. "As Sam put it, we are walking furnaces." He grinned at her and then tore into his food. He had waited too long for meat! He would hunt everyday for now on. No more apples and bean burritos. However, he found it very sweet that Mia had stocked up on food for him and tossed him snacks constantly throughout the day. Raechev had never taken care of him like a woman does for a man.

He paused.

His eyes roamed hungrily over Mia. She took care of him how he always thought his helpmate would. Curious.

Her brow was knit together. "You know I wish the Americans would know some of this stuff. I mean, you walk around Barnes and Noble and see all this occult stuff. Making it seem like Wiccans are nature, loving peaceful people, but when it comes right down to it, they're not. Wiccans are witches, and there is a good reason why witches have a bad name throughout history. I wish there was some bit of truth that could be told, or.... I don't know. Something that would wake people up to the deception."

Caleb popped up an eyebrow. "Well, the modern Book of Shadows does reference how the goddess Diana forced her followers to give her their 'due sacrifice.'" He waited for Mia to finish her monkey tail. He didn't want her losing her appetite. "Not that they told anyone what that 'due sacrifice' was."

Mia rubbed the grease from her chin. "What was the 'due sacrifice'?"

Caleb stared at her over the fire. "The young men who wanted to be her priests were castrated." Mia's face jerked in shock. "Then they had to run up to the top of a hill, holding their own severed genitalia. If they survived, without bleeding out, they tossed their dismembered piece onto the sacrificial fire burning at the base of her statue before having their wound sealed with pitch."

Mia gulped. Her eyes were ginormous. "Well, that's a bit different than the current Wiccans. Not much sacrifice there."

Caleb grinned. "Yeah, I'd say so." He threw the bones of his meal into the fire. "It's more out in the open down here, but these things happen in more places than you'd think."

Mia bit on her bottom lip as embers flew upward into the night sky. Caleb watched her. Her lips were quite plump. They had a seductive quality which underwrote her child-like pixie face. But it was her exotic black Asian eyes which always caught his attention. They seemed to eat her face up in comparison to how small the rest of her was.

She smoothed her hair back behind her ears. "You now, this is strange."

Caleb's eyebrows rose. "Strange?" He was thinking it was pleasant.

"Well," She threw her arms out to encompass their surroundings. "I'm used to cooking with Stacey for Sam while traveling. And I, the one to kill the food." She looked off to the side. "I guess it wouldn't be odd if you weren't a... male." She nibbled on her bottom lip and returned her eyes to him. "It's just so... weird."

Caleb did his best not to burst out laughing, but his grin was causing Mia's hackles to rise. "Uh, Mia. Men have been killing and providing the food for women for thousands of years. Then the women cook the food. It's quite normal. Natural even."

Her eyes took on a fiery cast, and she threw a pebble at him. "Out in the middle of nowhere and sleeping in a crevice?"

Caleb dodged her impotent missile and burst out laughing. "Yes, for thousands of years. Some would call them cavemen."

Fury rose through Mia's limbs, and she jumped to her feet and raced at him. "You're the caveman, old man!" She came flailing her martial arts tricks at him, but he easily battered them away while laughing at her. He wrestled her to the ground, rolling on top of her.

Suddenly, she froze.

Caleb froze.

That had been a very bad move. His mind drifted back to Mexico City and her screams not to touch her. He tried to move slowly off her, but she grabbed his tank top and yanked it up.

He froze again.

"Oh, my garsh. I'm so sorry. I forgot about your stitches."

Confused, Caleb looked down at her. Her eyes weren't terrified but concerned. She held up her fingers. His blood was on them. He looked down. Blood had seeped through his stitches.

Careful not to crush her, he got up slowly.

"Do you think we should wash it or just let it scab? I still have some water left."

Relief poured through Caleb. He had been so scared that the blossoming camaraderie had just been destroyed. He knew that she was beginning to trust him, and he didn't wish to damage that. "I think we should just let it scab. It was scabbed before. The stitches seem to have stayed intact."

Still on the ground, she was shaking her head back and forth. "I'm so sorry."

An overwhelming surge of protectiveness came over him. He stood there, looking down at her pixie face and frail body. Her eyes huge with concern for him. She hadn't froze for herself and her own fears which he knew had to be massive to give her nightmares every night, but because she was concerned for him. This was something new to him. Before, when he got wounded, Raechev had always acted like she was scared for him because he was so much weaker than her. It was always a constant reminder of how much stronger she was compared to him. He was the older, and yet Raechev had a way of making him feel diminished. He didn't want to have to admit it, but his sister saw the world through very selfish eyes. He guessed he was mostly to blame for that. But this tiny, urchin laid at his feet, and was concerned for him without a hint of selfishness.

Mia scooted up on one elbow. "Caleb? Are you alright?"

Caleb shook his head. "Yeah, yeah I am." He forced his eyes up and off her. "I, I just need a rest. I'm ready for bed. You?"

Mia nodded in agreement and stood to put out the fire. And Caleb was taken aback again. For all her black garbed, tattooed self, Mia quickly obeyed him. He had never really been obeyed before. Raechev always fought him, Ishtar always tried to control him, and Loki always knew more than he did.

She doused the fire and turned to him. "Ready?"

After he nodded, Mia headed into their crevice and holed up on the far side of the cave, giving him as much room as possible to lay down his massive frame. Which he did. She soon fell asleep, and Caleb rolled over to look upon her.

He was beginning to feel a connection with her. It was hard to explain since he knew very little about her. She almost seemed a different person, here, alone with him, rather than surrounded by her friends. But then, like he said, he didn't really know her, and she wasn't making it easy for him to get to know her. Oddly, her silence seemed to speak volumes about her, whereas some females who always talked, never really told you anything. Anything important. Did it ever matter what someone's favorite color was, what movies they liked, what their opinion was of everything in the world. Now that he'd met Mia, Caleb didn't think so.

He knew more about her than he knew about many females he'd known for centuries. Or maybe he just liked what he found in her more than what he'd seen in eons of acquaintances with other females.

With an unmotivated grace, she provided for his needs. Always getting him food. Taking care of his wounds. Not chastising him for crushing her, or fighting off a jaguar - Raechev would have complained about that. She allowed him to take care of her once she'd begun to trust him. Well, even before then. Not right away, but then again, he wasn't exactly human to her. But she had always taken care of his stomach. Not dramatically splurging on Betty Crocker home baked goodies, but with an efficient simplicity. Of course, he wouldn't mind being spoiled by huge farmer meals.

She was bluntly honest, not deceptive in the least. She had her secrets buried deep inside, but the way she hid them made him yearn to earn her respect enough for her to open up and share with him. When she did speak, she was honest. Mia didn't beat around the bush or make you wonder what she was hinting at. Coyness in females had never sat well with Caleb. She didn't flirt, play with a man's thoughts, or tease him with hope only to smash it to pieces when she began flirting with another.

Then there was her obedience. Simply, she was obedient. It

spoke more loudly about her than anything else. She didn't buck his authority much. She may pop one question from time to time or grumble, but when push came to shove, she obeyed, which seemed the most important. It was something that left Caleb relaxed and feeling respected. He didn't feel like he had to prove himself to her. Well, not since they had started the trip out alone together. But her understated submission affected him like nothing else ever had.

And then, there was her cute button nose. Playfully poking out under her dark Asian eyes. Situated in the most adorable face he'd ever seen.

Some of her hair had fallen over her face. He moved his hand and swept it behind her ear. She shifted. He froze. Her face moved towards the warmth of his hand. She scooted closer to him. Her arms reached and found his arm. She flipped over and nuzzled against it. Little by little, she slowly gravitated towards him till she was cuddled up beneath his shoulder. He slowly laid on his back, and she crawled up on top of him. A warm sensation nestled around his heart. A grin spread across his face as he remembered the complaints of Sam and Stacey because Mia always gravitated towards heat in her sleep. They were always complaining in the van while Mia just slept right through it.

He lifted his hand and stroked her silky, sable hair and then ran his fingers over her unbelievably soft skin. She burrowed further into him and he closed his eyes and soaked in her cool body temperature. With the heat of the jungle, she was cooler than the air. It was refreshing to his fevered skin.

*

When he awoke the next morning. She was gone. When he spotted her outside with some hand-picked edibles, she didn't speak to him. He decided not to say anything. She had been lying on top of him. She couldn't accuse him of doing anything. But he was feeling risky.

"You didn't awaken with nightmares last night."

Her hands stilled. She shrugged, then stood and walked to her backpack, putting her iBuds in her ears before plopping down to wait for him to be ready to leave.

He had a hankering to let her know that he knew her battery

was dead, but he decided to be chivalrous. He slurped down the berries she'd picked for him, grabbed his new backpack, and shot towards the jungle. Mia jumped to follow.

Caleb sauntered a long-legged stride. He could feel his body swaggering, and he grinned like a cheshire cat. He felt male. All male, baby.

Now, all he had to do was find the Olmec town.

He could hear Mia's huffing breaths behind him, and he slowed considerably. He had forgotten how short her legs were. He continued on, searching for landmarks that he might recognize, and delighted in the comfortable silence between them.

By the time they reached the remains of the Olmecs, dark storm clouds whirled and swung palm trees in unnatural ways.

Mia's eyes kept darting above.

Caleb kept pushing forward.

Within minutes, they reached the first statue. Mia froze, surprised.

A nine foot by nine foot, colossal stone head sat in front of them. The face looked negroid with a 1920s football helmet on. It was the strangest thing to see in the middle of the jungle in Central America.

Mia raised her hand, pointing at it. "African?"

Caleb nodded. He pulled her to another colossal head. This one had the same dimensions as the former sixty ton stone, but it was of a bearded Caucasoid with the same 1920s looking football helmet. He turned, bowing to her. "May I introduce the Olmecs."

A few sprinkles began to fall, so he took her arm and quickly guided her through the remaining colossal heads. They were all of proud Africans or bearded Caucasians.

She turned to him curiously. "How did they get so far from home?"

Caleb chuckled. "These are the star watchers. The Nephilim who left and sailed about teaching astronomy and bringing architectural triumphs to the indigenous peoples. You've been hearing about them for a long time. They came here, the same way the Tuatha de Danann went to Europe - 'in boats that moved without paddles.'"

She turned confused eyes to him.

"In boats carried by demons. It was a show of power to the

locals. Like they needed it being giants already."

"But I thought the ancient city..."

"Was the mecca for the Nephilim here in the Americas? To an extent. But the Olmecs were a bit different. They were set up more like a... monastery of sorts? Mortals would come seeking wisdom and aid. Only chosen wives were permitted to remain. It was an exclusive village, not a capitol. Eventually, the Nephilim passed, but the descendants still sought aid by them. Mortals would come and request knowledge from the descendants, and their ancestor's spirits would speak through their descendants."

"Oh," Mia paused, "like possession."

"Not like possession, actual possession. Or channeling"

Lightning crackled and thunder boomed above them. Mia threw another perturbed glance up to the threatening sky. "Uh, anything else we need here before finding shelter?"

Caleb smiled, grabbed her hand, and sprinted through the trees.

Stone altars and a grassed-over pyramid flew by as Caleb ran with Mia through the village. Finally, reed thatched huts came into view, but the heavens broke above them. Rain pounded down in a torrent that Caleb could barely see through. He knew that one of these buildings had to be open aired where they could stay till the storm passed.

He saw a small thatched building that acted as the museum's office, the shack where people could buy food which was thankfully still open, and finally an open shelter that wouldn't be closed up at night. Running inside, he laughed boisterously. He loved the rain. Mia sank down upon her knees, her chest heaving. He chided himself, he kept forgetting that she had short legs.

She opened her eyes and took in their temporary shelter. Images of feathered gods, serpent gods, feathered serpent gods and white bearded gods danced along the border. To the right was a short synopsis of how the mighty, giant bearded white gods were the legendary bringers of architecture and astronomy.

"So, is this it?" she asked panting.

Caleb frowned. Yes, this was it. It wasn't much, but it was intriguing, and it did meld everything together for her. She was getting an unique look at the ancestry of his people.

Where would he take her next? What would inspire her to

know more about him and possibly open herself up to him? He turned and faced south. Cuzco. He would take her to Cuzco, but first they'd have to pass over the Andes Mountains. Excitement coursed through his veins, igniting an unquenchable fire. Finally, a challenge.

CHAPTER 5:

CROSSING THE AMAZON

COLUMBIA, BRAZIL, PERU
CONTINENT: SOUTH AMERICA

Sweat coursed down Caleb's back and dripped into his eyes. Lifting his white tank top, he smeared the rivulets of salty perspiration from above his brows. He felt alive. Just him, the jungle, and Mia hacking their way through Elohim's grand creation. He was king of the world in this small patch of earth, surrounded only by Elohim's laws and the female who obediently and willingly met his needs in an unpretentious feminine way. Well, Mia couldn't meet all his needs according to Elohim's laws, but he still felt in control, trusted, respected, loved and valued.

They had cut their way through countless jungles, sometimes staying in caves, sometimes in small villages, and sometimes in large towns. His best guess was that they were somewhere in Columbia or Ecuador. The only negative coming from Mia was a disgruntled glance whenever she tried to check her cell phone. They rarely ever stayed any place where she could recharge the batteries, and then, they were often in remote areas that didn't receive coverage. Mostly, they were cut off from the world. A nagging concern surfaced intermittently, but Caleb shirked it off. Elohim would do, what Elohim would do. In the meantime, he would enjoy this small patch of heaven he'd been granted.

He turned behind him and gazed at Mia dutifully following him. He didn't think he'd find another female that suited him as much as she did. He didn't believe that any Nephilim females, who were still in their mortal bodies, hadn't already been selected as helpmates. So, there was really nothing for him to do but to enjoy Mia's company.

He pushed her hard. She didn't have the stamina or strength of Nephilim, but she trudged on like a warrior. He kept killing animals, and she kept cooking them. Once he'd discovered, that she really did sleep as dead to the world as Sam and Stacey complained, he'd picked her up and carried her through the jungles while she slept. He began to wonder if his strength really was at a normal mortal's because he didn't tire like she did, nor did he need as much sleep.

Each night he had picked up his speed and soon realized that he could run at a good pace without waking her. He did have the animal stealth that all Nephilim did. He had concocted a sling of sorts, like a hammock, that he tied over his shoulder. He would place her head near his heart, the steady beat seemed to soothe her, and wrapped her body around him within the sling. If she wasn't so short and petite, it wouldn't have worked, but it did. His body heat kept her wrapped around him and sleeping peacefully while miles swept by.

Overall, he was becoming quite attached to her, like a growth of sorts, on his body.... on his heart.

One night she had awoken while they traveled. Her eyes had flown open, fear making her heart pound. She quickly took in her surroundings, peeked out of the sling to see the jungle speeding by, then gave a long glare up to Caleb who was watching her closely. Eventually, she settled back into his body's warmth and fell back asleep. She never mentioned it. She never offered to hop into the sling before she fell asleep, nor did Caleb ever let her wake in the morning, sleeping in his personal hammock he'd built for her. They continued in their pretend world that it didn't occur, and Mia never mentioned that she never woke up where she fell asleep.

And much to Caleb's delight, Mia never woke with nightmares while wrapped around him. Without even trying, he gave her some peace.

Caleb stepped out of the jungle's dense growth and into the bright sunlight at the edge of a cliff. Elohim's creation was breathtaking. Down below him, an azure river carved its way through steep white cliffs be-speckled with jungle vegetation. They were practically standing amidst the clouds. He watched while the white billows moved, throwing the landscape into stark relief or demure shadows. Far ahead, he could see the snow peaked mountains of the Andes. It would be days before he reached those.

Mia grasped onto the back of his tank top and peered around him, trying to see the beauty past him. She gasped. Yes, it was that beautiful. Of all the places Caleb had traveled, he loved South America. He wanted to see her face, he could always return here, but he wouldn't always be able to see her face. Looking down, his heart clutched and a tenderness overwhelmed him. It wasn't often that a smile lit her features. She grinned up at him, her eyes shining, and laughter tore from her throat. Her laughter was dainty and feminine like her. It reminded him of a crystal creek gurgling joyfully over riverbed rocks. It made him think on stories of seductive pixies tempting mortals.

She patted his back, turned, and headed back into the jungle. Gazing time was over.

Straightening, he stretched. He was getting tired of walking, and it'd be pretty easy to find a downhill river to raft in. He decided it was time to canoe. He swung back into the jungle and decided to keep an eye out for somewhere he could get a boat.

By early afternoon, they had come across a village who was willing to let Caleb use their tools to build his own. Caleb gladly went to work, swinging the axe blade into the wood. Mia sat by waiting, patiently. She was actually kind of good at waiting. Perhaps, she had more experience with it than he thought she had. She didn't seem stressed, but relaxed, an ease that could be seen even from where he chopped down the tree. From time to time, she would reach down and pluck something near her feet, then continue on trying to sunbathe. Every once in a while, she'd pick her head up and ask if he wanted any help, but Caleb always shook his head. She returned to her previous activity, and let Caleb be the male. And Caleb appreciated that.

Raechev was helpful, but sometimes she was too helpful. Sometimes, a male just wanted to be and feel like a male. He wanted to provide, to take care of those he cared for. Females understood, it was called maternal instinct, and they craved to take care of their children as Elohim had created mothers to do. Well, it was the same with a male. It was a male instinct, and Caleb enjoyed being able to revel in it.

When one of the village children ran up and handed Mia a large, hot pink flower to put in her hair. She had giggled, thanked the child profusely, then did as instructed, even allowing the child to put the flower behind her ear for her. It was the first time Caleb had seen Mia in anything other than black. He liked it. He liked it a lot, and he swore that before their travels were over, he was going to see her dressed in a skirt... and in pink.

By late afternoon, he was filthy and covered in sweat, but feeling wonderful. He beckoned her over and pushed the canoe into the river. She climbed in and took her seat at the far end. He weighed a lot more than she did, but he had weighted the canoe to compensate for their extreme differences. He crawled in himself and pushed out.

Mia leaned forward and inspected the contents of the canoe. "Only one paddle?"

"Only one paddle," Caleb answered, while using that one paddle to help them down the river.

Mia squished her nose around a bit, then leaned back, propping her elbows up on the floor of the canoe. She popped one leg up and propped it over her other knee, bobbing the one leg up and done. Stretching her neck back to catch any stray warmth of sun, she settled in for a relaxing ride. "Don't you think we should at least call Sam or Stacey?"

Caleb watched the dappled sunlight play across her face as it broke through the jungle vegetation above them. The stream was narrow, only about ten feet wide. The water was a disturbing fluorescent green which would hide crocodiles or snakes from view, and the land was so close that any predator could easily hop into their birchbark vehicle. He would need to keep alert. The upside to the situation was that it was beautiful. The trees offered shade from the burning sun, and the jungle was so close that they could watch its beauty pass by.

"They are both with Nephilim that can fly fast enough to find us easily. Within twelve hours. Less time than it would take us to find a flight and fly to them in a plane. If they need us, they will find us."

"If they need us..," Mia mused.

Caleb gave her a scrutinizing look. They had mostly traveled in silence, but maybe this inactivity was going to open her lips. He almost chuckled. Perhaps, something of hers just always had to be moving. "If they need us."

Mia picked her face up and looked at him. "Thank you."

Caleb tried not to frown. "For what?"

"For... not needing me," she answered, then tilted her face back up to the sun.

Confused, Caleb tried to hide his perplexion. He needed her a great deal. He needed her to let him be the male. His need for her was growing. He had no clue as to what she was talking about. "Would you care to expound?"

She laughed, that happy twinkling sound again that nidgeled somewhere near his heart. "Sam needs me. She likes getting into trouble. She does it on purpose just to help her feel alive. So, I go on her trips with her as her protector. With you, I don't need to be in control or in charge in order to protect you. It's relaxing."

Caleb frowned. "And what of Stacey? Does she need you?"

Her head moved from one side to the other as if implying yes and no. "Stacey is a provider. She loves taking care of people. It's what makes her feel good, so I let her provide and pamper me, even if it irritates me." She gave Caleb a long measuring look. "I think you have that in common with her."

Caleb mused to himself. *And Mia identifies, and then gives people what they need.* "But doesn't Stacey need protecting too?"

Mia's bobbing leg paused. After a few moments, she answered, "Don't judge Stacey by her appearance."

Caleb thought that he shouldn't have judged Mia by her appearance.

"Stacey is... She is and isn't as naive and country bumpkinish as she appears to be. She is stronger than she looks, both emotionally and physically. She may not run towards what has hurt her to protect others, but she deals with her own past in her own way."

Caleb's brow creased. Unlike Mia, he thought. Mia ran towards what hurt her to protect others. That said a lot about Mia. Mia faced and dealt with things, and Stacey ran and hid from them. "Do you think she's dealing with it well?"

Mia chose not to speak for awhile. "One day, she'll have to face her past. Something will happen, and she will be forced to. It will stretch her in ways, she hasn't been stretched yet, and I fear it may change her forever. So I am fine with putting that off for as long as possible."

Since she was opening up, Caleb decided to ask a few questions. "Exactly, how are you and Stacey sisters."

"Adoption."

"You have a strong accent," Caleb probed.

"I was ten."

"From?"

"Laos."

"Did you grow up in an orphanage?"

Mia's steely eyes drove into him, chastising him for pushing.

Eventually, she whisked her hair back from her face and laid down. "I'm taking a nap."

And that was that, Caleb thought.

Late afternoon turned to sunset, sunset turned to twilight, and twilight turned to midnight. She persisted with her fake sleep. He allowed her pretense, but he had to admit that he enjoyed watching the colors of the sunset, twilight, and moon flicker over her as he paddled on.

By the next afternoon, they had left the mountains and entered the edge of the Amazon basin. He didn't mind this detour, it would keep them out of the northern volcanic region of the Andes. He steered them down the river, which primarily kept them heading in the same direction as their final destination.

Mia was awake and bobbing her leg again. "You know, my muscles are going to turn to mush."

Without sparing her a glance, Caleb continued paddling. "I like soft females."

Her leg stopped bobbing, and she shifted her knee to the side to look at his face, but he refused to meet the cautionary look she was throwing him. She snorted and resumed her normal posture.

Once hitting the river, they'd primarily fed on crocodile, and it was starting to bother Caleb's stomach. "I tell you what, I'll let you get the next croc."

Mia snorted inelegantly. "I'm a warrior, not stupid. I'll let you kill the crocs."

Caleb couldn't hide his grin. She didn't seem to like things that moved in water. She hid her fear well, but he could still see it.

The small river had turned into a much larger one. No vegetation gave them cover now, and Caleb could feel his shoulders burning. Mia also had a pleasant pink glow to her cheeks. The river had stretched out to about twenty feet across, and on land the trees were farther away. Only small bushes and marsh plants currently ran along the riverbeds. It kept them far from shade, but still gently flowing in the correct direction. Caleb looked up and noticed a few white clouds puffed above in the turquoise sky. Before, the small river had yielded a pleasant aroma of tropical flowers, now decaying flesh submerged in water assaulted their senses.

Caleb sniffed the air, wondering if the deaths were natural or from some chemical getting in the water. Out on the Amazon, it was kill or be killed, so it was possible that a bask of crocodiles had left some remains decomposing. He wiggled under his sweaty tank top. Deciding he'd prefer any breeze that may swirl by them, he yanked it off.

Mia sat up and stared at his chest. "I think those stitches can come out. I wouldn't want them to become permanent on you."

Caleb nodded and waited for her to slowly position herself in front of him. Wincing, she moved about, preparing to pull them out one by one. He felt a little bad knowing her body kept getting stiff with nothing to do for hours on end.

With each string she pulled out, Caleb focused not to show any form of pain. After she had a handful of bloody strings, she frowned, looking at the water. "It wouldn't be wise to toss them into the river, would it?"

Caleb grinned down at her. "Ah, there's nothing out there that I couldn't protect you from. Go ahead."

She gave him a measured look, letting him know that she wasn't exactly sure she fully believed that statement, before dumping them in the river.

"Maybe it'll bring us supper," Caleb joked.

Putting her dainty hand on his shoulder, she gently stood up and inched around him to get to the stitches on his back. Caleb smiled as he felt her tiny, cool fingertips gently tug each string out.

"Do you hear that?" Mia asked.

"Hear what?" Caleb asked back. She had stopped her delicate touches, and he wanted her to continue.

"Silence."

Caleb stilled to listen. No noises came from the jungle. It was an unnatural quiet - the type that alerted one that a predator was stalking its dinner, and the animals were hiding for their own protection.

"The land animals are quiet. It's probably a turf predator, not a surf one. Relax." Caleb, once again, paddled. After a minute had passed, he noticed she hadn't begun his stitch removal again and leaned back, putting his stitches more in her face. "They're done itching. It's definitely healed. It'll be good to have them all out." Her fingers still didn't move on his back.

Something jerked the canoe and ripples sped away. He could hear Mia gulp.

Caleb stiffened but didn't grow alarmed. "We'll just keep going. We probably just passed its path, and I'm not ready for supper yet. Are you?"

He couldn't hear Mia say anything, but he could imagine her shaking her head behind him.

"Why don't you finish up with the stitches?"

Without responding, Mia's frigid fingers once again began plucking out the strings, but he could tell that she was distracted now, and not taking pains to keep his pain down. He felt a little blood ooze from one of the holes.

"Mia, relax."

"The ripples are keeping pace with us."

He darted a look to the side. They were.

Mia's small hands grasped him where his love handles should have existed, the way he ate. He could feel her tensing into a combat position. Remembering Raechev, he knew women had a sixth sense when they were in danger. He wasn't quite willing to admit that they were in danger yet. It could just be another crocodile. A much larger crocodile, but one nonetheless.

"Shall we eat it for supper?" he joked.

"No."

He could tell by her voice, that she would not be joking about this... ever. "Okay, I'll look and see what it is, okay?"

"You are not going in there."

"I won't. I'll just stand."

"No, you will not! You will rock our canoe and tip us in," she snapped.

Mia was losing her cool, and she wasn't obeying anymore. *Interesting*, Caleb thought. He slowly moved his weight forward to get on the balls of his feet to stand up. Mia clung onto him, trying to force him to stay seated. Mia growled, "Caleb."

Choosing to defy her, he began to stand up. He just needed to know what it was. Her shaking arms were making him slightly imbalanced. She was going to be the one to capsize them if she wasn't careful. He'd do better if she wasn't clinging onto him, but down deep he liked it.

By the time he was fully standing, the ripples had circled in front of the canoe and were moving back to completely encircle them. His heart shuddered. He couldn't grow alarmed. It would scare Mia more. He had killed one of these before, but not one this large.

Stating calmly, Caleb informed Mia, "Here's the good news. I've killed one of these before."

Raising his arms to the side for better balance, he decided to attempt a look back at her. When he had stood, her hands had glided down his sweaty body and clenched onto the waistband of his khaki's, almost pulling them below modesty. She was staring, transfixed to the left where the ripples had been moving the most. Her face was pale.

"It's looking at me," she whispered.

Caleb's eyes shot to where she gazed. He couldn't see it from where he was. "Are you sure?"

"I can't see it, but I can feel it," she whispered again.

Caleb softened his voice, "Mia, stop looking at it. Look at me, Mia. Look at me."

Her bottom lip trembled. "I... I can't."

Crap. He knew these things had a mesmerizing stare. He had just never seen them ever need or choose to use it. And why had it chosen the smaller of the two meals? The canoe jerked; Caleb wobbled. It had hit the boat again. Mia scrambled to get a better grasp on Caleb, almost pulling him down into her lap, but he tightened his thigh muscles, refusing to go down.

He shot a look out over the water, plumbing its mud-murky depths. A barely distinguishable roll of yellow-brownish skin with black spots slinked below the surface of the water. Anaconda. He and Raechev had killed some that ranged from thirty-nine to fifty feet before, but this was even larger. If he didn't see it, he wouldn't believe it.

Below the water, it was curling its massive body in circles around and around the canoe, leaving no hope for them to make it to the shore. But with its length, they didn't stand a chance anyway. Caleb would have guessed the snake was at least a hundred feet, if not more. He'd rather fight ten Nephilim.

"Caleb?" a soft frightened voice called behind him.

"Yes?"

"I really enjoyed our time together," Mia whispered.

He stabbed a look behind him. The anaconda ricocheted the canoe, knocking him down. He fell back into Mia's lap. Deftly, she scrambled till every limb was wrapped around him. He shot a look out to where she stared. The snake's head had risen above the water and was keeping direct eye contact with her. He had to break their eye contact. It's reptilian black eyes kept its focus while gently swaying right and left, hypnotizing her.

It's head stood only six inches above the water. It slowly opened its mouth, as to test whether or not all of Mia would fit in one gulp. Jagged creme teeth surrounded the edge of its yellow jaws. Smaller rows of teeth continued back, throughout its entire head, before opening to the tunnel of its digestive track. Even Caleb had to shiver. As soon as it pounced, she was dead. And it would move lightning fast.

At least he was in the way. Maybe he could hold it back for awhile in time for her to escape.

A low seductive laugh echoed through the basin.

Goosebumps rose on Caleb's flesh.

"Clementia doesn't like your new playmate."

Clementia? Caleb's heart sank. Was she possessing the anaconda? Caleb's eyes darted towards the voice and spotted her. She looked exactly like Clementia with long flowing blonde hair and amethyst eyes, but her right breast had been cut off. An Amazon. They'd come upon the hidden kingdom of the Amazon women - the female Nephilim warrior tribe who refused to be submissive to males. Could things get any worse?

"Is she planning on killing her?" Caleb asked.

"I don't know, have you lain with her? Currently, as a snake goddess, Clementia wouldn't mind a human sacrifice," the unknown female Nephilim spoke.

"She's mortal. Of course, I haven't copulated with her," Caleb said placatingly. That was all he needed. A spurned, jealous female. Clementia had always wanted him, but he had never given in. Her constant lust for carnal pleasures always repulsed him. She had been more used than even his mother Ishtar. And then there had always been her decadent bingeing on mortal blood. It sickened him to watch the blood course down her chin and drip onto her breasts. Clementia had never given up, even negotiating with Loki in order to win Caleb. She'd made her last play on him at Nineveh, where Raechev had met Jordan.

"Not like you haven't lain with a mortal before, Caleb," the unknown female chided.

Caleb could feel Mia slightly withdraw from him. It bothered her that much? She was in mortal danger! And she began yielding him as her Nephilim shield when hearing he had done something he promised he had never done? He flinched. It was a trust issue. To Mia, the female's comment had just made him out to be a liar and untrustworthy. "That was before I became redeemed," he snarled, "You know it's forbidden to those who've repented."

"So you're saying, you don't have a softness for the Asian pixie?" the female mocked.

Caleb reached behind him and covered Mia's eyes. She jerked back. He whispered to her, "Stop looking at the snake. I need you to be alert. We're under attack. Great attack, worse than I'm sure you've ever seen. Now Mia, when I take my hand off your eyes, you must promise not to stare directly into the snake's eyes. Okay?"

He could feel her head move up and down, and he released her. He whispered, "Are you okay?" He felt her move slightly beneath him, unclasping her legs from around him. The glare of a dagger, that she unsheathed from her boots, relaxed him. Mia was back.

"If you don't mind, I'd rather have a go at the woman. I don't do snakes."

Caleb chuckled. "She's a Nephilim, Mia, an Amazon. You've heard of the infamous Amazons, haven't you?"

She whispered back, her breath tickling his ear, "Mmm, sounds like a challenge." She reached down and pulled another dagger out of her other boot and handed it to Caleb.

He grasped her hand tightly when she tried to hand him the weapon. It was the only reassuring nudge he could give. She used her whole body to squeeze him back. Inappropriately, he felt comforted. This was not a time to be less than battle wary.

Caleb used one hand to nudge Mia's legs and arms off him, so he could stand. He hadn't been able to think of a safe way out of this, so they would have to get out fighting. Slowly rocking the boat, Caleb stood.

Instantly, the anaconda lurched forward and smacked Caleb into the river with its nose. Water rushed over his vision. Blinded, Caleb thrust with his dagger, hoping he'd get lucky. Squeezed by unseen pressure, Caleb gasped, filling his lungs with water. His eyes popped open. Yellow-brownish snake skin twisted inches from his face.

Cords of steel around his chest shot him above the water line. Flailing, he saw Mia. She was wrapped in the anaconda's body. It choked her. He yelled, "Keep your mouth shut!"

Her bewildered eyes stabbed him. Her lips pressed into a harsh line. The snake tightened on her. She turned pale. It wrapped a fifth time around her frail body. Her eyes bulged. Her face tinted purple.

Caleb wrenched one hand out and stabbed the grossly enlarged snake. One coil loosened. Lightning fast, he swept a raking cut through six feet of snake flesh. It shifted, pained.

Caleb tossed his head back and glimpsed Mia. The snake had shifted her. Her face was blue. Horror spread through him, and anger like he'd never known exploded, vibrating his innermost being. He attacked with vengeance. Lacerated snake skin flew in chunks.

Mia'd been turned, her belly now facing the majority of the snake. Blood seeped through snake coils. Caleb couldn't tell whose blood it was. All he knew was that she needed air. Thrashing madly about, he did as much damage as possible.

Suddenly, the coils unsprung him, and he pitched into the river. Monstrous splashing blinded him when he rose. He couldn't see Mia. He grabbed the closest coil and stabbed, shredding its skin in raking slices.

Hisssssss.

Caleb pivoted and shot a look up. Mia clung to the snake's head, digging her dagger into its eye. The snake violently tossed its head, trying to dislodge her. She dug in harder, using her spare hand to grasp the snake's open mouth. Teeth pierced her flesh. The snake dove its tongue out and wrapped it around her eyes and head. She stabbed the other eye. The snake's tongue retrieved, then dodged around her neck, squeezing. Mia gagged. Her neck veins bulged. She lifted her arms and stabbed down hard into its skull. Its tongue loosened. Mia sliced into its brain, and it slumped. She wobbled in the air, then fell straight down into the river with the snake.

Caleb dove to recover her. The blood from the area would bring every carnivore in the area. Opening his eyes underwater was fruitless, everything was mud and blood. The snake convulsively twitched, constantly stirring up the mud, refusing to let it settle. Mia needed air, and she needed it now. He feared if he even got her to the surface Clementia or Kali would ambush a possession on her. She would need to take large gulps of air to survive this. It was a perfect strategy. While being crushed by the anaconda's coils, her mouth would fly wide open trying to breath, but they didn't know his Mia. She was tough and obedient. And currently, his.

The snake, moving uncontrollably in its death throes, whacked him hard from the side. He went down, flipped, and used the muddy bank to push himself back up. Where was Mia?

A tiny hand grabbed his arm. "Are you insane? Get out of the water!"

Reflexively, he hauled her into his arms and swam for the bank. She obediently wrapped her arms and legs around him. Sopping wet, he ran onto land, then sank to his knees. Mia unwrapped one leg, Caleb grabbed the other, forcing her to stop. Focusing on his breathing, he calmed his emotions. He had almost lost Mia.

She patted his back. "Um, where's your girlfriend?"

"Huh?"

"The Amazon with the seductive voice," she explained.

Caleb turned about, searching the embankments. Where was she, and who was she? These were both questions for them to focus on now. "Do you see Kali or Clementia's spirit?"

"Is that why you told me to keep my mouth shut?"

"It was a perfect ambush for possession, Mia," Caleb explained.

"Yes, it was," a seductive voice whispered.

Caleb jerked toward the voice and let Mia's leg go. He stood for another battle.

"Relax, I didn't come to fight you," the sultry blonde said as she ran her amethyst eyes over Caleb. She whipped a sardonic glance to Mia before returning her attention back to her prey.

"You look startling like Clementia," he accused.

The Amazon shrugged. "Are you going to hold that against me? After all, you did kill my pet. You owe me."

Caleb's head lowered, but his eyes targeted his enemy. He pushed Mia behind him. She resisted, but he was still stronger. "The anaconda?"

"Tzofi. We've been feeding her male Nephilim for a thousand

years."

Caleb squinted. Well, that would make sense with the snake's largess. Snakes continued to grow till they died. If it was eating Nephilim, the Nephilim flesh may have provided it with fleshly immortality. "And Clementia?"

"My sister is too blood thirsty for the locals. There really aren't that many tribes around here, and we couldn't have mortals searching for a mass murderer, now could we? We like anonymity. So, we told her to take Tzofi for a spin. No one around here gets suspicious of anacondas." The Amazon's eyes raked over Caleb's body. "You can call me Amynomene."

"The Blameless Defender," Caleb translated the meaning of her name.

"Yes, I'll let you live afterwards. You can go on your merry way."

Mia chirped in, "Great, we'll be on our way then."

Amynomene's eyes narrowed on Mia. "Amusing." She dragged a sardonic gaze back to Caleb. "Tell her to leave us."

Mia's face scrunched up in distaste. "Who do you think you are? You, you... uni-boob!"

Amynomene glanced down at her amputated breast. Amazons always cut off their right breast to assist them with the bow and arrow. "Warrior. All female warriors do so to increase their prowess in battle. It is a badge of honor."

Mia's lips twisted. "I am a warrior. And I can do so without chopping off my boobs!"

One eyebrow raised. Amynomene snorted, "There's nothing in your way to fight."

Mia's arms shot up, and covered her almost nonexistent rack. Her face flamed red.

Caleb wrapped a protective arm around Mia and inspected her bleeding hand that had been cut by the snake's teeth. Mia pulled away from him. He spoke to Amynomene, "You wouldn't do that to Clementia, and Mia's wounded. We'll be heading out now."

"I told Clementia she could watch," she purred. "Clementia agreed."

Mia's arms were still crossed over her chest. "Watch what?"

"Caleb pay me for killing my pet!" she screamed.

Mia jerked, surprised at the Amazon's reaction. "Well, gee,

how much does it cost?"

The Amazon turned negotiating eyes towards Caleb. "Ten years."

"In jail?" Mia asked.

Caleb tried to hide the truth. "Yes."

Amynomene clarified for Mia, "In my bed."

Caleb stiffened.

Mia stepped in front of Caleb, positioned for battle. "He's mine. Get your own hero."

A goofy grin broke across Caleb's face.

Amynomene snarled, "Over my dead body, mortal."

"Fine!" Mia raised her puny fists up to the Amazon's towering eight foot, four inch height. Amynomene was twice as tall as Mia with four times as many muscles.

Caleb grasped Mia around the waist, picking up her slight weight. She kicked out in frustration, trying to get back down to fight. Shaking his head, he easily moved her behind himself. "Pipe down, Mighty Mouse."

He turned back to the Amazon. "The answer is no."

Amynomene swiped her hair behind her shoulder. "Then die for your transgressions."

Without warning, her hair swipe had been to retrieve the sword attached to her back. She slung it sideways, arching for Caleb's still wounded chest. He leaned back, barely missing the point of its razor sharp edge. Hunched over, Mia ran between his legs, charged the Amazon, and staked her in the stomach, before jumping back to get out of her retaliatory swing.

Eyes wide open in shock, Amynomene clutched her profusely bleeding stomach. Caleb took the hilt of his dagger and smashed it against her temple. She fell to her knees, then fell face forwards.

Caleb grabbed Mia's uninjured hand, and ran her away from the land of the Amazons.

Mia looked back. "She's not dead, is she?"

"No, but she won't be following us for awhile. Come," Caleb swung her up onto his back. "We must get to a safe place for the night and let me nurse that wound."

She didn't say anything as she bobbed along, but he saw the blood splatter to the jungle floor as he sprinted. He had to get them out of there first. Mia was losing blood, and Amynomene or

Clementia, could bring in reinforcements at any time.

By nightfall, he had had found an excellent hideout. He dropped Mia to her feet. She wobbled and fell. She had been through much. He hoped the anaconda hadn't shattered her ribs and punctured any of her internal organs, but Caleb wasn't a doctor and didn't know how to check for that. He kneeled down and stretched out his palm. "Let me see your hand."

She put hers into his. There were two small teeth punctures that had gone straight through, but one very large one in the middle had to have moved one of her bones. He knew this was going to hurt. Closing his eyes and hoping Mia wouldn't hurt him, he began pushing her flesh, muscles, and bones around. She made no noise. He looked up. Her face was white. Quickly, lest he lose his resolve, he finished pushing the bones back where they were supposed to be. Then, he boiled some water, the best he could, to cleanse her wound from the river and jungle they'd passed through. He didn't have any antibiotics and could only pray to Elohim that she wouldn't become infected. Finally, as painlessly as possible, he stitched her up.

He didn't begin speaking till he was almost done. "I'm yours am I?"

Her pain laced eyes narrowed. Sweat beaded on her forehead. "Shut-up," she growled.

He couldn't hide his grin. "Your hero too, I remember."

She snarled, "Should have let her kill you. Have you to, for that matter."

"Your gallant Oh-Finely-Honed-Male-Specimen-of-Prowess," he teased.

She leaned forward and growled at him, then snatched her hand out of his. He lovingly nudged her leg with his own. She jerked up her knee and slammed her heel down on his calf, then pushed herself away, continuing to growl.

Smiling, he leaned forward and kissed her temple before standing up. "And your my little Mighty Mouse."

She pushed herself back into the corner to sulk. Her muttered grumbling echoed through the cavern.

Caleb popped his head out of the jungle to spy if anyone was staking them out. "Wish I could of thought to grab some of that anaconda meat for dinner tonight."

He turned back to Mia. She stuck her tongue out at him. Her sweat drenched hair clung to her face, which seemed even more puffy and swollen than when they had arrived. He didn't know if it was from pain or infection. Fear trembled throughout him. But there was nothing else he could do for it. "I'm going to find us food. You work on healing."

He caught and killed a few small animals. He didn't want her getting anemia too. Then he went in search of plants they could eat and luckily found some bananas. After heading back and cooking everything, he left her portion near her still grumbling personage and moved to the opposing side of the cavern to wait and watch.

She stared at him. Wouldn't even look at the food he'd provided.

"Do I need to feed you?" he asked.

A spark of fire leapt to her eyes, and she reached out her hand and ate. He watched her, enjoying the view, yet worrying about her hand. When she felt vulnerable, she became surly. Good to know.

When she finished, he moved back and knelt before her to rinse off her hand. Then returned to his dark corner and laid down. "I'm going to sleep. You coming?"

She started off a whole new volley of muttered grumblings and turned to look out the cave to the jungle. Caleb closed his eyes and waited.

Eventually, a small cool head was rested upon his shoulder. She curled her body towards him, laying her wounded hand on top of his scabbed-over chest.

He smiled.

*

The arctic winds cooled his brow, and the steep incline burned his muscles. His whole body was a mixture of extremes - fire and ice. Mia's short legs had given out on her a long time ago - whether from exhaustion from her injuries, the steep inclines, or the freezing weather, he didn't know. They had marched with determination up into the most beatific area of the Andes Mountains. Lava gurgling volcanoes heated some peaks, but the ice capped mountains were the constant in the terrain. Yet again, fire and ice.

The environment reminded him of Mia and himself. She was

cool in body temperature and demeanor while he had a burning furnace of a body. He never really saw himself as having a fiery temper, so maybe that connection didn't work, but Mia did have a fiery temper, and she could go from hot to cold with amazing swiftness. If nothing else, Caleb mused, their body temperatures were like fire and ice compared to each other.

Mia shivered. He wrapped his other arm around her, trying to give her more body heat. He wanted to kick himself. He kept forgetting that she was mortal. She didn't have a furnace temperature to keep herself warm in arctic climes. Each night, he and a fire kept her warm, but in the day, she struggled for as long as she could until he forced her into his cocoon. He shook his head. He hadn't even considered that all she had were tank tops and leather pants in her backpack.

He carried her slung around his chest like he carried her while she was sleeping. He strode about, without his tank top, hoping more of his body heat would warm her, but each day, she seemed more and more drained, more and more pale. It was only at night that she became decently warm. He knew he had to get her out of the snow and searched for the train that volleyed through the Andes. That was his goal, and it was just a bit beyond this last mountain peak.

The brown craggy cliffs loomed majestically around him, peeking out from snow enshrouded mounts. Clouds settled around his shoulders, and he pressed on. The azure sky enchanted his vision, but the glittering snow blinded him. The lack of oxygen made his lungs feel as if they were being scraped with glass.

Mia's teeth began to chatter. That was always a sign to him. He had to get her out of the cold. His eyes swung around, searching for a cave he could build a fire in. It didn't take long for him to spy one. His long lopes quickly carried him to their wind resistant shelter where he gently laid Mia down and ignited a fire.

Once the flames were modestly high, he stripped out of his trousers and helped Mia out of her shirt and pants. To use their body heat, he wrapped her around him, lying her on top of him, close to the fire. Then he spread out the only warm thing they had over themselves, an al paca fur blanket he'd bought in the last village they'd passed through. She shivered, but he could feel her skin warming even as she lay there.

He placed his arms around her and grasped her thigh to him. How long had they been traveling alone? His mind flew back over the weeks and collected enough data to surmise it'd been about six weeks or so. It should be about mid-December.

Mia wiggled a little, then relaxed into sleep. She had become ever more trusting through their trip. He kissed the top of her head, the only part he could reach. Lying back, he studied the cavern ceiling, then fell asleep.

*

He woke to a warm finger caressing his lips. He popped open his eyes to find Mia leaning over him. She still laid on his chest, but she had scooted up to gaze at him. A small smile played at the corners of her mouth.

"You rescued me from an anaconda," she murmured.

He half-smiled sardonically. "Yes, I did. It's about time you thanked me."

"You, you're my hero," she tentatively stated.

Caleb let out a masculine sigh of acceptance. "I suppose I am. You know, in the olden days, if someone saved a person's life, the rescued became their slave and companion till that debt was repaid. And with an anaconda..... I don't see that happening for the rest of your life, so I guess you're stuck with me."

Surprisingly, she didn't contradict him. Instead, she bit nervously on the bottom of her lip. "You're mine."

Caleb continued her steady gaze and answered solemnly, "I have no doubt that I am. Irrevocably."

She grinned impishly, then leaned down and kissed him. Her lips were warm, not chilled. Something he wouldn't have guessed since her fingers had always been cool even in hot climes. A shudder went through him, reminding him that he was playing with fire, but that was who they were, fire and ice. And it was only a kiss. He reached up and wrapped his whole palm around her dainty head, then took control and deepened the kiss. She submitted. Caleb's heart contracted. She tasted exactly as she smelled - fragile pink lotus petals surrounded in a sensual amber musk. Her lips were as soft as lotus petals and her skin as smooth as cashmere. A hunger he'd never known gripped him. He flipped her over. She giggled and stretched beneath him.

"Oh Caleb, I knew it would be like this," she crooned. She let his hands and kisses roam her body as she ran her fingertips enticingly along his scalp.

"I didn't, but I'm much pleased. Thought you'd be more of a tigress than a willing accomplice."

She sighed. "You know, I think I loved you the first time I saw you." She ruffled her hands though his hair. "Have been waiting ever since."

Caleb didn't know exactly what to say to that. It made no sense. He knew she hated him in the beginning. Well, was almost positive that she hated him. No, he was positive. And she wasn't happy that she got stuck with him for the girls' Nephilim match up. And then there was her yelling at him not to touch her because of whatever happened before he met her. Her words were confusing him, and he wanted to enjoy this moment, so he pushed himself back up and crushed his lips into hers, forcing her to stop talking. He let all his passion consume her in that kiss, and she giggled, wrapping her frail arms and legs around him.

She took his kiss more than returned it, but then she yanked his head up with her tiny fists balled into his hair. He stared down at her. She was utterly and shatteringly breaking his heart with her sex drowsed eyes and kiss swollen lips. She breathed heavily. "Caleb, Caleb look at me. It's me."

Breathing hard himself, he replied gravely, "Oh, I see you. I don't believe I've ever truly beheld you till now."

She laughed, then let his soul-searing impassioned lips come crushing back down for another haze inducing kiss.

Hours crept by. Caleb couldn't believe what was happening, nor how right it felt.

"I knew it was Ishtar's fault. Your mother always hated me."

Caleb froze.

He arched his back, lifting his head high above her. "Clementia!"

"What? I don't have a body anymore. Thor killed mine. This was the only way."

Mia's fearful, large eyes stared up at him. Caleb saw his dream wither before his eyes. Mia would never forgive him for this. He rolled off her, shaking his head in desperation. Rage consumed him.

Mia's body reached out for him, and he slapped it away. Grimacing, he hoped what he had to do wouldn't hurt Mia too much. He turned on his side and steeled himself.

Mia's wounded eyes, shot wide with fear. "No! No, not that way!" Mia's body flailed out as stiff as a board, her jaw dropping wide open. A loud gasp scratched deep in her lungs, then her body bowed backwards. An amethyst cloud-like entity seeped out of her mouth and hovered at the ceiling of the cavern.

"Mia?" Caleb's heart pounded. His blood rushed past his ears in deafening bursts. "Mia, *Ahuva. Chephtsiy-bahh.*" He caressed her face. "Come back to me."

Her eyelids fluttered open. She reached out her stitched hand towards him... then passed out.

Caleb gently picked up her wounded hand, and opened it to her palm to kiss it. He stared. The wound had grown angry and festered. Infection had set in. He glanced back up to Mia's face. He began lightly tapping her cheek, calling her name. She didn't wake. Suddenly, he realized why her skin had felt warm to him. Shock wracked him. How high was her fever? Was that why she was too weak to fight off a possession? Or even to awake with the arrival of a spirit? Caleb crawled over her, his light taps turned harder as understanding took hold.... she was unconscious.

Ahuva = Beloved
**Chephtsiy-bahh* = She is my desire.

CHAPTER 6

WINTER SOLSTICE

THE

BIRTH OF THE SUN-SERPENT GOD

KARNAK, EGYPT

KARNAK, EGYPT
CONTINENT: AFRICA

It was just after midnight, and the desert cold crept up John's spine. They had come to Karnak. He had been waiting forever to visit this great site, the most hallowed of places in Egypt, the designation of the center of the world. According to Egyptian myth, this was where Amun, the creator of the universe, first created himself and then all living beings. John shivered. Seker appeared pleased.

Most sites were not open at night, but tonight was different. Tonight, followers of Amun were allowed entree to worship Amun at his birth. The ceremonies enacted that night would be thousands of years old. At dawn, the winter solstice, which occurred on December 21st, would light up the Temple of Amun, the Egyptian god of the sun.

They stood on the eastern bank of the Nile. In ancient times, a ship would have been moored there to sail the idol down the Nile after sunset. Chanting was heard within the building, bringing John's attention back to the mighty structure before him. On either side of him, was a row of ram-headed sphinxes with small statues of the pharaoh between its paws, an image of the sun god Amun protecting his son, the pharaoh. Each sphinx was ten feet tall and sat on a seven foot dais. The graven images regally watched the precession of mortals entering the temple, threatening all who passed by. It was a warning, that they were entering a sacred place.

John couldn't count how many silent guardians there were as they passed amongst them, but the soaring brick walls of the first pylons loomed in front of him, beckoning him. As he continued onward, the chanting turned into hymn singing, and an uneasy crawling sensation encompassed his skin. Something didn't feel right.

Seker whispered reverentially, "The winter solstice, the birth of the sun, reminds us of life's renewal through death."

John trembled. Death was at death, not life.

They walked through the opening between the two pylons,

which acted primarily to keep the non-sacrosanct individuals in the courtyard and out of the holiest chambers. Once again, most of the walls were plain. The archways in and out of the smaller buildings were slightly wider at the base and smaller at the top, giving a grand impression that it was taller than what it was, an optical illusion to instill awe and wonder.

Seker pointed at a small plain building with three arches facing south. "That is the Shrine to Seti II. It has three chapels dedicated to Amon, his consort Mut, and their son Khonsu." He leaned in close, continuing to whisper, "Later I will show you the temple dedicated to Ptah, Sekhmet, and Nefertum. The statue of Sekhmet is glorious indeed. She was one of the most beautiful females to have ever existed." His eyes had taken on a dreamy quality, but he quickly cleared his throat and returned to their objective. "But not now. We don't want to miss any of the festivities."

Seker led John through the complex at Karnak. They passed by colonnades of papyrus-bud columns and ram-faced sphinxes, a kiosk where sacred boats waited to transport the spirits of the dead, and Osirid pillars. The chanting increased when they entered the Great Hypostyle Hall. It was a humbling room, where the worshipers of Amun had situated themselves. Every chamber was filled with colonnaded rows. There were no wide open spaces, and the soaring stone pillars blocked out the cold desert wind and steadied the flames of their candles.

John looked about himself. People from all races were there. He had half expected them to be all Egyptian, but he had been wrong. Each wore a semi-sheer fabric that hung from a golden neck torc. The robes were cinched at the waist by a gold rope. Most had on Egyptian styled wigs and cosmetics.

Seker leaned in and whispered, "All over the world this morn, pagans have gathered to worship in ancient ruins. They all worship the birth of the sun. Those here favor Egyptian pagan rites, but many go to Celtic grounds, Incan grounds, or wherever is closest, but most try to go to which culture they like the most."

Seker continued to lead him through the crumbling temple. As they passed more and more people, John noticed that the walls became more and more ancient. They were heading towards the oldest part. Seker pushed himself into a smaller chamber. It was completely black inside. John was pulled in after him.

Darkness surrounded him. John squinted but could see nothing, but he heard. Hymns were sung, and a flute played off to one corner. It seemed a bit strange to stand in a pitch black room with so many strangers about and not be able to see them. It sent a surge of anticipation tingling over his skin. Who would he see when the light revealed those around him? The harmonizing hymns only heightened the excitement, making him yearn for the gift which was to come - a bestowal of illumination and wisdom. This is what he had sought with his former girlfriend. This spiritual awe coming upon them and opening their eyes to truth and the world around them.

An hour crept by. John could tell the sun was coming. He could feel the awakening of the earth about him. The darkness lightened a fraction, and John could see an idol standing on the edge of the room, ensconced in an area for watching. It didn't look old, it appeared that someone had bought it for this occasion.

Physical bodies began to shift in the center of the room. John squinted. One by one, four torches were lit. The hymns stopped. The torches were positioned high, then slowly descended towards the floor.

Seker whispered in John's ear, "Symbolism. In Kore, the night-long vigil torchbearers descend into an underground shrine and bring up the image of their lord. Here, there is no underground chamber, so they just lower their torches and then raise them."

Indeed, the torches were being raised and something gold glittered. John moved about, trying to see between the people. He wanted to know what the image was. After stepping on two people's feet, he spotted it. It was small, and not what he expected. A wooden image of a child had five emblems of gold on it. The gold emblems were placed on its forehead, its two hands, and its two knees. All together, the gold reflected a five pointed star. The formation of the golden emblem, caught and held John's attention. It was a cross within a circle.

The torches went out. The room was thrown into darkness again.

Seker whispered, "We are in the womb, the most holy of holies."

Slowly, a sun's ray shot through the chamber. It's golden orange hue streaked through, illuminating some of the stone etched pillars.

The wooden image of the child was raised onto the the shoulders of the four torchbearers. They began a procession, carrying the child through the womb. When they came close, John leaned in to get a better look at the gold symbols. The cross was slightly twisted near the edges where it connected to the circle's ring. A shiver ran through John. It was a swastika.

Tambourines clanged, and flutes lilted over the assembled congregation. A happy hymn was begun and joined by everyone but him and Seker. The torchbearers carried the wooden idol, with a gold swastika inlaid upon its forehead, around the chamber seven times before carrying it out to the other congregants. Eventually, the torchbearers returned, and returned the image of the sun god to the center of the room.

"What, oh World Wise Ones, does this mystery imply?" a man in a dark green robe spoke from along one of the walls. His attire was similar to what a monk would wear.

John's eyes greedily roved over him and his fellow green robed monks who stood sentry on the perimeter of the womb chamber. Their hoods completely covered their faces, yet gold torcs could be seen glittering about their throats. The one who had spoken had gold-threaded Ogham script embroidered upon his robe. Though dressed like Druids, they had an emblem of a square and compass, a Freemason symbol, etched onto their robes, but inside the symbol was the image representing the Watchers, the angels who had originally left heaven to take up residence on earth.

John frowned. Taking a more scrutinizing inspection of the dark green robed sentries, he realized that most of them were taller than everyone present. He gulped. Were they mortals or Nephilim? All the mortals in the vicinity replied as one, "That today, at this hour, Kore - the Virgin Mother - has given birth to Aeo."

A loud celebratory noise was sounded throughout the temple, and then the sentries left. Everyone else followed them. John stayed where he was because Seker had, and Seker was staring at someone most intently. John flashed his eyes to Seker's curiosity. Samantha stood there, next to a tall man with burnished copper hair. Something seemed familiar about the man, but what was not familiar was his arm being about Samantha's waist. The man's long waves swept past his shoulders and rested on his bared chest. He was dressed for the ceremony too with a gold torc, a white leather kilt, and green teutonic tattoos circling his biceps. The only thing non-Celtic about him was a blackish stone bracelet with sapphire Hebrew symbols.

Samantha was gazing down at her fingers, which played about the man's belt. She seemed melancholy, but the slashing rising sun sent her sharp facial features into stark light and shadows emphasizing her unique bone structure. The man's eyes rested upon Seker.

No one spoke till the chamber had been emptied.

"Is it done?" the man asked.

John just couldn't get it out of his mind that he had seen this man before. He knew the man was somehow connected to the dig at Nineveh, but Thor and Nimrod had kept shoving needles in his face to make him pass out. He had to be one of the Nephilim. Was he protecting Samantha? Or was he staking his claim on her? And if he was, then he wasn't a redeemed Nephilim. John went cold. He really wished his friends were here.

"I have seen him," Seker answered.

"John?" Sam's face lit up.

The man turned questioning eyes upon Samantha, then glanced to John. He seemed to be measuring John, which made John feel even more vulnerable. The man squeezed his arm around Sam, kissed her temple, and gently commanded her, "Go and enjoy the feast while I talk to my old friend. Take the blond with you."

She beamed a smile up to him, then rushed over to take John by the hand and lead him out. When she let go of his arm, John turned to inspect her. Her eyes were haunted, and only a trace of a smile was hinted at.

VIRGIN MARY COPTIC ORTHODOX CHURCH ZEITOUN, CAIRO, EGYPT

Loki dragged his feet. Oh, how he hated this. After witnessing the pagan ritual at Karnak, Sam had demanded visiting a church as soon as possible. She said she had to cleanse herself from what she had just witnessed. Her dark chocolate hair was swept back into a tidy ponytail, and she wore a hot pink hoodie sweatshirt, jeans, and pink timberlines. She slanted him an annoyed glance, revealing the fact that she knew he was sulking. Her alluring eyes were more demure today since she wore no make-up, but it brought a quieter beauty upon her, more subtle, more innocent.

The towering white square structure ahead was softened by arched windows and a few rounded turrets. The coptic church had become famous in 1968 when the supposed Blessed Virgin Mother had come for the admiration and worship of her followers. She stayed for almost four years, appearing periodically to build her own hype. Pictures, video clips, and testimonies of healings had been taken and reported. One man had described the apparition as a radiating cloud of light that filled him with awe and wonder.

Loki snorted. Could have been any Nephilim spirit come to gloat and receive worship. Mortals were so quick to claim any supernatural entity they saw as coming from Elohim. It's what they wanted to believe. If it was pretty, then it was good. Didn't they read their own scriptures? Even Lucifere was recorded to be the most beautiful angel, and that doesn't quite match the mortal perception that beautiful supernatural entities are not evil. Lucifere masquerades as an angel of light. And healing? There's been occult healing since the beginning of time. And all it took was for a Nephilim spirit to reveal itself near a church, and everyone knelt and worshiped it. What a mockery to Elohim. Mortals worshiping the created in a house supposedly dedicated to worshiping only the Creator. Loki closed his eyes and quoted to himself. *The rest of mankind that were not killed by these plagues still did not repent of the work of their hands; they did not stop worshiping demons, and idols of gold, silver, bronze, stone and wood - idols that cannot see or hear or walk.* He had read the Book of Revelations so many times, he had memorized it.

Loki followed Sam into the church and jolted at the strong smell of incense. It was overpowering; however, the cathedral wasn't dark and gothic like most. White marble pillars held the arched ceiling aloft above dark wooden pews. The front portion, where the priests would stand, was glassed off with two paintings of the apparition of the Blessed Virgin Mary. The painting had a woman's body, but its face was of the bright cloud entity that had showed itself more than thirty years ago. Overall it was a bright, well-lit sanctuary because the white marble reflected the sun's light. The only colors, other than the dark pews, were the ones at the enclosed glass area.

Loki rambled behind Sam and sat down in a pew behind her. He thought it best not to bother her. She didn't bow her head. She just sat there looking, and he hoped she'd start her confessions or whatever she was planning on doing soon because he wanted to leave.

"It'll be Christmas soon," she whispered.

Loki rolled his eyes. *Mithramas.* "Aye, lass."

"We're supposed to be with family."

Loki's eyes narrowed. "Who be that? Stacey? Mia? Yer parents?"

She didn't speak. Instead, she leaned back and stared ahead of her.

Loki's gut reaction was that she was thinking of Nimrod.

"You don't like the Christian holidays do you?" She turned around and faced him. "You know, I don't believe you are a follower of God."

"Which god?" Loki asked.

"The fact that you have to ask that question proves the point that you do not recognize the one true God."

His eyelids lowered. "So *you* say."

"You know it wouldn't harm you to celebrate Christmas. It's a beautiful holiday. With ham, sweets, a beautifully decorated tree, lots of gifts, egg nog, and feasting. Lots and lots of feasting. Why don't you take me home, and we could celebrate with my family?" she pled. "We only go to one church service."

"'Depart from me, all ye who do iniquity, For ADONAI has heard the voice of my weeping.' Psalm 6:8. 'Then He will also say to those on His left, Depart from Me, accursed ones, in the eternal fire which has been prepared for the devil and his angels. Matthew 25:41'"

Sam's jaw dropped wide open. "Excuse me? You can't use those verses on me. Christmas is about the worshiping of Christ's birth."

"So *you* say," Loki demurred.

"So I say? Did you not witness that pagan ritual the other morn?" she spat.

"Aye, did *you*?" He sent her a measured look. "That ceremony has been practiced for thousands of years all over the world. Do ye really think it all to be a coincidence? For, dear Samantha, they were worshiping the birth of the sun god, the son of the Mother of God, the Queen of Heaven."

"That's not what's important. I'm thinking of Jesus when I celebrate. I can't help what those pagans do." She swung around to face the front and dismissed him.

"Ye are not to mind what the pagans do, nor are ye to enmesh any of their feasts and festivals with Elohim's. It is a sign that ye have fallen away from Truth."

Sam whipped around. "Are you calling me a pagan?"

"Samantha, take note of yer own scriptures. "'Concerning the coming of our Lord Jesus Christ and our being gathered to him, we ask you, brothers, not to become easily unsettled or alarmed by some prophecy, report, or letter supposed to have come from us, saying that the day of the Lord has already come. Don't let anyone deceive ye in any way, for (that day will not come) until the rebellion occurs and the man of lawlessness is revealed, the man doomed to destruction. He will oppose and will exalt himself over everything that is called God or is worshiped, so that he sets himself up in God's temple, proclaiming himself to be God. Don't you remember that when I was with ye I used to tell ye these things? And now ye know what is holding him back, so that he may be revealed at the proper time. For the secret power of lawlessness is already at work; but the one who now holds it back will continue to do so till he is taken out of the way. And then the lawless one will be revealed, whom the Lord Jesus will overthrow with the breath of his mouth and destroy by the splendor of his coming. The coming of the lawless one will be in accordance with the work of Satan displayed in all kinds of counterfeit miracles, signs and wonders, and in every sort of evil that deceives those who are perishing. They perish because they refused to love the truth and so be saved. For this reason Elohim sends them a powerful delusion so that they will believe the lie and so that all will be condemned who have not believed the truth but have delighted in wickedness.' 2 Thessalonians 2:1-12."

"What does that have to do with Christmas?" she snarled. "And anyway, the law is dead. The Bible says so."

Loki leaned forward. "Samantha, ye must start reading the Bible fer yourself and stop listening to man-made doctrines that deceive millions. Spiritual warfare is ALL about deception."

"God knows my heart! He knows I think of Him on Christmas," she ranted. "You preach legalism. Get thee behind me, Satan."

Loki's jaw tightened. He reached up and grabbed her ponytail, twisting it around his arm, pinning her in place. Then he leaned forward and whispered in her ear, "'Enter through the narrow gate; for the gate is wide and the way is broad that leads to destruction, and there are many who enter through it. For the gate is small and the way is narrow that leads to life, and there are few who find it. Beware of the false prophets, who come to you in sheep's clothing, but inwardly are ravenous wolves. You will know them by their fruits. Grapes are not gathered from thorn bushes nor figs from thistles, are they? So every good tree bears good fruit, but the bad tree bears bad fruit. A good tree cannot produce bad fruit, nor can a bad tree produce good fruit. Every tree that does not bear good fruit is cut down and thrown into the fire. So then, you will know them by their fruits. Not everyone who says to Me, 'Lord, Lord,' will enter the Kingdom of Heaven, but he who does the will of My Father who is in heaven will enter. Many will say to Me on that day, 'Lord, Lord, did we not prophesy in Your name, and in Your name cast out demons, and in Your name perform many miracles?' And then I will declare to them, 'I never knew you; DEPART FROM ME, YOU WHO PRACTICE LAWLESSNESS.' ' There will be weeping and grinding of teeth when you see Abraham and Isaac and Jacob and all the prophets in the Kingdom of God, but you yourselves being banished.'"

Tears streamed down Sam's cheeks. "Let go of me!"

He released her. She sat in silence, crying.

"Samantha, I did nay mean to harm ye, but to help ye. The Messianic Jews know when Yeshua was born. It was during the Feast of Tabernacles, the holy time set apart to celebrate when Elohim, in the form of Yehovah-Angel which is Yeshua's angelic form, came and dwelt amongst his people, guiding and instructing them on their daily lives, a constant communication between them. It is beautifully symbolic. The festival is done in memory of when their ancestors lived in the wilderness and Yehovah-Angel/Yeshua presented himself as a pillar of fire at night and a cloud by day.

The next time Yehovah presented himself to the Israelites during this festival was in the form of Yehovah-Man, his mortal form, revealing his name as Yeshua. And he, the Second Adam, the Son of Man, was born during the Feast of Tabernacles - when Elohim comes to dwell with His people to guide and teach them of His ways. Why would you want to celebrate his birth at the same time the pagans celebrate the birth of the sun god?"

Tears laced her voice. "What matters is in the heart."

He whispered, "What matters is obedience. Elohim hasn't changed, and he always demands obedience. 'Beware lest any man spoil you through philosophy and vain deceit, after the tradition of men, after the rudiments of the world, and not after Christ.'" He could hear her sniffles. "Ye like challenges Samantha, so I will give ye a challenge. You say that you are a follower of Yeshua, Jesus. Then I challenge ye to read all four gospels and write down each time Yeshua speaks of the law - whether we are to obey or dismiss it. Make two columns and separate them. Then we will talk. But first, you must do this. If you are a follower of Yeshua, then follow Yeshua, no one else. Not any disciple, or later apostle. Yeshua alone." He laid his hand gently on her shoulder. "Yeshua, himself, says that in the Last Day, his elect will be taught by the Father, not by man. Chuck the teachings and interpretations of man, Sam. Only believe the Word of God." He caressed her jaw. "Do we have a deal?"

Sam wiped the tears from her face and nodded in agreement. She folded both arms under her chest and slouched down in the pew. "At least you can't say anything about Easter."

Loki smiled, but chose not to say anything. He absolutely could speak against Easter. They hadn't even changed the name from the Celtic translation.

A bright white, glittering cloud settled beside him. *Loki.*

Isis.

Playing with mortals?

Was that you thirty years or so ago? he guessed.

Of course. I have always been denoted the Virgin Mother in Egypt. This is my home, and these are my people. They worship me still. You should hear the prayers they whisper to me. She giggled. *Do they pray to Elohim? Sometimes, but often they kneel in front of the Virgin and pray for MY aid.* She sighed. *I do miss direct adoration though. Watch this.*

"Don't...."

Isis' spirit slowly revealed itself visibly to mortals. Her glowing cloud-like form ethereally lit the area surrounding them.

Sam spun around, her eyes going huge. "Is, is that Nimrod?" she asked, her heart broken.

Loki grabbed her forearm and yanked her up. "No."

Isis cried bewildered, *Nimrod? Is Nimrod dead? It's not possible.*

Loki hauled Sam towards the front door of the cathedral. Yanking the door open, he shot one look behind him before pushing Sam out the door. Priests, nuns, and parishioners ran toward Isis' spirt, knelt down, and prayed, crying out to the Blessed Virgin Mother.

Loki's spirit clenched in disgust. He exited and slammed the door shut, yet Isis' giggles followed him.

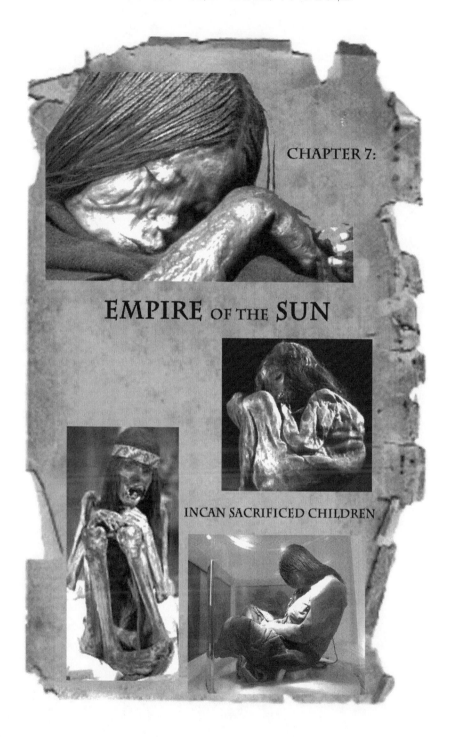

CHAPTER 7:

EMPIRE OF THE SUN

INCAN SACRIFICED CHILDREN

CUZCO, PERU
CONTINENT: SOUTH AMERICA

Caleb had held Mia throughout their long train ride to Cuzco. He had tried to buy tickets for the first class seats, but they had all been sold out. Instead, they had sat on metal benches amidst the peasants with their chickens, pigs, and farm animals. Mia never awoke.

Carrying Mia as a child in his arms, he stepped off the train and onto the outdoor platform. Below him lay the ancient city of Cuzco. Most modern buildings had swallowed up the old - entrenching and hiding its former grandness. Millions lived in the beige tenements that perfectly matched the beige, arid mountains surrounding it. To an airplane, the town would be camouflaged. The dry heat and lack of vegetation brought a thirst to Caleb's parched throat. He didn't understand why people would want to live in such an inhospitable location. Dust rose with each step he took, as he walked down the slope to the inhabited valley below.

The town was not pleasing to his eyes. Every building was made of yellowish beige bricks made from the mountains of which they matched. The roofs were tiled in the same dried mud. He felt like he was walking through a town made of dirt. He directly went to a herbal store and bought Elohim-made remedies for the infection, then quickly found the most opulent hotel he could. She would awake warm and well tended.

He headed toward Cuzco's central square where the city's famous cathedral and museums were located. Understanding tourism, he knew that there would be convenient transportation to Machu Picchu. He vowed that Mia would travel in as much luxury as could be afforded from here on out. Only two blocks away from the Plaza de Armas, the central square, he found the Hotel Monasterio - aptly named for what it used to be, a monastery built in 1592 on Incan foundations. The soaring building, even from the outside, was a romantic combination of the solemn colonial Jesuit seminary, the ancient Inca ruins, and modern luxuries for tourists. He was additionally pleased to learn of its unique bath butler service. He ordered one immediately set up for Mia.

His stomach grumbling, he turned away from the desk and headed towards their room. He nodded his head, knowing that Mia would like their accommodations when she awoke. The floor was made of dark grey stones made smooth and shiny with the passage of time. The walls were a mixture of Incan stone walls on the bottom and above, pink clay. Ginormous paintings of Christ's crucifixion loomed on every wall, one after another, adding to the solemnity of the hall. The paintings matched the pink clay walls and stones, blending in a romantic harmonious design. He followed the small stairway that led them to their room. A reddish pink carpet walkway rolled through the hall and up the stairs. On each step, on either side of the carpet, small candles had been lit, lighting the way to the massive dark wooden double doors that stood within a stone arch. Caleb hoisted Mia to his side and entered.

Hotel personnel were still bustling about preparing Mia's bath. Over twenty candles were lit near or around the ornate tub. Caleb watched as they poured in bath oils, salts, and lotus petals. He asked them to add extra salt to help Mia's body detox so it could function properly, the way Elohim had created it to function. Then he asked them to attain pure Frankincense and Rose oils and candles. They sent him baffled looks but did as asked. Caleb was ancient, and he knew the ancient ways were better than modern chemical ones.

Waiting for them to leave, he checked out the rest of the suite of rooms. The main room was made of grey stone with arched entrances. A fire burned in the hearth near a small wooden dining table and chairs. The clayish pink walls and Incan stone decor continued in the bedroom and bath and included the ceilings, which were held aloft by dark wooden beams. Sunlight gleamed from one window high above in the main room, but could not reach the windowless bedroom. He lowered Mia onto the dark four poster bed that had a clayish pink canopy. It was of Tudor design and centuries old. With no sunlight, he wouldn't need to close the canopy, but he did so anyway. He dropped their backpacks to the ground and went in search of a glass of water for her to take the herbs and vitamins.

By the time he was done getting the pills, teas, and broths down the unconscious Mia's throat, the maids were finished with the bath and had departed. He picked her up, unclothed her, and laid her in the steaming tub. Her hair curled around her ashen face, but she did not sweat. Caleb carefully cleansed her stitches and hand, vowing to do better the next time. After twenty minutes soaking in the salted water, sweat finally broke out on her flesh. Caleb heaved a sigh of gratefulness. He bent his head and cried.

He kept her in the bath for as long as he dared, then took her out, dried her off and swept her under the covers of the bed. He called down to the concierge desk for a sterilized needle and thread, then went about re-stitching the wound. Now that she had started sweating again. It would only be a matter of time.

When he had finished, he ordered three steak meals, a woman's night gown and a male's set of pajamas to be delivered and billed to the room. He wasn't used to ordering for females, so he explained Mia's petite form as best he could. Satisfied that, that would take awhile, he let out Mia's bath water, then began one of his own. He left out the bath salts and added extra bath oils instead. By the time he exited the tub, his orders had been delivered. He threw on the white pajama set that was blessedly the right size - good thing he had come to a five star hotel - before plowing through the three steak meals. When his stomach was content, he picked up a long, white, cotton nightgown and eased it over Mia's head and down her legs. With nothing else to do, Caleb pulled up a chair and sat, propping his legs up on the side of the bed.

By the time night had fallen, Caleb's limbs had grown stiff. He wanted to continue watching Mia. He didn't know how long he would have her. What if she never forgave him for what happened in the Andes? What if she no longer trusted him? His eyes kept drifting to the pillow on the empty side of the bed. That was where he wanted to be, but did he dare?

A shiver ran through Mia. Caleb sat up. Her lips trembled, but she continued to sweat. He knew that many people shivered when sweating from sickness. But was she getting better or worse? He leaned forward, flicked off the corner of the bed cover and saw that her night gown was soaked through, making it semi-transparent. Her shivers intensified. He threw the cover back over her and crawled into the other side of the bed. Pulling her into his embrace and tucking the covers securely around them, he slowly felt her shivers decrease as his body warmed her. He closed his eyes. Whether or not she forgave him would only be important if she survived.

"*Ahuva. Chephtsiy-bahh.*" He kissed the top of her head. "Come back to me."

*

Days passed before Caleb ventured out of the room. He had grown too restless. He left Mia a note telling her to order whatever she desired and that he would be back shortly. He scurried out, desperately needing to stretch his long legs and feel his muscles moving again. He traipsed the two blocks to the Plaza de Armas, the Plaza of Arms. It used to be the center of the Incan city and twice its current size. Caleb stood as if he could see the two worlds merged on top of each other. This great city had once been the capital of the Incan Empire, which ranged from the Andean mountains to the Pacific Ocean. It encompassed vast regions of today's Peru, Ecuador, Bolivia, Columbia, Chile and Argentina.

He closed his eyes and memory transported him back to 1296, when he and Raechev had first passed through this area. He remembered the Pasto, the Caras, the Pazaleo, the Puruha, the Canari, and the Palta - the most important clans of the Incas. The power amongst the peoples was somewhat balanced being a dual system of chieftains and land-holders that oversaw the crop cycles. The mountains had been full of terraced farming. Their main vegetables being maize, beans, squash, potatoes and quinoa. It was much greener back then compared to now. Back then, they had taken care of their land, building a vast and complex irrigation system. Now, those budding farmlands lay fallow, covered in dust.

Each area had its own local sacred *Huaca*, a large stone or megalith inhabited by a spirit who mentored the entire village. The *Huaca* was often carried into battle and sometimes married to a human fourteen year old girl. Caleb shivered at the memory. A child willingly given to a spirit. If it was a fallen angel, the child-bride was ravished and often died in childbirth. The Indians called these occurrences 'giant matings' because a giant would often be produced to fight for them during wars. In battle, a warrior would be possessed and fight another possessed warrior from the enemy territory. He remembered watching the Puruha sacrifice high-born virgins and the best llamas of sacred herds to their Huaca.

Every tribe partook of ancestor worship through the use of *conopas* - small stones carved into llamas passed down from one family to the next. They asked wisdom from the ancestor spirits residing in their family conopas. Across the empire, the king imposed the worship of Inti - the sun god - whom he was a descendant of. Like the Egyptian pharaoh and Japanese Emperor, he called himself the 'child of the sun' and received worship from his subjects.

Caleb opened his eyes and gazed at the plaza before him. Remnants of the Conquistador invasion lingered. They had reduced Cuzco's plaza, 'the heart of the puma,' in size by building some political buildings and two cathedrals. It was a Conquistador tradition to build a plaza of arms in the center of each conquered town. If under attack, the square was where arms would be passed out and military orders given while priests could bless the soldiers before going to kill the natives.

Today, Caleb had to stay on the sidewalk to not get hit by a car. The square had a road along its perimeter with a garden and benches in the center. He sprinted to the lawn, then slowed down to enjoy what was probably the only green spot in the entire town. Wide grey sidewalks crisscrossed the green square and centered on a fountain, which gurgled life sustaining water in the middle of a desert mountain range. As Caleb walked around, he noted that each grassy area included a landscaped symbol - a cross within a circle, the symbol of the sun god. His eyes lifted to the two Catholic cathedrals along the square's perimeter. Things had changed, yet stayed the same.

Turning away, he glimpsed a native woman wearing a straw hat and a short flaring full skirt. In her hands was a small stone llama, smoothed through centuries of family members caressing it to ask their ancestor spirits for guidance. Even here, in front of the symbols and cathedrals, Caleb felt out of time and place. Her lips moved but no words came out. She was praying to her ancestor. Something he had seen often in Asia, Africa, Europe, Australia and the Americas. All over the globe. The mixture, of the worship of the sun god and spirits - that resided in stones, had been practiced since before he was born and was continuing on.

He glanced to *La Caterdral*, where the palace of the Incas had once stood. It's beige stone walls rose in a perfect square. It appeared more of a fortress than a church. Two tower outlooks sat on each end of the structure's front. No fancy statues had been carved into its facade. Only pointy spirals rose along the top and the outlooks, and only one non-clay color, green, was painted over the three wooden doors.

He shifted his eyes to *La Compania*. It wasn't as old as *La Caterdral*, but its former structure had been created by the same bricks. It had been built in 1571 by the Jesuits during the reign of the last Incan emperor, but it had been destroyed in an earthquake in 1650. After a quick reconstruction, it had become one of the most beautiful cathedrals in South America. Its facade was sculpted majestically with soaring bell towers. Its wooden doors were a bluish green that blended more aesthetically. Domed ceilings could be seen in several places and a triple arched facade of a smaller portion was seen to the right. Caleb decided to enter this one.

It was pitch black inside. The only light came down from the dome and lit an impressive golden wall. The wall had so many gold frames of saints that Caleb couldn't tell who was who. There were pillars and arches and icons - all in gold. Is this what had happened to some of the Incan gold? Now used to glorify a sun god with another name? The entire back wall behind where the priests stood was covered in gold as well. The light reflected off the gold and lit the front part of the church, and caused everything else to be in silhouette. This is why it seemed pitch black where he stood. On the stage, priests rushed about arranging things for an upcoming event. Caleb shot a look to the hospitality table and noted the announcements for a midnight mass on Christmas Eve. Was it December 24th already?

He chose a seat near the back and sat. Grief overwhelmed him. It always came back to this. Again and again and again. Sometimes it looked hopeless. The enemy always winning. Masses of people willingly blinding themselves. The blind leading the blind. That was what grieved him the most. So many people out there really and truly thought that they were obeying Elohim, but deep down he knew the truth. They listened to what their pastors and elders said, the same thing that had been said and believed for over a thousand years. Tradition does not make truth. They practiced and believed things not in their Bible but what was decided by Graeco-Roman Catholic philosophers. But they were to follow Elohim's commands not the philosophies of man's interpretations.

Caleb had always thought that Elohim was very clear on what he wanted, and he wanted obedience.

His eyes feasted on all the gold before him, and he couldn't stop his mind from drifting back to Moshe. The Israelites had built a golden calf in Elohim's honor and prepared a celebration, declaring it a 'feast to the Lord.' Using a golden calf, the Egyptian idol of sun-worship, was not seen as fitting to Elohim. He was a jealous god and did not see the feast as truly being in his honor. The Egyptian sun god came from the womb of Isis, the ancient Egyptians' Virgin Mother.

From Caleb's perspective, it was the commingling worship of the sun god with Elohim which caused his chosen to abandon the true faith. The commingling caused them to fall away. Their desire to enjoy the pagan rituals and festivities overrode their obedience to Elohim. Each time a king erected sun worship, the nation was split, judged by a prophet, and forewarned of their impending captivity. Then they were dispersed throughout the world, kicked out of their Promised Land.

Caleb's heart became even more resolved when he remembered Loki's story. Those who had disobeyed Elohim and mingled sun worship with a feast to honor Elohim were condemned to wander the desert, never to enter the Promised Land, and were even blotted out of the Book of Life. It was a harsh lesson, but it served as a warning.

Caleb whispered under his breath, "They joined themselves also unto Baalpeor, and ate the sacrifices of the dead. Thus they provoked him to anger with their inventions: and the plague brake in upon them. Then stood up Phinehas, and executed judgment: and so the plague was stayed. And that was counted unto him for righteousness unto all generations for evermore. They angered him also at the waters of strife, so that it went ill with Moshe for their sakes: Because they provoked his spirit, so that he spake unadvisedly with his lips. They did not destroy the nations, concerning whom the LORD commanded them: But were mingled among the heathen, and learned their works. And they served their idols: which were a snare unto them. Yea, they sacrificed their sons and their daughters unto devils, And shed innocent blood, even the blood of their sons and of their daughters, whom they sacrificed unto the idols of Canaan: and the land was polluted with blood.

Thus were they defiled with their own works, and went a whoring with their own inventions. Therefore was the wrath of the LORD kindled against his people, insomuch that he abhorred his own inheritance. And he gave them into the hand of the heathen;"

Caleb felt his spirit squirm. His anger and grief at those who professed to worship Elohim had turned his innards to a cold stone chamber. He rose and walked out, passing through the garden and refusing to turn and look back. He knew. He didn't have to see. Behind him stood layers upon layers of sun worship masked in a great deception. The ancient occult symbol of the sun god, the Black Sun, as a cross within a circle, was everywhere: mixing the old and the new. He didn't glance at the woman still rubbing her *conopa*. Nor at the nun who rubbed a saint's pendant as she prayed to it - a dead mortal or a false god made saintly by Catholic means of joining all religions into one. It was the universal religion. Polytheism enmeshed with monotheism.

He wanted to return to Mia, but it hadn't been that long. He decided to be nice to his heart and allow a quick peek before heading out again. What he found was nothing different. She hadn't even moved while he was gone. After ordering in a very large lunch, he took off for the museums.

He didn't really think that he'd find anything he didn't already know, but he needed something to distract him. Anyway, weren't people supposed to wake up when you weren't expecting them? Then again, Mia probably wouldn't appreciate feeling like she'd been watched while she slept. He grimaced. She'd probably yell at him for bathing her himself. He'd bathed and bought her a new dry night gown each night. He'd have done it twice a day, but he was scared Mia would have deemed that unnecessary, then attack him on his motives.

Loping up the stairs, he turned onto the second level for the traveling exhibit and paused. Clear cases of sacrificed Incan children were on display. Solemnly, he walked up to the first case. A fifteen-year-old girl sat cross-legged, her back leaning against an unseen wall. Her head was rolled forward, and her hands rested peacefully in her lap. She was slightly plump and very healthy looking. Her skin was perfectly intact, and her shiny black hair hung in numerous braids. It was as if she'd just fallen asleep and no time had passed. Overall, she was lovely, for they only sacrificed beautiful virgins to the sun god.

Caleb glanced at the placard beside the case. Llullaillaco Maiden. Llullaillaco was a volcano in northern Argentina that soared twenty-two thousand feet above sea level. He read that the two other children in the museum room had been found with her. All three frozen mummies had begun as peasants and rose in social status when chosen to be sacrificed. They were underfed vegetarian peasants who were fattened up with maize and dried llama meat starting a year before their death. Then science was able to report, that in the final four months of their lives, the children began practice pilgrimages up the volcano from Cuzco, a 300 mile trek. Each child had died alone, or perhaps within eyesight of the frozen corpse of another. Although the scientists could not say exactly how the children were sacrificed, one of them had received a killing blow to the head. Caleb wondered if the child had fought against those who had led him to his death. One of them appeared to have been drugged and left to succumb to exposure. While the last of the five hundred year old mummies, an even younger boy, had been suffocated with a cloth tied so tightly around him that his ribs had been crushed and pelvis dislocated. Many more mummies remained on the volcano, but the tribal natives refused to allow any more be taken.

Turning to the next case, Caleb settled his eyes on a six year old girl. He read that in her digestive system, she had less traces of maize beer and coca leaves, the substance of cocaine. However, she had high concentrations of the drugs that alleviated symptoms of altitude sickness that were also used to mellow them into compliance. It was recorded that attractive peasant children were normally selected around the age of four and raised by priestesses. Some were offered as wives to nobles, some became priestesses, while others were sacrificed. Caleb leaned in to inspect more closely. The adorable child still had coca leaves on her lips and a slight indentation on her cheek from sleeping against her shirt. Her soft brown robe dropped down to red and brown striped sandals. The thin, cold air had preserved her better than the Egyptians had preserved their pharaohs. Blood was frozen in her heart, and all her internal organs were still fully intact. Caleb sighed as he read the last placard. According to Incan belief, the physically perfect children did not die, but became spirit guardians of their villages.

Caleb quickly looked around the rest of the museum, thankful that nothing had been preserved like this from his mother's days. He wouldn't want any sins of his to be made public like this. Near the door, he passed a young couple who were looking at the mummies. Their reverential faces and whispers of the holiness and beauty of the ancient religion made Caleb grit his teeth. How could anyone think human sacrifice was anything other than a travesty? He left them murmuring their respect and awe of the great ancient Incan religion, the Empire of the Sun.

He left the museum disgruntled and walked around searching for something else to do. He came across some native women selling colorful skirts, blouses and short sweaters. He quickly bought some for Mia, then decided to head back.

When he walked into the room, his heart jumped. He thought he saw her hand move, but he was wrong. Depression beginning to descend, he kicked their backpacks under the bed and ordered room service. He really needed her to wake-up. Being confronted with his past was something he couldn't handle alone.

He pulled up his normal chair, leaned over her, and moved some of her hair from her face. Reaching down to her frail hand, his thumb caressed her palm before completely covering it. She was a mixture of Snow White and Xena, Warrior Princess. She embodied contradictions. Her tough physical appearance hid the soft, giving heart beneath. He was glad he had been allowed the chance to get to know both sides of her, and he liked both of them.

Tiny, cool fingertips moved within his palm. Caleb looked up to her face. There was no change. "*Ahuva. Chephtsiy-bahh*," he whispered. "Come back to me."

Her tiny eyelids, covering her large exotic Asian eyes, fluttered, before slowly opening. She looked dazed, still feverish. "Caleb?"

Tears sprang to his eyes. "Yes."

"I'm parched."

Caleb jumped up and fetched her some water. After helping her to drink a whole glass, he laid her back down. Her eyes slowly moved around the romantic chambers. "Where are we?"

"Peru. Cuzco to be exact."

An unbelieving look fell over her features. "We walked all the way to Peru?"

Caleb felt like pointing out that he had done most of the

walking, but he wisely chose not to comment on that. "We took the train once you became feverish."

Her brow creased. She spoke perplexed, "Thanks?"

Caleb moved to sit on the bed next to her. "Do, do you remember anything?"

Her eyes fluttered closed again. "Like the anaconda or your girlfriend?"

He jumped up and moved to get some fruit left over from breakfast. "You need to eat. Eat something before you fall asleep again."

"No," she muttered.

"Yes." He brought her some strawberries and a banana. He thought the potassium would be good for her since she'd been sweating so much. He poked her in the side.

"Stop," she muttered.

"I'll keep poking till you eat," he asserted.

Her eyelids opened, her brows drew close together, then she reached up for the banana. Caleb smiled, then cut a piece of banana off and held it to her lips. Her hand dropped and her mouth opened. He fed her. She ate all he had given, then returned to sleep. Caleb didn't dare wake her for her nightly bath. She was too alert now, but he did hope that she would wake again before nightfall.

She didn't.

Worried that her memory would return when she awakened the second time, he stayed awake throughout the night keeping vigil. He wouldn't lay beside her. She no longer shivered from her fever. It had completely broken. She was now sleeping a healing sleep.

Around three in the morning, she sat up. Caleb watched her from the dining table in the main room. She looked around herself, down at her white nightgown, then up to meet Caleb's gaze.

"I'm wearing white."

Caleb fought his smile. "And you look like an angel." Or a bride.

She snorted. "I'm sure you've seen an angel. I look nothing of the like." She ran her hand through her mussed hair. Caleb couldn't tear his eyes away from her. "You have seen an angel, haven't you?"

Caleb shook his head. "I've seen Jordan turn into the appearance of an angel, but I've not seen a real one."

Mia grunted. "Where are my clothes?"

Caleb chose his words carefully, so he wouldn't lie. "They've been misplaced."

Mia shot him a knowing look. "Misplaced?"

"The backpacks," Caleb answered.

"And the clothes I was wearing here?" she implored.

Caleb stumbled. Now, that was a problem. "Misplaced."

Her eyes narrowed. "Well, what am I supposed to wear? I can't fight off your girlfriends in this."

Caleb didn't know if that was a barb or not. Standing, he walked over to the bed. "I bought you some clothes. Don't worry. Do you want something to eat? The hotel has twenty-four hour food service."

She chuckled. "You are always thinking about food. Okay, but I'm tired of being in bed. Order whatever."

Caleb nodded, then quickly ordered some fruits, breads, and juices to be delivered to the patio area outside. "Come. Let's get some fresh air."

Startled eyes turned to him. "In this?"

He turned a meaningful look to her. "Which is more modest than what you normally wear."

She bit her bottom lip, then scooted out of bed. The long white nightgown danced down her frail body and hid all her curves. She looked like an innocent child caught doing something naughty. When she hesitated a bit in her walk, he quickly discerned that she probably just realized that she wasn't wearing any underwear. He waited for her to make a comment. Apparently, she chose avoidance. She took a small step forward and faltered. Caleb rushed to her side and held her to him. Leaning her against him, so she could still walk, he led her out of the bedroom and into the inner courtyard. Her eyes soaked in the majestic and romantic beauty of their hotel. It was a meeting of three worlds they walked through: the ancient Incas, the Conquistadors, and modern luxuries.

The inner courtyard boasted a large gurgling fountain. It sat in the middle of a white flower garden, but it did have a large tree, and some small bushes and ferns as well. There were a few tables and benches, and Caleb saw that one table already had their food setting on it. They were fully enclosed by four two-storied walls, each composed of multiple pillared archways revealing open hallways leading to other rooms. The moonlight shone down, creating a mystical other-worldness.

Mia tugged Caleb so that they could walk through the grass. He could see her toes curl up to the dew covered greenery as she slowly made her way to the table with food. When they arrived, he helped her to sit down, then poured a glass of grapefruit juice for her. She ate in silence, taking in her surroundings. Her feet dangled like a child's from her seat.

Caleb respected her decision and remained silent.

When she finished, she leaned back. She kept her eyes averted from him. Caleb didn't take his eyes off her.

After an hour, she spoke, "You used my body to be with your girlfriend."

He tensed. He didn't like how she worded that. "I thought it was you."

Her eyes stayed averted. After a few minutes, she spoke again, "So I become willing, and you become unrighteous?"

Caleb sucked in his breath. "It was only kissing. I am forbidden to mate with a mortal."

She lowered her voice solemnly, chastising him, "It was more than kissing."

Caleb grimaced. He had wondered himself if he would have been able to stop. If he hadn't realized it wasn't Mia, he doubted he would have had that kind of self-control. "I stopped." He ran his hand through his hair. "As soon as I realized it wasn't really you, I stopped."

Her eyes turned to him. "So you wouldn't have stopped if you thought it was me?"

Caleb's heart stuttered. Her sleep drowsy eyes played havoc with his mind and her question left him paralyzed on how to honestly answer. "I would *like* to say that I would have had the strength to stop, but I am not sure. I've never been where I am now."

Her brow creased in confusion.

"I'm in love."

She averted her gaze again, her leg started swinging like a child.

Caleb waited.

By the time she found her voice, the light of a new day was just beginning to spread above them. "When I was ten, Stacey's dad found me. He bought me from a Laotian prostitution ring. My mother had been kidnapped for sex trafficking. She looked young, childlike, and was Asian. She was much desired."

Wrath filled Caleb. His blood boiled like it had never done before.

She whispered, "Stacey's family thought that they had rescued me before the same could be done to me." Her dainty, child-like chin dipped to her chest. "I try to imagine it was so."

They *thought* they'd rescued her before? In other words, they hadn't. She had been forced, before the age of ten, to be a prostitute. Vile emotions ripped through him, he bolted and dropped to his knees inches from her. Vomit spewed out of his mouth. His emotions had never made him physically ill before. He wiped the vomit from his lips and turned to face her. Tears streamed down her cheeks.

On his knees, he crawled to her and reached for her hand. She jerked it back.

"Don't. I know what you think of me now."

Horror shone from his eyes. "No. No, Mia. That wasn't because of you. It was because I couldn't stand the image of another man touching you. Hurting you."

Her wide eyes kept moving from one far away object to another. She wouldn't look at him. He could see the fight within her. She did, and she didn't believe him.

A rosy sunrise burst over the roof and lighted the courtyard. She shot him a look. Her eyes took over her whole face. The blinding light vanquished all shadows. They stared at each other. Her secrets bared to the bright light of day.

Jerking herself up, she began walking away. "At least that solves the first problem. I'm going back to bed. I want my strength back as soon as possible."

What, to fight him off? To be able to resist him? To ignore him like she had in the beginning of their travels with that accursed iPod? And what was the first problem? He racked his brain. Him desiring her? Not being able to stop himself from making love to her? Loving her? Exactly which 'problem' was she referring to because it had better not been his statement about him loving her. That was not a problem. It was a blessing. A blessing he was overjoyed to have felt. Blessed that Elohim had allowed him to know what it felt like to love someone romantically. And one day, he vowed he would know what it was like to make love to a woman he loved.

He bunched his fists in anger, hit the table, and shattered it.

CHAPTER 8:

CUZCO, PERU

INTIHUATANA STONE
OPENS VISION TO THE SPIRIT WORLD

MACHU PICCHU, PERU

Mia slept through most of the day. Her silent tears dampened her cheeks. Caleb could barely stand to gaze at her thusly.

When dusk fell, Mia awoke. Her eyelids slowly drifted open to find Caleb watching her. She turned immediately, so he couldn't see her face. Her stiff shoulders held, then she abruptly sat up.

"Mia, nothing's changed. Your confession doesn't alter how I feel."

She answered sternly, "Where are my clothes?"

"In a bag in the bathroom."

She stood and forcibly marched herself to the bathroom. Slamming the door, she disappeared. Caleb could hear her running water. Hear her get into the bath. Hear the water slosh about the tub. He closed his eyes, trying to keep the image of her in the bath out of his mind. It was torture.

Eventually, a loud gasp came from the bathroom. The door edged open to reveal a slick Mia modestly shielding herself. Her eyes shot daggers at him.

"What is this!"

"Clothes."

"It's, it's pink! A skirt!" she hissed.

"It's local." He held up his hands as if he was blameless, as if he couldn't easily have found something more befitting her normal garb at a five star hotel.

Growling at him, she slammed the door shut. Caleb got excited. He was going to finally see her in a skirt... and in pink. He'd been waiting days for this.

When she emerged, his heart clenched. Lightning shot from her eyes, but the pink sweater and white peasant blouse brought out her natural pink rosy skin. She seemed beautifully flushed. Kittenish even. The native skirt was so full it stood out from her body and fell just below the knees to reveal perfectly formed calves and dainty feet. Her skirt was patched together with various colors and hues of pinks ranging from the most vibrant fuchsias imaginable to the softest pastels on the color chart. He grinned from ear to ear.

She stomped to the table, dropped her nightgown, whirled to face him, then darted for the door. "Let's go."

Caleb had enjoyed the whirl. The skirt had slightly lifted and revealed a little more leg. "Where are we going?"

"Out. Out of the hotel. Off the premises."

Caleb grabbed his wallet. Whether or not she felt the same, to him this was their first date. He quickly caught up with her and tugged on her sleeve to slow her down. She had definitely gotten her energy back. After exiting the hotel, she made an immediate stop. In front of her sat three native women dressed in the local garb. All three wore sandals, the big flouncy bright multi-colored skirt, the white blouse, the matching sweater cardigan, and a matching hat. The hats were, simply, large pieces of matching fabric with fringe that sat limply on their heads. All three women grinned and nodded excitedly at Mia.

She gulped, "Thank you for not buying the hat."

He leaned down and whispered in her ear, "My pleasure."

She fidgeted from the tickling whisper then shot him a look. "Where to?"

Smiling, he tugged her towards the Plaza de Aramas. When they rounded the curve, her jaw dropped. It was truly breathtaking at night. The fountain and cathedrals were lit by golden lights making the beige structures turn to gold. The square appeared to be a garden set in the midst of a golden city. The Empire of the Sun was famous for its gold, and this square did history justice. A band played in the corner and couples strolled hand in hand. This was a South American custom. Single women and men would sit in the center of the square, meander about the garden, and check each other out. When a man favored a woman, he would approach her and ask her to take a stroll. The outskirts of the square were side-walked and reserved for these couples getting to know each other. No man was going to be approaching Mia. He grabbed her hand and headed for the perimeter sidewalk. An ancient romantic song began filtering around them, and Caleb's heart soared.

"Where are we going?"

"Here. We're coming here. It's a cultural tradition," he explained. This was where future married couples met and announced their intentions to the whole city. It was a primal thing. A man staking his claim on the woman of his choice. It made some men take note and press their own intentions, but Caleb would fight for Mia. No one would be bothering them. No men were allowed to interrupt the stroll. Other men weren't allowed to approach the woman until she returned to the garden, and if she never did, then a marriage was in the works. Caleb reached down and wrapped his arm around Mia, pulling her close into the side of his body.

"Aren't you getting hungry?"

Caleb sighed. "Can't you just enjoy a romantic stroll?"

Her eyes got large, and she bowed her head. "Romantic?"

He reached up and played with her hair. "Yes, romantic." She kept her head bowed. "Why don't you look up at the stars. They're brilliant up here in the Andes."

She tilted her face, it glowed with moonlight.

"Your head's blocking half my sight," she complained.

"Then gaze at me," he flirted.

And surprises of surprises, she did. He didn't know how long they walked. He just remembered walking, holding her in his arms, and getting lost in her eyes while soft music played and a cool breeze ruffled their hair. It seemed a lifetime.

Eventually, his stomach growled, and Mia giggled. "Time for food."

Reluctantly, he decided to agree with her. Keeping his arm around her, he led her to an outside cafe where he could keep their memory close to the most bonding experience of his life. It seemed odd that something so simple could have such a profound effect. They ordered and ate in silence. No words needed to be said. He just gazed at her, and she mostly returned the gaze, when she wasn't blushing or looking around her.

When the band began playing dance tunes, he whipped her back out to the garden and swung her around in his arms. Her laughter rose to the heavens and sent his spirit spiraling to catch up. Her warrior abilities enabled her to learn the Peruvian dances quickly, and they moved about with an uncanny elegance as if they'd been dancing together for centuries. Her smile enveloped her face and made her eyes twinkle. She was a different person in his arms tonight. Jubilant, carefree, and - if he wasn't mistaken - in love. Something inside him shifted. A fear grew, a fear of losing her. It cut like shards through his lungs. Terror gripped him. He couldn't lose her. He couldn't lose this.

He twirled her in his arms and another burst of laughter ripped through her. This was exactly how he wanted to always think of her. In this moment, at this time.

When she began to grow tired, he spun her around and headed her back to the hotel. When they arrived in their bedroom, an awkwardness descended. She began nervously fidgeting, then quickly announced that she would change into her nightgown.

Caleb disrobed and hopped into bed. He didn't want a fight on who would or would not be sleeping in the bed. She appeared, the long white nightgown flowing gently over her curves as she walked towards him. She paused just outside the bedroom, deciding. "We're only sleeping."

"Sleeping," Caleb agreed. He waited, watching her watch him. Taking a deep breath, she hastened into bed and pulled the sheets up to her chin. She laid flat on her back as far away from him as possible.

"You know, you gravitate towards heat when you sleep," he reminded her.

"I know."

He glanced at her tiny fists balled up at the edge of the sheet below her chin. Her knuckles were white. "We've slept together countless times."

"I know." Her fingers didn't loosen.

"You even laid on top of me and nothing happened," he emphasized.

"I know!" she gritted out of clenched teeth.

Caleb turned onto his side and looked down at her. Using one finger, he caressed her face. "Just one kiss."

"No."

"One close mouthed kiss? Like siblings. A generic farewell before night separates two people," he begged.

She shot him a disgruntled look.

He leaned down for his goodnight kiss, taking her silence as acceptance. A petite, cool finger was shoved against his lips. "No. I will not risk you damning your soul."

Keeping eye contact, he seductively kissed her finger. She didn't loosen her arm. Resigning, he flopped back on the bed and ran his hand through his hair. He threw off the hot covers that trapped his body heat inside and tried to fall asleep.

His mind began wandering over his life, his regrets, and Mia. He was only one generation from aging. He'd be considered mortal if he was only one generation down, and he would have been allowed to have Mia in the way he wanted her - as his helpmate. Just one generation away. It seemed so close yet so out of reach. But then, he would have died thousands of years before Mia was born. He would never have found Elohim in a short mortal's lifespan with Ishtar as a mother, and he would have died a very sad and alone male. He had never been happy in those first few centuries of his life. It was Elohim, then Raechev, which had granted him his true first glimpses of peace and purpose. Caleb had to retract one statement. His father had made him happy. A deep, soul wrenching anguished sigh ripped through him. He would just have to take the good with the bad. Some things couldn't be changed, just accepted - his past and Mia. She was a blessing, and he would gratefully accept any form of affection and time she would give him. They had so much in common that she didn't even know. He understood her better than she realized, and she understood him more than any other person ever had... or ever could.

Mia gravitated towards him. She rested her tiny head on his chest and molded herself along his side. He smiled. "Ahuva. Beloved."

A cool finger ran over the sapphire tattoo. Caleb jolted. She was still awake? Her cool finger slowly moved down and became her whole hand. She lovingly ran her hand down his six pack then to the opposite side of his waist. He swiftly inhaled as her hand and fingers continued their exploration along his chest before returning to a place near her chin.

She slightly turned her head and kissed his chest. She whispered, "Goodnight."

Caleb wanted to do something in return, but he knew she wouldn't let him. He decided to say something instead. "You are not the only one who hides from their past."

"Okay," she said in a tone commanding him to continue.

"I, I did many things before I became redeemed," he hedged.

"I can imagine," she replied sardonically.

"I've never been in love. Never even had a relationship before," he admitted.

"You were a one-night-stand kind of guy?" she asked.

"Well, that's all that was needed."

"What do you mean, 'that was all that was needed.'" Her voice at first hard, became soft. She whispered sympathetically, "Were you used?"

"No, my mother was the self-proclaimed goddess Ishtar. She was the goddess of love, sex, fertility and war. She mandated that all virgins sacrifice their virginity to strangers at her temples before being united in marriage."

Mia didn't speak for a long time. Then she asked in a masked voice, "How did that affect you?"

"Well, many of the mortals were unkind, hurried and dirty. I at least gave them pleasure and eased their breach."

Mia stilled to a statue.

Suddenly, she jerked upright in bed. "Let me get this straight. You did nothing to stop the forced prostitution of innocents. And even joined in?"

Caleb sat up. "Mia, it wasn't prostitution." He reached his hand out and placed it on her back.

She lurched off the bed, spun around, and spat at him, "Of course, it was prostitution. Or rape. Which word would you prefer?"

"They were willing."

"They were forced! Child prostitutes are not willing; they are forced!" she screamed.

"Mia!" How could he get her to understand what it was like back then. It was thousands of years ago. Things were so different. He always knew it wasn't right, but he fully believed that he was helping them by not hurting them. He jumped off the bed and reached out to her.

She swung her hand around, obstructing his attempt to touch her and ran into the main room. When he chased after her, she picked up a vase and threw it at him. It smashed into the wall near his head. He froze. She had picked up another vase and was eyeing him, ready to smash another one if he came any closer.

He asked menacingly, "Do you want the doors closed?" He referred to the glass French double doors separating the bedroom where he was and the main room where she stood. They had yet to be closed during their entire stay. He did not enjoy the symbolism of that move, but he couldn't see her calming down any time soon.

"I'll do it. You get in bed and stay there," she ordered.

He complied.

She turned off the lights and paused before closing the glass doors. "You are not to touch me unless I give you leave. Understand?"

"Understood."

He heard the latch click, her crawl onto the sofa, then sobs rip through her. He flinched. Pain. He had caused her irrevocable grief. Gone was the laughing Mia. Now, he listened to the wailing cries of a girl who'd lost her innocence before she should have known what innocence was. His attempt to bridge a connection of past regrets and pains had backfired. And it was all his fault. He had failed.

*

They rode in silence on the train. She had remained distant all morning. Neither was she amused when she had demanded her clothes back and saw him retrieve them from under the bed. Now, she sat staring out the window as they slowly ascended the Andes heading for Machu Picchu. It seemed... the mountains pierced the sky as the clouds descended.

When the train stopped, they continued on in silence. It was a long hike up to the ancient city in the clouds. His lungs hurt from lack of oxygen, and he could hear Mia panting. She had grown paler, but she trudged along, the trooper she always was.

Finally, they broke through and stared down at the stone ruins below. Before them, rocky jards of mountain impaled the heavens, many of their summits hidden by clouds. Near one of these mountainous spikes, the city sat on a lonely flat precipice. The ruins matched the stone and were accented by bright green tufts of grass. In the center, was a large grassy square, what used to be their plaza. In some areas the city's walls fell off directly into clouds. In other areas, steep terraced gardens led a hike-able approach.

Caleb yearned to take a big breath, but it was fruitless. The air was thin. They were over nine thousand feet above sea level. His eyes slid to Mia once again, but she had her back turned towards him as she inspected their upcoming excursion. She examined it reverently.

Machu Picchu was known to be a sacred city to the Inca, and it had never been found by the Conquistadors. It couldn't be seen from below. You had to know the intricate way there, or you would never find it. It was completely hidden from the world and didn't need it. The town was completely self-sufficient, and with its agricultural terraces and natural springs, it was able to adequately feed everyone living in the five square mile fortress. It had over one-hundred-fifty houses. Down below, the majestic Urubamba River helped create the clouds which further immersed the city in its cloak of invisibility. And before them, these clouds still enshrouded the former temples, palaces, storage rooms, and baths.

"Well, I suppose they were protected up here. Who'd still have breath to fight once getting here?"

Had she just called a truce to their fight? Of course, Caleb didn't see it as a fight, he saw it as a terrible mistake that he was paying drastically for. His eyes dropped to the sapphire butterfly on her lower back, once again visible by her black leather pants and black tank top. She had fully armed herself with daggers and other smaller weapons that he hadn't known she'd been carrying in her backpack. When he asked her why she was preparing for battle, she threw him a dangerous look and muttered something about how his girlfriends kept showing up.

There was one thing that he was grateful for. She'd left the iPod at the hotel. He had seen her pick it up, think about it, then lay it back down.

She moved on without him. Descending down into the haunted town. It wasn't only clouds that moved about the ancient city, but terrestrial spirits as well. He wondered how many Nephilim floated about. Too many for him to try to count. They passed fifty-ton grey granite stones ingeniously built into walls and buildings so that not even his dagger could fit between them - no mortar needed.

He just wanted to make sure Mia was aware of what they were entering. "Do you see..."

"Your buddies?" she cut him off. "Yeah, I see them."

He followed her, letting her take the lead as they entered the city. The ruins were well preserved. Silently, she moved about the grey ruins, leaving footprints in the lush grass by her small black combat boots. No one disturbed them. No one had gotten off the train. Caleb had thought that odd but was delighted with the outcome. They were alone. In the clouds. In a sacred city. Surrounded by spirits.

Should they be alarmed?

She tossed him a paper bag, shocking him out of his thoughts. When he opened it, he found food. Hope blossomed in his chest. "Do you want some?"

She shook her head and continued her perusal.

They walked the ruins for two hours before finding the *Intihuatana Stone*, the Hitching Post of the Sun. Someone had roped off this particular megalith.

"Why does this seem important?" she asked.

"On the spring and fall equinoxes, the sun rests on the top. The worshipers 'hitch' the sun here for a short while to visit with their god and bask in its majesty."

"Sorry I asked," she muttered. She slowly spun around taking in the spirits that had surrounded them near the sacred stone. "What's up with them?"

He was amazed that even after her possession, she did not show her fear - if she was even afraid. Caleb wasn't sure that she was. "Shaman legends say that when a sensitive person touches their forehead to the sacred stone, the *Intihuatana* opens one's vision to the spirit world."

"And..."

"They know you're sensitive to the spiritual realm," Caleb finished for her.

Mia's eyes shot out a challenge to the spirits. "Well, I see more than I care to. I won't be touching my forehead, so you can just scatter." She mumbled under her breath, "And I don't like being possessed."

So, Caleb thought, she knew. When a spirit possessed a person, that person was able to see the spiritual realm like the spirit could. It was why Paul cast out the spirit of divination from that one fortune teller. And once the spirit had been cast out, she could no longer divine the future. She hadn't been a born seer. Mia was. She was ripe for any spirit to desire. Jealousy burst through Caleb. She was his. No other Nephilim, whether in flesh or in spirit, could have her.

She turned and left the area. "Why are so many buildings missing their roofs?"

"This place was for the devout to study the stars. Overall, it was an astronomical observatory." Caleb followed her, now keeping a vanguard of protection about her. No spirit was going to touch her.

"I'm done. Are you done?"

"Yeah. I'm done," Caleb said, relieved.

Traipsing down the grey stone ruins, Mia hopped from one level to another in her pursuit to get back to the train. When they reached the main plaza, she stilled. Her head moved from right to left looking for something she was not seeing.

The hairs on the back of Caleb's neck stood on end.

Swoosh.

Swoosh.

Swoosh.

Whatever it was, was behind them.

Mia turned around and swore. "You are so much more trouble than you're worth." She pulled out one of her daggers. She yelled out, "What do you want?"

Caleb slowly turned. Three Amazons stood there, outfitted in combat gear. They wore short silk tunics, as light as cobwebs and almost as sheer as them. Their shifts barely fell below their buttocks, giving them freedom of ease for kicks, sprints, and leaps. Leather straps crisscrossed their chest, allowing arrows and a sheathed sword to hang down their back. Bows were grasped in their hands. Their skin glowed ethereally beneath long silken locks of hair, and their eyes sparkled with determination. Any man would appreciate their appearance, but Caleb was not one of them.

The tallest one answered, "What belongs to us. Caleb." She was nine feet tall with glittering turquoise eyes and flaxen hair. Beside her, two fellow Amazons stood. One with amber eyes, bronzed skin, and chestnut hair. The other with jade eyes and red hair. All three were missing their right breast.

Mia sighed frustratedly. "He *belongs* to you?"

"Caleb," the leader called, "We will not have speech with this dust mite any longer. You will come with us."

Mia's whole body went rigid, her back ramrod straight. Her eyebrows rose disdainfully. "Dust mite?"

Caleb stood firmly. "I will not submit."

The leader prowled in front of them. "Surely, your father spoke of how well we treat our male Nephilim guests."

"He was always complimentary," Caleb conceded.

"We have needs too, Caleb. And our ranks have grown thin. We need more Amazons." She leapt onto a stoned wall.

Mia whispered under her breath to Caleb, "I thought Amazons were female warriors. Why would they want you?"

The blonde looked Mia up and down. "Not to fight, imbecile. To father more Amazons. We need his seed."

Mia's face flamed to life, her lips quivered in anger. "He's not yours to command!"

The leader turned her attention back to Caleb. "Leave with us, and she will not be harmed."

Mia threw herself in front of him. "Over my dead body!"

"As you wish."

A spear sailed directly for Mia's heart. Caleb somersaulted over Mia and swatted it away just in time. His eyes darted to the brunette who'd thrown it.

The blonde let out a sultry laugh and sat down on the wall. "We will get what we desire." She whistled a tropical bird call, and seven more Amazons jumped over the walls. They encircled Caleb and Mia.

Caleb's hopes fell. "Mia, *ahuva*..."

Mia pulled out two black throwing-stars from beneath her belt. In the center was the emblem of a ninja dragon, and each of its four points was curved like a machete. They were so small, they fit within her tiny palms. Their razor sharp edges glittered, ready to tear flesh open. She yelled, "He is not your whore!"

The blonde lazily dangled her leg. "If he doesn't want payment, we won't give it to him. But nonetheless, he'll receive payment in pleasure."

"Bitch!" Mia snarled. She shifted to throw her first star when Caleb caught her wrist.

"This is death, Mia," he whispered in her ear. "We can both survive this."

Huge eyes turned up to him. "You're willing to do this?"

"If it saves your life, yes," he answered solemnly.

Her eyes narrowed. "Because *you want to*. It's every man's desire to have a beautiful harem."

"How little you know of men, Mia." He pulled her into his embrace. "Some men are not good men, but most men desire a loving relationship with only one woman. A woman's heart does not soften if she knows he sleeps with others. It brings out their cattiness. We are relational beings too. We desire a spiritual bond with only one other - our helpmate. And as much as you disbelieve it, only sex with the one we truly love would ever be a spiritually bonding love making." He ran his hand over her cropped black hair. "I want that bond with *you*, not them."

Mia's eyes grew soft and her lips parted.

"She has much courage," the brunette said.

Caleb's eyes snapped to her. He knew that sometimes Amazons took women into their ranks. Women who were great warriors. Sometimes, giving them male Nephilim lovers to build their army, other times assigning them guard duty of their private lair. That would never happen to Mia. He glared at the brunette who was probably the real leader.

The red haired one spoke, "I heard Loki has come to Cuzco. Perfect timing."

"She will not be given to Loki," Caleb spat. "If she lies with anyone, it will be me!"

The brunette purred like a kitten. "Two male Nephilim. Our future just keeps getting better and better."

A small, cool hand grasped his bicep. Caleb gazed down into Mia's eyes. She asked, "Do you really not want them?"

"No," he whispered, "only you."

She turned her face away from him, her head bowed, her eyes downcast. Her two hands rose, fell, then settled at either side of his waist, grasping him. His hands fell to her shoulders. They stood there, in silence, waiting. Her breathing slowed to silence.

Then, lightning fast, Mia blazed a throwing-star into the jugular of the brunette. Surprised, her amber eyes huge, she sunk to her knees, blood spurting out, and spraying her white tunic red.

With another quick twitch, Mia sent her other star tearing into the blonde's skull, right above her eyes, immediately severing the connection between the two halves of the brain. A perfect lobotomy. Blood geysered out of the wound as she sank to her knees, catatonic. Whirling around, Mia planted her back against Caleb's chest.

Two down, eight to go.

A sharp stab informed Caleb that the Amazons behind him had dug a sword into his back. It was a shallow thrust. They wanted him alive and functioning.

Mia pulled out two more throwing-stars and took aim. Moving in a whirlwind motion, she released the stars at a higher velocity than she would have been able to do by arm strength alone. Two more Amazons fell to their knees. Down to six.

The red head jerked her chin. Arms closed around Caleb's, pulling him back, leaving Mia's back exposed.

They pulled him down hard. He shoved himself further and rolled back up, smacking his feet against one of their jaw. He heard it crack. Claws raked his face, aiming for his eyes.

He swung his dagger around in a large, sweeping motion, bludgeoning the tip into the temple of one. Blood coated the dagger's handle. His fingers slipped off. A knee drove into his back. His face plowed through dirt and grass. He threw his weight to the right. The knee and a foot pinned him down. He swore.

He flipped his head. Sightless eyes stared at him. They glittered like the rubies they were. Blood dripped over them. His dagger still protruded from her temple. He wrenched it from her and back stabbed the thigh holding him down. A yelp of pain rent the air. His head got shoved into the dirt again. Dirt blinded him. He jerked his hips and imbalanced the wounded Amazon. Flipping, he leapt off the ground, his arms reaching out to encircle her neck. Her eyes grew wide when air choked out of her. They fell to the ground. Caleb landed on top of her, his weight crushing her. Her wind knocked from her. Her face turned red, then purple. She raked her claws through any piece of flesh she could find, but Caleb kept hold, squeezing tighter and tighter. Her chest heaved, lifting him off the ground. He threw more weight on her to hold her still. She arched her back, stretched to get away from him. Caleb gritted his teeth. A snarl ripped from his throat. She flailed one arm, then died.

Four left.

He flipped over and searched for Mia.

Mia did several backflips while spears sailed past her petite frame. She was heading for the red head. In her final backflip, she landed and swept a roundhouse kick into the red head's side. Mia was extremely short compared to the Nephilim, and she only had mortal strength. This wasn't like watching Raechev. Raechev was short for a Nephilim but she had Nephilim strength. Mia was a mortal fighting Amazon Nephilim. Fear engulfed him.

Mia attacked with a hook kick. The red head dropped and came up under her leg. Mia fell to the ground. The red head yanked her up tight. Mia grappled the Amazon down into a locked position and began a choke. The Amazon threw Mia off her.

The red head is the leader. Caleb knew for sure now. He rose and had a stinking cloth shoved over his nose and mouth. He was grasped from behind. The stench overrode him. His vision blurred. He threw his weight into breaking the grasp. He stumbled back. His head woozed. He tripped and fell. His vision turned black and white, then blackness consumed him.

*

Pain ricocheted through his body. The stench burned his nostril and lungs. With his eyes closed, he listened to his surroundings. He heard feet trod from left to right. Sandaled feet. Not Mia. Was he in their lair already?

He opened his eyes. An Amazon anxiously stared out the window of an intact grey stone chamber. He was still at Machu Pucchu. Night had fallen. Moonlight streamed through the one window sending a ghostly shimmer upon the darkened room. Brilliant stars blazed from the skies.

He heard more feet approach. He closed his eyes.

"She took out Tereis." It was the voice of the red head, the leader.

"Tereis? How?" the guard asked.

"She's doing some new type of fighting. It looks Asian. She's an excellent warrior," the leader replied.

"Well, she is Asian," muttered the guard.

"Every blow I land, she deflects," the leader said frustrated. "You should have seen her. She's short, yet she jumped and kicked me in the face. She's not even five feet. I'm eight. It is such a shame to kill her."

"Do we have to?" the guard asked.

Silence fell. Caleb grew nervous. Had they noticed he wasn't unconscious?

"We need children. She won't let us take Caleb while she breathes." The leader stated. "I actually respect her."

"How did she take out Tereis?" the guard pried.

"She shoved the base of her palm up her nose. The bone went straight into her brain." The leader moved about the chamber. "Watch your face. That is what I warn." She knelt down in front of Caleb. "Why do you think he matters so much to her?"

The guard giggled. "Mayhaps, he pleasures well."

He could hear the leader moving about to peer around him. She ran her hands over his body searching for weapons. Grunting, she stood.

"Zerynthia was speared by her own weapon."

"Zerynthia too?" the guard asked alarmed. "So it's just us?"

"Just us," the leader confirmed.

Caleb hid his grin. Down to two. Mia was doing well.

He began wondering why the leader had come back. Was it to check on the guard? Him? Why would the leader show Mia where he was being held? His breathing stilled. It was a trap.

The wind blew eerily outside and whisked through the ghostly ruins. Caleb could almost imagine ghostly fingers moving through his hair. He didn't like it here, and he was worried for Mia. There was no way he could break out of his confines. She was all alone.

He sat on the ground, his back leaned against one of the corners. The females were silent. Apparently, the guard had been silenced by fear. Fear of a mortal, a petite five foot mortal. Fear of his Mia, his *Ahuva*.

"You give yourself away. Are you thinking of her?"

Caleb refused to answer the red head.

"I have excellent senses. Your heart slowed and your face became peaceful."

Caleb remained silent.

"You have every right to be proud of her. I'd be proud of her if she was mine," the leader mused. "She hides her tiny body, dressed in black, in the shadows, where the moon cannot lay her bare." She walked closer to him, farther away from the door and window where the guard nervously stood. "She's like a phantom tonight. Earlier in the bright light of day, her fighting technique was new and intriguing. None of us could get our hands on her. But now, she stalks the shadows, waiting for us to separate. Then without warning, she attacks from the shadows before we even know she's in arms length."

When Caleb did not speak, she moved away. He swore to remain supposedly unconscious, just in case Mia needed him for a surprise move.

Hours ticked by.

The moon's beams became stronger. His muscles stiffened.

Had Mia left him? She had said that he wasn't worth the trouble. Did she really believe that? Raechev had said that often enough, but he knew she had always been teasing him. She was his sister. They both needed each other. But Mia didn't need him. She had lived her whole life without him. She had a family and two best friends. Angered, he made a silent pact that if she had left him, he would find her and force her to stay with him. She had less than a hundred years to live. For all he knew, he still had thousands of years. She could endure spending her lifetime with him.

Fear gnawed at his belly.

"Ooph."

Caleb opened his eyes just in time to see the guard hit the ground. Mia had thrown a stone hard enough through the window that it had knocked the guard out. The leader positioned herself firmly in front of him. Her eyes darting between the door and window. Her whole body was alert.

Caleb couldn't hide his smile. It would be mighty scary to know that someone could through a stone so hard that it could kill. Especially, when you couldn't even see the person who'd throw it.

"Show yourself. You act cowardly."

Oh. Caleb knew that was going to ruffle Mia's feathers.

"Are you a warrior or a coward?" the leader yelled.

The leader was trying to provoke Mia into making a mistake. Mia was being wise, and the leader knew it. She was mortal. They Nephilim.

"Do you prefer hand to hand combat?" Mia called from outside.

"No!" Caleb yelled. Mia could not handle the leader's strength. She was the leader for a reason.

"Hand to hand," the red head repeated.

"No weapons. None whatsoever," Mia demanded.

"Warrior to warrior. I like that. Skill on skill." The leader smiled knowing she had won.

"No, Mia," Caleb commanded.

Mia walked in, her eyes blazing with an intensity Caleb had never seen. Her whole mind and body was focused on her adversary. She didn't acknowledge Caleb. But the focus was unnerving even to him. She stopped just inside the door. Her legs were splayed wide. Her arms, stiff and straight, were held slightly off her body. Her head was barely bowed. Determination vibrated from every tense muscle and shone from her eyes. Caleb sat transfixed.

The leader dropped each of her weapons to the ground.

Mia flexed her hands. They opened, then fisted, then opened again.

They stood only two feet apart.

Mia took one step forward, her hands continuing to flex.

The Amazon took the other step forward.

They were one foot apart.

Suddenly, the Amazon dropped to her knee, her arm whipping out.

Mia struck straight in front of her, nailing the Amazon with a palm heel strike. Her skull burst open.

Caleb gulped. The red head laid at his feet, blood, flesh, and brains fell out of her shattered skull. "How, how did you do that?"

"Martial arts. I was breaking ten cement blocks with my elbow back in junior high. I take self defense very seriously."

Stunned. Caleb could only stare at her. In a haze he saw her walk towards him, drop down, and untie him. She gazed at him. He stared amazed. She reached forward, wound his tank top in her tiny fist and yanked him towards her, giving him a searing kiss. Too shocked to respond, Caleb just accepted it. Finished, she dropped him back against the wall, got up, and left.

"Let's go. I'm hungry," she yelled as she exited the chamber. Caleb scrambled up and raced after her.

He could still barely believe his eyes. He followed her as she headed for the train stop. Why they were heading there, he didn't know. Trains wouldn't begin again till morning. And the ruins were pretty. Now that his shock had begun to wear off, he began wondering why they hadn't stayed in the romantic environment.

Reaching forward, he clutched her back to him. Flipped her and molded her to his body. He swept his lips down to continue the kiss, but she wiggled out of his hold. "What?"

"Let me down," she demanded.

"You started it," he retorted angrily.

"You didn't reciprocate."

He crushed his lips against hers. She fought him, pounded his chest, then finally kneed him in the groin. He went down like a sack of potatoes. "Mia!"

"Caleb!" she mocked.

"What's, what's wrong with you!" he screamed.

Fury shot over her face. She turned and stormed off. "Nothing. Nothing is wrong with me. You're the damaged goods!"

Remorse smacked him hard. "That's not what I meant. You just kissed me! That gives me permission to kiss you back!" Painfully, he got up and limped after her.

"Privilege revoked!" she yelled, shaking her fist high in the air.

He stomped down the mountain and caught up with her at the train station. She sat, her knees held tightly to her chest by her arms. She seemed unapproachable. In a moment, his mind flashed to the iPod she had left behind. He softened. "I enjoyed the kiss. Will I be getting another one?"

"I, I just thought I deserved something for saving your arse from being forced into debauchery."

"Would you like another reward?" he asked, smiling.

"Silence too much to ask?" she replied sarcastically.

He plopped down beside her. "Thank you."

"I do whatever I can. They were going to whore you amongst themselves," she muttered.

"Yes, they were. But I had a hero. A mighty angel to guard my virtue," he teased.

She stiffened. "You dare to mock me?"

Caleb knew that wouldn't be wise. What were the bones and strength of Nephilim when she could burst cement blocks. No wonder she walked the earth without fear. Except her fear of vulnerability. Not physically, but emotionally. She had turned surly again. She was protecting her heart. Caleb fought his grin. She was fighting her own heart. Even with the information shared last night, her heart was still attached to his.

"You are cold. I'm going to warm you."

She cast him an untrusting look.

"It is the least I can do in the mountain coldness." He held up his hands in defeat.

She narrowed her eyes and searched his face for duplicity. Then she jerked her chin in acceptance. He moved behind her and wound his body around her. Her tiny body slowly stopped shivering and relaxed. Soon, her head fell back against his shoulder.

Caleb enjoyed holding her throughout the night and watching the stars shine magnificently above. His breath caught when the sun rose. He nudged her awake, and she gasped. They sat amidst the clouds, struck pink and orange by the rising sun. It was glorious. After the sunrise had passed, she returned to sleeping.

He woke her when it was time to board the train. She moved onto an empty bench and sat so that he could not sit beside her. Accepting his fate, he sat opposite her and propped his legs up on her seat. He couldn't hold her, but he could watch her.

The train cab jerked and rumbled its way back down to Cuzco. She kept her eyes averted. He waited over an hour before attempting his question.

"Why did you stay? You could have left me."

She continued staring out the window at the passing Andes Mountains. After half an hour, she answered, "Your spirit is like the ocean: steady and soothing."

Satisfied, Caleb relaxed for the rest of the journey.

CHAPTER 9:

CUZCO:
NAVEL OF THE UNIVERSE

Mia twirled around and leaned over the flowerpots. She stared intently into the octagon shaped structure. He smiled. She'd worn the pink skirt and sweater combo he had purchased for her.

"Cuzco means navel. This city, this spot, was believed to be the center of astronomy, the navel of the universe." His eyes roamed up her well formed calves, the full and swaying skirt, the pink sweater, and her bowed head. Her hair had been growing out and currently reached a little past her shoulders. Caleb liked it, but he missed being able to see the back of her neck.

This was the third place they'd visited that day. They had started with the Incan palace ruins, then visited the Temple of the Virgins of the Sun, and currently stood inside the ruins of the Temple of the Sun. Pizarro had looted this temple more than any other. It had been the center of the Inca's religious life. Although a church had been built over it, earthquakes had destroyed most of the church, but the Incan temple to Inti, the sun god, stood perfect and unaffected.

Caleb's mind drifted back to when Raechev and he had visited during the empire's peak of existence, before it was plundered by Spain. They had crossed the final crest of hills to find many buildings burning as bright as the sun, appearing to have been dipped in golden fire. Four thousand priests and virgin priestesses moved in and out of a golden temple that acted as an astronomical observatory and calendar. It precisely calculated precessional movements of the stars. The walls of the temple had been covered in over seven hundred sheets of pure gold, weighing about four and a half pounds per sheet. Walls and floors were completely covered in gold, and facing the rising sun was an immense golden image of the sun covered with emeralds. Spreading out from the temple, were forty-two lines, portraying the rays of the sun. These lines shot out for hundreds of miles, signifying universal alignments. *Huacas* (spirit megaliths) ran along these lines which pointed out solstices, equinoxes, and heliacal rise positions of stars and constellations.

Caleb opened his eyes. Mia still stood at the *Cuzco Cara Urumi,* the Uncovered Navel Stone. Currently, it was all grey rock, but during the Empire of the Sun, this courtyard had been at the heart of the Temple of the Sun. Each wall and floor had been covered in pure gold, and at the center of this courtyard, had been an octagonal stone coffer covered with one-hundred and twenty-one pounds of pure gold, representing the sun itself. It was said that the actual sun, descended to this gold sun.

"It's empty. I don't get what's so special," Mia mused, still intently staring into the empty stone coffer where the golden sun had once sat.

"It was once filled with gold, and sacrifices occurred here."

"Sorry I asked," she muttered.

"The priests would predict world cataclysmic events, and the Sun-King believed that he could stop time by sacrificing children tied to the stone before you. Their souls migrating to heaven. The souls of the dead becoming souls in the sky."

"Like I said, sorry I asked," she mumbled.

The Druids also had worshiped the sun god, but they had built blazing fires during their child sacrifices. It was believed that when the fruit of the body was offered, it covered for the sin of the soul. According to Mosaic law, scapegoats had been sent out on Yom Kippur, the Day of Atonement, as a symbol of sin being cleansed from the people. But the Druids had perverted it and offered children in mockery. And as the Hebrew priests were required to eat of the sacrifice, so too were the Druids to eat of the human sacrifices. That is why the term Priest of Baal/God became known as Devourer of Human Flesh.

Mia's somber voice interrupted his thoughts. "I don't understand why everyone keeps trying to kill or sexually sacrifice innocents in ancient times. It just seems so much more evil."

Caleb's eyes softened. "Only in ancient times?"

Mia's eyes slowly drifted to him.

"Traces of Moloch persist in your own nation. The Land of the Free permits the ancient rite of sacrificing one's own babe for material or financial gain. No difference. Women abort their own babe to further their careers, social acceptability, or personal needs." Caleb shuddered as memories of Molech worship assaulted his mind. Even the Israelites had fallen when they'd stopped reading the Torah, the laws of Elohim. "Let's talk of something else shall we?"

Mia twirled to face him. She bit her bottom lip. She'd been avoiding various topics that Caleb would have liked to broach, but they'd come to an excellent truce. She needed time, and he would give it to her. She was worth the wait.

"So, are Nephilim responsible?"

He chuckled. "Of course. Remember Tiahuanaco, near the shores of Lake Titicaca?"

Her eyebrows smushed up. "Where we went with Raechev?"

"Exactly. Well, that is where the Incas inherited their knowledge on astronomy, from people coming from the great port of Tiahuanaco." Caleb had no problem keeping his mind focused on the present with Mia's flushed pink cheeks captivating him.

Mia tilted her her head to the side. "Ah, yes. The white giants who sailed around the world teaching pyramid building and sun worship."

"And astronomy, astrology, witchcraft, the Cult of the Stones, spiritism, human sacrifice, and all forms of the occult," Caleb added.

"Great guys," Mia teased.

"But there were some redeemed ones," Caleb defended.

"That were tempted by Amazons," she probed.

"That rejected the sexual offerings of Amazons," he reminded.

Mia shoved her dainty foot in front of her. Her eyes drifted down to watch her foot nervously move about the edgings of the stones. Her distraction didn't seem to be working too well because Caleb could see her jugular pounding heavily. Her heart beat was increasing.

He drew near her and wrapped his arms around her waist. He kissed the top of her head. "*Ahuva. Chephtsiy-bahh,*" he whispered. "Come back to me."

"What here?" she whispered.

He murmured into her hair, "Here. At the heart of the Incan Empire, and the navel of the universe."

She raised her hands and grasped his waist. Her forehead fell onto his chest.

"Which leads to the navel of the world."

Caleb raised his head. Loki. He stood with a loving arm encircled about Sam.

"Is that what you search for?" Caleb asked him.

"Mia?" Sam asked stunned.

Mia turned shy eyes to Samantha.

"You're wearing a skirt. And pink. And your hair's long," Sam stammered. "And you're in a man's arms."

Mia fidgeted. Her face flamed hot pink.

Caleb protectively wrapped her in his arms.

Loki's eyebrow rose.

"Nothing's happened. I haven't fallen," Caleb defended himself.

"Not for long by the looks of it," Loki retorted.

Sam raced towards Mia. Mia met her halfway. They hugged, cried, and embraced. They were so caught up in their own reunion that neither paid attention to the growled discussion occurring between the men.

"You have no right to lecture me," Caleb threatened.

Loki walked to Caleb, so they could speak without the women hearing. "Matters not anyway."

Caleb spoke aghast, "You *have* turned."

"Sam, why... What about Nimrod? Have you forgotten him so soon?" Mia asked, jerking Caleb's attention away for a moment.

Sam murmured resolutely, "Nimrod's dead. I chose to embrace life, Mia."

Loki's smoldering eyes warned Caleb. "The time has come. The prophecy is at hand."

"Whose prophecy?" Caleb asked.

"The Lamb's." Loki darted a look to Sam before continuing, "When the mightiest hunter dies for love and is returned obedient unto Elohim, Nephilim and man are one."

"What does that mean?" Caleb asked confused.

"It means you may take Mia as your helpmate."

Caleb let his hungry eyes rove over Mia's face. Hope blossomed.

Loki continued, "It means the Lamb's sacrifice has been extended to us. It means Elohim no longer enforces our separation from mortals. The end has drawn nigh. We are in the last mortal generation. The seventh millennium is about to dawn."

"Caleb!" Mia called out excitedly. "Thor and Stacey are engaged!"

Shock slammed through Caleb. Was Loki telling the truth or

trying to get him to fall? He turned beseeching eyes to Loki. "What do you know, Loki? What are you doing? And most importantly, what are you scheming?"

"The possibility for full restoration, from all the curses, for mankind and Nephilim alike, is at hand."

Caleb looked perplexed.

"Adam and Eve were created to live forever. It was the curse, the effects of the curse, that aged them and caused them to get sick and die. The Bible prophesies that when the fullness of the gentiles has come, the Unlawful One will be revealed. Adam and Eve were kicked out of the heavenly dimension when they broke the law. Just like every spirit being is kicked out of the heavenly dimensions when they break the Kingdom of Heaven's laws... including our angelic fathers. It will be like in the days of Noah. How long did they live? Without generational curses upon generational curses piling upon them? Mortals have a chance to be fully restored to what they were created to be before Adam and Eve ever broke a law. It is prophesied that the believers who live through the tribulation will live and rule with Yeshua here on Earth for a thousand years." Loki's eyes glittered brilliantly. "And that extends to us as well. Both halves of our DNA and bloodlines can now be fully restored as well through repentance. It is about to get really exciting, Caleb. Really, really, exciting."

"But... How?" Caleb stammered.

Loki grinned. "When the blindfold of the deception of the Unlawful One is removed, the Word of YHVH will speak to the elect. The answers are already in Scriptures, and revelations will once again pour forth." His eyes became solemn. "It is all about repentance, obedience, and faith."

Sons of God Series

To Kill A Goddess (1)
To Lure Your Prey (2)
To Seduce & Sacrifice (3)
To Wield the World (4)
To Challenge the Devil (5)
Secrets of the Sons (6)
Secrets of the ... (7)

Questions? Intrigued by what you read?
Contact Rebecca on her blog where she posts research, insights, and
tidbits from her research and travels.

For speaking engagements visit

rebeccaellenkurtz.com

Turn the page

for a sneak peek
at Rebecca Ellen Kurtz's next novel in the
Sons of God Series

To Challenge the Devil

Garden of Eden

Beautiful rays highlighted the Tree of Life.

The archangel Rapha-el turned to the right, then to the left. No one was near. He floated nearer, then tentatively stepped as the mortals did. It was different, unique. He smiled to himself.

He allowed his glance to behold the majesty that Elohim had created. He was surrounded by lush vegetation, a gurgling brook, sweet smelling roses, and a cool gentle breeze that flowed over his skin. Little by little, he allowed his form to harden like man's so that he could feel the world as man did. Once he had felt sorry for Adam, but now, Adam had Eve. They were perfect together. Their bodies, temperaments, emotions, and perspectives perfectly balanced and complimenting the other, together making a perfect blend of a whole being, a being more closely reminiscent of Elohim himself. The logic and warrior of man softened by the nurturing and vulnerability of woman.

Spirit beings were different. They were hermaphrodites, both male and female. Some looked more male while others looked more female. When they chose consorts, it was for alliances and friendship. But Elohim had taken the female portions out of male, so they were two halves needed to make a whole. Adam was created a hermaphrodite, but Elohim had taken Eve out of him, so they needed the other to be one and balanced.

A noise startled him. Surprisingly fast, Rapha-el shifted his body back to its spirit state, then hid himself behind some foliage. He liked watching. The mortals had been made of spirit, soul, and flesh. That way they could live in both realms. They saw and functioned in both realms, but they were to rule the physical realm. They were to take dominion and keep the Fallen from destroying creation. Elohim had trapped the Fallen in the firmament dimension which went into the earth a few levels and all the way up to the outermost part of the atmosphere, yet they were trapped to this one planet. Yet not all of the Fallen had been trapped, but that would be for another tale.

Elohim demonstrated how earth was to be governed. The **Kingdom of Heaven** was to be duplicated on Earth. "As it is in Heaven, so shall it be on earth," Elohim had said. Elohim spent time personally instructing Adam on establishing the govermental protocols for the **Kingdom of Heaven on Earth** where Satan ruled. Earth was his planet, and Elohim had created Adam to subdue the ruler, who was Fallen. Elohim manifested himself each twilight, at the cool of the eve, to commune with his created mortals.

It was the woman who approached. She was inspecting the fruit, looking for something to eat. Her gaze fell upon the fruit of the Tree of the Knowledge of Good and Evil. A small glimmer of joy flitted across her face. The glance was not from curiosity, but of a memory. A memory of Elohim forbidding them to it. Rapha-el was familiar with the joy that would move across the mortals' faces whenever they thought of their Creator, and that is what happened now. It was beautiful, almost as if the law itself was a tie between Creator and created, a romantic reminder of the presence of one's life in the other, and an ongoing decision to love the other in respect and obedience.

From behind the Tree of the Knowledge of Good and Evil stepped Satan. His onyx eyes, sable hair, and pale chiseled face stood in contrast to the bright red cape that hung down his back. He did not shine forth a bright light, for only those who were able to merge into the **Kingdom of Heaven on earth** reflected the glory of Yehovah. The Fallen had been kicked out of the heavenly dimensions, therefore they didnot reflect the glory of Elohim, yet they did ethereally glow for they were made of flame.

From behind Satan emerged his consort, the Morning Star. Rapha-el caught his breath. She was so beautiful. The most beautiful entity Elohim had ever created. Her skin was a unique lustrous mixture of pearl and diamonds, her eyes glittered in amethyst, emerald and turquoise hues, and her hair was long and wavy, appearing to be spun silver. Her wings matched her eyes, but nothing compared to her facial structure and sultry lips. She was the embodiment of perfection. A dream only to be had when Elohim blessed you. She had doted on Elohim's attention and love, but she had also noticed how other angels wanted to dote on her. Her beauty gave her power. The power and adoration went to her head, and the created began to take credit for the work of the Creator's hands. When her proud heart began a stench in heaven, and some angels began coveting her attention more than Elohim's, they were thrown from the heavenly dimension. She was jealous for Elohim's attentions, and jealousy is the root of every evil thing. She used her beauty to control and manipulate, and many were ready to war for her.

Satan and the Morning Star despised Adam and Eve. Not only were they Fallen and Satan trapped, but they were put under Adam and Eve's authority. They were forced to submit to other created beings on their planet of imprisonment.

Eve gasped at Morning Star's beauty. Adam joined her side and stared in awe himself. There she stood, the most glorious, the most gorgeous, the best work of the Creator's hands. Morning Star smiled benevolently, then gracefully walked around both of them, hypnotizing them with her beauty.

In a slightly petulant and bored voice, Satan asked, "Did Elohim *really* say, you are not to eat from this?"

The woman jerked. "We may eat from the fruit of the trees of the garden, but about the fruit of the tree in the middle of the garden Elohim said, 'You are neither to eat from it nor touch it, or you will die.' 'Tis a law of the **Kingdom of Heaven**."

Morning Star seductively ran her finger down Eve's arm, then Adam's.

Satan raised his eyebrows, then leisurely leaned back against the forbidden tree. "It is not true that you will surely die." Satan snatched a piece of fruit and bit into it. "Elohim knows that on the day you taste of its flesh, your eyes will be opened to more than what you see, and you will be like Elohim, able to judge good and evil."

Rapha-el stood ramrod straight, watching the temptation. Every entity had free will. He would not interfere, but he studied Satan and Morning Star's tactics. First was to question the laws of Elohim. Then ease them by saying that Elohim would not punish as promised. Then Satan had given the reason why she would benefit from breaking Elohim's laws... to gain wisdom, to be able to judge for themselves. Overall, Satan removed the penalty of law-breaking.

Adam and Eve kept looking back and forth to each other, then to Satan and Morning Star.

Rapha-el stood painfully still. He wanted to warn the humans of what happened to those who broke Elohim's **Kingdom of Heaven** laws.

Rapha-el was distracted by movement to the right. Another entity lurked but kept in the shadows, hiding itself, refusing to reveal himself. It was the Lawless One.

Satan stepped forward and lifted the fruit up to Eve's lips. Gently, he caressed her hair and face before willing her to bite. She complied. Smiling in triumph, he tossed the fruit behind him and kissed her deeply.

Morning Star took her cue and did the same with Adam.

Rapha-el shook his head. They were not to taste the forbidden fruit. The seed, and the fruit of these seeds, these compromising unions, these illegal covenants, would destroy mankind's authority to rule.

Rapha-el turned away. It had been an act of war. Before, they had only been tossed from heaven, but this, this was willingly and actively destroying Elohim's creation. This was rebellion to his laws. Rapha-el glanced to see if the Lawless One continued to lurk in the shadows, but instead he glimpsed the glory of Yehovah fading from Adam and Eve. No longer did they reflect the glory of Elohim. They were so entranced with their activity, that they did not even notice that they were being dispelled from the **Kingdom of Heaven**. Why would Adam and Eve believe that mortals were an exception to governmental protocols of the **Kingdom of Heaven**? Every entity who broke the **Kingdom of Heaven**'s laws was kicked out of the **Kingdom of Heaven on Earth**.

Sighing, Rapha-el analyzed the battle strategy of deception. First, make it believable that Elohim would not punish those he loved, then help mortals rationalize why it would be beneficial to sin.

Rapha-el turned his back. He groaned inwardly and began walking away. He wouldn't return till the cool of the evening, and he would see what Elohim would do.

"Where are you?" a loving voice asked.

Rapha-el returned, this was it. Elohim had come. He flew as fast as he could to the place of the voice, and he was not alone. Many angels were in attendance, all wondering what Elohim's reaction would be. The humans stood there, their heads bowed. Their eyes downcast, and why not? They could no longer see into the heavenly dimensions. What was there to look at? They heard a voice, but could not see Yehovah.

The man spoke, "I heard your voice in the garden, and I was afraid, because I was naked. Your glory has left me, so I hid myself."

Elohim asked quietly, "Who told you that you no longer reflected my glory?"

A long silence developed.

Elohim asked, "Have you tasted from which I ordered you not to?"

Rapha-el was perplexed. Elohim already knew the answer. Why would he ask?

The man pointed to his wife. "The woman you gave to be with me - she weakened, which enticed me."

Rapha-el was disgusted. The man was to be the leader, he was the elder, and he quickly pushed the guilt onto the younger. Elohim was asking, hoping that the man would repent, but he did not. Elohim always gave a chance for repentance. But accountability was needed for repentance. Instead, he blamed another for his failing. Already the one given authority was dropping the very reason why Elohim would entrust one to have authority.

Then Elohim turned to the woman. "What is this you have

done?"

"The being tricked me, so I ate."

Rapha-el flinched. The being tricked her? It didn't trick her. It flat out said that Elohim was a liar, that the woman should trust his rationalizations and truths over Elohim's laws and promises of consequences for disobedience. There was no tricking. Elohim had issued a law, and the woman had disregarded it. She knowingly chose her personal desires and rationalizations to break Elohim's laws, and inside she had been telling herself that Elohim would not punish her as he promised. And once again, like Adam, when given the opportunity to repent, she had not.

Then Elohim turned to Satan. His sigil stood out prominently on his forehead - an onyx solar ring with a cross inside it. "I am what you made me. I am 'Accuser.' I am to accuse those who deserve to be accused. In your courts, I bring the charges of the Accused, of those unworthy to be allowed into the heavenly dimensions. I am to tempt to see what your holy and righteous are really made of. To see if they are worthy. I did not force them. There was no rape. They chose with free will. And they chose to listen to my counsel instead of yours. My wisdom gives them freedom to judge for themselves, and they judged your law..... silly. Pretentious. Unworthy to be kept. Not important enough to adhere to. They judged you, O Almighty. They sat in judgment of you." Satan smiled. "They must see themselves to be as wise as you. Your equal. A god."

Elohim's voice sounded grief stricken, and all the heavenly entities leaned in closer for the verdict. The entire universe waited for the pronouncement for this new sin. What would Elohim do? Adam and Eve had made an alliance, a covenant, with those in rebellion. It was an act of war. Breaking Elohim's laws was rebellion. "Because you have done this, you are cursed. I will put animosity between you and the woman, and between your descendant and her descendant."

Rapha-el's jaw dropped. Cursed. Satan had been cursed! There was no more room for repentance or mercy. No entity had ever been cursed before! Rapha-el shook. Some of the angels who had fallen backed away. Fear of being cursed as well, frightened them. Rapha-el knew that some would come back to Elohim now, but others would continue to follow Satan (the Accuser), Morning Star, and the Lawless One.

Cursed. Satan's eyes raked over the woman and ended on the woman's groin. "She carries my seed now, and Morning Star carries Adam's."

Elohim continued, "The Second Adam, the Son of Man, will bruise your head, and you will bruise his heel."

Satan narrowed his eyes. There would be another son of God since Adam fell. Yehovah always had to give an opportunity for restoration. It was what He saw as fair, just, and merciful.

"I will greatly increase your pain in childbirth. You will bring forth children in pain. Your desire will be toward your husband, but he will rule over you," Elohim spoke to the woman before turning to the man. "Because you listened to what your wife said and broke the law which I gave you, the ground is cursed on your account; you will work hard to eat from it as long as you live. It will produce thorns and thistles for you, and you will eat field plants. You will eat bread by the sweat of your forehead till you return to the ground - for you were taken out of it; you are dust, and you will return to dust."

Rapha-el shook his head. Elohim did as he had promised. There were consequences for breaking his laws and not repenting of it. Laying blame when called to Judgement Day, crying someone had deceived them, did not withhold promised consequences. Children knew their father's voice. The mortals had willingly chose to listen to Satan's interpretation of Elohim's law rather than simply obeying. Satan had become their father, their teacher, and their downfall.

Sources Consulted for "To Wield the World"

Angus, Colin Simpson & Robertson. *Adam in Ochre: Inside Aboriginal Australia*. 1962.

Anitei, Stefan (Science Editor). *The Time of the Megaliths: The monuments of the European Neolithic*. 2008.

Bacchiocchi, Samuele, *From Sabbath to Sunday*. 1977.

Bible.

Bonanno, Anthony. *Archaeology and Fertility Cults in the Ancient Mediterranean*. 1986.

Charlesworth, James H. *The Old Testament Pseudipigrapha Apolcalyptic Literature & Testaments*. 1985.

Cooke, Jean, Kramer, Ann and Rowland-Entwistle, *History's Timeline*. 1996.

Cotterell, Arthur and Rachel Storm. *The Ultimate Encyclopedia of Mythology*. 2006.

Cumont, Franz Valery Marie. *The Mysteries of Mithra*. 1903.

Eliade, Mircea, John C. Holt, Rosemary Sheed. *Patterns in Comparative Religion*. 1963.

Eusebius. *The History of the Church from Christ to Constantine. 1989.* (Andrew Louth)

Forlag, Paul. *Journal of Prehistoric Religion*. 1998.

The Gallic Wars By Julius Caesar. Translated by W.A. McDevitte and W.S. Bohn. 1869.

Gonzalez-Wippler, Migene. *Book of Shadows*. 2005.

Gray, John. *Near Eastern Mythology*. 1988.

The Greater Key of Solomon. Translated by Lauron William De Laurence. 1914.

Guaitoli, M.T. and Rambaldi, S. (Eds.). *Lost Cities from the Ancient World*. 2002.

Holmes, Thomas Rice. *Caesar's Conquest of Gaul*. 1899.

Jones, David M. and Molyneaux, Brian L. *Mythology of the American Nations*. 2001.

Kahn, Michael. *"Incan Children were 'Fattened Up' Before Being Sacrificed."* London. Reuters. 2006.

Kennedy, Ph. D. D. James. *The Real Meaning of the Zodiac: Special TBN Edition*. 1989.

Knight, Christopher and R. Lomas. *Uriel's Machine: Uncovering the Secrets of Stonehenge, Noah's Flood, and the Dawn of Civilization*. 1999.

MacCulloch, J.A. *Religion of the Ancient Cults*.

Mead, G. R. S. *The Mysteries of Mithras*. 2001.

Mellor, Ronald and Podany. Amanda (Eds.). *The World in Ancient Times: Primary Sources & Reference Volume*. 2005.

Miller, Hamish and Paul Broadhurst. *The Sun and the Serpent*. 1990.

More, Sir Thomas. *Utopia*. 1516.

Nabarz, Payam. *The Mysteries of Mithras: the Pagan Beilief that Shaped the Christian World*. 2005.

Newton, Michael. *Raising Hell*.

Oakes, Lorna and Gahlin, Lucia. *Ancient Egypt*. 2005.

Petrie, Flinders & Sir William Matthew. *Egypt and Israel*. 1911.

Pritchard, *The Ancient and Near Eastern Texts* (2 volumes). 1950.

Recent Advances in Indo-Pacific Prehistory: Proceedings of the International Symposium Held at Poona, December 19-21, 1978. Ed V. N. Misra and Peter Bellwood. 1985.

Rhys, Sir John. *Celtic Britain*. 1884.

Rolleston, Thomas William. *Myths and Legends of the Celtic Race*. 1911.

Sacred Destinations. http://www.sacred-destinations.com/malta/tarxien-temples

Sergi, Giuseppe, *The Mediterranean Race: A Study of the Origin of European peoples*. 1901.

Seven Wonders of the Ancient World. Discovery Channel Premiere. Questar Video Collection.

Squire, Charles. *Celtic Myth and Legend*. 2001.

Testament of Solomon. Trans. F.C. Conybeare. 1898.

Thompson, Ruth, Williams, A.and Taylor, Renae. *The Book of Angels*. 2006.

Torah: The Five Books of Moses. The New JPS Translation of The Holy Scriptures According to the Traditional Hebrew Text. The Jewish Publication Society. 1992.

Ulansey, David. *The origins of the Mithraic mysteries: Cosmology and Salvation in the Ancient World*. 1991.

Wikipedia.

Woolf, Greg, (Ed). *Ancient Civilizations: The Illustrated Guide to Belief, Mythology, and Art*. 2005.

Zohar: Bereshith to Lekh Lekha/The Sepher Ha-Zohar (Book of Light). By Nurho de Manhar. 1900-14.

TO WIELD THE WORLD

26156826R00200

Made in the USA
Charleston, SC
26 January 2014